ALONE

BY

MARION HARLAND

OF

RICHMOND VIRGINIA

"Through long, long years, to seek, to strive, to yearn
For human love,—and never quench that thirst;
To pour the soul out winning no return—
O'er fragile idols, by delusions nursed,—
On things that fail us, reed by reed, to lean,
To mourn the changed, the far-away, the dead,
To send our troubled spirits through the unseen
Intensely questioning for treasures fled."

HEMANS.

DEDICATION

To my Brother and Sister

It is meet that those whose sympathy has been dew and sunshine to the nursery plant, should watch over its transplantation into the public garden. And as this Dedication is the only portion of the book which is new to you, you do not require that it should remind you of the welcome stormy evenings, when I laid down my pen, to read to you the chapters written since our last "select party;" how the fictitious names of my real characters were household words to our trio: and your flattering interest—grateful because sincere—stimulated my flagging spirits in the performance of my task. You know, too, what many may not believe—with what misgivings it was entered upon, and prosecuted; what fears of the licensed critic's ban, and the unlicensed public's sneer;—above all, you comprehend the motive that held me to the work—an earnest desire to contribute my mite for the promotion of the happiness and usefulness of my kind. Coming as it does from my heart—penned under the shadow of our home-altar, I cannot but feel that the mission of my offering is to the hearts of others,—ask for it no higher place than the fireside circle. Readers and judges like yourselves, I may not, do not hope to find; but I trust there are those who will pardon the lack of artistic skill in the plot, or the deficiency of stirring incident, in consideration of the fact, that my story is what it purports to be, a simple tale of life—common joy and sorrow, whose merits, if it has any, consist in its truthfulness to Nature, and the fervent spirit which animated its narration.

MARION HARLAND.

Richmond, 1854.

CONTENTS

ALONE

CHAPTER I

The Sermon was over; the funeral psalm chanted brokenly, by reason of quick-drawn sobs, and bursts of tender remembrance; the heart's tribute to the memory of the departed. "The services will be concluded at the grave," pronounced the clergyman in an unwilling voice; and a shuddering awe fell, as it ever does, upon all. "The Grave!" Even in the presence of the sheeted dead, listening to the rehearsal of excellences lost to earth,—set as living stars in a firmament of unchanging splendor;—we cannot comprehend the dread reality of bereavement. Earth smiles the same; familiar faces surround us; and if the absence of one is painfully noted, the soul would fain delude itself with the belief that his departure is not forever;—"he is not dead, but sleepeth." But "the Grave!" These two words convey an irrevocable sentence. We feel for the first time the extent of the gulf that separates us from the clay, beloved, although inanimate; the dissevering of every bond of companionship. For us the earth has, as before, its griefs, its joys and its duties;—for the dear one—but a grave! The story of a life is ended there. The bearers advanced and took up the coffin. They were no hired officials, performing their work with ill-concealed indifference, or faces robed in borrowed lugubriousness; but old family servants, who had sported with the deceased in infancy; faithfully served her in later years, and had now solicited and obtained this mournful privilege. Tears coursed down their dusky cheeks as they lifted their burden and bore it forth from the portal which seemed to grow darker, as she, the light of the dwelling, quitted it, to return no more. They wound through the flowery labyrinth whose mazes were her care and delight. The dews of evening were beginning to descend upon the thirsting petals, and in the breezeless air hung, in an almost visible cloud, the grateful return of spicy and languishing odors. A tall rose tree drooped over the path, and as the bearers brushed by its stem, a shower, like perfumed snow-flakes, lay upon the pall. The end of the journey was reached; a secluded and beautiful spot in the lower part of the garden, where were many mounds clustered together—graves of a household. A weeping willow, years before, a little shoot, planted by the hand of the wife to mark her husband's resting-place, now grown into a stately tree, swept its feathery pendants above her pillow. The cords were lashed around the coffin, and the word given to lower it into the pit; when—with a shriek that chilled the blood of the bystanders—a slight figure darted forward, and clasped it in her arms. "Mother! oh mother! come back!" Men of iron nerve bowed in childlike weakness, and wept, as this desolate cry rent the air. She spoke not another word, but lay, her cheek to the cold wood, enclosing the colder form, and her fingers interlocked in a vice-like grasp. "Ida! my child!" said the old minister, bending to raise her; "She is not here. She is with her God. Can you wish her again upon this sinful earth?" His consolation was addressed to an ear as dull as that of the corpse. In that outburst of frenzied supplication, consciousness had left her. "It is best so!" said the venerable man. "She could not have borne it else."

The ceremony was concluded—"dust to dust—ashes to ashes;"—and the crowd turned sorrowfully away. It was not in pity for the orphan alone. There were none there who could not recount some deed of love or charity done by her, whom they had given to the earth. Since the deaths of a fondly loved partner and three sweet children, Mrs. Ross had sought balm for her wounds, by binding up those of others. Environed by neighbours, whose position and means were more humble than her own, she had ample exercise for her active benevolence;—benevolence evincing itself,—not in studied graciousness and lavish almsgiving, but in kindly sympathy, and those nameless offices of friendship, so easily rendered, so dear to the recipient. "Her children shall rise up and call her blessed," was the text of her funeral discourse, and the pastor but uttered the feelings of his auditory, when he called the community in which her blameless life had been passed, her family—loving her, and through her, united together in bonds of fraternal affection. In this genial clime, had Ida Ross been nurtured;—beloved for her mother's sake, as for the warm impulses of her generous nature; petted and indulged; yet obeying the least expression of her parent's wishes, not in slavish fear, but a devotion amounting to worship. She had no companions of her own age who were her equals in education or refinement, and from intimate connection with vulgarity she shrank instinctively. Her pride was not offensively displayed. No one could live in the sphere of which Mrs. Ross was the ruling power and feel aught like superciliousness or contempt of inferiors. From infancy, Ida was her mother's companion; at an early age her confidante and co-adviser; had read her pure heart as a richly illuminated missal, from which self-examination and severe criticism had expunged whatever could sully or disfigure. Can we marvel that she shrined her in her heart of hearts as a being more than human—scarcely less than divine?

That mysterious Providence who guides the fowler's messenger of death to the breast of the parent bird, leaving the callow nestling to perish with hunger, recalled the mother's spirit ere her labor of love was completed. Ida was an orphan in her fifteenth year;—the age of all others when a mother's counsels are needed;—when the child stands tremblingly upon the threshold of girlhood, and looks with wondering, wistful eyes into the rosy vista opened to her sight. Babes in knowledge, nine girls out of ten are grown in heart at fifteen. A stroke, whether of extraordinary joy or sorrow, will oftentimes demolish the gew-gaws of the child, and reveal instead, the patient endurance, the steady faith, the all-absorbing love of a woman. A week had passed—a week devoted by the bereaved to thoughts of, and weepings for the lost, by others to preparations for her residence among strangers. Years might elapse before her return. That night, as stealthily as though seeking a forbidden spot, she trod the path to her mother's grave. It was clear starlight, and she sat down beside the newly sodded mound, and rested her brow upon it. Cold—cold and hard! but it entombed her mother;—aye! and *her* heart! for what had she to love now? There was no loving breast to receive that aching head;—no solace for the wounded spirit. The dew-gems lay freshly upon the grass;—for her the dewiness of life was gone;—earth was one vast sepulchre. She looked up to the stars. In the summer evenings her mother's chair used to stand in the piazza, and she sat at her feet, her eyes fixed alternately upon her angelic face, and the shining orbs above them. Mrs. Ross loved to think of them as the abodes of the blest; the mansions prepared for those who had sojourned in this sin-stained world and yet worn their white robes unblemished; and the theory was confidently adopted by the imaginative child. She drank in descriptions of the glories of those celestial regions until her straining eyes seemed to catch a glimpse of a seraph's glittering robe, and she leaned breathlessly forward to hear the music of his golden harp. But to-night the sparkling smiles of those effulgent ones, "forever singing as they shine," were changed to pitying regards as they beheld her so sad and lonely;—the gleam of the seraph's wings was dimmed; his far-off melody plaintive and low, and the burden of his song was "alone." The wind waved the willow-boughs, and a whispering ran through the leaves—"Alone—alone!" The words were so audibly breathed that the girl started in her delirious sorrow, and gazed wildly around. "Oh mother! cannot you leave Heaven for one short minute to comfort your child? Who will love her now? Alone, all alone! mother! *dear* mother!"

CHAPTER II

Two persons sat in the parlor of a handsome house situated in a pleasant street of the capital of our Old Dominion. The afternoon of a summer's day was deepening into twilight, but the waning light sufficed to show the features of the occupants. There was no hazard in pronouncing them father and daughter. The square forehead, indicative rather of keenness of perception and shrewd sense, than high intellectual faculties; the full, grey eye; flexible lips, and heavily moulded chin were the same in both, although softened in the younger, until her face might have been deemed pretty, had the observer omitted to remark an occasional steel-like spark, struck from the clear eyes, and a compression of the mouth, betokening a sleeping demon whom it would be dangerous to arouse from his lair. A turbulent light flashed there now. She had thrown herself into the corner of a sofa, after many restless wanderings through the apartment, and the shapely foot, oscillating rapidly, beat with its toe, a tattoo agitato upon the floor. Her father was immersed in thought or apathy. She repeated a question in a voice which savored of peevishness, before he withdrew his eyes from the watch-key, the twirling of which had been his occupation for a quarter of an hour. "At what hour will your ward arrive, sir?"

"She must be here in a short time. They have travelled slowly. The journey might have been accomplished as well in one day, as two."

"You said her escort was a clergyman, I think. Gentlemen of the cloth are not famous for inconveniencing themselves to gratify others," responded the young lady. "They inveigh against the emptiness and vanity of sublunary things; yet I know no class of men who enjoy 'creature comforts' more."

"Confounded humbugs!" was the rejoinder, and a muttered something about "priest-craft" and "blind leaders of the blind" finished the sentence so charitably begun.

Another pause was ended by the daughter. "Miss Ross' father was an early friend of yours,—a college chum,—was he not?"

"He was,—and a clever fellow into the bargain;" said her father, with a touch of feeling in his tone. "At his death, he left to me the management of his child's property,—(a snug operation I have made of it, too!) In the event of the mother's decease, I was appointed sole guardian, an office for which, it must be said, I have little partiality. If Mrs. Ross had given her up to me ten years ago, I might have made something of her; but she said a mother was the proper guide for her daughter. Women are wonderfully self-sufficient,—always undertaking what it would puzzle sensible men to do, and perfectly satisfied with the style in which it is done." If there was any meaning in the severity of this remark, the face and voice of the listener betrayed no consciousness.

"How old is Miss Ross?"

"What is your age?" and seeing her hesitate—"What does the Family Bible say? I want no school-girl airs."

"I am fifteen sir," raising her eyes coolly to his.

"And she is two months younger. A pretty time I shall have for six years; unless she takes it into her head to marry before she is of age. Very probably she will; for her fortune, although small, is large enough to attract some fool, too lazy to work, and too ambitious to remain poor."

"Is she pretty?"

"How should I know? I only saw her at her mother's funeral, where she got up quite a scene—fainting and such like. I came away the next day, and she was still too unwell to leave her room, they said."

"Romantically inclined! Pity she should be doomed to uncongenial associations!"

"You would indeed have profited little by my instructions if your mind were infected by these whimsies," said her parent, with a self-gratulatory air. "I pride myself upon your superiority to the generality of your sex, at least, in this respect"—

"There is a carriage at the door," interrupted the other, in an unvarying tone, and without changing her posture. The host met, in the entry, an elderly gentleman and a young girl, whom he saluted as "Mr. Hall" and "Miss Ross," introducing them to "Miss Read, my daughter." Ida glanced timidly into the face of her guardian, and then hastily scanned that of his daughter. That the scrutiny was unsatisfactory, was to be read in the deeper sadness that fell over her countenance, while the sinking lashes, and trembling lip showed how sharp was the disappointment. Youthful and inexperienced as she was, her heart told her that the bruised tendrils which had been torn from their original support could never learn to twine around these gelid statues.

"You will remain to tea, Mr. Hall," said Mr. Read, as the good clergyman arose.

"I thank you, sir; but our journey has been fatiguing owing to the extreme heat. I find myself in need of rest,—and my charge here requires it more than I do."

"You will call before you leave the city. May we not hope for the pleasure of your company to dinner to-morrow?"

The invitation was accepted; and after a silent pressure of the hand from Ida, and a courtly bow from father and daughter, Mr. Hall took his leave.

"Miss Ross would perhaps like to make some alteration in her dress, Josephine," Mr. Read said; his manner testifying how necessary he esteemed the proposed measure. Miss Read rang for a light, and signified to Ida that she was ready to show her up stairs. Any change from the bleak formality of their presence was a relief; and she longed to be alone, if but for half an hour, that she might give way to the emotions which had been rising and beating, through the livelong day, choking and blinding her. But Miss Read summoned a servant, whom she ordered to wait upon Miss Ross, now and in future; and seated herself in a rocking-chair to watch the progress of the toilette. Mechanically Ida went through the torture of dressing. There are times when it is such;—when the manifold details, heretofore so engaging, are to the preoccupied and suffering mind, like the thorn of the prickly-pear, too small to be observed, but pricking burningly in every fibre and pore. It was a woman— a sister—a girl as young as herself—perhaps as tender-hearted, who sat there. Why not, with the unrepressed sorrowfulness of a child, bury her face in her lap, and sob, "I have lost my mother!" to be fondled and comforted into composure? It would be sacrilege to ruffle the elegant propriety of her figure; and the glassy eyes said, by their tearless stare,— "Between you and me there is a great gulf *fixed*!" One weakness Ida could not overcome; the repugnance to beholding herself in her mourning garments. They as yet reminded her too vividly of the bier and the pall. She averted her eyes, as she stood before the mirror, to put the finishing stroke to her apparel. "I beg your pardon," said the calm voice of Josephine. "Your collar is all awry. Permit me"—Ida submitted in silence, while her volunteer assistant unpinned, and re-arranged the crape folds, but as she gathered them under the mourning brooch, a tear, large and pellucid, dropped upon her hand. It was but a drop of salt water to Miss Read, and she wiped it off, as she asked her guest "to walk down to tea." To the new-comer, the palatable food was as the apples of Sodom—bitter ashes.

She could not swallow or speak. Her companions ate and chatted with great gusto. The ill-humour of an hour since had passed away. This exemplary daughter was her father's idol, when contrasted with other, and less favored girls. She was formed in his image, and when the plastic mind was wax to receive, and adamant to retain impressions, he moulded it after a pattern of his own. He taught her deceit, under the name of self-control; heartlessness, he called prudence; veiled distrust and misanthropy under clear-sightedness and knowledge of human nature. All those holy and beautiful feelings which evidence to man his kindred to his Divine model and Creator, he tossed aside, with the sweeping condemnation—"romance and nonsense!" The crying sin was to be "womanish;"—"woman" and "fool" were synonymes, used indiscriminately to express the superlative of ire-exciting folly. He delighted in showing things as they were. Men were machines, moved by secret springs of policy and knavery; the world a stage, viewed by others in the deceptive glare of artificial lights, and so made attractive. He had penetrated into the mysteries behind the curtain, and examined, in the unflattering day, the clumsy contrivances, gaudy daubing and disgustful hollowness of the whole. Fancy and the pleasures of imagination were empty, bombastic names; he would have seen in Niagara only a sizeable fall, and "calculated," amidst the rushing shout of its mighty waters, as to the number of cotton-mills it would turn, and the thousands it would net him, could he transport it, patent right secured, to Virginia. He tore the cloud-covering from the storm-god's brow, and beheld a roaring, vaporing giant, whose insane attacks might be warded off by philosophical precautions, and discretion in the disposition of lightning rods.

The party returned to the parlor. "You play, I presume, Miss Ross?" said her guardian. Inexpressibly hurt by this new proof of insensibility to her situation, Ida faltered an excuse of fatigue and want of practice; and with a very perceptible shrug, he addressed his daughter. "What apology have *you*, Josephine?" She replied by going to the instrument, but had just taken her seat, when the door opened to admit three visitors—two school-fellows of Miss Read's, and their brother. "The Misses and Mr. Talbot" were presented in due form to the stranger, who had risen to leave the room. Josephine saw the movement, and arrested it by the introduction. No attention was paid to her; and in the midst of the lively conversation, she seized an opportunity to speak aside to Josephine. "I wish to retire, if you please." Josephine started. If not so measured, the tone was as haughty as hers, at its proudest pitch. With a word of apology to her guests, she led the way into the hall, and lighted a lamp. Ida took it from her. "I will go up without you. Good night." She walked up the staircase with a steady step, for she was followed by a gaze of wonderment and anger; but when her chamber was gained, she sprang through the door—locked and double locked it, and dashed herself upon the floor. A hurricane raged within her—grief, outraged feeling and desperation. The grave had gorged her past, black walls of ice bounded the future. Meanwhile the sound of jocund voices came up through the flooring; bursts of laughter; and then music; brilliant waltzes and triumphant marches, to where the orphan lay sobbing, not weeping, with hysterical violence; her hands clenched upon her temples, through which each convulsion sent a pang that forced from her a moan of anguish.

"She is a weak, foolish baby! it will take an immensity of schooling to make her endurable;" said Mr. Read, when the guests had gone.

"She has temper enough, in all conscience!" rejoined Josephine, and she related the scene preceding her withdrawal.

"Bad! bad!" ejaculated the senior, with a solemn shake of the head. "I admire spirit in a girl; but a woman should have no temper!"

CHAPTER III

In a crowded school-room, on a glorious October morning, a student was penning, with slow and heavy fingers, an Italian exercise. A physiognomist's eye would have wandered with comparative carelessness over the faces,—so various in feature and character—by which she was surrounded, and found in hers, subject for curious speculation; wondering at the contradictory evidence her countenance and form gave of her age; the one, sombre in its thoughtfulness, its dark eyes piercing through his, into his soul, said twenty—perhaps thirty—the lithe figure and rounded limbs, sixteen; but most, he would have marvelled at the listlessness of her attitude; the lack of interest in her occupation and external objects, when every line, in brow, eyes and mouth, bespoke energy; a spirit strong to do or dare; and which, when in arms, would achieve its purpose, or perish in the attempt. The hand moved more and more sluggishly, and the page was marred by blots and erasures. Thought had the crayon, and dark were the shades that fell upon the canvass. "Seventeen to-day! Who remembers that it is my birth-day? There are none here to know or care. If I were to die to-morrow, there is not a creature who would shed a tear above my corpse. I wish I could die! They say such thoughts are sinful, but annihilation is preferable to an aimless, loveless existence. Oh! this intolerable aching, yearning for affection—it is eating into my soul! gnawing, insatiable longing! can I not quiet you for an instant? I have intellect—genius—so says the world. I have sacrificed to knowledge, reason and poesy;—praying, first, for happiness, then comfort, then forgetfulness—to cast myself down, the same heart-sick, famished creature! Our examination was an imposing affair. The élite of intelligence and fashion honored us with their presence. The prizes for which others had expended sleepless nights and toilsome days, were for me, who had scarcely put forth an effort; and as the music swelled out to celebrate my victory—blent with the applause of my critics, my heart beat! I had not felt it before for a long, long time,—and as in a lightning flash, I saw what I might—what I would have been, had the sunshine of love been continued to me. But the pitchy cloud rolled over the dazzling opening, and I was again a stranded wreck upon a barren shingle—the wailing monotone of the deep in my ear. I read to them, that a tile was once cast upon an acanthus root, and the hardy plant thrust its arms in every direction, until they felt the light, then coiled in spiral waves, to convert their oppressor into a thing of beauty;—and bade them recognize in the Corinthian capital, an emblem of Truth, which had in all ages owed much of its transcendent loveliness to the tyranny that sought to stifle its growth;—and when I pointed to it as a type of our national freedom, I was forced to stop,—for snowy handkerchiefs perfumed the air, and eager hands beat a rapturous 'encore;' and I was reading a written lie! for my heart was dying—puny and faded—beneath its weight. Intellect! a woman's intellect! I had rather be little Fanny Porter, with her silly, sweet face, and always imperfect lessons, than what I am. She has a father, mother, brothers, sisters, who dote upon her. Nourished upon fondness, she asks love of all, and never in vain. If I could dream my life away, I should be content. I love to lock my door upon the real world, and unbar the portals of my fairy palace—my thought-realm. Those long delicious reveries which melt so sweetly into my night-visions—and the blessed rainy days spent by Josephine in worsted work! Yet all this is injurious—I am enervating my mind—destroying every faculty of usefulness. To whom can I be useful! 'Do your duty in your home'—said the sermon last Sabbath. I have no home—no friends— I am cut off from my species. Tired of the world at seventeen! weary of a life I may not end! Seventeen! seventeen! would it were seventy or seven! I should be nearer my journey's end—or once more a happy child, nestling in my mother's bosom!"

"Forgive me," said a gentle voice, "but your exercise is not finished, and it is near Signer Alboni's hour." The speaker was the owner of the adjoining desk. As their eyes met, hers beamed with sympathy and interest. Ida knew nothing of the wretchedness expressed in her features, but she felt the agony at heart, and taken unawares, she could not entirely repress the tide that sprang to her lids at this unexpected kindness. Ashamed of what she had been "schooled" to consider a weakness, she lowered her head over her writing, until the long curls hid her face. "Signor Alboni, young ladies!" called out Mr. Purcell, the principal of the seminary. Ida surveyed the unsightly sheet in dismay, but there was no time for alteration, and she repaired with the rest to the recitation-room.

Signor Alboni was a gaunt, bilious-looking Italian, whom a residence of ten years in America had robbed of all national characteristics, except a fiery temper. The girls feared and disliked him; but he was a popular and efficient teacher, and in virtue of these considerations, Mr. Purcell was inclined to overlook minor disadvantages. Ellen Morris, whose fun-making propensities no rules or presence could restrain, soon set in circulation a whispered report, that their "amiable professor had had a severe return of dyspeptic symptoms since their last lesson;"—and "don't you think he has a queer taste? They say his favorite drink is a decoction of saffron, spiced with copperas! No wonder he looks so like a piece of new nankeen." Then an impromptu conundrum, pencilled upon a fly-leaf, went the rounds of the class. "If a skeleton were asked to describe his sensations in one word, whose name would he pronounce?" Black, brown and sunny tresses were shaken, and smiling mouths motioned,—"We give it up." Ellen scribbled the answer,—"All-bone-I."

It is a singular fact, that when one person is the unconscious cause of amusement to others—although ignorant of their ridicule, he often experiences an odd feeling of displeasure with himself and the whole world,—a sudden fit of spleen, venting itself upon those who richly deserve the wrath, which in his sane moments, he acknowledges was unprovoked. It was impossible for the signor to observe the laughing faces that sought refuge behind open books and friendly shoulders, for he was occupied in the examination of the pile of manuscripts laid upon his desk, yet his brow was more and more wrinkled each second, and when he spoke, his tone was, as Ellen afterwards described—"as musical as that of a papa lion, administering a parental rebuke to his refractory offspring."

"Miss Porter!"

Poor Fanny's eyes started from their sockets, as she uttered a feeble response.

"Receive your exercise," tearing it in half, and giving her the fragments. "Remain after school-hours, and re-write it; also prepare the next one in addition to your lesson for to-morrow. Miss Morris, where do you purchase your ink?"

"Of Messrs. Politeness, Manners & Co.," she retorted, with an innocent smile. "You never deal there, I believe, sir?"

"Silence!" vociferated the infuriated foreigner. "Rest assured, Miss, I shall report your impertinence to Mr. Purcell. Miss Carleton!" and Ida's neighbour replied. "I find no important errors in your theme, but your chirography lacks dignity and regularity."

With a respectful courtesy, the paper and hint were received; and if a smile played around her mouth, as she contrasted her delicate characters with the stiff, upright hand, in which the corrections were made, he did not see it.

"You had some incontestable reason for omitting to write, Miss Ross," with a sardonic grin; "into its nature I shall not inquire, but plead guilty to curiosity to know the name of the friend who did your work, and appended your name to his or her elegant effort."

Ida was not of a disposition to brook insolence, and she answered with spirit,—"The exercise is mine, sir."

"By right of possession, I suppose?"

"It was written by myself."

"Do I believe you, when my eyes tell me this is neither your hand-writing or style? Who was your accomplice in this witty deception?"

"SIR!"

"Who wrote this theme?" he thundered, maddened by her contempt.

"I have told you—*I* did. No one else has seen it."

"You lie!"

With one lightning glance, she arose; but he placed himself between her and the door.

"Let me pass!" she ordered.

"Signor Alboni!" said Miss Carleton, who had before endeavored to make herself heard, "I can certify to the truth of Miss Ross' statement. I saw her commence and complete her manuscript."

"Aha! yet she says it has been seen only by herself. You must tutor your witnesses more carefully. They convict, instead of exculpate."

"If you hint at collusion between Miss Ross and myself, I can say that we never exchanged a word until an hour since. My desk adjoins hers; it was this circumstance which furnished me with the knowledge of her morning's occupation."

"I beg you will not subject yourself to further insult, upon my account," interrupted Ida, whose figure had dilated and heightened during the colloquy;—then to him—"Once more I command you to stand aside! If you do not obey, I shall call Mr. Purcell." As if he had heard the threatened appeal, the principal appeared in the doorway, in blank astonishment at the novel aspect of affairs. Alboni commenced a hurried jargon, inarticulate through haste and rage; Ida stood with folded arms, her countenance settled in such proud scorn as Lucifer would have envied and striven to imitate. The prudent preceptor perceived at a glance the danger of present investigation; and abruptly declaring the lesson concluded, appointed an hour on the morrow for a hearing of the case. That evening, for the first time in many months, Ida voluntarily sought her guardian's presence. Josephine was in her room, and he was left to the enjoyment of solitude and the newspaper. He arose at the approach of his visitant, and offered her a chair. In these little matters of etiquette, he was particular to punctiliousness; carrying his business habits of law and order into every thing. The paper was replaced upon the stand; the spectacles wiped and returned to their case; and those matter-of-fact eyes raised with an interrogative look.

"You have been informed of the altercation that occurred in the Italian class to-day?" Ida said, waiving the preliminary remarks.

"Josephine mentioned it."

"May I ask what was her version of it?"

"It was a statement of *facts*."

"Doubtless. Then, sir, you are aware that I have been wantonly and grossly insulted by a man for whom I have no respect; that in the presence of the entire class, I was forced to listen to language, which, uttered by one man to another, would be met by prompt chastisement; you are furthermore advised of the *fact* that he, whose duty it is to protect those whom he instructs, instead of compelling the creature to apologize upon his knees, 'postponed inquiry until to-morrow.'"

"And very properly, too."

"Unquestionably, sir!" with the sarcastic smile which accompanied her former assent. "My object in seeking this interview, is to request your attendance upon that occasion. I shall not be present."

"And why not?"

"Because, sir, I will not be confronted with that odious reptile, and give my testimony in his hearing. Judging from the past, and the knowledge of mankind I have acquired under your tuition, nothing that I can say will avail to secure me justice. Mr. Purcell cannot obtain a better teacher, and it is as politic in Alboni to remain. There will be an amicable settlement; and my word will be a knot in the chain of satisfactory evidence they will elicit. The young ladies will, of course, side with 'the gentlemen.'"

"But why am I to be there?—to receive Alboni's apology?"

"I want none, sir—I will hear none. I have been called a *liar*! his pitiful life could not expiate the offence!"

"You are savage, young lady! you wish, perhaps, that I should pistol him."

"I thank you, sir, for recalling by your ridicule, the remembrance that this is a business interview. What I ask is this:— that you announce to Signor Alboni the termination of my studies with him, and pay his bill."

"Do you know, that although it is only the second week of the session, you will be charged for the term?"

"I do, sir."

"What if I refuse to discharge the debt?"

"I shall liquidate it with the money intended for my personal expenses."

"And if I forbid this, and command you to continue your lessons?"

"I shall refuse obedience to a demand you have not the right to make."

"Miss Ross! do you know to whom you are speaking?"

"I address Mr. Read."

"And your guardian, young lady!"

"The guardian of my property, sir."

"You are under no obligations to me, I suppose."

"None that I am conscious of. You are paid for your services and my board."

"There are cares for which money can offer no adequate compensation."

"Indeed, sir! I thought gold a cure for every ill; a reward for every toil. But we are digressing. You will do as I wish?"

"Resume your seat, if you please! The hope that I might have regarded your request favorably, is lessened by your unbecoming deportment. You are ignorant of any benefits I have conferred upon you! Since you will have a debit and credit account, I will enlighten you on this point. You came into this house two years ago—a romantic, sentimental, mawkish, spoiled child; weeping at every word which happened to jar upon your exquisite sensibilities; an unsophisticated simpleton; a fit prey for any bungler in deception; unformed in manner; womanish in feeling, and extravagant in expression. You have now, although but seventeen years of age, more sense and self-possession than most women of double your years; control the weaknesses which rendered you so ridiculous; are accomplished and respected; in short, I say it without flattery to myself, or to you, bid fair to fill your position in society creditably. You have still obstacles to surmount; but I have judged your failings leniently, attributing them, mainly, to the defects in your early training. If your mother had had the wisdom and discretion"—

"Stop, sir, stop!" exclaimed the girl, rising from her chair, and trembling in every limb with excitement "Take not the name of my holy mother upon your lips—still less cast the shadow of reproach upon her conduct! You have taught me the corruption of human nature,—have crushed all the warm affections I had been instructed to cherish;—have made the life my young mind pictured so inviting, a desert waste, inhabited by wily monsters;—but over the wreck there shines one ray, the memory of an angel lent to earth! For her sake I live among those whose form she wore, but with whose foul hearts hers could have had no fellowship. You tell me she was like the rest, that the religion, in her so lovely, is a delusion—and I answer, I do not believe you. In her name I refute your vile sophisms! Heaven knows how little I have profited by her counsels and example. I loathe myself! 'A woman,' you said! rather a fiend! for such is woman when she buries her heart, nor mourns above its grave. 'Control my feelings!' I do! I have driven back the tears until the scalding waves have killed whatever in my soul could boast a heavenly birth. There is nothing there to prove my relationship to my mother, but her memory. When that is destroyed I shall go mad. I am on the verge of insanity now—I often am! I do not doubt your assertions as to your, and shame on me that I should say it, *my* brethren; for in yourself I see all the traits you ascribe to them. Woman, you say, belongs to an order of yet inferior beings; and in your daughter I have an illustration of this; for she inherits her father's character, combined with a meaner mind. You consider that I owe you respect,—I do not! I am superior to you both, for I still struggle with the emotions our Creator kindled up within us, and sent us to earth to extinguish. Within your bosoms there are only cold ashes. Frown as you please! your anger intimidates as little as your ridicule abashes. The idea once entered my mind that I could win you and your child to love me. I could laugh at the thought; that was in my sentimental days, when I deemed that the desolate orphan must find affection somewhere. My most 'extravagant' imaginings never paint such a possibility now. I have done. We understand each other. The contempt you had for the 'mawkish' baby, cannot equal mine for you. You will say no more of obligation and respect. I *despise* you, and I owe you nothing?"

"Is the girl mad in good earnest?" gasped the cause of this burning torrent, as the door closed upon her. "She's a dangerous customer when her blood is up—a perfect Vesuvius, and I came near being Herculaneum or Pompeii. I've seen Ross in these tantrums, when we were chums together. She looked like her father when she said she was my superior. Bah!" He picked up his "Enquirer," but the political news was stale and vapid: the "Whig" was tried with no better success. In the centre of the racy editorial, and oddly mixed with the advertisements, was that incarnation of pride and passion, which through her eyes, more plainly than her lips, said, "I despise you, and I owe you nothing." Thus stood her part of the account he had proposed to examine.

CHAPTER IV

Miss Carleton acknowledged the appearance of her desk-mate on the succeeding morning, by an inclination of the head and a smile; and nothing more passed between them until the hour for Italian. She paused, seeing that Ida retained her seat. "Are you not going in?" she ventured to ask.

"No."

There was a moment of hesitation, and she spoke again. "I would not appear to dictate, but do you not fear Mr. Purcell may construe your non-attendance into disrespect to himself?"

"I fear nothing," was upon Ida's tongue, but her better nature would not allow her to return rudeness for what, suspicion could torture into nothing but disinterested kindness. With a gleam of her former frankness she looked up at her interlocutor, "You do not know as much as I do, or you would understand the inutility of my presence at the trial which comes off this morning. I would avoid a repetition of yesterday's scene. One will suffice for a life-time."

"You met then with insult and injustice. To-day, Mr. Purcell will shield you from both. As a gentleman, and a conscientious judge, he cannot but see that Alboni's attack was uncalled for, and decide against him."

"No man is conscientious when his conscience militates against his purse and popularity." Miss Carleton seemed shocked, and Ida added, hastily, "Our views upon this, as upon most subjects, are very different, I fancy; therefore, discussion is worse than useless. In this instance, my determination is taken;" and she opened her book.

"I will not attempt to shake it," replied her companion. "But suffer me to hope for a longer conversation at some future time, upon these topics, concerning which you think we differ. There may be some points of agreement, and I, for one, am open to conviction."

Again was Ida thrown off her guard, and the smile that answered irradiated her face like a sudden sunbeam. But when her class-mate had gone, she thought,—"Weak fool! the reserve I have striven for two years to establish, melted by a soft speech of a school-girl. She is one of the would-be 'popular' sort, and would worm herself into confidence by an affectation of sympathy and sweetness."

"Miss Ross," said Mr. Purcell, a while later, coming up to her desk, "you will do me the favor to meet me in my study at two o'clock."

At the time designated, she walked with a stately tread through the long school-room, unabashed by the hundred curious eyes bent upon her; for a summons to "the study" was an event of rare occurrence, and had been heretofore the harbinger of some important era in the annals of school-dom. Ida was prepared for every thing partiality could dictate, and tyranny execute; but Mr. Purcell was alone, and his demeanor anything but menacing. "He thinks to cajole me," whispered the fell demon Distrust, and her heart changed to steel.

"Miss Ida," began the principal, mildly, "this is your third session in this institution, and I can sincerely declare that during that time, your propriety of behaviour, and diligence in study have not been surpassed. I have never had a young lady under my care, whose improvement was more rapid—of whose attainments I was more proud; but I regret to say, never one whose confidence I failed so signally to gain. A teacher's task, my dear Miss Ross, is at best an arduous one, but if he receive no recompense for his toil in the affection of those for whom he labors, his life is indeed one of cheerless drudgery. You appear to regard me as a mere machine. For a time I attributed your reserve to diffidence, and trusted that time and my efforts would dissipate it. On the contrary, the distance between us has increased. You hold yourself aloof from your school-mates, repelling every offered familiarity, yet I have seen you weep after such an act. Your cheek glows with enthusiasm when your favorite studies engage your mind, and you relapse into frigid hauteur when recalled to the actual world around you. You have feeling as well as intellect—you are acting a part assumed from some unaccountable fancy; or, I would rather believe, put upon you by necessity. The evidence of your want of reliance in my friendship which you have given me to-day, has determined me to speak candidly with you. I would not wrest a confession from you which you might afterwards repent, but I entreat you to look upon me as a friend who has a paternal love for each member of his numerous family, who desires to see you happy, and asks—not your confidence, but that you will let him serve you."

Ida sat like a statue. He resumed in a tone of disappointment—

"As to the unjustifiable charge brought by Signor Alboni—I am aware how galling is even the appearance of humiliation upon so proud a spirit. I have investigated the matter carefully. The testimony of your friend, Miss Carleton, would of itself have been sufficient to exonerate you. It was confirmed by the voice of the class, and the inevitable consequence is, that Signor Alboni no longer has a place in my school. I can safely promise that the teacher I have selected in his stead, will oppose no impediment to your progress."

Shame for her unjust accusations, and remorseful gratitude pierced Ida's bosom. Greatly agitated, she approached her instructor, when Mr. Read walked in;—a cynical iceberg! Every generous emotion—all softness vanished on the instant. His inquiring glance encountered one as freezing. "I will not detain you longer, Mr. Purcell," she said, as if concluding a business arrangement. "As nearly as I can understand, your object in sending for me was to secure me as a pupil of the new language-master. Having undertaken the study of the Italian, I prefer going through with the course. Mr. Read will settle the terms. Good afternoon, gentlemen;" and with the mien of a duchess she left them.

Mr. Read "had been delayed by pressing business. Miss Ross requested him to see Signor Alboni—was sorry he was late—presumed all was right, etc.," and walked out again. Mr. Purcell was too much hurt, and too indignant at his pupil's conduct, to care whether he stayed or not.

The misguided girl had alienated a true friend, and she knew it—felt it in her heart's core. In the solitude of her chamber she wept bitter tears: "I have cast away the gem for which I would sell my soul! While I thirsted for the waters of affection, I struck down the hand that held them to my lip. It is my fate—I was not born to be loved—I hate myself—why should I inspire others with a different feeling?"

In vain she tried to reason herself into a belief of Mr. Purcell's insincerity. Truth speaks with a convincing tongue, and she knew that the imputation of interested motives she had hurled at him in the unfortunate revulsion of feeling, was unfounded.

In intermission next day, a note was laid upon Ida's desk, inscribed in towering capitals, to "Misses Ross and Carleton;" It ran thus:—

"At a large and enthusiastic meeting of the Italian class of Mr. Purcell's Young Ladies' Female Seminary, convened on yesterday afternoon, the succeeding resolutions were proposed, and carried unanimously:

> "*Resolved*, That whereas, Miss Ida Ross and Miss Caroline Carleton, members of the aforesaid class, have, by their spirited independence delivered us from an oppression as grinding as that under which our

Revolutionary forefathers groaned, a vote of thanks shall be tendered them in the name of their compatriots. And—

"*Resolved*, Moreover, that we bind ourselves to assist them by our united suffrages in the attainment of any honor for which they shall hereafter be candidates, whether the dunce-block or the gold medal.

ANNA TALBOT, *Chairman*.

ELLEN MORRIS, *Secretary*.

The event which had elicited this public manifestation, was to Ida, connected with too much that was unpleasant, to allow her to smile at the pompous communication. She passed it gravely to her neighbor. She laughed at the ludicrous repetition of feminist in the second line, and at the conclusion, bounded upon the platform where stood Mr. Purcell's desk, and commenced a flourishing harangue "for herself and colleague," expressing their gratitude at the flattering tribute from their fellow-laborers, and pledging themselves to uphold forever their honor and lawful privileges. "In the language of your eloquent resolution, my sisters, we form a 'Young Ladies' Female Seminary'—womanfully will we battle for woman's rights."

"Hush-h-h!" and Mr. Purcell was discovered standing behind the crowd. He stood aside to let the blushing orator return to her seat, remarking in an under-tone as she passed, "I must take care to enlist such talents in my service—I shall be undone if they are directed against me."

"Oh Carry! what *did* he say?" whispered Fanny Porter.

"Nothing very dreadful," she returned, laughingly. Ida looked on in surprise, Josephine with scorn; but to the majority, this little episode in their monotonous life was a diverting entertainment.

"Give me a girl who is not too proud to relish a joke," said Ellen Morris. "Ida Ross is above such buffoonery. She would not have demeaned her dignity before the school."

"But Carry spoke for her too," said Emma Glenn, a meek, charitable creature: "Perhaps modesty, not pride, kept her silent."

"Fiddlesticks!" was the school-girlish rejoinder.

Ida had missed a chance for making herself popular. The girls were moved to admiration by her manner of resenting Alboni's rudeness, and their joy at getting rid of him, assumed the shape of gratitude to their champion. She was for the hour a heroine, and might have retained her stand, but for her cool treatment of their advances. She saw, without understanding the reason of the change, that there was now a mingling of dislike in their neglect; and as she sank in their esteem, Carry mounted. Mr. Purcell never noticed her out of the recitation room—Mr. Read was more lofty—Josephine more contemptuous than ever. Inmates of one house—occupying adjacent chambers—sitting at the same board at home, and within speaking distance at school, the two girls had not one feeling in common—a spark of affection one for the other. Open ruptures were infrequent now, although they were innumerable during the first months of their companionship. They appeared together in public—this Mr. Read enjoined "It was due to his reputation, people should not say that his daughter's privileges exceeded his ward's." Further than this he did not interfere. He saw them only at meal-times, and in the evening; then Josephine presided over the tea-tray with skill and grace, and amused him, if he wished it, by reading, singing or talking. Ida did as she pleased. There were no requirements, no privations. In the eyes of the world her situation was unexceptionable. They knew nothing of the covert sneers which smiled down any tendency to what the torpid minds of the father and daughter considered undue enthusiasm; their sarcastic notice of her "singularities," their studied variance with her views;—but to her, bondage and cruelty would have been more tolerable. Yet this mocking surveillance—this certainty of ridicule, could not always check the earnest expression of a grasping intellect and ardent temperament; and there were not a few who frequented the house, who preferred the piquancy of her conversation, when they could draw her out of the snow-caverns of her reserve, to the trite common-places and artificial spirits of Miss Read.

Among these was Mr. Dermott, an Irish gentleman of considerable scientific renown, and a traveller of some note; hard upon forty years of age, but enjoying life with the zest of twenty. Ida's intelligent countenance had pleased him at their introduction, and having letters to Mr. Read, he embraced every opportunity to improve the acquaintance.

"I shall not go to school to-day," said Josephine, one morning, "father expects Mr. Dermott and several other gentlemen to dine with him, and I cannot be spared. He says you must come home in time for dinner."

"As school breaks up at three, and you will not dine before five, there was no need to issue the command;" said Ida, irritated at her arrogant tone.

"Very well, I have delivered the message."

Mr. Read was dissatisfied that his ward did not enter the drawing-room until dinner was announced. "It did not look well,"—and her nonchalant air and slight recognition of the party, did not "speak well for his bringing up." But the current veered before meal was over. The fowls were under-done, and the potatoes soaked. His glance of displeasure at his daughter was received with such imperturbability, that he chafed at the impossibility of moving her, and his desire to render somebody uncomfortable. The latter wish was not left ungratified. One after another felt the influence of his lowering brow, and imitated his silence, until Mr. Dermott and Ida were the only ones who maintained a connected conversation. He talked fluently with the humor peculiar to his countrymen, and had succeeded in interesting his listener. She had naturally a happy laugh, which in earlier years rung out in merry music; and as the unusual sound startled him from time to time, Mr. Read took it as a personal affront. Could not she see that he was out of temper? He had punished the rest for the cook's misdeeds, how dare she, while they sat 'neath the thunder cloud of his magnificent wrath, sport in the sunshine? It was audacious bravado. She should rue it ere long. Josephine readily obeyed his signal to leave the table, so soon as it could be done with a semblance of propriety. "I will hear the rest, by and by," said Ida to Mr. Dermott, "*au revoir*." Neither of the girls spoke after quitting the dining-room. Josephine lay upon a lounge, with half-closed lids, apparently drowsy or fatigued, in reality, wakeful and watching. Ida walked back and forth, humming an Irish air—pleased and thoughtful. Then taking from the book-case a volume of "Travels," she employed herself in looking it over. "See!" said she, at Mr. Dermott's reappearance, "it is as I thought. This author's account varies, in some respects, from yours; and at the peril of my place in your good graces, I must declare my prejudices to be with him. A spot so celebrated, so sacred in its associations, cannot be as uninteresting as you would have me to think. Come, confess, that the jolting camel and surly guide were accessories to your discontent."

Josephine lost the answer, and much that followed. She was joined by young Pemberton, a fop of the first water, with sense enough to make him uneasy in the society of the gifted, and meanness to rejoice in their discomfiture and misfortune. For the rest, he was weak and hot-headed, a compound of conceit and malice. Time was when he admired Ida. He had an indefinite notion that a clever wife would reflect lustre upon him; and a very decided appreciation of her more shining and substantial charms.

Her repulse was a mortal offence: small minds never forget, much less pardon a rebuke to their vanity, and he inly swore revenge. But how to get it? She rose superior to his witless sarcasms, and more pointed slights; reversing the arrows towards himself, and his mortification heated into hatred. Josephine was aware of this feeling, and its cause; and while despising, in a man, a weakness to which she was herself a prey, foreseeing that he might prove a convenient tool, she attached him to her by suasives and flatteries.

"It is a positive relief to talk to you, Miss Josephine," he yawned, "I am surfeited with literature and foreigners. These travelled follows are outrageous bores, with their bushy moustachios and outlandish lingo. How the ladies can fawn upon them as they do, I cannot comprehend."

"Do not condemn us all for the failings of a part. There are those who prefer pure gold to gilded trash."

"For your sake, I will make some exceptions," with a "killing" look. "But what do you imagine to be the object of that flirtation? No young lady of prudence or proper self respect, would encourage so boldly the attentions of a stranger. Supposing him to be what he represents, (a thing by no means certain,) she cannot intend to marry him—a man old enough to be her father!"

"But, 'unison of tastes,' 'concord of souls,' etc., will go far towards reconciling her to the disparity of years," observed Josephine, ironically; not sorry to strike upon this tender point. He tried to laugh, but with indifferent success.

Ida's voice reached them, and they stopped to listen.

"I am afraid my conceptions of Eastern life and scenery are more poetical than correct. I picture landscapes sleeping in warm, rich, 'Syrian sunshine,' 'sandal groves and bowers of spice,'

'Ruined shrines, and towers that seem
The relics of some splendid dream,'—

such a Fairy Land as ignorance and imagination create."

"The Utopia of one who studies Lalla Rookh more than 'Eastern Statistics,' or 'Incidents of Travel,'" said Mr. Dermott, smiling. "Yet Moore's descriptions are not so much overwrought as some suppose. His words came continually to my tongue. He has imbibed the true spirit of Oriental poetry; the melancholy, which, like the ghost of a dead age, broods over that oldest of lands; the passion flushing under their tropical sun; their wealth of imagery. Lalla Rookh reads like a translation from the original Persian. The wonder is that he has never been self-tempted to visit the 'Vale of Cashmere' in person."

"Campbell, too, having immortalized Wyoming, will not cross the ocean to behold it," said Ida.

There was a consultation between the confederates, and Pemberton crossed to Ida's chair, with a smirk that belied the fire in his eye.

"Excuse me, Mr. Dermott,—Miss Ida, I am commissioned to inquire of you the authorship and meaning of this quotation—

'Deeply, darkly, *desperately* blue!'"

It is impossible to convey a just impression of the offensive tone and emphasis with which this impertinence was uttered. The quick-witted Irishman saw through the design in an instant. "It is from a Scotch author," said he, before Ida could reply, "and the rhyme runs after this fashion—

'Feckless, fairlie, farcically fou!'"

and not deigning a second glance at the questioner, he continued his account of a visit he had paid to Moore. The object of this merciless retort stood for a second, in doubt as to its meaning, and then walked off, still in incertitude. Ida's laugh, while it might have been in response to Mr. Dermott's story assured Josephine that her end was unaccomplished, before her messenger had delivered his lame return.

"She understood me, and it cut pretty deeply, but that puppy of a paddy answered for her. He repeated the next line, too, 'from a Scotch author,' he said, but I believe he made it up."

"What was it?" asked Josephine.

"'Fairly, farcically fou,' or something like that. If I were sure that last word meant fool, I would knock him down. Do you understand Scotch?"

"No," replied Josephine, vexed, but afraid to excite him further. "He is beneath the notice of a gentleman; we can let him alone."

But Ida's share in this was not to be overlooked. Josephine appeared as usual at breakfast: talkative to her father, and taciturn to her female companion. At length she inquired, meaningly, "by the way, Ida, when does your travelled Hibernian 'lave this counthry?'"

"If you speak of Mr. Dermott, I do not know."

"Is it not remarkable," said Josephine to her parent, "that polish and purify as you may, you cannot cure an Irishman of vulgarity? Irish he is, and Irish he will remain to the end of the chapter."

"Dermott behaves very decently, does he not? His letters of recommendation—introduction, I would say, describe him as a pattern gentleman."

Josephine lifted her brows. "It is a misfortune to be fastidious; my education has rendered me so. I cannot tolerate slang or abuse, especially when directed at a superior in politeness, if not in assurance."

"What now?" demanded Mr. Read, impatiently; and Ida, unable to hear more in silence, started up from the table.

"Wait, if you please," said Josephine, with that metallic glitter of her grey eyes. "I wish you to repeat your friend's reply to Mr. Pemberton, when he was the bearer of a civil message from *me*."

"I heard no message of that description," retorted Ida, unmoved.

"He did not repeat a line of poetry, and ask the author's name, I presume?"

"He did."

"And you furnished the required information?"

24

"I did not."

"Mr. Dermott did, then. What was his answer?"

"I do not choose to tell. *I* am not in the habit of playing spy and informer."

"Then I shall repeat it. *I* am not in the habit of winking at impudence or transgressions of the most common laws of society. What do you say, sir, of a man who, in the presence of ladies, calls another a 'farcical fool?'"

"That he is a foreign jackanape. He never darkens my door again. You heard this?" to Ida.

"I did not, sir, but Mr. Pemberton displays such penetration in discovering, and taste in fitting on caps that could suit no one else so well, I am not inclined to contest his title to this latest style."

"I do not wonder at your defence of your erudite suitor," said Josephine, laying a disagreeable stress upon the adjective. "If he were to single me out in every company, as the one being capable of appreciating him, I, too, should be blinded by the distinction attendant upon my notoriety. But as His Highness never gives token, by word or deed, of his consciousness of the existence of so unpretending a personage, I may be pardoned my impartial observation and judgment. I do not expect you to forbid his visits, sir, but I wish it understood that *I* am not at home when he calls."

"And that you reject his attentions?" asked Ida, dryly.

Josephine did not like her smile, yet saw no danger in replying—"assuredly!"

"It is a pity," was the rejoinder, "that your resolution was not postponed until Tuesday."

"And why?" said Mr. Read.

"Mr. Dermott informed me last night that he had secured three tickets for the concert of Monday evening, and requested permission to call for Josephine and myself. I told him that she had expressed anxiety to attend, and that I was disengaged. She was not in the parlor when he left, and he entrusted the invitation to me. He will be here this forenoon for her answer. As things now stand, his visit will be extremely mal-apropos. I shall decline for myself; she can do the same."

Josephine prudently lowered her eye-lids, but her lips were white with rage. She had especial reasons for desiring to go to this concert. Every body was running mad after the principal performer:—absence from necessity would be a pitiable infliction;—to stay away from choice, irrefragable proof of want of taste. To be escorted thither by Mr. Dermott, would give her an éclat the devotion of a score of Pembertons could not produce. In seeking to mortify another, she had pulled down this heavy chagrin upon her own head,—common fate of those who would make the hearts and backs of their fellows the rounds of their ladder to revenge or to fame.

Even Mr. Read was momentarily disconcerted. "I will procure you a ticket," he said, consolingly.

That tongue was used to falsehood, yet it did not move as glibly as was its wont, as she replied, "I do not care to go, sir."

"That is fortunate," said Ida, "as every seat was taken yesterday. You do not object to my withdrawing *now*?"

The shot had gone home; her enmity was gratified; she had not been anxious to attend from the first, and therefore was not disappointed; she did not suffer from pained sensibility; the frequency of these encounters had inured her to ambushed attack; she was fast becoming a match for them in stoicism, and surpassed them in satire; in this skirmish she had borne flying colours from the field; but had the contrary of all these things been true, she could not have been more wretched. She hated, as spirits like hers only can hate, her cold-hearted persecutors, and exulted in their defeat; yet close upon triumph came a twinge of remorse and a sense of debasement.

"I am sinking to their level! I could compete with them upon no other ground. They are despicable in their worldliness and malice; shall I grovel and hiss with them? It seems inevitable—debarred as I am from all associations which can elevate and clear my mind. Oh! the low envy in that girl's face as she named my 'suitor!' Destitute of mental wants herself, she thinks of nothing but courtship and a settlement! But this matter must be arranged."

She opened her writing-desk. Her chamber was her retreat and sanctum, and she had lavished much taste and time in fitting it up. All its appurtenances spoke of genius and refinement. With a poetic love for warm colors and striking contrasts, crimson and black relieved, each other, in her carpet and curtains. The bedstead, seats and tables, fashioned into elegant and uncommon forms by her orders, were draped and cushioned with the same Tyrian hue. Books and portfolios were heaped and strewed upon the shelves and stands; and in one corner, upon a wrought bronze tripod, was an exquisite statuette—a girl kneeling beside an empty cage, the lifeless songster stark and cold in her hand. Several of Ida's schoolmates were with her when she purchased it from an itinerant Italian. They saw in the expression of hopeless sadness, only regret for her bird. Ida noted that her gaze was not upon its ruffled plumes, but to its silent home; and that one hand lay upon her heart. Looking more narrowly she discerned upon the pedestal the simple exclamation, "*Et mon coeur!*"

Henceforward it had become her Lares. She had scattered flowers over it, kissed it weepingly, and with lips rigid in stern despair, laid her hot brow to the white forehead of the voiceless mourner. She must have something to love, and the insensate image was dear, because it told of a grief such as hers. Now, after she dipped her pen in the standish, she paused to contemplate it,—the red light bathing it in a life-like glow,—and the blood receded from her face, as she uttered aloud its touching complaint, "Et *mon* coeur!"

Writing a note to Mr. Dermott, in which; without stating her reasons, she declined his offer, she dispatched it by one of her own servants, lately promoted to the office of Abigail, and attired herself for a walk. It was Saturday, and the weather faultless. A sigh of relief escaped her when she was in the outer air—she was free for a while. The streets were densely peopled—dashing ladies, and marble-playing urchins, glorying in the holiday; bustling, pushing men, and lazy nurses lugging fat babies; and through the incongruous crowd the pale thinker threaded her way, jostling and jostled, wrapped in herself, as they thought but of their individual personality, with this difference—they seemed happy in their selfishness; she was miserable in her isolation. She did not see that Pemberton passed her with a stiff bow, which, in punishment for her non-recognition, he resolved should be exchanged for a decided "cut" at their next meeting; did not catch Mr. Purcell's eye, as forgetting her rebuff in his pleasure at espying one, who could rightly value the prize he had discovered in an antiquated volume, musty with age, he beckoned to her from the door of the bookstore; did not hear Emma Glenn's modest "Good morning, Miss Ida," although she liked the child, and would have loved her if she had dared. She turned from the busy thoroughfare into an unfrequented street, keeping the same rapid pace; the mind was working, the body must be moving too—on, still on, with unflagging speed—'till she found herself upon the summit of the hill overlooking the lower part of the city, and near the old church-yard. She stopped, and looked in. A flight of steps led up to the burying-ground, several feet above the level of the walk. What tempted her to ascend? She had been there before, and was not interested—yet the irresolution ended in her entrance. It was very still in that Acropolis of the dead: the long grass, yellow in the October sun, waved without rustling; the sere leaves drifted silently to the ground; from the mass of buildings below her arose only a measured beat rather than hum—as regular, and not louder, than the "muffled drum" within her bosom. The warring elements of discord sank into a troubled rest, but their conflict was easier to be borne than the reaction that succeeded.

"Free among the dead;" forgotten as they, she sat upon a broken tombstone, in the shadow of the venerable church, with sorrowful eyes which looked beyond the city, the river, and the undulating low-grounds skirting its banks.

She had said to herself an hundred times, "I cannot be happy; it is folly to hope." But this morning she felt she had never until now relinquished hope; that despair, for the first time, stalked through the deserted halls of her heart, and the dreaded echo "alone" answered his footsteps.

It is easy to give up the world, with its million sources of delight, to share the adverse fortunes of one dearer than all its painted show; it is sweet to bid adieu to its frivolities, for the hope of another and a "better," but

"When the draught so fair to see
Turns to hot poison on the lip;"

when the duped soul cries out against the fair pretence that promised so much and gave so little, when it will none of it, and puts it by with loathing disgust;—yet resorts to nothing more real and pure;—what art can balm a woe like this?

A click of the gate-latch, and voices warned her that her solitude was about to be invaded. "I will wait here half an hour," said familiar tones. "Thank you," was the reply; "you need not stay longer; if she is at home I shall spend the day." "Very well; good bye," and Carry Carleton ran up the steps. Retreat was impossible, for their eyes met at once, and to the new visitor the meeting appeared to give satisfaction.

"I am, indeed, fortunate," said she, saluting Ida, and taking a place beside her, "I expected to pass a solitary half-hour. One of the girls came with me to the gate. She has gone to see her aunt, and may not return to-day. This is a favorite spot of mine. I am laughed at for the choice, yet it seems I am not as singular as they would have me believe. Do you come here often?"

"This is only my second visit."

"Indeed! But it is a long walk from your house. I live nearer, although on the other hill."

"I understood you were from the country," said Ida.

"So I am—but my sister resides here, and hers is another home to me. I *love* the country, yet I like Richmond. It is a beautiful city," she continued, her glance roving over the landscape.

"Outwardly—yes."

"You do not think the inhabitants adapted to their abode, then?"

"I do not know that they are worse than the rest of mankind. It is a matter of astonishment to me, that this globe should have been set apart as the theatre for so depraved a race."

"I don't know," said Carry, cheerily. "I find it a nice world—the best I am acquainted with; and the people harmless, good creatures—some dearer to me than others; but I entertain a fraternal affection for all."

"I have read of philanthropists," said Ida; "but you are the sole specimen I have seen. And this universal love—is it content to exist without a reciprocation?"

"The heart would be soon emptied were this so," returned the other, her bright face becoming serious. "There are many who love me; if any dislike, I am in blissful ignorance of the sentiment and its cause."

"But if your friends were removed, and replaced by enemies?"

"I would teach them friendship. My affection for the dead would make me more desirous to benefit the living."

"And if they would not be conciliated—if upon the broad earth you had not an answering spirit?"

"I should die!"

"How then do I live?" nearly burst from Ida's heart, but she smothered it, and replied, "It is easier to speak of death than to brave it."

"Death! did I say death?" exclaimed Carry. "I saw life as it would be were I bereft of father, sister, friends—and I said truly that it would not be worth the keeping—but death! I would not rush on *that!* I have such a horror of the winding-sheet and the worm!" She shivered.

"Yet you like to be here?"

"Yes. This is a sunny, cheerful place, with no fresh graves to remind one that the work of destruction is still going on. I love life. Others may expose its deceits, and weep above its withered blooms; I see blue sky where they fancy clouds. It is the day—the time for action and enjoyment; who would hasten the coming of the night—impenetrable—dawnless!"

"'To die—and go—we know not where!'"

quoted Ida. "That line conveys all that I fear in death. There have been seasons when the uncertainty shrouding the abyss beyond alone prevented my courting its embrace. Were it eternal forgetfulness, how grateful would be its repose. Looking around me here, I think of calm sleepers under these stones, hands folded meekly upon bosoms that will never heave again; of aching heads and wearied spirits at rest forever."

"You are too young to covet this dreamless slumber," said Carry "With your talents and facilities you have a work to do in this world."

"What can I do? and for whom?"

"Why—for every body."

"Too wide a scope—define. For example, what are my school-duties, setting aside my studies?"

"We can help each other," was the modest rejoinder. "We can impart pleasure, and avoid giving pain. Not a day passes in which we cannot add a drop of sweet to the appointed draught of some one of our fellow-creatures."

"Apropos to honey—it suggests its opposite, gall, and our ei-devant professor. I have not thanked you for your generous interference in my behalf, on the day of our fracas," said Ida, with an ease and cordiality that surprised herself.

"You magnify the favor. I spoke the truth. To withhold it would have been dishonesty."

"Dishonesty!"

"Your character for veracity was assailed. I had the proof which would establish it. I should have felt like a receiver of stolen goods had I concealed it."

"Moreover, to your philanthropy, I was not an individual, but the impersonation of the sisterhood;" said Ida, jestingly.

"Perhaps so," returned Carry, in a like strain. "You remember the 'Young Ladies' Female meeting.'"

"That was a piece of Ellen Morris' grandiloquence. Do you know, I envy that girl her faculty of creating mirth wherever she goes!"

"I had rather be Emma Glenn," said Carry. "One is witty, the other affectionate, and they will receive respectively admiration and love."

"I do not quite agree with you. Ellen's high spirits will carry her through many a sharp battle, from which Emma's sensitive nature would never recover. To combat with the world one should have no heart; and I heard a clergyman once say that a woman had no use for sense."

Carry laughed. "Between you, you would represent us as a superfluous creation. Yet woman has her sphere, no less than man; and if he conquers in his by might of purpose and brute strength, she guides, instead of rules in hers, by love and submission. As for the world, that semi-fabulous ogre, supposed to live somewhere, all out of doors, whose cold charities are proverbial; who eats up widow's houses, and grinds the poor; we have no dealings with it. It is, to my notion, an innocent bugbear, kept by the men, to prevent us from meddling in their business matters; and to melt flinty-hearted wives into pity for one, who has been fighting this monster all day, and has now to drink smoked tea, and eat burnt toast for supper."

"Are you ever sad?" questioned Ida.

"Not often, why do you ask?"

"You appear so light-hearted. I was at a loss to determine whether it was natural or feigned."

"My spirits are good, chiefly from habit, I believe. My father is remarkably cheerful. It is a maxim of his, that we are unjust, when we cause others to do penance for our humors; they have trouble enough of their own to bear. Controlling the manifestations of temper and discontent, is generally followed by the suppression of the feelings themselves. It has been so with me."

"See that burlesque of life!" said Ida, pointing. "Children turning somersets upon a tomb-stone!"

The tomb was built with four brick walls, supporting a horizontal tablet; and upon this flat surface, the irreverent youngsters were gambolling. One, the most agile, and the leader of the troop, was, as she spoke, in the act of performing a vehemently encored feat, viz.: throwing two somersets upon the marble, another *in transitu* for the ground, and a fourth, after landing upon the turf. Two were accomplished in safety, the third was a flying leap, and he did not move afterwards. The children screamed, and the girls ran to the spot. In falling, he had struck his head against a stone, and was senseless, the blood gushing from a wound in, or near the temple. Carry rested his head upon her arm, and with nervous haste, unbuttoned his collar. "Where are his parents?" inquired Ida. But they only cried the louder. "I fear he is killed!" said Carry. Ida shook her purse at the terrified group. "Who will bring me a doctor,—who, his mother?" Her collected manner tended to quiet them, as much as the clink of coin. Half-a-dozen scampered in as many directions, and she ordered the rest off, without ceremony. There was no rebellion. Each had a misgiving that he was to blame for the casualty, and they were glad to skulk away.

The handkerchief which Carry held to the gash, was saturated, and Ida supplied hers. He showed no sign of life, except that Ida imagined that she detected a feeble fluttering of the heart. Carry wept as though her heart would break. "Poor little fellow!" she exclaimed repeatedly. Ida did not shed a tear, but her compressed lips and contracted brow said this did not proceed from insensibility. "I cannot bear this suspense," she said. "I will look for a doctor myself, if you are not afraid to stay here alone."

"No, go!"

She met the medical man at the gate. It was Mr. Read's family physician, who chanced to be in the neighborhood. "Oh, Dr. Ballard!" exclaimed Ida. "I am rejoiced to see you!"

"And I am always happy to meet Miss Ross—but what is this about a boy killed? None of your friends, I hope."

Ida explained, as she led him to the scene of the disaster. It seemed ill-timed to the agitated girls, to see him touch his hat, with grave courtesy, to Carry, as he stooped to make an examination. "He is not dead," he said, feeling the pulse and heart; "but it came near being an awkward hurt. Miss Ross, I will trouble you to call one of those boys, and send him for my servant, who is in the street with my carriage. If I only had some soft linen!" looking around. Ida took an embroidered scarf from her neck. He tore it into strips, rolled them into a ball, and bound it tightly upon the cut. "Where does he live?" he asked.

The information was furnished by the boy's mother, who hurried up at this instant. She, with her reviving son, were put into the carriage, and the doctor stepped in after them.

The girls had no inclination to linger in the church-yard. The conversation, during their walk, ran upon the accident; but as they parted at the corner of the streets diverging to their separate abodes, Carry expressed a strong desire for the continuation of the acquaintance. "We have had an odd talk this morning;" said she smiling; "I would not have you regard it as a fair sample of my conversational powers."

Ida walked homeward with a lightened spirit. "Odd" as was their talk, and alarming as was the incident which interrupted it, she was better for both. There was a charm in Carry's frankness, which beguiled her confidence, and her cheerful philosophy was a pleasant, if not a prudent rule, for making one's way in life. She dwelt upon her declaration, that each day brought its opportunities for benevolent deeds; and her conscience responded joyfully to the appeal, "Have I contributed my drop of sweet to-day?" by pointing to her exertions for the relief of the unknown sufferer. Carry had praised her presence of mind, and the doctor complimented her warmly. "If I have not given pleasure, I have mitigated pain."

The struck chord ceased to vibrate as she reached the house where she had suffered and learned so much. When she came down to dinner, she was impassive and distant. Mr. Read vouchsafed to inquire if she had seen Mr. Dermott. She replied in the negative.

"I thought there was an arrangement to that effect;" said he, sneeringly.

"I addressed a note to him which made his call unnecessary."

"I do not presume to meddle with your correspondence, Miss Ross;" with "immense" stiffness; "but I trust neither my name, or that of my daughter was contained in that communication."

"I am responsible for my actions, sir; it is certain I never thought of referring them to your influence. I suppose Mr. Dermott is satisfied,—*I* am."

CHAPTER V

Mr. Purcell, himself an able connoisseur and liberal patron of the fine arts, never suffered a suitable occasion to pass, without endeavoring to implant, and cultivate like tastes in his pupils. No "Exhibition" or Collection was recommended unadvisedly. He justly considered a relish for a vicious or false style, worse than none. So well was this known, that the girls were equally eager to examine what he esteemed worthy of their inspection, and to avoid that which he condemned. An artist visited the city, and advertised a set of "choice paintings, on exhibition for a few days." They were much talked of, and the scholars impatiently listened for the verdict of their principal. There were many smiling faces, when he announced, that he accepted, with pleasure, the polite invitation of the artist to himself and the members of his school. "The pictures were the work of a master hand;—he recommended them to their careful study." That afternoon, the studio was full. Some went from curiosity; some to be in the fashion; comparatively a small number through genuine love for the art. Among the latter class was Ida Ross. Bestowing little notice upon her acquaintances present, she passed around the room, intent upon the object which had drawn her thither. She was not disturbed; her reserve repelled, and her intellectual superiority awed; she knew—and they knew that though with, she was not of them; as an institution, they were proud of her; as individuals, with a very few exceptions, they disliked and envied her.

The proprietor, or a gentleman, supposed to be he, was at a desk, writing. He must have possessed the power of abstraction in an extraordinary degree; for the chattering about him resembled the confabulations of a flock of magpies, more than the conversation of decorous young ladies. Groups came and departed; and Ida did not mark the changes, until, diverted from the contemplation of a splendid landscape by the sound of her own name,—she perceived a group near by, composed of four or five girls and as many young men, none of them her well-wishers or admirers;—their attention divided between herself, and a sketch of St. John's church. Josephine was the magnet of the circle, and behind her, was the smirking Pemberton. A single glance took in all this, and features and expression were immobile as before. It was Josephine's voice she had heard;—its tones higher than usual. She neither desired, nor affected concealment.

"As I was saying, the church-yard has been converted into a gymnasium. The cry is no longer, 'Liberty or Death!'—but 'Leap Frog or die!'"

A general cachinnation applauded this felicitous hit.

"On Saturday last"—continued the narrator—"the unrivalled troupe were in the midst of one of their most elaborate performances, encouraged by the presence—I am not sure, but assisted by a select company of spectators. I need only specify Miss Ross and friend, name unknown—to assure you of the high respectability of the assemblage. Smiled upon by beauty, and animated to superhuman exertions by soft glances from one, perchance too dear to his youthful heart,—the chief of the band threw his whole soul into his lofty undertaking, and alas! his body, also! He arose, like the Phoenix, from the ashes below, but to seek the earth again, having fallen from the frightful height of three feet. He lay upon the sod without sense or motion. The spectators pressed around,—but, breaking through the throng, came the fair nymphs aforesaid. One pillowed his head upon her arm, and drenched his dusty brow with tears; her comrade wrung her hands, and shrieked for 'help! lest he die!' The crowd, at a respectful distance, looked on; venturing a whisper, now and then, to the purport that 'it was as good as a play, and cost nothing.' Warm brine and sounding air are poor medicines for a cracked skull; and the sufferer remaining insensible, a frantic damsel was seen, vaulting over tomb-stones, bonnetless and shawlless, on the most direct route to the gate. A gallant man of healing was passing, and him she conducted to the prostrate hero. Handkerchiefs and scarfs were stripped from necks and arms to staunch the trickling gore; and supported by his affectionate nurses, the interesting youth gained his carriage. Miss Ross returned home with swollen eyes and downcast air. The afternoon, evening, and most of the next day were spent in retirement. This was a grief sympathy could not assuage."

"Did she tell you of it?" asked one.

"No. Madam Rumor is my informant, and her story is vouched for by a gentleman, an eye witness of the catastrophe."

In this lamentable caricature, there was so little truth, and so much less wit, that it should have been beneath the contempt of her, at whom it was aimed; but the ridicule was *public*. Her bonnet hid her face, but the angry blood surged over her neck in crimson streams. There was vengeful fury enough in the grasp, which drove the nails through the paper she held, into the palm, to have swept the tittering clique from the earth at a stroke. Whatever purpose of retaliation sprang into life, it was nipped in the bud. The desk of the supposed artist was in a niche; and the projecting wall concealed it from the view of the party. He was almost in front of her; and her burning eyes were arrested as they encountered his. There was no scorn, or none for her, in that regard; but warning, interest and inquiry were blended with such earnestness, that, like the charmed bird, he could not move or look away. Even when he cast his eyes upon his work again, she did not, at once, withdraw hers. He might have been thirty; was pale, and not handsome, yet anything but ordinary in his appearance. If his countenance had betrayed emotion the previous moment, it vanished as his pen began to move. He was the automaton scribe, and the subdued Ida, drawing her shawl around her, quitted the place, without exchanging a syllable with any one.

The spell of the silent rebuke was speedily dissolved, yet she was grateful that it had restrained her hasty retort. The heated in a quarrel, are always the defeated. Morbid sensibility is the engenderer of suspicion,—and vice versa; the two act and react, until a smile, a look, is the foundation of weeks—it may be, of years of wretchedness. To such a mind, ridicule is a venomed dart, piercing and poisoning, and pride but inflames the wound. Dr. Ballard had showed the courtesy of a gentleman, and the kindness of a friend in his intercourse with Ida. Unconsciously, she had come to like, almost to trust him—and this was at an end. He, and he, only, could have provided the outline of the narrative she had heard. She set her teeth hard, as she recalled her agitated greeting at the gate; and his composure; her subsequent offers of assistance—"officious"—she called them now,—and his calm acceptance. But it was base and unmanly, to make capital for sport of the weakness of a woman—a child, compared with himself! "They are all alike—I must believe it! with hearts rotten to the core! Heaven have mercy on me, until I am as callous as they!" And when he called, at some personal inconvenience, to impart the intelligence of her "protegé's" recovery, she met him with a haughtiness that surprised and angered him; and his futile attempt to throw down the barrier, resulted in his cutting short the interview. He had told Mr. Read of Ida's adventure; but not in the spirit in which its events were coarsely retailed. He lauded her kindness and self-possession, in terms too extravagant to suit the zero humanity of her guardian's narrow soul;—as he wound up the story to his daughter— he "was not a man to get up a fit of heroics, and had no idea that Ballard had so much palaver about him."

If his vile doctrine were indeed true, if all men were alike, and like him, who of us would not unite in the orphan's prayer—would not cry, with her, in despairing bitterness, "Heaven have mercy upon us, until we are as callous as they!"

She had no mercy upon herself. There was an unholy joy in ruthlessly trampling upon the few flowers that grew in her path: the ebullition of a desperate despair, as when one is tortured by a raging tooth, he probes, and grinds and shakes the offending member, self-inflicting yet more exquisite pain, but bearing it better, under the insane impression that he is wreaking revenge upon its cause; saying, with the poor Dutchman, "ache on! ache on! I can stand it as long as you can!" And "ache on! ache on!" said Ida to her heart, "the nerve will be dead by and by!"

We consign to the lower pit of darkness the bloody demons, cloaked in priestly stole, and "speaking great, swelling words of wisdom" and peace, who tore limb from limb upon the rack, in "zeal for the Faith!" but for him who pours out his atheistical misanthropy,—deadening, petrifying the soul, and blinding the eyes, until in this, our lovely earth, they see but a mighty charnel-house, full of nameless abominations; who traduces God, in despising His noblest work, and says: "Behold the Truth!" the murderer of the *heart*,—what shall be his portion!

Carry Carleton's liking for the company of "that proud, disagreeable girl," and her defence of her when attacked, was a nine days' wonder. True, "she loved everybody," but here she manifested partiality, far more than accorded with her schoolmates' notions of justice and reason. Carry was unwavering. "I like her," said she, one recess, when her corps of affectionate teazers hung on and about her. "It wounds me to hear you speak disparagingly of her. You must admit that she has redeeming traits. She is one of our best scholars, and if inaccessible, is upright and honorable, and will not stoop to do an ignoble action."

"Yes," said Emma Glenn, happy to add her mite of praise, "Don't you remember she found Julia Mason's composition behind a desk in the cloak room, and brought it in examination day, although she knew that she was her most dangerous competitor for the prize? I'm afraid I should have been tempted to keep it, or leave it where it was."

"I should not be afraid to trust you, dear," said Carry. "You are too ready to commend such conduct in others, to act a contrary part yourself. As for Ida—have any of you reflected how much of what you call her pride you are accountable for?"

"We! how!" was the unanimous exclamation.

"I know my misdeeds are legion, and my good works, like Parson Wilkins' text, 'way off and hard to find,' but 'evil,' indeed, as well as 'few, have been the years of my pilgrimage,' if I had anything to do with the 'formation of Ida Ross' character!" said Ellen Morris, clasping her hands deprecatingly.

"Ellen! Ellen!" remonstrated Carry, "think what effect a remark like that would produce! Would it increase her confidence in you or us? Would she not avoid us more then ever? She is an orphan, and should be dealt with more charitably, than if her feelings had expanded in a home like yours."

"You do not believe she could love anybody!" said one of the group.

"Certainly I do, and I mean she shall love me. You would make the same resolution, if you knew her as I do."

"An idea strikes me, Carry," said the incorrigible Ellen.—"She and we have affinity for each other—water and oil—you are the alkali, which is to reconcile us; we shall be a soap manufactory, to cleanse and regenerate the world."

"A little vinegar facilitates the process, does it not?" asked Carry, good-humoredly.

"You have come to a poor market for it, my good Alkali; upon second thoughts, you must leave me out of the combination altogether—salt, Attic, particularly, being detrimental to the integrity of the article in question."

"Soap boiling and Attica!" said Anna Talbot, who was reading a little apart, "your conversation takes an extended range to-day, young ladies."

"Both are warm places," returned Ellen. "Our imaginations needed thawing after perching so long upon the North Pole, *id est*, Ida Ross."

"You have offended Carry," said Emma, apprehensively, as the former walked towards the other room.

"Not offended, but grieved," she replied, with sweet gravity. "I should not love Ellen as I do, if I did not believe her heart to be oftener in the right place than her tongue."

She passed into the recitation room, and there, her head bent upon a desk, was Ida! Carry was transfixed with dismay. The door was a-jar—she had heard it all! But the relaxed limbs—the unmoving figure—was she then asleep? A minute's stay confirmed this opinion; and greatly relieved, she tripped lightly out by another door. Ida did not sleep. She had left the larger room at the close of morning recitations, seeking in the comparative quiet of this, some ease from a severe headache. She did not think of concealment. After the gossip of the thoughtless circle turned upon herself, she still supposed that her vicinity was known; that their pretended unconsciousness was a covering for a renewal of mortifications. To move would have been matter for triumph, she was not disposed to supply. So unjust does suspicion make us!

Carry's disinterested vindication electrified her. To risk the forfeiture of the favor of the many, for one who had never conferred an obligation—whose good will could profit her nothing! in her experience, the act lacked a parallel. "Can it be," she thought, with stirring pulses, "can it be that I may yet find a friend?" then, as Carry's "I am resolved she shall love me," reached her, she bowed in thankfulness. "I will trust! will stake my last hope of ever meeting a kindred spirit upon this throw—will let her love me if she will, so help me God!" It was no light vow.

Carry's intrusion was unobserved; she was only sensible of the incalescence of her frozen heart. The afternoon was cloudy, and her maid was surprised to see her mistress preparing for her promenade.

"Indeed, Miss Ida, you'll get caught in the shower; 'twont be no little sprinkle, neither. When its starts to rain this time o' year, it never holds up."

"Oh, well!" returned Ida, familiarly, "if we have another deluge, I may as well be out of doors as in. But give me my cloak, Rachel, I must have a short run before it sets in."

Josephine crossed the hall as she was going out. She stared, but made no remark upon her unseasonable excursion. It was less wonderful than the smile and nod she received. "It is pleasant," said Ida to herself, "yet they talked of rain!" But the storm was not to be delayed by inward sunshine. The smoky fog grew denser; through the ominous calm which pervaded the city, the roaring of the distant "Falls" was distinctly audible; cows stood, solemnly herded together, the vapor from their nostrils scarcely thicker than the surrounding atmosphere; and an occasional rain-drop trickling down their roughened hides. Then the pavement was spotted with the precursors of the prognosticated deluge, and a dash of spray into Ida's face restored her to the perception of her actual position: a mile from home, night and a tempest approaching. Ere a dozen steps were retraced, she was met by the shower,—November rain, cutting and numbing as hail. Her veil, flimsy defence for her face, was dripping in a moment, and the water streamed in miniature cascades from her bonnet and shoulders. Bewildered and dizzy, she sprang, without a thought, except the instinct of self-preservation, into the shelter of a friendly porch. She laughed, despite her uneasiness at her situation. "Wet, not quite to the skin, but more damp than is comfortable; sans umbrella, over-shoes, carriage or servant, and where, I cannot precisely determine."

"Walk in, *do!*" said a pleasant voice behind her. A lady was holding the open door. "I thank you," Ida began, when a figure glanced out of the entry. "Why, Ida! my dear creature! how wet you are! don't stand there a moment. I am so glad you ran in! This is my sister, Mrs. Dana—my friend, Miss Ross—now we will go directly up stairs, and take off your damp things!" and in the confusion of congratulations and regrets, Ida did not know where she was, until she was seated in Carry's room; both sisters occupied in divesting her of such portions of her apparel, as were likely, by their humidity, to endanger her health.

"You are very kind," she said; "but I cannot wait to have these dried. I must go home."

"Impossible!" cried the impulsive Carry. "I will not hear of it. Just make up your mind to stay in your present quarters until clear weather."

"Let me insist upon your staying, Miss Ross;" said Mrs. Dana. "I will send a messenger to your friends to inform them of your safety."

"She will stay," said Carry, looking very positive.

Ida yielded with secret pleasure. Her guardian angel must have guided her into this haven. Mrs. Dana was Carry's senior by ten years or more, and resembled her more in voice and manner, than feature. They had the same kind eyes and dimpling smile. Having seen her guest comfortable, she gave her into Carry's charge, and went to forward her message to Mr. Read. "How it rains!" said Carry, drawing aside the curtain. "It is lucky you came when you did. Did you know we lived here?"

"No, it was entirely accidental. I was walking, and did not notice the clouds until the shower came; then I took refuge in the nearest house."

"A happy accident for me," said Carry. "I despaired of ever persuading you to visit me. This storm was sent for my express benefit. Sister and I are never tired of each other's company; but the little ones demand much of her time; and brother John—Mr. Dana, often brings home writing, or is detained at the store late at night, in the busy season, and I am rather lonely."

"You are bent upon convincing me that all the obligation is on your side," returned Ida: "but compare the mermaid-like fright which shocked you, with the decent young lady before you now, and recollect that my gratitude is proportionate to the improvement."

A pretty little girl, about five years old, crept into the room.

"Come to aunt, Elle!" said Carry. "And speak to this lady."

The child came up timidly to Ida, and slid her plump hand into hers. She did not struggle, as she lifted her into her lap, but looked steadfastly at her with her soft black eyes. "What is your name?" asked Ida.

"Elinor Dana," she answered, in her clear, childish voice.

"Elinor!" repeated Ida, and the little one felt herself pressed more closely to her breast."

"Do you like it?" inquired Carry.

"It was my *mother's* name!" was the low reply. Elle put up her lips for a kiss. She saw a pained look flit over the countenance of the visitor, and administered the only panacea she possessed.

"Is she your sister's oldest child?" asked Ida, repaying the caress.

"Yes. She has two younger; a boy and a girl. The babe is my namesake."

"My brother is named Charles Arthur; after uncle Charley and uncle Arthur," ventured Elle.

"And you love him very dearly,—do you not?" said Ida.

"Yes ma'am; I love papa and mamma, and aunt Carry, and uncle Charley, and uncle Arthur, and grandpa, and sister and brother," said the child, running over the names with a volubility that showed how used she was to the repetition.

"Will you love me too?" asked Ida. The anxiety with which she awaited the reply will not be sneered at by those who have been, like her, starvelings in affection.

"Yes, you too, but I don't know what to call you."

"My name is Ida."

"Miss Ida, or cousin Ida?"

"Cousin!" exclaimed Ida, catching at the word. "Call me cousin!"

"Elle claims as relatives, all whom she loves," observed Carry; "and we encourage her in the practice. Miss is formal; and the absence of any such prefix gives a disrespectful air to a child's address."

"She speaks of her uncles. Have you brothers?"

"She alludes to Mr. Dana's brothers," said Carry, with a slight blush, which Ida remembered afterwards. "They were wards of my father's; and we regard them as a part of the family."

Ida amused herself by coaxing forth Elle's prattle; and related, as reward for her sociability, a marvellous fairy tale, which expanded her eyes to their utmost circle, and interested even Carry. Mrs. Dana entered at the finale.

"Papa has come, Elle, and would be happy to see Miss Ross. Tea is ready, too. I hope she has not annoyed you,"—to Ida.

"Annoyed! oh no, ma'am! we are good friends, and have had a nice talk, have we not, darling?"

Playing with a child is a very puerile amusement—what room is there for the exercise of the reasoning faculties; what opportunity for gaining new views of the world or of truth? Still Ida was happier, and she was silly enough to think, wiser. A germ was set, which should be developed by and by.

Mr. Dana was in the supper-room. He was tall and dark, grave-looking when silent; but as he acknowledged the introduction to herself, and stooped to kiss Elle, his smile rendered him exceedingly handsome. The proud tenderness of his wife was beautiful to behold; and he unbent all that was stern in his nature, in her presence, or Carry's. The repast went off delightfully. There were no sarcastic flings at society and individuals, and clash of combat, imperfectly drowned by courteous phraseology, such as characterized similar occasions at Mr. Read's. Free to act and speak, without dread of criticism, Ida acquitted herself well. She and her entertainers were equally charmed; and Carry sat by, contented with the success of her benevolent efforts. Mr. Dana's business required his attention immediately after supper; Mrs. Dana sat with the girls awhile, then repaired to her nursery. "We shall not be troubled by visitors to-night," said Carry. "What say you to adjourning to our chamber? It is more snug than these empty parlors."

They visited the nursery in their way. Elle opened her eyes as her friend kissed her coral lips, but their lids fell again directly, and her "good night" died in a drowsy murmur. The boy was sleeping soundly, and little Carry lay quietly wakeful upon her mother's lap. "These are my treasures," said the fond parent, smiling at Ida's admiration of the group.

"Treasures she would not barter for the wealth of both Indies," added Carry. "You are a diplomatist, Ida, you have found sister's blind side by praising her pets."

"You, who are so accustomed to these pretty playthings, do not know how lovely they are to one who is not so favored," replied Ida.

"Ah! there you are in error. No one can love the sweet angels as I do, except the mother who bore them. Now," continued she, when they were in their room, taking from a wardrobe two dressing-gowns, "I move that we don these, and make ourselves comfortable generally."

And cozily comfortable they appeared, ensconced in armchairs, in front of that most sparkling of coal-fires; a waiter of apples and nuts sent up by thoughtful Mrs. Dana, on a stand between them; shutters and curtains closed, and the storm roaring and driving without.

"I no longer wonder at your cheerfulness, since I have seen your home," said Ida. "All the good things of life are mingled in your cup."

"You are right. I am very happy, but not more so than hundreds of others. My contentment would be grievously marred, if I suspected this was not so."

"Fraternizing again. I have reflected and observed much since our talk in the cemetery, and am almost persuaded that you have chosen the easiest method of living; that 'where ignorance is bliss, 'tis folly to be wise.' Your system has brought most pleasure thus far, whether it will endure the test of time and experience, is another question."

"You alarm me," answered Carry. "Your vague hints excite my curiosity, yet do not indicate the description of dangers I am to encounter. Let us understand each other—as the Methodist class-leaders have it, 'tell our experiences.'"

"Mine may be briefly summed up," said Ida, sadly.

'The frigid and unfeeling thrive the best;
And a warm heart in this cold world, is like
A beacon light;—waiting its feeble light
Upon the wintry deep, that feels it not—
Trembling with each pitiless blast that blows,
'Till its faint fire is spent.'"

"You have known this?" asked Carry.

"In all its bitterness!"

"And the writer felt, or thought he felt the force of their meaning, when he penned the lines. Have you ever met with a warm heart besides your own?"

"Yes, one—the home of excellence and affection."

"Then, 'this cold world' has produced three, to whom its biting atmosphere was uncongenial—may there not be more? I look into my bosom, and discover there charity and good-will towards men; why should I deny the existence of like feelings in those who are partakers of the same nature, in all other respects?"

"Fair logic; but let us examine facts. Take an example so frequently cited, as to appear hacknied, yet none the less true to nature. Your wealth, or situation, or influence enables you to benefit those who style themselves your friends. You are courted, beloved, popular. A change in these adventitious circumstances alters everything. With unabated desires for love or distinction, you are a clod of the earth, a cumberer of the ground. The stream of adulation flows in another direction; former acquaintances pass you with averted eyes, or chilling recognitions; you are sought by no new ones. Men do not go to a barren tree, or a dried fountain. You shake your head;—this is not a fancy sketch. Listen to a leaf from my history. Until two years ago I never received a harsh word, or an unloving look. My mother was the benefactress of the poor, for miles around, and I was her almoner. Blessings and smiles hailed me wherever I went. I had no conception of sorrows she could not alleviate; and I remember thinking—foolish child that I was! that her empire of hearts was worth the glory of an Alexander or Napoleon. She died! and where are the fruits of her loving kindness? If her memory lives in another breast than that of her only child, I do not know it!"

There were tears in Carry's eyes, already, and the slight tremor of her speech was grateful music to the orphan's ear.

"You quitted your home, and all who knew her, and came to a strange city, where it was necessary for you to earn love as she had done. I have no doubt, nay, I am sure, that by the creatures of her bounty, her memory is preserved as a holy thing; and that they are ready to extend the affection they had for her, to her child. Here, she was comparatively unknown. To carry out your metaphor of the tree, the graft cut from the parent stock must bear fruit for itself. I know the world is generally selfish, but I am convinced that our reprobation of it often arises from the growth of a similar weakness in ourselves. May it not be that the dearth of love, so painfully felt by you, proceeds in part, from the ignorance of your associates as to the real state of your mind, or from an exacting spirit in yourself! Pardon my freedom; it is meant in kindness."

"I thank you for your candor. The truth, if unpalatable, cannot offend."

"Then, trusting to your forbearance, I will go more into particulars. To curry favor, in school, or elsewhere, is as repugnant to me as to you; but do we sacrifice self-respect, by swaying to the popular voice, when no abandonment of principle is required? or play the hypocrite, in concealing prejudices and humors that conflict with the sentiments of others; in uniting, with apparent willingness, in the common cause? We cannot like—we may help all. I say it in humility—there is one rule by which I do not fear to be judged: 'Whatsoever ye would that men should do unto you, do ye even so to them.'"

"I understand your allusions. You think my reserve proceeds from pride alone. What if I were to tell you"—and her voice sank, "that haughty as I seem, I would cringe—lie in the dust—to the most inferior of my daily companions, if she would give me love. Believe me, it is this unquenchable thirst—this longing for what is unattainable by me, which has forced me to court its opposite—hate! I will not lay my heart bare to those who would spurn it. It is said, the hind seeks an obscure covert, to die from the wound for which his unhurt comrades would shun him. You cannot know—it would be improper for me to recount my fruitless endeavors to win the coveted blessing, at any price, even the loss of the self-respect you imagine I value so highly. It is enough that experiences, such as I hope may never be yours, have taught me to entrench myself in my fortress of self-confidence, from whence I hurl disdain upon besieging powers. I am thought independent; the world has made me so. No woman is independent from nature or choice."

Carry looked musingly in the fire. "I am not certain," she said, "that I have a right to repeat what was told me, by one who never thought that you would hear it. I do not see, how ever, that it can do harm, and I wish to show you, that I am not ignorant of some of your trials. A friend of mine, whose name I am not at liberty to mention, was in F——'s painting-rooms on the afternoon of your visit. The artist was an acquaintance, and having letters to write, he offered to occupy his desk while Mr. F—— should seek recreation. He was an auditor of Josephine's Read's garbled story of our church-yard adventure; he had heard a true statement from me. Had my name been used, as it would have been if she had known who your companion was, he would have spoken. As it was, his indignation nearly got the better of his prudence. He identified you as the heroine of the tale, by the significant gestures and winks of the ill-mannered party, and commended your equanimity and forbearance."

"He did not add, that his timely warning suppressed the responsive storm?" said Ida.

"Why! did he speak?"

"No. He only looked, but such a look!"

Carry laughed. "He is a strange mortal! But to return to yourself. These exhibitions of depravity and cold-heartedness, are not adapted to raise our estimate of mankind; yet even then, there was *one* present, who was on the side of right and humanity; who saw no cause for mirth in the sufferings of a child, or the anxieties of two inexperienced girls."

"Dr. Ballard did, it seems," said Ida, the gloomy look returning.

"Did Josephine hear of the affair from him?"

"I suppose so. Who else knew it?"

"True. But is it not more probable that she gave it her own coloring, than that he made a jest of us? We will lean towards mercy in our judgment."

"You are a veritable alchemist," said Ida. "You would ferret out gold, even in the dross of my character."

"Try me!" replied Carry. "But bear in mind, nothing is to be secreted; no hard thoughts or jaundiced investigations. All must be cast into the crucible."

"And tried by what fire?" inquired Ida.

"Love!" said the warm-hearted girl, kneeling beside her, and winding her arms about her waist. "Love me, Ida! and if I prove heartless and deceitful, I will cease to plead for my brothers and sisters."

The glad tears that impearled her bright locks, replied.

CHAPTER VI

"Teach me to gain hearts as you do!" Ida prayed, on the memorable evening of the storm, and Carry answered, blithely, "Love, and live for others!"

To her, natural disposition and practice made the task easy; for her pupil, it was arduous beyond her worst expectation. Her reputation was established; the wall she had erected between herself and her associates, was not to be undermined or scaled in a day. Her overtures of familiarity and service was unskilfully made; her very timidity construed into labored condescension. "It is a hopeless endeavor—they will never care for me!" said she, despondingly—once and again, and Carry still predicted—"Love will win love. Persevere!" The birth and growth of their attachment was remarkable. Dissimilar in mind; made more so in manner, by education and circumstances, there existed from the earliest stage of their friendship, perfect confidence in each other's affection. Carry had an infallible perception of genuine worth, hidden though it might be; and Ida clung drowningly to this last anchor—the sole tie that connected her with her race. Like most deep feelings, its current was noiseless. They were much together;—that was not strange, since their studies were the same. They had separate compartments of one desk; and none marked how often one book was conned by both; brown and fair curls mingling; and hands clasped in mute tenderness. Still less did they dream of the miraculous confluence of the sun-bright stream with the turbid torrent, and the wondrous music of their flow.

They were sitting thus one forenoon, when an assistant teacher drew near, and inquired if there were a vacant seat in their vicinity.

"A new scholar!" buzzed from fifty tongues; and the eyes of our two students strayed with the rest, to the door.

"Miss Pratt, young ladies!" introduced Mr. Purcell.

The girls arose, in conformance with their custom of reception, and bowed to the figure that followed him into the room. She was short and fat—"dumpy," in vulgar parlance; and so homely, as to countenance Ellen Morris' report to another department—"that the farmers in the neighborhood where she was 'riz,' had forwarded a petition, beseeching her to return, their corn having suffered greatly from the depredations of the crows since her departure; a thing unheard of, previously, in that part of the country." Her eyes were small and grey; her nose a ruddy "snub;" her lips curiously puckered up; and her skin might have owed its dappled red to the drippings of the carroty frizette overshadowing it. Her dress was showy and outré; a rainbow silk trebly-flounced; an embroidered lace cape; white kid gloves; a gold cable of startling dimensions; two bracelets of corresponding size, and different patterns; a brooch that matched neither, and out-glittered both; while blue, green, and red stones, with heavy settings, loaded the thick fingers to the knuckles.

Awe of their preceptor in some, good breeding in others, prevented any audible outbreak of amusement; but what school girl on the *qui vive* for diversion could keep from smiling? Mr. Purcell frowned as his eye travelled from one mirthful face to another, but a twinkle from Ellen Morris' dancing orbs neutralized the effort; and there was a perceptible twitch of his risible muscle as he rapped for "order." Ida and Carry had not escaped the contagion, an indulgence for which they reproached themselves.

"Poor girl!" whispered Carry. "She knows no better. She is to be pitied instead of laughed at." And Ida thought of *her* loneliness, upon her induction into these strange scenes. "I can lessen her discomfort, and, uninfluenced by prejudice, she will be thankful, perhaps will become fond of me."

Carry read her resolve in her thoughtful survey of the stranger; but while she loved and honoured her for it, her heart misgave her as she looked more attentively at the object of the purposed charity. Her physiognomy was not more irregular than unpleasant in its expression. She had opened a book, to be in the fashion in this as in every thing else, but her regards were wandering around the room in scared yet unblushing curiosity, flustered at being in a crowd, without a doubt as to her ability to cope with the best of them. Before the exercises of the forenoon were concluded, she was summoned to see a visitor, and did not reappear before intermission. Then Ida, having occasion to go into a small room, where bonnets and cloaks were hung, found her standing at the window, crying. She wheeled about sharply on hearing a step; her eyes swelled almost out of sight, and her whole appearance frightful in its disorder.

"What do you want?" she asked, querulously.

"I did not know you were here," said Ida. "What is the matter? Are you sick? Can I help you?"

"No. My pa's gone away!" A fresh burst.

"Gone! where?"

"Gone home! and I don't want to stay in this nasty, mean place. I don't want to go to school no more—nowhar!"

To hint at the obvious propriety of the deprecated measure was a temptation policy bade her resist, and Ida was actually nonplussed in casting about in her mind for appropriate consolation.

"You will like us better than you expect," she said, rather awkwardly; "and your father will come soon to see you again—will he not?"

"Yes; he's comin' next week. He is a representative!" mouthing the word magniloquently.

"A—what?"

"He belongs to the legislater. Lor! didn't you know that?"

"No," replied Ida, humbly; "I am so little conversant with State affairs. You will be glad to have him so near."

"I don't care much about it; I want to go home and stay with ma!" beginning to sob. Neither her unpolished manners, nor her accent, combining, as it did, the most vicious of Virginia provincialisms, with the gutturals of the African; nor her noisy grief, could make Ida forget that she was a home-sick child—weeping for her mother! *She* too had mourned, and "refused to be comforted, because hers was not." Miss Pratt's sorrow, however, was very garrulous.

"Now, at home," she continued, "I did jest as I pleased; I lay down most all day. Ma said reading was bad for my head; and so 'tis; it makes me as stupid as I don't know what; and ain't no use besides. I can play on the pianny; gentle*men* don't care for nothing else when they go to see the ladies. You all don't have no beaux while you're at school, do you?"

Ida smiled at this unlooked for query. "We do not have much leisure for amusements," she rejoined.

"And can't you go to the theatre, and to shows and parties?" asked Miss Pratt, alarmed.

"There are no rules on the subject; but it is thought that a young lady is better fitted to go into society, when her mind and manners are formed by time and study."

"Mine are enough formed, I know," complacently glancing from her attire to Ida's plain merino, and black silk apron. "How awful ugly all the girls dress! Ain't none of 'em rich?"

"I believe so; but the school-girls here dress simply."

"*I* shan't! My pa's able to give me decent clothes, and I mean to have 'em. I don't like Richmond a single bit. Nobody don't take no more notice of me than if I wan't nobody— no better than other folks."

"You are not acquainted yet. There are some pleasant girls amongst us; and you will love Mr. Purcell."

"Is he strict, much? Does he make you get hard lessons?"

"He is very kind and considerate."

"I despise teachers and books. Thank patience! I am going to turn out after this session. Ma was married at fifteen, and I'm going on seventeen."

"I am quite seventeen, but I am not tired of books. When I leave school, I shall adopt a regular plan of study and reading."

"*Good* gracious! Why, don't you expect to get married? What are you going to learn so much for? I reckon you're going to teach school."

"No; I study because I like to do it."

"Pshaw! you talk like your teacher was in the room. I don't believe *that*."

"The school-bell!" interrupted Ida, happy to be released.

Miss Pratt hung back. "I don't want to go where all them girls are. Will Mr. What's-his-name be mad if I stay here?"

"He will probably send for you."

"Then I might's well go now. I don't care—I'm as good as any of 'em."

"What, and who is she?" inquired Carry, when school was out.

"A silly, neglected child," responded her friend. "Shamefully ignorant, when we consider her father's station. He is a member of the legislature."

"Ah! can it be the delegate from A——? I have heard of him. He is a clever politician, and an educated man. I am astonished!"

So were all who made the acquaintance of his daughter. Mr. Pratt had done his best to serve his country and increase his fortune. The rearing of his children was confided to a weak and foolishly fond mother. The only girl was alternately stuffed and dosed, until the modicum of intellectual strength nature might have granted her, was nearly destroyed; the arable soil exhausted by the rank weed growth. It was just after his election to the House of Representatives, that the father made simultaneously two astounding discoveries—that physically, his daughter was no longer a child, and that she was a dunce. He had paid a teacher to superintend her education, and supposed she had done her duty; whereas, the prudent governess, having little more sense than her pupil, and loving her ease fully as well, had enjoyed her sinecure of a situation with no compunctious visitings of conscience. She acted "according to Mrs. Pratt's instructions." It was a thunderbolt to the feminine trio when the Representative introduced a bill of amendment, paid the soi-disant instructress for the work she had not performed, informing her that her services were at an end; and ordered the mother to resign her spoiled child to him, "he would see what could be done towards redeeming the time." He carried his point in the teeth of a windy and watery tempest, and "Miss Celestia Pratt" was duly entered on the roll-book of Mr. Purcell's justly celebrated institution. She soon ceased to complain that she was not noticed. The second day of her attendance she fell in with Ellen Morris and her coterie. By the time the half hour's recess was over, they were enlightened as to her past life, and future aspirations, and supplied with the material of a year's fun-making; while she was reinstated in her self-consequence, and ready to strike hands with them in any scheme they chalked out.

"It is a shame," said Ida, who, with Carry kept aloof, silent spectators. "Cannot she see what they are doing?"

"It will be a severe, but perhaps a salutary lesson," replied Carry.

"But the poor creature will be the butt of the school."

"And of the community," said Carry. "I have reasoned with Ellen;—she is not evil disposed, but would compass sea and land for as rich a joke as this promises to be. My influence can effect nothing."

"What if I warn the girl?" said Ida. "Must she pay the penalty of her parent's fault?"

"My darling," returned Carry, affectionately, "I am learning prudence from you, and I verily believe I have imparted to you some of my inconsiderateness. What hold have you on this Miss Pratt's confidence? Ellen and her clique are as likely to be in the right as yourself. In her estimation they are more entitled to credence. They play upon the string of self—you will utter a distasteful truth. Let her and them alone, except so far as your individual self is concerned. Attract each one to you, and you may be the means of bringing them together."

Ellen Morris burst into the school-room one morning in a gale of excitement.

It was early, and none of the teachers were present, the girls were gathered in knots about the stove and desks.

"Oh girls!" she cried, "I hurried to get here before my angel Celestia. I have the best thing to tell you. You must know she and I were invited, with several others, to take tea at Uncle James' last evening. We had not been there long before aunt said that Mr. Dermott was expected. 'I have it,' thought I. I gave Celestia a nudge, 'Do you hear that?'

"'What?' said she.

"'The great traveller, Mr. Dermott, is to be here presently. Ain't you glad?'

"'Who is he? I never heard of him.'

"'Oh Celestia! and you a representative's daughter! and he invited expressly to meet you— it is well no one overheard you—and you have not composed your conversation either? What will you do? He is one of the famous authors you hear so much of. They will make a statue of him when he dies, like Washington in the capitol, you know.'

"'You don't say so!'

"'Yes, and he has seen the seven wonders of the world, and elephants, and rhinoceros, and polypi, and hippopotami, and Dawalageri, and anthropophagi.'

"'*Good* gracious!' said she, looking wild, 'You reckon he will speak to me? *do* tell me something to say!'

"'Could you repeat those names?'

"'*That* I couldn't, to save my life!'

"'Well,—let me see,—you must be very sober and wise; only saying 'yes' and 'no,' till he gets to talking of books. Then is the time to show off. Literary people never inquire what you remember in a book, if you say you have read it.'

"'Yes,' she struck in, with a grin. "So when he asks me if I've read them he's talking about, I'm a-going to say 'yes'—(you know she is always 'going, going, gone.') 'He ain't a-going to catch me, I'll show him!'

"'Right,' said I; 'and question him about two or three, which you name yourself; that will finish the business.'

"'I don't know none.'

"'Don't you? Then I will write off a short list. Keep the paper in your hand; and when he is fairly under way talking, you steal a sly peep at it.' Oh! it was enrapturing to see how she held on to that slip of paper! poring over it every five minutes before Mr. Dermott's arrival, and once in two minutes afterwards. She would study it for a second, then her lips would move, until the time for another peep; she was getting it by heart, staring at him all the while. By and by he happened to be near her; and said something about the Panorama. She had been on tiptoe for the last hour, lest her trouble should be thrown away; and resolved not to lose this opportunity, she spoke out as loudly as addressing a deaf person—

"'Mr. *Dermarck!* have you ever read Plutarch-es Liv-es, Homer's Eyelids, Dance's Diving Comedy and Campbell's Gratitude of Wimming?' I wish you could have seen him!"

"O Ellen! Ellen!" chorussed twenty voices; and the crowd rocked in uncontrollable merriment. Carry, and one or two more were grave; and an indignant voice said, "How wickedly heartless!"

There was no mistaking the meaning and emphasis of the interjection. Ellen crimsoned to the roots of her hair. She retorted with a spirit entirely opposite to her usual sportive gaiety. "One, whose lowest thoughts soar so far above the common herd, as Miss Ross, cannot be expected to understand a piece of harmless pleasantry."

Ida had unluckily employed the oft-quoted words, "the common herd of mankind," in a written composition; and this was not the first time it had been used as an offensive missile. "One must stoop low indeed, Miss Morris," was the instant rejoinder, "to see harmless pleasantry in a plot for the disgrace of an unoffending school-mate."

"Ida! Ellen!" exclaimed Carry, laying her hand upon Ellen's mouth, and stifling her reply. "For my sake, girls—if not for your own—say no more! Ida! what have you to do with this miserable affair?"

"I have done!" said Ida, bitterly; "Defence of right and truth is better left unattempted *here*!"

The girls fell back as she crossed to her seat. The sentence sank into every mind; and the expression of each one showed that she appropriated it. Carry's head dropped upon Ellen's shoulder; and sullenly vindictive as was the latter, she was not unmoved by the quiver of the slender frame. Mr. Purcell's entrance put an end to the scene. That was a wretched day to more than one heart. Ida's was well-nigh bursting. It mattered not that her prospects of popularity were, for the present, shipwrecked; that her resolutions of patience and gentleness had broken, like dry straws, at the breeze of passion;—Carry was wounded— perhaps offended—perhaps estranged! "Still, what have I done?" whispered pride, "spoken truth, and defended the absent!" But conscience answered—"Anger, not justice was the prompter," and again, every feeling merged in one—"What will Carry think?" She did not offer her book as usual—did not meet her eye. She would have read no resentment there; the pale, sad face told of suffering, with no admixture of baser motives. The intermission was dull. Miss Celestia's extravagant description of "the party," and "the gentle*men*" she "was interduced to," hardly excited a smile. A nameless depression was upon all. Ellen, their ringleader in mischief, and Carry, the willing participant in their innocent pleasures, were wanting from their band. They remained at their desks, seemingly engaged in study, until almost school-time, when Carry went around to the other, whispered a word; and they left the apartment together. They returned arm in arm, as Ida, who had gone home in recess, more to be quieted and refreshed by the cool air, than for luncheon,—entered from the street. She remarked their affectionate air, and happier faces with goading envy. "Ellen is worth conciliating. It would be dangerous to break with her. There can be no hesitancy, with the fair words of the crowd in one scale—and Ida Ross, unknown and unbeloved, in the other. Be it so!" But awakened affection had had a taste of its proper nutriment, and was not to be famished into silence. The afternoon wore heavily away in the unspoken anguish of love and pride and suspicion. Careless of remarks or conjectures, she declined dinner, and retired at once to her chamber, when she reached home. It might have been one hour;—it might have been three, that she had knelt or laid upon the floor, her head upon a stool, before the mourner for the dead bird;—weeping and thinking, and seeming to grow a year older with each flood of grief; when there came a tap at the door. "Josephine!" was the first thought—to spring to the mirror, brush the tumbled hair, and dash rosewater over the discolored cheeks, the work of the next minute; then she said sleepily—"Who is there?"

"It is I—Carry!"

The bolt was withdrawn, and the intruder lay, sobbing upon her breast.

"Oh, Ida! how could you be angry with me?"

Ida struggled with the answering drops, but they *would* come.

"I thought you had thrown me off, Carry!"

"You could not—after my note."

"Your note!"

"I slipped it into your French Grammar, as it lay open before your eyes; and you shut the book and put it aside,—I supposed to read it at your leisure."

"I did not see it."

She went to her satchel, and brought forth the Grammar. "There it is!" said Carry, as a folded paper fell from within it. "Do not read it. I will tell you its contents. I asked your forgiveness for interrupting you so rudely this morning; but these public disputes lead to so much evil. Ellen was wrong; she has said so to me; and is ready to be your friend, if you consent. Her conduct was blameably thoughtless; and her quick temper could not submit to a rebuke so openly administered. I was abrupt, but it was not because I was angry with, or did not love you. Ellen's taunt was extremely provoking"—

"Stop! stop! Carry! It is I, who should sue for pardon, and excuse, if I can, my unbecoming heat, and after doubts of your friendship. I cannot tell you what a fearful warfare has waged within me;—how much incensed I was to see you and Ellen come in so lovingly, at noon;—how Ishmael-like I felt;—every man's hand against me, and mine against the universe, and Him who made it," she added, with an intonation of awe. "Can you love me after hearing this, Carry?"

"Always—always!"

Ellen was amazed, that afternoon, on being summoned to receive visitors, to find in them her two class-mates, and more astounded to hear from her antagonist of the morning, a frank and graceful apology for her hasty strictures upon her conduct and words. Ellen was, as she phrased it, "great upon high-flown speeches; but this was an extraordinary occasion, and demanded a deviation from ordinary rules; so I condescended, for once, to make use of simple language."

If simple, it was satisfactory, and they parted most amicably. It was past sunset, when the friends arrived at Mr. Read's door. Ida stood upon the steps, watching Carry, as she tripped away into the dusk. Others would have seen only a pretty girl, with a smile like May sunshine;—to the fond eyes that followed her, she was an angel of love, upon whom nothing of evil could gaze without adoration and contrition;—and now the light of a new blessing beaming upon her brow—the blessing of the peace-maker!

CHAPTER VII

Spring had departed, and the good citizens of Richmond complained as piteously of the heat, as though every zephyr that awoke for miles around, did not sweep over their seven hills freighted with the perfume of gardens and groves, instead of the reeking odors of a thronged city. And in our day, as then, airy, spacious villas are forsaken, while their infatuated denizens hie away to pay $50 per week, for a genteel sty, six feet by ten; with the privilege of eating such fare, as in the event of its appearance upon their own boards, would find its way back to the place where it was concocted, accompanied by an anathematised warning to the cook;—and of gulping down unwholesomely-copious draughts of a nauseous liquid, which the stomach neither relishes, nor needs. There is dancing "all night, 'till broad day-light," a dusty drive to assist the digestion of a breakfast, one's common sense, no less than the digerent organs assures him is insured against chylifaction; promenading until dinner, which meal is taken in full dress;—another drive, or an enervating siesta, and it is time to dress for supper; then dancing again; and at the end of "the season," the fashionable votaries return, jaded and debilitated, to home and comfort, and tell you, with a ghastly smile, that they have been ruralizing at the "Carburretted, Sulphuretted, Chalybeate Springs." Ruralizing at the Springs! sketching a landscape from an Express train—sleeping in a canal-boat—reciprocating ideas with a talkative woman!

Mr. Read came home to tea, on a sultry July evening, with some crotchet in his brain. That could be seen with half an eye; and Josephine was affable to a distressing degree, to coax the stranger into an earlier incubation, than would occur without artificial warmth. The effects of her Eccolodeon were presently apparent.

"When does your session close, Josey?" he inquired.

"On Friday, sir."

"Then you will be on your head to quit town, like everybody else."

"I have no solicitude on the subject, sir. I am as indifferent to it, as to many other things people rave about."

"You are your father's child, cool and hard!" observed her parent, with a gratified look.

"But for a novelty, what say you to a trip to Saratoga?"

"I should like it, sir,—if you accompany me."

"I have business which takes me in that direction, and I thought, as you are to 'come out' next winter, it would sound well to have made your début at such a fashionable place."

Josephine smiled; she could appreciate this argument. The journey was discussed—the expenses, dress, appearance, etc. Ida sat by, taciturn and unconsulted. She had a motive in remaining. Finally, she contrived to throw in a word.

"I wish to inform you of *my* arrangements for the summer, sir, if you have time to listen."

"Yours! they are the same as ours, of course. Do you imagine that I would permit my daughter to travel without a female companion, or give her an advantage, you are not to share!"

The latter clause was so clearly an afterthought, and dove-tailed so oddly with its antecedent, that Ida's smile was almost a sneer.

"I am sorry, sir, that you are disappointed in your calculations; but as Josephine has a maid, I do not deem my attendance indispensable. If I leave town, I shall go in another direction, unless you positively forbid it."

"And what place is to be honored by your preference? May I presume to ask?"

"I shall go home with Miss Carleton."

"Ahem! I comprehend. I should have anticipated this from your overpowering intimacy. You have played your cards badly, Josephine. Why have you not ingratiated yourself with some 'divine creature,' who has a rich papa? It is a capital means of extending one's acquaintance, and sparing one's purse. How long do you intend to sponge—to remain, I mean, with *your friend*, Miss Ross?"

"I may not return before Christmas. I hear that the holidays are celebrated with much style and festivity, in the country," she replied.

Mr. Read suppressed something very like an oath, at her calm assurance.

"When do you go?"

"Next Monday. Dr. Carleton is expected daily. Did I understand you to say, that you did not object?"

"Confound it! what do I care where, or when you go?"

"Oh Carry!" apostrophized Ida, shutting herself in her room. "Even you could not be charitable and forbearing here. It is hard! hard!"

"That is unquestionably the most wrong-headed girl I know," said Mr. Read, to his daughter.

"I am heartily glad she is not going with us," was the answer. "She would be of no use to me, and an additional care to you."

"Maybe so, maybe not. Her travelling expenses would not have come out of my pocket; and there are advantages, sometimes, in having two ladies, a larger and better room, and such like; you pay the same price, and have twice the value of your money. You understand?"

"I don't care. I had rather sleep upon a pallet in a loft, by myself, than in the handsomest room in the house, with her for a room-mate. It frets me, though to see her airs! I wish the law allowed you absolute control."

"It won't do with her. If she suspected a design on my part to abridge her liberties, or defraud her of her dues, she would as lief enter a complaint against me as not. She has the temper of the Evil One; and watch as you may, will get the bit between her teeth."

The carriage was at the door by six o'clock on Monday morning. Ida was ready; but her trunk was strapped on, and her maid seated upon the box with the driver, before she appeared. The truth was, she dreaded to meet Dr. Carleton. She did not recollect her own father, and had no agreeable associations connected with any who bore that relation to her young acquaintances. She was inclined to look upon the class, as a set of necessary discords in life; Mr. Read being the key-note. Carry often spoke of her surviving parent with earnest affection; but Ida attributed this to a charity, that beheld no faults in those she loved. The thought of her ride and visit would have been unalloyed, but for this idiosyncrasy. "If he were like Mr. Dana!" she said, going slowly down stairs. He was in the porch, with Mr. Read and Carry. "My friend Ida, father," said Carry. He was not like Mr. Dana,—better than that! He was the image of Carry—her eyes, mouth and smile—his locks, although silvered by years, must in youth have waved in the same golden curls. He was handsome yet, how could he be otherwise! and had she failed to love him at sight, the unaffected geniality of his salutation would have captivated her. She had not a care in the world, as she reclined in the carriage, beside Carry, the revolving wheels bearing her towards the country. Mr. Read and his feminine prototype were sign-posts, marking rough and miry roads she had travelled; they were troubles no more; she was leaving them behind.

There had been a thunder-storm in the night, and in that brief fit of passion, nature had wept away every unkind or unpleasant emotion. The sky wore that rich, soft, transparent hue, which imparts its own pureness to the soul of him, who looks upon it; smilingly luring it to soar away, and "steep itself in the blue of its remembered home;" the forest-leaves glittered with rain-diamonds, and the bird-matin was warbled by a full orchestra. And on, through the slants of sunlight, and the alternations of deep, green shade; with the old, familiar chirpings in her ear, and the touch of the loved one's hand upon hers, rode the orphan; very quiet, through excess of happiness; afraid to speak or move, lest this should prove a never-to-be realized dream, whose awaking should bring bitter, hopeless yearnings!

Little by little, Carry broke up her musings; and her father seconded her. He was prepared to like his daughter's friend, and there was that in his eye and voice, which made Ida forget, as she had done with Carry,—that she was talking with a stranger.

"That is a fine specimen of your favorite tree, Ida," observed Carry, pointing to a majestic pine, grand and solitary, at the entrance of a grove of oaks.

"And superb it is, in its loneliness!" said Ida.

"Farmers would cavil at your taste," remarked Dr. Carleton. "'Pine barrens' are proverbial. A thick growth of them is an unmistakeable sign of poverty of soil. Nothing else can extract sustenance from the worn out ground."

"That is why I like them, sir. There is sublimity in their hardy independence, taking root, as you say, where pampered, or less robust vegetation would perish, and with never-furling banners, stretching up boldly towards the stars."

"They are emblems to you—of what?" asked the Doctor.

"Of the few really great ones, who have demonstrated that human nature is not of necessity, vile or imbecile, or yet a debtor to accident, for its spice of good."

"The gifted,—or the fortunate?"

"The *resolute*,—sir. They, who have riven the shackles of low birth or poverty, and made for themselves a glorious name—out of nothing!—have done it by the naked force of *will*. Call it 'talent' or 'genius,' if you choose;—upon analyzation, you will resolve it into this one element of character."

"It is a sorry task to pick flaws in your beautiful analogy," said the old gentleman. "You may not be aware that your pine, sturdy as it appears, is less fitted than any other tree, for standing alone; its roots running out laterally from the trunk; and lying near the surface of the earth. Cut down the outer row which have kept off the tempests, and helped to support him, and the first hard wind is apt to lay him low."

"And so there are fates, against which the mightiest of mortal energies are powerless. Leave the pine unprotected, and if it survive one blast, it strikes its roots deeper and deeper into the ground, until it has strength to brave an hundred winters. Adversity, if it does not kill—strengthens."

"Do you favor the philosophy, which teaches that a certain amount of trouble is necessary for the complete development of character?"

"Whether necessary or not—it comes. That is not a matter of hypothesis; but I have seen some, who, I did not think, required discipline; and many more, who wanted softening, instead of hardening."

"Is hardening the legitimate effect of sorrow?" asked he, more gravely. "When the chastening is guided by love, does it not melt and refine? Are strength and hardness synonymous?"

"I question the difference, sir,—as the world goes."

"Instead of referring to 'the world,' in an abstract sense—judge we of the influence of trials, by what we know of ourselves. I never tasted real happiness, until I learned to bear grief, by submitting to the will of Providence."

"And one affliction has embittered life for me!" returned Ida, gloomily.

"Poor child!" then recollecting himself, he addressed Carry in a jesting tone. "And you—Miss Carry—what is your vote upon this important question?"

"I have had no trouble, sir," replied she, lightly, "except school-quarrels. You would not class them in the category of tribulations."

There was sadness in her father's look of love, as he answered, "I hope you may long be able to say so, dear!"

Carry brushed away the mist from her lashes. "'A consummation devoutly to be desired,'—as Charley, or Shakspeare would say. Where is he, father?"

"Who? Shakspeare or Charley?"

"The latter, of course. Apart from his probable location being more easily decided upon,—he is, to me, the more interesting of the two."

"He is somewhere in the Western part of the State;—travelling, partly for pleasure. John told you, that they have committed the New York branch of the business to Mr. E——, and that Charley will in future reside in Richmond."

"Yes, sir. I was glad to hear it; I understood, however, that this change would not be made before Fall. In the interim, are not we to be favoured with his company?"

"I trust so. It will seem like old times for us all to be together again."

"I hope he will come while you are with us, Ida," said Carry. "I am so anxious you should know him!"

"You have seen him, surely, Miss Ida?" said Dr. Carleton.

"I have not yet had that pleasure, sir."

"He is an original worth studying."

"I can credit that. Elle's panegyrics would have created a desire to see this nonpareil of an 'Uncle Charley,' and Carry has raised my curiosity to the highest pitch, by naming him as the successful rival of Shakspeare."

"Oh!" cried Carry, laughing. "I said more interesting to *me*. Charley is one of my pets; and I am afraid I have presented you with an erroneously flattered picture of him. You must not look for an 'Admirable Crichton.' He is not one to please the fancy on a slight acquaintance."

"Is he as handsome as his brother?"

"Which brother?" inquired the Doctor; and Carry blushed.

"I have met but one," said Ida. "I consider Mr. John Dana very fine-looking."

"I will repeat Charley's ideas of what he styles, his 'personal pulchritude,'" responded Carry. "He says he thanks Heaven he is not handsome. To endow him with a moderate share of beauty, some one would have been deprived of his, or her good looks. No broken hearts are laid at the door of his conscience." 'Yes'—concluded he, triumphantly—'A man ought to be grateful for ugliness; and I am persuaded that not many have as much cause to rejoice on that score as myself!'"

"He is not homely," said her father, warmly.

"Ah father! other people tell a different story."

"That may be; but where you find one handsomer face than his, you see a thousand destitute of its intelligence and agreeableness."

"Granted. Homely or not, I prefer him to any doll-faced dandy of my acquaintance."

"He is fortunate in his advocates," said Ida. "He has the art of making friends."

"Because he is such a firm friend himself," replied Carry. "Yet some will have it that he is frivolous and unfeeling. The only satirical remark I was ever guilty of, was extorted by an aspersion of this kind. A lady was offended by a playful bagatelle of his; and thinking that I would be a sure medium of communicating her wrath to its object, criticised him unsparingly. She ridiculed his person and manners;—I said nothing. She said he was bankrupt in chivalry and politeness. I smiled; and she blazed out a philippic against his 'disgusting levity and nonsense—he had not a spark of feeling, or grain of sense—intelligent indeed! for her part she had never heard him say a smart or sensible thing yet.'—I put in my oar here—'You will then allow him one talent, at least; the ability to adapt his conversation to the company he is in.' I repented having said it; but it quieted her."

"You did not reproach yourself for taking the part of your friend!"

"No, but I might have done it in a less objectionable manner. It did not alter her feelings to him, and caused her to dislike me."

"How is it, sir, that I hear so much more of this one of your former wards, than of his younger brother?" said Ida to the Doctor.

The question was innocently propounded, and for an instant, she was puzzled by the quizzical demureness, with which he glanced at his daughter.

"This is a serious charge, Carry. Your predilection for one old play-fellow should not make you forgetful of another."

She was looking down, touching the shining tire of the wheel with the tip of her gloved finger. The truth beamed upon Ida; and with it a thousand little circumstances she had been blindly stupid not to understand before. Her intelligent eye said the mystery was explained, but she forbore to say so in words. Dr. Carleton went on in a changed tone.

"Arthur is not a whit behind his brothers in sterling worth, or personal graces. He is associated with me in the practice of medicine, and unites a skill and prudence, rarely found in one so young. He is popular, and deservedly so."

Carry bestowed a grateful smile upon him, and was answered in the same mute language. In such desultory chat, the sunny hours ran out They travelled well; only stopping an hour to dine and rest; yet twilight saw them eight miles from their destination. Each was disposed to silence, as the light grew dimmer; and when the moon smiled at them above the tree-tops, she elicited but a single observation of her beauty. The road was lonely and sheltered; bordered by forests on one side, and thicket-grown banks on the other; the soil sandy and heavy; the tramp of hoofs scarcely heard, and the wheels rolling with a low, crushing sound, that, to Ida, was not unmusical. Silver willows, and twisting 'bamboo' vines, and the long-leaved Typha Latifolia edged the road; and she watched through the openings in the woven screen, for a glimpse of the stream that watered their roots; sometimes deceived by the shimmer of the moon upon the leaves; sometimes, by the white sands, until she doubted whether there was indeed one there;—when the gurgling of falling waters betrayed the modest brooklet, and it widened into a pretty pool; the moon's silver shield upon its bosom. The thicket became taller, and not so dense; tulip trees and oaks in place of the aquatic undergrowth; and between them the fleeting glimmerings of the sky were, to her, an army of pale spectres, marching noiselessly past; no halting or wavering; on, on, in unbroken cavalcade, "down to the dead." And memory, at fancy's call, produced the long roll of those who had gone to the world of shades;—the master-spirits of all ages;—the oppressed and the oppressor;—the lovely and the loved;—had joined that phantom procession;—how few leaving even the legacy of a name to earth! With the Persian Poet, her heart cried out—"Where are they?" and echo answered—"Where are they?" And thought poured on thought, under the weird influence of that enchanted night, until the shadowy host was the one reality in the landscape; and one and another beckoned and waved to her, as they defiled by. She came near shrieking—so startled was she—as a horseman reined up at the window. The moon was at his back; but showed every lineament of her countenance. He raised his hat. "Miss Ross, I believe. I fear my sudden appearance has alarmed you."

"Arthur! my boy! how are you?" exclaimed Dr. Carleton, extending his hand, which was as eagerly seized. "Miss Ross—Dr. Dana."

"Miss Ross will excuse me for having anticipated the introduction," said he, bowing again, and rode to the opposite side of the carriage. The greetings there were more quiet; but it needed not Ida's delicate ear to detect the feeling in the voices which tried to say common-place things. Arthur had much to say to the doctor, and once in a while a remark for her—Carry remaining in the back-ground.

"Were you uneasy that we did not arrive?" asked Dr. Carleton.

"Not uneasy—but restless; and to relieve my impatience rode out to meet you."

He was first on this side—now on that—as the highway afforded him room; but Ida could not get a view of his face. His figure was good, and he sat his horse well;—upon these facts, and such impressions as were made by a pleasant voice and gentlemanly address, she was obliged to form her opinion of his personal appearance, until more light should be shed upon the subject. The house appeared, approached by a shady lane, and so embowered in trees, that only the chimneys were visible from the main road. Carry's tongue was unloosed as she bounded into the midst of the sable throng that swarmed about the carriage. Arthur exclaimed merrily at the clamor of blessings and inquiries.

"Will you accept me as your attendant, Miss Ross? The ceremony of reception will last some time."

But Carry was in the piazza as soon as they were.

"Thank you, Arthur, for taking charge of her. Welcome to Poplar-grove, dear Ida! May you be as happy here as I have been!"

"Amen!" said Dr. Carleton and Arthur, heartily.

Carry acted like a wild creature all the evening. She half-carried Ida to her chamber, and kissed her over and over.

"Now, darling!" she ran on, strewing their shawls and bonnets in all directions. "You see I have no idea of putting you off, company style, in another room. You will be with me morning, noon, and night. My dear, dear room! how natural it looks! and to think I am never to leave it again!"

"Bless your heart!" said a middle-aged mulatto woman, whose mild and pleasing face struck Ida as much as her motherly kindness to her young mistress, "You are not half so glad to get back as we are to have you here."

"Hush, Mammy! you will make me cry. Comb my hair—will you? Not that I do not believe you could do it, Sally; but it used to be Mammy's work."

"Thoughtful of others still," reflected Ida, as the girl Sally displayed a double row of ivories, at Carry's apology. "Can nothing make her selfish?"

"We won't waste time by an elaborate toilet, dear," said Carry, seeing Ida deliberating upon two dresses. "Father will be too much engaged with his supper to notice our dress. Wear the plain white one; it is very becoming; and remember, you are in the back-woods."

Arthur was in the parlor when they descended. He looked as happy as Carry, and "almost as good," thought Ida. She was not *de trop*; it might have been a brother and sister who strove to convince her that this, their home, was hers for the time-being. The supper-table was set with taste and profusion. Ida wondered whether the ménage were entirely controlled by coloured servants. She learned afterwards that "Mammy," trained by Mrs. Carleton, and until that lady's death, her constant attendant, was housekeeper.

"You have not much affection for a city life, Miss Ida," said Arthur, continuing a conversation commenced in the parlor.

"No. I am country-bred, and cherish a preference for the scenes of my childhood. Perhaps," she said, ingenuously, "the fault is in myself. I did not want to live in Richmond, and determined not to like it."

"And are your aversions so strong that the manifold attractions of the metropolis cannot shake them? or, are you countrified upon principle?"

"I have not given the city a fair trial. It has occurred to me lately that my weariness of it proceeded from monotony rather than satiety. There is little variety in school life."

"Except when we regard it as the world in miniature," said Arthur. "It is different, doubtless, in 'Young Lady Establishments,' but we boys contrived to maintain a healthy circulation, one way or another."

"Is it not a popular fallacy that school-days are the happiest of one's life?" asked Ida.

"Unquestionably," rejoined he, promptly. "As well say that Spring is the farmer's happiest season. He has the pleasures of hope, the delight of viewing his whitening harvests in futuro; but there is severe, unromantic drudgery; suspense and boding fears for the result. The 'harvest home' for me!"

"And when is that!" questioned Ida.

"Now!" said he, with emphasis.

"What do you mean?" inquired Carry.

"That you and Miss Ida begin to reap from this date. To dispense with this inconvenient metaphor, your actions will be the proof of what your lessons have been; every day your knowledge and principles will be brought into play,—you will be binding up sheaves of worthy or of evil deeds."

"You are trying to terrify us," said Carry. "Don't you wish yourself at school again, Ida!"

"Are *you* sorry you're a-goin' to turn out!" replied Ida, in a peculiar tone.

"Oh, Celestia!" exclaimed Carry, with a burst of laughter.

"Who? what?" said her father.

"One of our school-mates, father; who, hearing another say that she was sorry to quit school, went through the house the day we were dismissed, asking each one confidentially, 'Are *you* sorry you're a-goin to turn out?' grief at such an event being, in her code, a more heinous sin than to dance at a funeral."

"Who was she?" asked Arthur.

"Miss Pratt—Celestia Pratt."

"Daughter of the member from A——?"

"The same—what do you know of her?"

"I met her once at a ball," he replied.

"Were you introduced?" cried both girls in a breath.

"Yes; and danced with her."

"Enough!" said Carry. "We will not pursue the subject."

"As you please," he returned; "but if I am not mistaken, as Sir Roger says, though with a different meaning, 'much could be said on both sides.'"

CHAPTER VIII

Poplar-Grove was comparatively a modern place; having been built by the present proprietor at the time of his marriage. The house was of brick, large and commodious; and flanked by neat out-houses and servants' quarters, presenting an imposing appearance, an air of lordly beauty. The shade trees were forest-born; the maple, oak, beech, and fairest of all, the tulip-poplar. Excepting in the green-house, on the south side of the mansion, and a rose-creeper that climbed upon the piazza, not a flower was tolerated within the spacious yard, and the sward was always green and smooth. Dr. Carleton's seat was the pride and envy of the country. "No wonder," growled the croakers; "a man with a plenty of money can afford to be comfortable." *They* lived in barn-like structures, treeless and yardless; (and who that has travelled in our commonwealth, but knows the heart-sickening aspect of these out-of-door habitations?) raising vegetables, because they must be had to eat; planting orchards, and suffering them to dwindle and pine, for want of attention; and existing themselves after the same shambling style, because they "had it to do;" content to "get along," and not feeling the need of anything higher, until the buried—not dead—sense of the beautiful was exhumed by the sight of the work of taste and industry; and the stupid stare was succeeded by jealous repinings, and the writing down of a long score against Providence. "I tell you what, my friend," the doctor said to one of these murmurers, "instead of harping so much upon one P, try my three, and my word for it, your wishes will be fulfilled sooner by fifty years—they are, Planting, Perseverance and Paint."

In the garden, beauty and utility joined hands, and danced together down the walks. There were squares of thrifty vegetables, deserving a home in the visioned Eden of an ambitious horticulturist; and the banished floral treasures here expanded in every variety of hue and fragrance. There grew hedges of roses, and the dwarf lilac, and the jessamine family, the star, the Catalonian, the white and yellow, thatching one arbor; while the odorous Florida, the coral, and the more common but dearer English honeysuckles wreathed their lithe tendrils over another; and ever-blowing wall-flowers, humble and sweet, gaudy beds of carnations, and brightly-smiling coreopsis, and pure lilies with their fragrant hearts powdered with golden dust—a witching wilderness of delights. Trellises, burdened with ripening grapes, were the boundary line between the garden and the orchard. The same just sense of order and well-being regulated the whole plantation. Kindness was the main-spring of the machinery, but it was a kindness that knew how to punish as well as reward.

"Do you believe in the unity of the human race?" asked Ida, one evening, as she and Carry were taking their twilight promenade in the long parlor.

"Assuredly; but what put that into your head just now?"

"I was thinking of your father; and trying to realize that he belongs to the same species with others I could name. I am compelled to the conclusion that he is an appendix, a later creation, a type of what man would have been had he not 'sought out many inventions.'"

"And what new instance of his immaculateness has induced this sapient belief?"

"I was sitting at the window this afternoon, before he went out, when I heard him call to little Dick to bring his saddle-bags from 'the office.' The boy scampered off, and presently appeared running, still holding the precious load with great care in both hands. 'Steady, my lad,' said your father, and as the warning passed his lips, Dick tripped his foot, and came down—the saddle-bags under him. He cried loudly, and your father ran to pick him up— what do you suppose he said!"

"Inquired if he was hurt, of course."

"He did—but reflect! every phial was smashed, and that is no trifle this far from the city, I take it. Yes—he set the little chap upon his feet, and asked after the integrity of his bones; and when he sobbed, '*I* ain't hurt, sir—but de bottles—dey's all broke!' patted him upon the head, and bade him 'stop crying—master isn't angry—you won't run so fast next time,' and let him go. Then, kneeling upon the grass, he unlocked the portable apothecary-shop, and pulled out gallipots and packages, fractured and stained in every imaginable shape and manner—looking seriously perplexed. 'This is an awkward business,' he said, aloud; 'and my stock is so nearly out! but accidents will happen.'"

"And is that all?" said Carry.

"'All!' I have seen men affect forbearance, and talk largely of forgiveness, when they wanted to 'show off,' but he did not know that I was within hearing. Some other principle was at work. I wonder," she said, with a short laugh, "what my esteemed guardian would have said upon the occasion! He punishes a menial more severely for an accident, or thoughtlessness, than for deliberate villany."

"I do not pretend to uphold Mr. Read's doctrines or practice. I am afraid he is thoroughly selfish, and Josephine is too close a copy of him to suit my fancy—but why think or speak of them? Did you not promise to see life through my spectacles awhile? There is a hard look in your eye, and a scorn in your tone, when you refer to them, that repel me. It is so unlike you!"

"So *like* me, Carry! My character is velvet or fur—stroke it in one direction, and you enhance whatever of beauty or gloss it possesses; reverse the motion, and you encounter rough prickles, and in certain states of the atmosphere, more electricity than is agreeable or safe. I am not changed. The hand of affection is gliding over me now; you may do what you will with me."

"But you are happier than you used to be?"

"I am—happier in you! Do you recollect the stormy November evening when you 'took me in?' Cold, and wet, and shivering as was the body, the heart stood more in need of comfort; and you warmed it—taught me that woman is woman still—brow-beaten, insulted, crushed! The poor, soiled flowerets of love will smile, despite of all—in the face of him, or her whose pitying hand lifts them up. Carry! you do not know what depends upon your fidelity! Have you not read in that most wondrous of books, how the evil spirit returned to the house, which, in his absence, was swept and garnished, and that the latter end of that man was worse than the first?"

"Ida! my own friend! how can you hint such frightful things? I *do* love you—very dearly? You cannot doubt me."

"Not now. But will the time never come, when other claims will dispossess me of my place? Do not despise me, darling! Do not impute to me the meanness of being envious of your happiness. I rejoice with, and am proud for you—proud of your choice. He is all that a man should be—let me say it—I have never told you so before;—but is it true love expels friendship? You will be as dear to me married as single; why should your affection decrease?"

"It will not!" Could it be the modest Carry who spoke? "Judge for yourself. Arthur and I have loved from childhood. He spoke to me of his hopes two years ago, but father exacted from us a promise that no love but that of brother and sister should be named between us until my school-days were at an end. Yet I knew that I was not a sister to him; and, to me, he was more than the world besides:—and with this sweet consciousness singing its song of hope and blessedness within my heart, I found room for you; and lover and friend were each the dearer for the other's company. You will understand this some day, dear Ida. You are made to be loved—you cannot exist without it, and you will achieve your destiny."

"That love is to be my redemption, Carry. In the upper region of the air there is eternal calm and sunshine, while the clouds brood and crash below. Such calm and light shall my love win for me. I have dwelt for years in the black, noisome vapors—I am rising now! Is it not Jean Paul who says—'Love may slumber in a young maiden's heart, but he always dreams!' I have had dreams—day visions, more transporting than any the night bestows. I have dreamed that my wayward will bent, in glad humility, to a stronger and wiser mind;— that my eye fell beneath the fondness of one that quailed at nothing; that I leaned my tired head upon a bosom, whose every throb was to me an earnest of his abiding truth; and drank in the music of a voice, whose sweetest accent was the low whisper that called me 'his own!' These are not chance vagaries; they have been the food of my heart for long and dreary months; angel-voices about my pillow—my companions in the still twilight hour— summoned by pleasure or pain, to sympathise and console. Then my breast is a temple, consecrated to an ideal, but none the less fervent in the devotion offered therein; the hoarded riches of a lifetime are heaped upon his shrine. I have imagined him high in the world's opinion; doing his part nobly in the strife of life;—and I, unawed by the laurel-crown—unheeding it—say, 'Love me—only love me!' I love to fancy, and feel him present, and sing to him the strains which gush from my soul at his coming. This is one."

She left Carry's side. A lightly-played prelude floated through the darkening room, then a recitative, of which the words and music seemed alike born out of the impulse of the hour:

Thy heart is like the billowy tide
Of some impetuous river,
That mighty in its power and pride,
Sweeps on and on forever.
The white foam is its battle crest,
As to the charge it rushes
And from its vast and panting breast,
A stormy shout up gushes.

"Through all—o'er all—my way I cleave—
Each barrier down-bearing—
Fame is the guerdon of the brave,
And victory of the daring!"
While mine is like the brooklet's flow,
Through peaceful valley's gliding;

O'er which the willow boughs bend low
The tiny wavelet hiding.
And as it steals on, calm and clear,
A little song 'tis singing,
That vibrates soft upon the ear,
Like fairy vespers ringing.
"Love me—love me!" it murmurs o'er,
'Midst light and shadows ranging,
"Love me," It gurgles evermore,
The burden never changing.
Thine is the eagle's lofty flight,
With ardent hope, aspiring
E'en to the flaming source of light,
Undoubling and untiring.
Glory, with gorgeous sunbeam, throws
An Iris mantle o'er thee—
A radiant present round thee glows—
Deathless renown before thee.
And I, like a shy, timid dove,
That shuns noon's fervid beaming,
And far within the silent grove,
Sits, lost in loving dreaming—
Turn, half in joy, and half in fear,
From thine ambitions soaring,
And seek to hide me from the glare,
That o'er thy track is pouring.
I cannot echo back the notes
Of triumph thou art pealing,
But from my woman's heart there floats
The music of one feeling,
One single, longing, pleading moan,
Whose voice I cannot smother—
"Love me—love me!" its song alone,
And it will learn no other!

There was a long stillness. Carry was weeping silently. She was a novice to the world, and believed that many were guileless and loving as herself; but she felt, as she listened to this enthusiastic outflow from ice-girt depths, unfathomable to her, unsuspected by others, that terrible woe was in reserve for the heart so suddenly unveiled. There was, about Ida, when her real character came into action, an earnestness of passion and sentiment that forbade the utterance of trite counsels or cautions; the tide would have its way, and one must abide its ebb in patience. Her first words showed that it had retired.

"I appear strangely fitful to your gentle little self, dear one. It is seldom that I yield to these humours. You have pierced to the bottom of my heart to-night;" linking her arm again in Carry's. "Forget my vehemence, and believe me if you will, the iceberg people say I am."

"Never! oh, Ida! Why do yourself such injustice? Why not let your friends know that you have feeling? They would love you but the more."

"Do not believe it. I should be sent to the Insane Hospital. Hearts are at a discount in the market just now, and hypocrisy above par."

"There you go!" exclaimed Carry. "One moment all softness—the next, an ocean is between us. Contradictory enigma! If I loved you less, I should be angry. You read every leaf of my heart as easily as you unfold a newspaper; and just as I fancy that I have the key to yours, it is shut close—a casket, whose spring I cannot find."

"Or like an oyster," said Ida. "Apropos de bottes—here come the candles, harbingers of supper, and I hear our brace of Esculapii, upon the porch, ready to discuss it."

Carry asked herself if it could be the impassioned improvisatrice, who charmed her father and Arthur into forgetfulness of professional anxieties, and the attractions of the inviting board, by her brilliant play of wit, sparkling and pleasant as foam upon champagne, without its evanescence. The gentlemen admired and liked her. That they unconsciously identified her with Carry, may have accounted for this, in part, but most was owing to her powers of pleasing. An inquiry, made with extreme gravity, as to the number and welfare of their patients, was the preface to a burlesque sketch of the saddle-bag scene; in which, not a hint of the reflections it inspired, escaped her; and when she described the doctor's rueful countenance, as he held up the neck and stopple of a large phial, saying dolefully, "The Calomel too, and three cases of fever on hand!" Arthur resigned knife and fork, in despair of eating another mouthful, and Dr. Carleton drew out his Bandanna to wipe off the coursing tears.

"Hist," said Ida, her finger uplifted, "some one is coming!" The roll of an approaching vehicle was plainly heard; the coachman's sharp "Whoa!" followed by a cheer, in sound like a view-hallo, but it said, "Ship ahoy!"

"Charley! Charley!" screamed Carry, upsetting the tea-urn on her way to the door, pursued by Arthur and Dr. Carleton. Ida went as far as the porch. She heard Mrs. John Dana's voice, then her husband's; and Elle's incoherent response to the efforts made to awaken her; but the stranger was chief spokesman. "Look after your wife and the baggage, John; I will disembark the lighter freight. Elle! Elle! don't you want to see Aladdin's lamp? Aha! well, here is something prettier—Aunt Carry, and a nice supper. Charley! you monkey! wide awake as usual! Feel if you have your own head, my boy! People are apt to make mistakes in the dark. Give me that small-sized bundle, Jenny—you'll lose it in the weeds, and then there will be the mischief to pay. One, two, three, all right!" And with the "small-sized bundle" in his arms, he marched up the walk, Carry scolding and laughing.

"Charley! you are too bad! give her to me—a pretty figure you are, playing nurse!"

"He has carried her, or Elle, before him, on the horse, all the way!" said Mrs. Dana. "Ida, my love, how do you do?" warmly kissing her. John Dana shook hands with her, and Elle cried, "Cousin Ida! *you* here at grandpa's!"

Charley gave a comic glance at his burden, when he was presented; but his bow was respectful, and as graceful as the case admitted. Ida hardly saw him until the second supper was served; Carry insisting that she should occupy her accustomed seat, and go through the form of eating. Elle petitioned for a chair by her, and the three brothers were together on the opposite side of the table. They were an interesting study. John, with his strong, dark, yet singularly pleasing physiognomy, was the handsomest; but his precedence in age, and perhaps rougher experiences in life, had imparted an air of command, which, while it became him well, deterred one from familiarity. Charley was so unlike him, that the supposition of their being of the same lineage, seemed absurd. His hair and complexion were many shades lighter, and the features cast in a different mould, his eyes the only fine ones in the set. He was not so tall, by half a head, and more slightly built. Arthur was the connecting link; with John's height, and Charley's figure; the perfect mouth and teeth of one; the brown eyes of the other; and hair and skin a *juste milieu* between the two. Ida's attention was most frequently directed to the new-comer. She thought him more homely than his brothers; and it certainly was not a family resemblance that troubled her with the notion, that she had seen him somewhere not very long ago—when, she could not say—except that his expression was not the same as now. Heedless of her observation, he rattled on; doing ample justice to the edibles, in some unaccountable manner; his gastronomical and vocal apparatus never interfering; yet withal, he was an excellent listener; and allowed the rest of the party to say whatever they wished. "He would be worth his weight in gold to a comic almanac-maker," thought Ida, as he dashed off caricature and anecdote, conveying a character in an epithet, and setting the table in a roar, by a grimace or inflection. His pictures, however, were coloured by his gay mood; there were no frowning portraits, and their smiles were all broad grins.

"You have not learned to love buttermilk, yet, Charley?" said Carry, as John called for a second tumbler of the cooling beverage.

"Can't say that I have. Did I write you an account of my begging expedition?"

"Begging! no—tell me now."

"It was in the Valley. Fitzgerald and I—you know Fitz., Arthur—were on a hunting frolic. We went up on the mountains, and fell in with game in abundance, but despicable accommodations. We were at it for three days. The first night we 'camped out,' gipsy style; built a rousing fire to scare the wild beasts; wrapped our dreadnoughts around us, and 'lay, like gentlemen taking a snooze,' feet towards the fire, and faces towards the moon. I had made up my mind that there would be precious little romance, and less comfort, in this very roomy hotel; but Fitz. was sentimentally inclined, and I let him alone. 'A life in the woods for me!' said he, as he stretched himself upon the ground. I was fast asleep in two minutes, so far as sounds went. 'Charley!' he exclaimed, at my heavy breathing. 'Pshaw! he's off! he has no more poetry in him than there is in a—rock!'"

"I guessed that he was helped to this illustration, by his discovery of the quantity of the substance in the soil thereabouts, for he shifted his position. He was tolerably still for about five minutes; then there was a jerk, and 'I have not picked the softest spot, surely!' After another season of quiet came, 'How he sleeps! If he were to swap sides with me, he would not be disturbing the echoes in that style!'

"A brief objurgation to an unnamed annoyance, was comment fourth. I slept on perseveringly. He bore it for an hour, and then got up and mended the fire, by which he was moodily seated, when I awoke from my first nap. 'Hallo!' said I, rubbing my eyes, 'Is it morning?' 'No! and what's more, I don't believe it's ever coming?' with a savage accent. 'Ah well! just hail me when it does break,' and I dropped back 'That is more than flesh and blood can bear!' said he, with awful deliberateness, 'Here I can't get a wink of sleep, and you are snoring away with a forty horse power. Maybe you think you are on a feather bed, man!' fiercely ironical.

"'A feather bed!' just opening my eyes—'a feather bed is nothing to it, Fitz.'

"'I *believe* you!' he said.

"The morning did come, and we had splendid shooting, and happened on a log cabin that night, where we were permitted to lodge, leaving most of our game for its mistress, who refused money for her hospitality. By three o'clock of the last day, we turned our faces towards home, and by rare luck, overtook a man who lived upon Fitz.'s farm, him we loaded with our guns and game-bags, he being on horseback, and fresh, we on foot and tired. Presently a traveller passed us, crossing to the other side of the road, and eyeing us suspiciously. 'Fitz.,' observed I, 'How hard that man looked at you. You are not exactly in holiday trim, my dear fellow!'

"'I haven't seen any man, or thought of myself, I was too much absorbed in conjecturing how such an ugly creature as you, was ever raised—you couldn't have been, except in Eastern Virginia.'

"After some sparring, we laid a bet as to how the people of the first house we came to, would decide the question of our comparative beauty, 'I have it!' said he, 'We are foreigners; talk the most villainous jargon you can invent, and trust me for the rest. We shall hear criticisms enough, I'll warrant.'

"We were ripe for fun; and reaching a small farm-house, Fitz. opened the gate. 'Recollect we know no Inglese!' We were grotesque figures, wearing bell-crowned hats of white felt, drab wrappers, coated with mud, and green-hunting shirts. Add a beard of three days' growth, and brigandish mustachios, and you have our 'picters.' The men were off at work, but the women peeped at us from all quarters. Fitz. walked meekly up to a girl who was washing in the yard.

"'*Avezyouvuspaimum*?'

"'What!' said she, wringing the suds from her hands.

"'*Wevusivusfaimetsoif*,' winking at me for confirmation.

"'Yaw! pax vobiscum!' returned I, in imitation of poor Wamba; and pointing into my throat.

"'Two forrinners,' said an older woman. 'Come, see 'em, chillen.'

'You are hungry, ain't you?' said the girl.

"'*Novuscomprendum*.'

"'And thirsty, too?' to me.

"I put my finger to my mouth, with a voracious snap. Away she ran, and was back in a minute, with a plate of cold Irish potatoes and a bowl of buttermilk; a younger sister following with another."

"What *did* you do?"

"I drank it! absolutely! I, who had never looked at a churn without shuddering. I desired to make a favorable impression. The children were gaping at the sights; and I contrived, before handing the bowl to one of them, to drop a piece of money into the milk left in the bottom 'for manners.' I wished it back in my pocket, as the old hag, after a prolonged stare, pointed her skinny hand at me, '*Sary, I think this 'ere one is rayther the wuss looking, don't you*?'

"Fitz. burst into a laugh, that scared them all in one direction, while we beat a retreat in the other."

"A hearty laugh helpeth digestion," said Dr. Carleton, setting back in his chair. "Miss Ida, if you and Charley will undertake my practice, I am in hopes that the casualty of the afternoon will be less disastrous than we apprehend."

"What casualty?" asked Charley.

The doctor explained:

"And you seize upon a prime lot of choice spirits, as a substitute for your tinctures and drugs. Fie, Doctor! I thought you were a temperance man!"

"I have the best right to your services," said Carry, clasping her hands around his arm, and walking with him towards the parlor. "And I forewarn you, I have enough for you to do. Ida and I have moped here for a fortnight, without a single frolic, and with an alarmingly scanty supply of beaux."

He looked down at her, as he would have done at Elle.

"You ride, do you not?"

"There is a pleasant fiction that we have morning excursions, daily; but history records but three such felicitous events."

"Where was Arthur?"

"Hush, my dear sir, the country is sickly; and——" she said, *sotto voce*, "He will not hear of father's going out after nightfall; and they have had several difficult cases, of late, demanding almost constant attendance."

"Then, if you are willing, I will enter upon my duties as escort, to-morrow morning."

"Oh! not so soon! you may have time to recover from your fatigue."

"Fatigue! fudge! I could dance all night. Are you fond of riding, Miss Ross?"

"I used to like it; I am sadly out of practice now."

"A fault easily cured, if you are not timid."

"Not she!" said Carry; "and want of practice notwithstanding, she is a better horsewoman than I."

This was demonstrated in the course of the first ride; and both improved rapidly under the tuition of their self-constituted instructor.

John returned to the city; Arthur's time was never at his own disposal; the care of the girls devolved entirely upon Charley. From the moment of his arrival, Ida studied him intently, and each hour brought difficulties, instead of elucidation. Easy and kind, always at their service; and performing the tasks assigned him, as if they were real pleasures, he was nothing of a "ladies' man;" eschewed gallant speeches, and consigned flatterers to the tender mercies of Mrs. Opie. She felt that he was affectionate, but would have been at a loss to produce proof thereof. He never let fall a syllable of endearment, yet Carry and the children read something in his face which said more. His tastes were cultivated, and his mind well-informed, but he set at naught the laws of conversational etiquette; his sayings had as marked a style as his features; a style, which those who did not know better, termed "droll," and those who did, dubbed "Charley's;" it was referable to no thing or person else. His candor was not his least remarkable trait. He was obstinately silent when appealed to for an opinion, or gave it rough-hewn; no rounding-off of sharp corners; no filling out here, or sloping in there, so as to fit neatly to another's. He made no distinctions of rank; pulled off his hat to the meanest field-hand, with as gentle courtesy as though he had been the President; and severed the thread of her most sprightly narrations, to thank the ragged urchin, who unfastened gates, or let down drawbars, in their desultory excursions.

"He is one of the best of men," delivered Mammy, as foreman of the kitchen jury. Ida smiled at the harum-scarum figure, which arose in her mind, in opposition to the image of sanctity, Mammy's description should have summoned.

"You do not do him justice, Ida," observed Carry.

"My smile was not of unbelief, but amusement; I like him. There is a rich vein of quaint humor in his mind; and his unebbing spirits entitle him to the honors of the laughing philosopher."

"He is more than that—"

"Who was it I heard wishing for a frolic?" asked Charley, coming in. "I met a boy with a basket full of perfumery and white satin ribbon, at the gate. I had to stand between him and the wind, while he gave me these. 'Miss Carleton'—'Miss Ross'—'Dr. Dana *and brother*,' they would swindle a fellow out of his birth-right! 'Mr. and Mrs. Truman solicit the pleasure—' hum—no doubt they will be overjoyed—'evening, 27th August'—what is it, Carry?"

"We were talking of it this morning, the bridal party given to William Truman and lady."

"Whom did he marry?"

"He isn't married at all; on the 26th, he is to conduct to the hymeneal altar, the beautiful Miss Sophia Morris, of Richmond, Virginia."

"No newspaper reporter could be more explicit. You will go?"

"That depends upon Miss Ross' inclinations, and somebody's gallantry."

"Poor dependence—that last! Do you know the bride elect—that is to be?"

"The bride elect, that *is*—is sister to a school-mate of ours; and I have some acquaintance with herself."

"Ellen will be with her sister," said Ida. "I shall enjoy meeting her. Her laugh will carry us back to days of yore."

"To days of yore," said Charley, balancéing to an imaginary partner. "Is it three or four weeks since you parted! In a young lady's calendar, a month is an age, six months eternity. You look upon me as a miracle of longevity, do you not?"

"As old enough to be less saucy," said Carry. "Do you know that this habit of catching up one's words is very rude?"

He threw a quick glance to Ida. "Miss Ross is not offended, I trust. Nothing was further from my intention than to wound or offend. I am too prone to speak without thought. Forgive me this time."

"Upon two conditions."

"Name them."

"First, that you never again imagine an apology due, when no offence has been committed; secondly, that you drop that very punctilious 'Miss Ross,' and adopt your brother's manner of address."

"Agreed! to both. If I presume upon my privileges, I rely upon you for admonition."

"And this party?" said Carry. "Sit down and be a good boy, while Ida and I talk it over."

He brought up a stool in front of their sofa, and, knees at a right angle, feet close together; and folded hands, waited humbly for the crumbs that might be flung to him.

"It is eight miles off," said Carry, "but there will be a moon—"

("Most generally is!")

"Be quiet, sir! it will be moonlight, and the road is level and dry—"

("It stops at the creek to get a drink!")

She aimed a blow at him with her fan, which he dodged.

"I am so little acquainted with them," objected Ida.

"That's nothing. Mr. and Mrs. Truman are the most hospitable of human beings, and Mary is a lovely girl—"

("Per latest steamer from Paradise.")

"We must go. Sister is here to keep father company. Now the last query—what shall we wear?"

("The first shall be last.")

"White muslins," returned Ida.

"Yes; and the thinnest we have. Nothing else is endurable this weather—"

("Except iced juleps!")

"Arthur!" cried Carry, with a pretty affectation of vexation. "Come in, and keep your brother quiet!"

"What is he doing? he seems very harmless," said Dr. Dana, stepping through the window from the piazza.

The maligned individual applied his fist to his eye. "I ain't a-touching nothin!"

"I am security for his good behaviour," continued Arthur, laying his arm across his shoulder. "Proceed with the case in hand."

The rival merits of peach-blossoms and azure were set forth; bandeaux preferred to curls—the gentlemen giving the casting vote;—kid and satin slippers paraded—Charley advocating "calf-skin;"—a muttering of "patriotism" and "domestic manufacture," checked by a pinch from his brother;—every knot of ribbon;—each bud and leaf of the bouquets were settled to the taste of the fair wearers before the council adjourned.

CHAPTER IX

The most spacious of Mrs. Truman's chambers was prepared for the ladies' dressing-room, on the evening of the party; and there were no spare corners, although several of the neighbours offered their houses for the use of those who dared not tempt the chance of crumpled robes and disarranged coiffures; the probable consequence of a ride eight or ten miles in gala dress. Every stage of the toilet was in progress, from the chrysalis of the dressing-gown to the full-winged butterfly, the sylph, who, with a dainty adjustment of her diaphanous drapery, and a last, lingering look at the flattering mirror, declared herself "ready."

Ida and Carry were bent upon dressing alike; no easy matter to do, consistently with their perceptions of colours and fitness. No one hue became both; no they proscribed the prismatic tints and appeared in virgin white. Carry was beautiful as a dream of Fairy Land. The plump, white arms were bare to the shoulder, and without other ornament than their own fairness, except a chain of gold, attached to a locket, containing her parents' hair. This she never left off. Snowy gloves hid hands, softer still; the exquisitely-fitted corsage, and the waist it enclasped, were the admiration, and, if truth must be told, the envy of the bevy of talkative damsels; but few remarked upon these after a sight of her face. Her hair would curl, do what she would; the rebellious bandeaux refused to be plastered upon the blue-veined temples, but rippled and glittered, like nothing but a stream, golden in the sunset. The most artful *soupçon* of rouge was a palpable counterfeit compared with her living bloom; pearls lay between the ruby lips; and a spirit, more priceless than gold or rubies, or pearls beamed from the liquid eyes. Ida looked forward with delight to Arthur's exultant smile, when he should behold her; and Carry, alike forgetful of self, was lost in gratified contemplation of the elegant figure of her friend. With not a tithe of the beauty of half the girls present, her tout ensemble was striking and attractive. The haughtiness which held the crowd at a distance, gave a high-bred tone to her bearing, and one sentence, uttered in her clear voice, and a smile dispelled all unfavourable impressions.

Arthur and Charley were at the foot of the stairs.

"What a Babel!" said Ida, as they entered the thronged rooms.

"And what a waste of breath!" replied Charley. "There is neither sociability, or rational enjoyment, to be had in these very large assemblies."

"I rather like the excitement of the crowd;" said Ida, "it affects me strangely, but agreeably; with the same sensation the waves may feel in their sports,—a tumultuous glee at being a part of the restless whole,—never still, and always bounding onward."

"How do you account for it? Is it magnetism—animal electricity?"

"Perhaps so. If, as some contend, we are electrical machines, the revolving currents of the subtle fluid must operate powerfully upon the system of each, in a crowd like this. But to leave speculative ground—perilous to me, inasmuch as I do not know what I am talking about—"

"And I understand the science less," interrupted he. "You remember the Scotchman's definition of metaphysics—what were you going to ask?"

"Why you dislike these scenes? I fancied you would be in your element."

"Excuse me for saying that I suspect you class me among amphibious creatures—a *sui generis*—equally at home in the air, earth, and water, and not over-well qualified for any of these states of existence."

Ida would have disclaimed; but he had come too near the mark; the eyes that asked a reply were penetrating as laughing; she was thankful that the bridal party released her from their regards.

"The bride is pretty," he observed, when the confusion was a little over.

"Tame praise for such beauty," said Ida.

"What then? superb—magnificent? and if I wish to describe the Alps or Niagara, can you help me to a word?"

"You do not affect the florid style now in vogue?"

"No. It is the vice of American language and literature. We 'pile on the agony,' until the idea is smothered; plain words lose their meaning, become too weak to go alone, and have to be bolstered up by sonorous adjectives."

Ida smiled, and turned her head to look for Ellen Morris. Charley remarked the movement, and imitated it.

"Ha! can it be!" he exclaimed.

"What!" she questioned.

"I cannot be mistaken! it is he! What wind has blown him hither? An old—I thought, a transatlantic friend; the gentleman with the moustache, conversing with one of the bridesmaids."

"Ellen Morris! I see him; but he deserves more than the doubtful designation of the 'gentleman with the moustache.' Who, and what is he?"

"An artist and poet, just returned from Italy, and the hero of divers adventures, which, as you love the romantic, I may relate to you in my poor way some day. His cognomen is Lynn Holmes."

"He looks the poet; how handsome!"

"'Tame praise for such beauty,'" quoted Charley, with mock gravity.

It was, when applied to the face and form before them. He was not above the medium height; symmetrically proportioned, hair purplish in its blackness, the arched nostril, and short upper lip indicative of spirit end gentle birth, and the rich, warm complexion had caught its flush from Italian suns. Its rapid fluctuations, plainly visible through the transparent olive of his cheek, spoke too, of passions kindled by that burning clime. But his eyes! Ida's were darker, as she gazed into their midnight—large and dreamy and melancholy! a world of unwritten poetry; but when did poet have, or artist paint such!

"What is the conclusion of the whole matter?" asked Charley, patiently.

"That you should speak to your friend;" letting go his arm. "I shall not mind your leaving me alone."

He replaced her hand. "Content yourself. Miss Morris will not thank me, if I intrude at present. There is time enough. Pity he has chosen a starving profession."

"And why 'pity,' if in so doing he has followed the beckoning of genius! He has hearkened to, and obeyed the teachings of his higher nature. Can they mislead?"

"When we mistake their meaning. Genius steers wildly astray if the compass-box of judgment is wanting. My remark was a general one"—seeing her grave look. "Holmes is one of the gifted of the earth; and when I lamented his choice of a profession, I did not censure him, but the public. He ought to have a nabob's fortune to perfect his schemes; and he will not make a living. Men squander thousands for the intellectual gratification of a horse-race; an exhibition in which, I allow, the brute is generally the nobler animal;—and knowingly brand him 'a verdant 'un,' who expends a quarter of that sum in works of art. Will you dance? I hear a violin."

"I think not. It is too warm."

"To say nothing of the crowd. In dancing, as in most things, I prefer standing upon my own footing—not upon other people's toes."

Nevertheless, there were those present who could not withstand the allurement of a "hop," under any circumstances; and by snug packing on the part of the soberly-inclined, while numbers sought the freer air of the passages and piazzas, room was made for a set. Ellen Morris joined it, and Mr. Holmes had time to look about him. His start of delight as he recognised Charley, and the heartiness of their greetings, showed their mutual attachment; and imagining that they would have much to say after a lengthy separation, Ida would have fallen in the rear, had not Charley forestalled her by a prompt presentation of his friend. They exchanged, indeed, one or two brief questions and replies; but these over, she was the centre of attraction. The panting, heated dancers tripped by, commiserating, if they noticed the "hum-drum" group at the window; never thinking that, demure as they appeared, there was more enjoyment in that secluded recess, than in the entire mass of revellers besides. There are harmonies in conversation, the arrangement of which is wofully disregarded. Accident had collected a rare trio. The artist talked as he would have painted; descrying beauties everywhere, and bringing them together with a masterly hand;

only tolerating deformity, as it displayed them to more advantage, and shedding over all the mellow glow of his fervid imagination; startling by paradoxes, to enchant by the grace and beauty of their reconciliation. And Charley, with a cooler brain and wary eye, was ready to temper, not damp his enthusiasm;—not to dam the rushing flood, but lead it aside into a smoother channel. Ida thought of the compass-box, and charmed as she was by the eloquence of this modern Raphael, acknowledged the justice of the simile. For herself, appreciative and suggestive, she fanned the flame. Her sympathetic glance and smile, the quick catching at a thought, half unuttered; the finish and polish his crude ideas received from her lighter hand, could not but please and flatter. How grating was the interruption!—

"Mr. Dana! not dancing!"

"No, Mr. Truman, but exceedingly well entertained."

"Hav'nt a doubt of it! hav'nt a doubt! but there's a young lady—a stranger—who wants a partner for the set that is forming, and as your brother is engaged—to dance, I mean—with Miss Somebody—I forget who—I thought as an old friend, I would make so free as to call upon you, ah—ah—she being a stranger, you understand, ah—ah—"

"Certainly sir, of course, where is she?" said Charley, swallowing his chagrin, in his willingness to oblige the embarrassed host. "Charles Dana, having gone to see his partner, desires the prayers of the congregation," he said aside to his companions, before plunging into the throng.

"'O, rare Ben Jonson!'" said Mr. Holmes, as they disappeared.

"And most incomprehensible of anomalies!" responded Ida.

"The dross is upon the surface—refined gold beneath. Have you known him long?"

"But a fortnight."

"You have not mastered the alphabet yet. Bright and dancing as is that eye, I have seen it shed tears in abundance and softness, like a woman's. His tongue knows other language than that of flippant trifling."

"He is a universal favorite. I am surprised he has never married."

Mr. Holmes was silent. He even looked pained; and Ida, conscious that she had unwittingly touched a sore spot, took up the strain Mr. Truman had broken. She was in the Coliseum of Rome; when among the moving sea of faces precipitated upon the retina, yet nothing to the brain, unless, perhaps, making more vivid its conceptions of the multitude, who once lined the crumbling walls of the amphitheatre—one arrested her attention. The subject was thrilling; the speaker's description graphic and earnest;—it was unkind, and ungrateful, and disrespectful—but laugh she must, and did, when in Charley's partner she beheld Celestia Pratt! Her first emotion was extreme amusement; her next, indignant compassion for him thrust into public notice as the cavalier of a tawdry fright; for the thickest of satin robes, and a load of jewelry, that gave plausibility to the tale of Hannibal's spoils at Cannæ, betrayed, instead of cloaking vulgarity. He was playing the agreeable, however, with, his wonted sang-froid, varied, as she judged from his gestures, by gratuitous hints as to the figure and step. In trying to efface the remembrance of her rudeness from Mr. Holmes' mind, and watching the oddly matched pair, she passed the time until the set was finished. Arthur approached, and the gleam of his white teeth upset her acquired gravity.

"Caught," said he, as Mr. Holmes walked away, "just as I was. I secured a partner directly I saw her; and Mr. Truman, hearing from her that I was an acquaintance, put at me two minutes later."

"He said you were engaged—to dance."

"Here he is! Charley, I thought you declined dancing."

"So I did. I consented to please Mr. Truman."

"Had you ever seen your partner before?"

"No. I know what you are at, Art., but I cannot laugh with you. I am sorry for her."

"You shame us, Mr. Dana," said Ida, frankly. "I will make amends for my uncharitableness, by fighting my way, single-handed, to the farthest end of the room, to speak to her, if you say so."

"And I, not to be outdone, will dance with her," said Arthur, with a martyr-air.

"I absolve you," said his brother. "She is a queer fish, I own," in his light tone. "Have you spoken to Holmes?"

"Yes. He says he has partly resolved to winter in Richmond. He is a groomsman; but the party disband to-morrow; only Miss Morris attending the young couple to their home up the country. I have invited Lynn to spend some time with us, before he settles to business."

"Will he come?"

"Probably."

A succession of introductions and beaux engaged Ida until supper. She forgot her purpose of speaking with Celestia, and would not have remembered her again that evening, had she not been made aware of her proximity at table by something between a grunt and exclamation, forced through a mouthful of cake.

"Lor! if that ain't Idy Ross!"

She had a saucer of ice-cream in one hand, and a slice of fruitcake in her left; so she stuck out a red elbow in lieu of either; which unique salutation Ida pretended not to see.

"How are you, Celestia? When did you come into the neighbourhood?"

"I jest got down yesterday. You see," in a stage whisper, "I heard of this party better'n a fortnight ago, and ma and I set our hearts 'pon my coming; so I had this dress made (it cost four dollars a yard!) and *happened*, you know, to pay a visit to Cousin Lucindy Martin's, jest in the nick of time, and Mrs. Truman, found out, you know, that I was there, and sent me a 'bid.' Didn't I manage it nice?"

"You appear to be having a pleasant time."

"O, splendid! I've danced every set. Thar's a heap of polite beaux—ain't there?"

"Miss Ross, what shall I have the pleasure of helping you to?" asked Mr. Euston, Ida's escort.

She named an article, and Celestia twitched her arm—"Who's that?"

"Mr. Euston," said Ida, distinctly.

"Is he your beau?"

"No."

"Then you'd as lief as not interduce me, hadn't you? He's the loveliest thing I ever saw."

Ida flushed with disgust and vexation; the insufferable conceit of the girl, her bizarre appearance, and harsh tones drew the notice of many to them; and her horror of ridicule was strong upon her.

"Miss Ida," said Charles Dana, across the table. "Will you eat a philopoena with me?" As he tossed the almond, she marked his expression, and the scene in the painting-room, Josephine's derision, and the rude mirth of her supporters, her hurricane of rage and the commanding look that said to it "Be still," all rushed over her like a whirlwind, and departed suddenly. Mr. Euston was bowing with the desired delicacy; Celestia, serenely expectant, and with the mien of one who confers a favour upon both parties, she complied with the fair lady's request. Mr. Euston was handsome and gallant; he immediately dipped into his stock of pretty sayings, and presented one of the most elegant. The recipient fluttered and prinked, and baited another hook; and Ida stole a look at Charley. Her not recognizing him before was no marvel; she could hardly persuade herself that her conviction of a minute before was not an illusion; so impervious was the Momus mask. He was frequently near, and with her, in the course of the evening: but no sign betokened a suspicion of her perplexity. He was gayer than his wont; when sheer fatigue drove the votaries of pleasure from the festive hall, his spirits were at their meridian. He had passed most of the day on horseback; had talked and danced and stood for six hours; yet he sent off carriage after carriage with a lively adieu; and seeing his own party seated in theirs, vaulted into the saddle, as for a morning gallop. He cheered the weary travellers so long as he could extort replies from the lagging tongues, and serenaded them the rest of the way with snatches of melody fantastic as his mood.

"Why have you and Charley preserved such a mysterious silence respecting our former meeting?" inquired Ida, when she and Carry were laid down to sleep.

"He charged me not to name him, if I heard the matter alluded to; and, since we have been at home, enjoined secrecy more strictly, saying the incident was better forgotten than remembered," said Carry, dozingly.

This was Thursday. On Saturday the young artist made one in their midst. In his school-days he was a welcome guest at Poplar-grove, spending a portion of his vacation with his friend Charley, and the lapse of years had not rusted the hinges of the hospitable doors, or those of the master's heart. He was received and cherished as of old.

Mrs. Dana looked into the girls' room before retiring. Ida was brushing her hair; Carry watching and talking to her. "Yes," said she, complacently, appealing to her sister for confirmation. "I flatter myself our party could not be more select or composed of choicer materials. Four beaux—including father—handsomest of all; and but two belles—three— pardon me, Mrs. Dana. It may be a century ere we are again so blessed; and we must go somewhere, or do something to exhibit ourselves. Ida may have Charley and father, if she will leave the Italian and his lamping eyes to me."

"And Arthur—why is he neglected the division of spoils?" asked Mrs. Dana.

"I make him over to you. Brother John commended you to his care."

"Mammy applied to me for numberless passes, to-night. There is a big meeting at Rocky Mount. The servants will attend en masse, to-morrow; why not follow their example?" said Mrs. Dana, with playful irony.

"We will!" exclaimed Carry, clapping her hands. "I'll ask father this minute."

"But, my dear sister—"

"Don't say a word, Jenny; Ida would like to go, I am sure."

"When I understand the character of the entertainment; I shall be qualified to express my wishes."

"Why," answered Carry, tying the cord of the wrapper she had cast around her. "They preach a little, and sing and shout; and in intermission, we have grand fun."

"Fun! at church!"

"That is not the word precisely; but everybody meets everybody else, and we have an hour for talking and eating. How happens it, that you are a novice? you are country-born."

"I was never at a big meeting, notwithstanding."

"An additional reason, why we should be on the spot to-morrow. I will be back directly." In five minutes she returned, blushing and laughing.

"Would you believe it? When I knocked at father's door, Arthur opened it. I slunk back in the dark, and asked for 'Marster.' 'Doctor,' said he, 'Martha wants to see you,' and sauntered off. Didn't father stare, and I laugh, when I ran in! The stupid creature! to be fooled so easily!"

"The meeting!" said Ida.

"All's well! Father was afraid we might be tired, if we stayed to both sermons; but I assured him that was impossible. I hope it will be a fine day!"

She was gratified; but the weather was not brighter than the faces gathered upon the piazza, at a shockingly unfashionable hour. It was six miles to Rocky Mount; and as Charley observed, "seats in the dress circle would be at a premium, two hours before services begun."

"'Marster' does not accompany us," said Arthur, significantly, as he handed Carry into the carriage. She was too much confused to reply; but Ida and Mrs. Dana laughed outright.

"Papa and myself, having no vagrant propensities, will go to our own church," answered the latter. "And if you have waited upon the young ladies, I will thank you to put me into the gig, Dr. Dana."

Mr. Holmes accepted a seat with the ladies; Charley and Arthur were on horseback. It is doubtful if one of the merry riders realised, for an instant, the sacredness of the day, or that they were bound to a place of worship. It did not occur, even to Dr. Carleton, that their glee, innocent and proper upon ordinary occasions, now verged upon sinful levity. He saw in it, the buoyancy of youth under the influence of agreeable company, and a cloudless day. They would be subdued by the exercises of the sanctuary; and he drove along, his large heart full of love and praise to Him who had showered these gem-sparkles into his chalice of life; the young people beguiling the length of their journey, by a running fire of badinage, puns and serio-comic discussions; embarked, to all intents and purposes, upon a party of pleasure.

"Behold Rocky Mount!" said Arthur, pointing to a rising ground, tufted by a clump of oaks.

"Where is the church?" inquired Ida. "I can distinguish people and horses, but no house."

"After we get there, I will lend you my pocket microscope," responded Charley. The brown walls of a small building, in the centre of the grove, were visible, as the road wound around the hill; but its dimensions were as great a puzzle as its absence would have been. Carry came to her aid.

"They preach out of doors, my dear."

"Out of doors!" this was a charming novelty.

"'The groves were God's first temples,'" she repeated softly, and Lynn continued the noble lines—

"Ah, why
Should we, in the world's riper years, neglect
God's ancient sanctuaries, and adore,
Only among the crowd, and under roofs
That our frail hands have raised?"

Charley smiled dubiously, but held his peace. The crowd thickened with their advance. Horses were tethered in solid ranks to the trees; children straying frightfully near to their heels; wagons and carriages almost piled upon each other; and men, white and black, stood about everywhere. The driver reined up, twenty yards from the arbor erected under the trees.

"Drive up nearer, Tom!" said Carry.

"He cannot," replied Arthur, letting down the steps. "Look!"

There was a quadruple row of vehicles on three sides of the arbor, the fourth being, at considerable pains, left open for passage. Several young men dashed to the side of the carriage, with as much empressement as at a ball, and thus numerously attended, the girls picked their way through the throng and dust. No gentlemen were, as yet, in their seats, and our party secured a vacant bench midway to the pulpit.

"Don't sit next to the aisle," whispered Arthur.

"Why not?" questioned Ida, removing to the other extremity of the plank.

"Oh! it is more comfortable here. We will be with you again presently."

"That is not all the reason," remarked Carry, when he was gone. "This railing protects us from the press on this side; and our young gentleman will not permit any one to occupy the stand without, but themselves."

"Will they not sit down?"

"No, indeed! there will not be room. Then the aisles will be filled with all sorts of people, and our dresses be liable to damage from boots and tobacco juice."

"Tobacco juice!" was she in a barbarous country! As Carry predicted, their three attendants worked their way, between the wheels and the people, to where they sat. Charley crawled under the rail, and planted himself behind them.

"I can keep my position until some pretty girl dislodges me," said he. "The denizens of these parts have not forgotten how to stare."

He might well say so. A battery of eyes was levelled upon them, wherever they looked. The tasteful dress and elegant appearance of the ladies, and their attractive suite, were subjects of special importance to the community at large. Although eclipsed in show by some present, theirs was a new constellation, and they must support observation as they could. They stood fire bravely; Ida was most unaccustomed to it, and she found so much to interest and divert her, that she became unconscious of the annoyance after a little.

"Are those seats reserved for distinguished strangers? have not we a right to them?" designating a tier in front of the speaker's stand.

"They are the anxious benches," returned Charley.

"Nonsense!"

"So I think. The brethren dissent from us. I am not quizzing. That is the name."

"The mourners—the convicted occupy them," said Carry.

"Are they here?" inquired Ida, credulously. It was preposterous to conceive such a possibility in this frivolous loud-talking assembly.

"Not now;" answered Charley. "But when they crowd on the steam, you will witness scores."

"Fie! Charley? it is wicked to speak so!"

"I am just as pious as if I did not, Carry. I'll wager my horse—and head too—that by to-night, Miss Ida will agree with me, that these religious frolics are more hurtful to the cause they are intended to advance, than fifty such harmless affairs, as we attended on Thursday night."

"I am not solemnised yet;" said Ida.

"You are as solemn as you are going to be. You may be excited, or frightened into something like gravity. Two, three, four preachers! That's what I call a waste of the raw material. What a flutter of ribbons and fans! The congregation reminds me of a clover field, with the butterflies hovering over its gaily-colored, bobbing heads. Handsome ladies by dozens! This county is famed for its beauty, and but one tolerable-looking man in its length and breadth!"

"Why, there is Mr. Euston—what fault have you to find in him?"

"He is the honorable exception. Whom did you think I meant?" smiling mischievously at Carry's unguarded query. "Art. here, is passable. Modesty prevents my saying more, as we are daily mistaken for each other. The music strikes up;—rather quavering; they are not in the 'spirit' yet. They never get to the 'understanding.' I must decamp. Those fair ones are too bashful to look this way, while I am here."

He was on the outside of the rail, sedate and deacon-like, in a minute. Unsuited as his remarks were to the time and place, they were less objectionable than the whispers of the ladies who dispossessed him;—critiques upon Susan's beaux and Joseph's sweethearts; upon faces, dress and deportment; a quantity of reprobation, and very sparse praises.

The preacher was an unremarkable man, who delivered, in a sing-song tone, an unremarkable discourse; opposing no impediment to the sociability of the aforementioned damsels, except that they lowered their shrill staccato to a piano. The gentlemen whispered behind their hats, notched switches, and whittled sticks. The hearers from Poplar-grove, albeit they were gay, youthful, and non-professors, were the most decorous auditors in their part of the congregation. Another minister arose; a man not yet in his thirtieth year, his form stooped, as beneath the weight of sixty winters. The crowd stilled instantly. He leaned, as for support, upon the primitive desk; his attenuated hands clasped, his eyes moving slowly in their cavernous recesses, over the vast assemblage. "And what come ye out into the wilderness for to see?" he said, in a voice of preternatural sweetness and strength. "Aye! ye are come as to a holiday pageant, bedecked in tinsel and costly raiment. I see before me the pride of beauty and youth; the middle-aged, in the strength of manliness and honor, the hoary hairs and decrepid limbs of age;—all trampling—hustling each other in your haste—in one beaten road—the way to death and judgment! Oh! fools and blind! slow-worms, battening upon the damps and filth of this vile earth! hugging your muck rakes while the glorious One proffers you the crown of Life!" The bent figure straightened; the thin hands were endowed with a language of power, as they pointed, and shook, and glanced through the air. His clarion tones thrilled upon every ear, their alarms and threatenings and denunciations; in crashing peals, the awful names of the Most High, and His condemnations of the wicked, descended among the throng; and those fearful eyes were fiery and wrathful. At the climax he stopped;—with arms still upraised, and the words of woe and doom yet upon his lips, he sank upon the arm of a brother beside him, and was led to his seat, ghastly as a corpse, and nearly as helpless.

A female voice began a hymn.

"This is the field, the world below,—
Where wheat and tares together grow;

Jesus, ere long will weed the crop,
And pluck the tares in anger up."

The hills, for miles around, reverberated the bursting chorus,

"For soon the reaping time will come,
And angels shout the harvest home!"

The ministers came down from the stand, and distributed themselves among the people; bowed heads and shaking forms marking their path;—a woman from the most remote quarter of the throng, rushed up to the mourner's seats, and flung herself upon her knees with a piercing cry;—another and another;—some weeping aloud; some in tearless distress;—numbers knelt where they had sat;—and louder and louder, like the final trump, and the shout of the resurrection morn, arose the surge of song;—

"For soon the reaping time will come
And angels shout the harvest home!"

Carry trembled and shrank; and Ida's firmer nerves were quivering. A lull in the storm, and a man knelt in the aisle, to implore "mercy and pardon for a dying sinner, who would not try to avert the wrath to come."
Sonorous accents went on with his weeping petition;—praying for "the hardened, thoughtless transgressors—those who had neither part nor lot in this matter; who stood afar off, despising and reckless." Again rolled out a chorus; speaking now of joyful assurance.

"Jesus my all to heaven has gone—
(When we get to heaven we will part no more,)
He whom I fix my hopes upon—
When we get to heaven we will part no more.
Oh! Fare-you-well! oh! fare-you-well!
When we get to heaven we will part no more,
Oh! Fare-you-well!"

Ida's eyes brimmed, and Carry sobbed with over-wrought feeling. Arthur bent over the railing and spoke to the latter. He looked troubled,—but for her: Lynn stood against one of the pillars which supported the roof; arms crossed, and a redder mantling of his dark cheek; Charley was cool and grave, taking in the scene in all its parts, with no sympathy with any of the phases of emotion. The tumult increased; shouted thankgivings, and wails of despair; singing and praying and exhorting, clashing in wild confusion.
"You had best not stay here," said Arthur to Carry, whose struggles for composure he could not bear to see.
"Suffer me to pass, Dr. Dana;" and a venerable minister stooped towards the weeping girl. "My daughter, why do you remain here, so far from those who can do you good? You are distressed on account of sin; are you ashamed to have it known? Do you not desire the

prayer of Christians? I will not affirm that you cannot be saved anywhere; 'the arm of the Lord is not shortened,' but I do warn you, that if you hang back in pride or stubbornness, you will be lost; and these only can detain you after what you have heard. Arise, and join that company of weeping mourners, it may not be too late."

Carry shook her head.

"Then kneel where you are, and I will pray for you."

She dried her tears. "Why should I kneel, Mr. Manly? I do not experience any sorrow for sin."

"My child!"

"My tears are not those of penitence; I do not weep for my sinfulness; I can neither think nor feel in this confusion."

The good man was fairly stumbled by this avowal.

"Have you *no* interest in this subject?"

"Not more than usual, sir. My agitation proceeded from animal excitement."

"I am fearful it is the same in a majority of instances, Mr. Manly;" said Arthur, respectfully.

"You my perceive your error one day, my son; let me entreat you to consider this matter as binding up your eternal welfare; and caution you not to lay a feather in the way of those who may be seeking their salvation."

Arthur bowed silently; and the minister passed on.

Dr. Carleton retired early that evening with a headache. Mrs. Dana was getting the children to sleep; the young people had the parlor to themselves. Charley was at the piano, fingering over sacred airs; psalm tunes, sung by the Covenanters, in their craggy temples, or murmuring to an impromptu accompaniment, a chant or doxology. All at once he struck the chords boldly, and added the full powers of the instrument to his voice, in the fine old melody of Brattle Street. Lynn ceased his walk through the room, and united his rich bass at the second line; Arthur, a tenor; Carry and Ida were happy to be permitted to listen—

"While Thee I seek, protecting Power,
Be my vain wishes stilled;
And may this consecrated hour
With better hopes be filled.
Thy love the power of thought bestowed,
To thee my thoughts would soar;
Thy mercy o'er my life has poured,
That mercy I adore.
In each event of life how clear
Thy ruling hand I see!
Each mercy to my soul most dear.
Because conferred by Thee.
In every joy that crowns my days,
In every pain I bear,
My heart shall find delight in praise,
Or seek relief in prayer.

When gladness wings my favored hour,
Thy love my thoughts shall fill;
Resigned—when storms of sorrow lower,
My soul shall meet Thy will.

My lifted eye, without a tear,
The gathering storm shall see;
My steadfast heart shall know no fear,
That heart will rest on Thee!"

"There!" said Charley, "there is more religion in that hymn than in all the fustian we have heard to-day; sermons, prayers and exhortations. Humbug in worldly concerns is despicable; in the church, it is unbearable."

"Consider, Charley, that hundred of pious people believe in the practices you condemn. Some of the best Christians I know were converted at these noisy revivals," said Carry.

"It would be miraculous if there were not a grain or two of wheat in this pile of chaff. I never attend one that I am not the worse for it. It is a regular annealing furnace; when the heat subsides you can neither soften or bend the heart again—the iron is steel. What does Miss Ida say?"

"That sin is no more hateful, or religion more alluring, for this Sabbath's lessons; still, I acquiesce in Carry's belief, that although mistaken in their zeal, these seeming fanatics are sincere."

"You applaud enthusiasm upon other subjects, why not in religion?" asked Lynn, "if any thing, it is everything. If I could believe that, when the stormy sea of life is passed, heaven—an eternal noon-tide of love and blessedness would be mine—a lifetime would be too short, mortal language too feeble to express my transport. There is a void in the soul which nought but this can satisfy. Life is fresh to us now; but from the time of Solomon to the present, the worlding has nauseated at the polluted spring, saying, 'For all his days are sorrow, and his travail grief; yea, his heart taketh not rest in the night.' I envy—not carp at the joys of those whose faith, piercing through the fogs of this lower earth, reads the sure promise—'It is your Father's good pleasure to give you the kingdom.'"

"You do homage to the beauty of the Faith, by whomsoever professed. I note its practical effects; judge of its genuineness by its workings. For example, the Old Harry awoke mightily within me, in intermission, to see Dick Rogers preaching to Carry, threatening her with perdition—she, who never in her life, committed a tenth of the sin he is guilty of every day He has been drunk three times in the last month; he is a walking demijohn, his hypocrisy a shame to his grey hairs. And James Mather—he would sell his soul for a fourpence, and call it clear gain. Sooner than lose a crop, he forces his negroes to work on Sunday—can't trust the God of harvest, even upon His own day. The poor hands are driven on week-days as no decent man would do a mule;—he let his widowed sister go to the poor-house, and offered to lend John five thousand dollars, the next week at eight per cent. I have known him since I was a shaver, and never had a word from him upon the 'one thing needful,' except at church. And he was in the altar, this morning, shouting as though the Lord were deaf!"

"Charley! Charley!"

"Facts are obstinate things, Carry. Next to being hypocritical ourselves, is winking at it in others. The church keeps these men in her bosom; she must not complain, if she shares in the odium they merit. They are emphatically sounding brass."

"Let them grow together until the harvest," said Arthur. "It is a convincing proof of the truth of Religion, that there are careful counterfeits."

"I do not impeach the 'truth of Religion.' You need not speak so reproachfully, Arthur. I believe in the Christianity of the Scriptures. What I assail, is intermittent piety; springs, whose channels are dusty, save at particular seasons;—camp-meetings and the like; men, who furbish up their religion, along with their go-to-meeting boots, and wear it no longer. Their brethren despise them as I do; but their mouths are shut, lest they 'bring disgrace upon their profession.' It can have no fouler disgrace than their lives afford. I speak what others conceal; when one of these whited sepulchres lifts his Bible to break my head, for a graceless reprobate, I pelt him with pebbles from the clear brook. Look at old Thistleton! a mongrel,—porcupine and bull-dog;—pricking and snarling from morning 'till night. A Christian is a *gentleman*; he is a surly growler. Half of the church hate, the other half dread him; yet he sits on Sabbaths, in the high places of the synagogues, leads prayer-meetings, and weeps over sinners—sanctified 'brother Thistleton.' He thunders the law at me; and I knock him down with a stout stick, St. John cuts ready to my hand;—'If a man say, I love God, and hate his brother, he is a *liar*!' I hush up Rogers, with—'No drunkard shall inherit the kingdom;' and Mather, with, 'You cannot serve God and Mammon.' They say I am a scoffer;—I don't care. Now"—continued this contrary being, passing into a tone of reverent feeling;—"There is my kind guardian. I don't believe he ever shouted, or made a public address in his life. He *lives* his religion; a child can perceive that the Bible is a 'lamp to his feet;' a pillar of cloud in prosperity; a sun in adversity. I saw it when a boy, and it did me more good than the preached sermons I have listened to since. He called me into his study the night before I left home, and gave me a copy of 'the book.' 'Charley, my son,' said he, 'you are venturing upon untried seas; here is the Chart, to which I have trusted for twenty years; and have never been led by it, upon a quicksand. Look to it, my boy!' I have read it, more, because he asked it, than for its intrinsic value; that is my failing, not his. I have waded through sloughs of theories and objections; but hold to it still. Especially, when I am here, and kneel in my old place at the family altar; hear the solemn tones, that quieted my boyish gayety; when I witness his irreproachable, useful life, I say, 'His chart is true; would I were guided by it!' No—no—Art.! I may be careless and sinful;—I am no skeptic."

"A skeptic" exclaimed Lynn. "There never was one! Voltaire was a fiend incarnate; a devil, who 'believed and trembled,' in spite of his hardihood; Paine, a brute, who, inconvenienced by a soul, which would not sink as low as his passions commanded, tried to show that he had none, as the easiest method of disembarrassing himself. That one of God's creatures, who can look up to the glories of a night like this, or see the sun rise to-morrow morning, and peep, in his insect voice, a denial of Him who made the world, is demon or beast;— often both. 'Call no man happy 'till he dies.' Atheists have gone to the stake for their opinions; but physical courage or the heat of fanaticism, not the belief, sustained them. We have yet to hear of the infidel, who died in his bed,

'As one who wraps the drapery of his couch
About him, and lies down to pleasant dreams.'"

"It is a mystery that one can die tranquilly," said Carry.

"I have stood by many peaceful death-beds," returned Arthur. "I never wish so ardently for an interest in the Redemption, as when I watch the departure of a saint. One verse is in my mind for days afterwards. I repeat it aloud as I ride alone; and it lingers in my last waking thought at night:

'Jesus can make a dying bed
Feel soft as downy pillows are;
While on his breast, I lean my head,
And breathe my life out sweetly there.'

"And why do you not encourage these feelings?" asked Charley, bluntly. "I call that conviction; a different thing from the burly of this morning. You want to be a Christian;— so do I sometimes; but you are a more hopeful subject."

"I am by no means certain of that. You would never abide with the half-decided, so long as I have done. You are one of the 'violent,' who would take the kingdom of Heaven by force."

"How strange!" said Charley, thoughtfully.

"What is strange?" inquired his brother.

"Here are five of us, as well-assured of the verity of Christianity, and God's revealed Word, as of our own existence; the ladies, practising every Christian virtue; Lynn, prepared to break a lance with infidelity in any shape; you, like Agrippa, almost persuaded; and I, stripping off the borrowed plumage of those who have a name to live;—yet we will be content to close our eyes in sleep, uncertain of re-opening them in life;—unfit for Death and Eternity!"

He turned again to the piano; Arthur quitted the room; Lynn gazed out of the window, with working features; Carry shaded her eyes with her hand; Ida felt a cold awe creeping over her. 'Death and Eternity!' had she heard the words before? how out of place in the bright warm life they were leading! Here were true friendships, tried and strengthened by years; young love, joying in his flowery course; refined and congenial spirits; the luxuries of wealth and taste;—how unwelcome the hand that lifted the drapery which enveloped the skeleton! 'Death and Eternity!' The spell was upon the scented air; the moon threw shadows upon the grass, as of newly heaped graves; and the vibrating cords spoke but of the one awful theme!

CHAPTER X

"Our last ride—can it be!" said Lynn, when the horses were brought to the gate, early in a September afternoon. Ida smiled faintly. The parting of the morrow, was, to her, the death of a summer's day, to be succeeded by wintry darkness. Not even Carry knew how the prospect oppressed her.

Lynn saw that his remark was injudicious, and endeavoured to atone for it, by the most delicate assiduity of attention. Their liking had matured into an attachment, which might have been predicated upon their consonance of feeling and sentiment. Her calmer judgment gave her the ascendancy, which belonged of right, to the masculine mind; he did not look up—she could not have respected him if he had; but he consulted and appealed to her, as a brother would ask counsel of an elder sister. She learned to imitate Charley, in curbing his impetuosity; and he chafed less at her soft touch upon the rein. No bantering checked the growth of their friendship; they were, for the time, members of one family; Lynn and Charley were no more to the disengaged young lady than Arthur.

Their excursion was to a splendid mansion, fifteen miles from Poplar-grove, lately completed, and not yet occupied by a wealthy landed proprietor, the Croesus of the county. Arthur had seen it, and carried home such a report of its stately grandeur, that a visit was forthwith projected. Nature was in one of her richest autumnal moods.

"She dies, as a queen should—in royal robes,"—said Lynn. "Note the purple haze upon those hills, and the yellow glory that bathes the foreground! I would sacrifice this right arm, could I first transfer that light to canvass. Loveliness like this maddens me with a Tantalus frenzy. To think that it must fade, when it should be immortal! I would have it ever before me."

"It lives in your memory. That is a pleasure, time nor distance diminishes."

"I am not satisfied with this selfish hoarding. A voice is ever urging me on,—'Create! create!' it cries; and while my pencil moves, I am a creator; exulting in the pictures graven upon my soul, as no parent ever joyed over a beloved child. 'They are mine—mine!' I repeat in an ecstacy. I have wept above—almost worshipped them! Then comes the chill, grey light of critical reason, as when you awake at morning, and see things as they *are*: the soul-pictures are beauteous still:—my copy the veriest daub!"

"The keenness of your disappointment is an augury of success. The lithography is perfect—you must not despond at the failure of one proof-impression. Your mortification is a greater triumph than the complacency with which a mediocre genius surveys his work."

"You remember Sheridan's maiden speech," said Charley.

"I have read of Demosthenes'," replied Lynn.

"Sheridan's was a similar case. He was hooted at for his presumption; his first and second attempts were wretched: and his friends advised him to retire from the rostrum forever. 'Never!' said he, striking his breast. 'It is *here*, and shall come out!'"

"A glorious 'coming out' it was!" responded Ida. "What do you say now?"—to Lynn.

"That it is *here*!" returning her bright look. "Was ever man more blessed in his friends? More fortunate than Adam, I take my guardian angels with me, from the Paradise I leave to-morrow."

"You must array one in a less questionable shape, if you would have men admit his angelic relationship," said Charley, with a grimace. "What are you looking at?"

Lynn did not reply. They were upon a hill; and some object in the valley beneath fastened his gaze. The pensive cast of his features bordered upon gloom, as they neared it. Ida saw only a graceful knoll, bounded, except towards the west, by a chain of more imposing eminences. A monarch oak stood in isolated sovereignty upon its summit; it had shaded a dwelling, for one chimney yet remained; and the sickly herbage of the slope was not the produce of a virgin soil. Lynn stopped. Not a word was spoken, his eyes were too full of tender sadness; the man—not the artist, looked from them.

"A lonely tree, and a desolate hearth-stone!" muttered he. "It is prophetic!"

"Is the spot known to you?" asked Ida, gently, as they rode on.

"It was my birth-place."

"I had forgotten;" said Charley. "You were very young when you left it."

"But I remember it. I could point out to you the very place where my mother taught me to walk;—a grass-plat before the door:—she upon the step, my father kneeling at a short distance, and each tempting me to undertake the journey from one to the other. They are gone! parents, brother, sisters! there is but one puny scion of a noble line remaining!"

Ida turned her face away. The sad story everywhere! Was there justice—there was *not* mercy—in thus rending away the sweetest comforts man can know,—while avarice, and pride and malevolence rioted in unharmed luxuriance. Earth was a cheat, and happiness a lie!

"This is a fine piece of road," said Charley, "and we are jogging over it, like Quakers going to market. I say! Art.!"

"Well!" answered his brother, who was some yards in advance.

"Don't you think your Rosinante would be benefitted by a taste of the spur?"

Oh! the delight of a sweeping gallop in the open country! the elate consciousness of strength and liberty, as the magnificent animal beneath you exerts every thew and sinew in obedience to your voice and hand; you and he together forming one resistless power, free as the rushing air—able to overleap or bear down any obstacle! The jocund tones wafted back by the breeze attested the efficacy of Charley's prescription.

"That bend hides 'the Castle;'" called out Arthur.

"I will be the first to see it!" exclaimed Carry, and as the turning was gained, she raised herself from the saddle. It was an unguarded moment;—the horse circled the bend in a run; and she was thrown directly in the road of the trampling hoofs behind. Charley's horse fell back upon his haunches;—there was giant might in the hand that reined him;—an inch nearer, and she was lost! for his fore-feet grazed her shoulder.

"My dearest love!" cried the agitated Arthur, raising her in his arms. "Thank God! you are not killed!"

"I am not hurt, dear Arthur! you are all so frightened! it was very careless in me. Indeed I do not require support—I am not injured in the least!"

"Are you sure?" questioned Ida, anxiously: "or do you say it for our sakes?"

"I was never more free from pain. And I am able and ready to go on!"

"You were her saviour!" Arthur griped his brother's hand, with a trembling lip.

"No thanks! I would not run down a cow or sheep if I could help it."

Arthur's even temper was tried by this speech, and the more, that it wounded Carry.

"Coarse! unfeeling!" thought Ida. She grudged him the eloquent affection of Lynn's glance. "I do not care to go further;" said she, when Carry was reseated.

"What! turn back within sight of the Promised Land?" said Carry. "Do not cause me to feel that I have spoiled your afternoon's pleasure! Oscar and I will not part company again so unceremoniously,—will we, old fellow? Allons!" and she shook the reins gaily. The rest followed with reluctance, and for awhile, very soberly. The thought of what might have been the result of the accident, she treated so lightly, precluded jest, and they would not speak of it seriously. By tacit consent, it was not referred to again. Lynn recovered himself first; he forgot everything but the fair domain they were entering; and his raptures awakened the others to its attractions. The house was a princely pile, rearing its towers from the midst of a finely-wooded park. The architecture was Gothic, and perfect in all its parts, even to the stained windows, imported, at an immense expense, from abroad. A village at the base of the hill, was peopled by the negroes, of whom there were more than an hundred connected with the plantation. The equestrians rode up the single street. Good humour and neatness characterised the simple inhabitants; children drew to one side of the road, with smiles and courtesies; the aged raised their bleared eyes, to reply to the respectful salutations of the young riders; through the open doors were seen clean, comfortably-furnished rooms;—in most, the tables were spread for the evening meal, and the busy housewives preparing for their husband's return from field or forest.

"These are thy down-trodden children, O Africa!" said Ida, sarcastically.

Lynn fired up. "They are the happiest beings upon the globe."

"So far as animal wants are concerned," subjoined Arthur.

"I do not accept of that clause. They are happy! They have a kind and generous master; every comfort in health; good nursing when ill; their church and Bible, and their Saviour, who is also ours. What the race may become, I do not pretend to say. These are far in advance of the original stock; but their intellectual appetite is dull, and I dare affirm that in nine cases out of ten it is satisfied. I never knew a master who denied his servants permission to read, and many have them taught by their own children. The slave lies down at night, every want supplied, his family as well cared for as himself; not a thought of to-morrow! he is secure of a home and maintenance, without disturbing himself as to the manner in which it is to be obtained. Can the same be said of the menial classes in any other country under the sun?"

"American as ever!" smiled Carry.

"And Virginian as ever! The Old Dominion is my mother! he is not a loyal son who does not prefer her, with her infirmities and foibles, to a dozen of the modern 'fast' belle states. The dear old creature has a wrinkle or two that do not improve her comeliness, and adheres somewhat pertinaciously to certain obsolete ideas, but Heaven bless her! the heart is right and sound!"

Ida's eyes sparkled—

> "'Where is the coward would not dare
> To die for such a land!'

Is not this scenery English, Mr. Holmes? We seldom see so large a tract, under as high cultivation, in this quarter of the globe; and where will we find another palace and park like that?"

"Mr. Clinton intends to stock the park with deer," said Arthur. "That will bring before you yet more vividly the 'Homes of Merry England.'"

"If an English landscape, it is an Italian light that gilds it," replied Lynn. "The highlands upon the other side of the river are Scottish; and the tropical growth of the tobacco fields would not be out of place under the Equator."

"Shocking your gleanings, then, you return to what Charley calls 'the original proposition,' and pronounce it American scenery," concluded Arthur.

"Precisely. One need not go abroad in quest of natural beauties. The fairest are culled for his native land."

"What a romantic creek! that *is* English!" exclaimed Ida. "I have G. P. R. James for authority; a rocky ford; a steep bank on either side; tangled undergrowth—and actually, a rustic foot-bridge! Oh! for the solitary horseman!"

"There he is!" ejaculated Charley, and from the hazel-boughs emerged an old negro, mounted upon a shaggy donkey, a bag of corn behind him.

"There is but a step, etc.," said Ida, despairingly. "It is my fate always to take it."

With a hearty laugh, they wheeled their horses. Charley and Ida had the lead. Exhilarated by exercise and the scenes through which they had passed, and accustomed to chat familiarly with him, she ran on for some time without remarking that she received monosyllabic replies.

"You are tired," she observed.

"Not at all."

"Out of humor, then?"

"Do I look so?"

"Not when you smile; but you are not making yourself agreeable."

"I did not know that I had ever succeeded in doing so."

"What! when Mr. Holmes says you are the only man who is never otherwise!"

"He is partial. You can teach him better."

"The intimacy between you two mystifies me more and more. He is all fire and impulse; you—"

"A galvanised icicle! Do I freeze you!"

"No. That is most wonderful of all. I am not afraid of you—although I have a cowardly horror of being laughed at."

"A 'horror' you should overcome; it proceeds from vanity. Like most of us, you are not apt to do or say things which you consider particularly silly; and are offended that the public sees them in that light. Lynn is afflicted similarly, in a still greater degree. It will get him into trouble yet."

"He is too independent to vacillate on account of ridicule," said Ida.

"Men style the peevish resentment such dispositions exhibit, '*honor*,'" returned Charley, with a half bitter emphasis. "It is one of the million misnomers with which they deceive themselves."

"Among the number I may place my mistaking conceit for sensibility?"

"And concealment of one's feelings for *in*sensibility," he added.

"You misunderstood me, Mr. Dana. I do not think you have a heart of adamant—"

"But that I have *none*," he interrupted; his kind glance blunting the edge of his words. "We shall understand each other better by and by. You spoke of James a while ago; do you like him?"

"No. He has two defects which spoil everything he writes, at least to me—verbosity and affectation."

"Not to mention self-plagiarism; but that is a common fault. When an author has exhausted his capital, he had better suspend honorably and wait until he has funds in hands to recommence operations, than drag on, 'shinning it,' in mercantile phrase, until the reading world dishonors his notes. Instead of this, James, and a score more of our popular writers are palming off upon us, duplicates and re-duplicates of their earliest productions. We encounter continually some old acquaintance in a different attire, and under an 'alias.' Warmed-over dinners are good enough in their place, but when we pay the same price, we have a right to be dainty. Dickens, himself, is not free from this charge."

"Oh! do not say so! I will not hear a word against him. He says much that seems irrelevant, and occasionally a thing that is provokingly absurd; but it is grand to see how, in the dénouement, he catches up these floating, apparently useless threads, and weaves them into the fabric. He works with less waste than any light author of the day; all is smooth and firm; no ragged edges or dropped stitches. And if his charming creations are set before us more than once, they can well bear a renewal of acquaintanceship."

"But not in a disguise which is less becoming than the dress in which we first knew them. When we cry 'encore,' we ask for a repetition, not an imitation—too often a burlesque."

"But," persisted Ida, warm in defence of her favorite Boz, "where shall we discover new phases of human nature? The fault is that so many men are copies of others; we must not censure the painter for lack of originality, who writes above his sketches, 'taken from life.' Who ever reads a new love story? and love is not the only passion which is the same the world over."

Charley leaned forward to brush a fly from his horse's ear.

"Are there no peculiarities in your lot?" he inquired.

"Perhaps so," she replied, startled by the home-thrust.

"Your character is not the reflected image of another's; you have never seen one who felt, thought, and acted exactly as you do; or who would have been your prototype, had your outward circumstances been alike. The Great Original is not a servile copyist."

The sun's rim was below the horizon, as they passed Lynn's birth-place; but a parting ray shot through the western gap upon the knoll—the solitary bright spot in the landscape. They went rapidly by; but Ida was grateful that his recollection of it should be linked with that fragrant eve, and gleaming farewell smile.

"It is singular that in our rides we should not have taken this road before," said Charley. "It is, just here, a mere bridle path, but I thought we had scoured the country."

"Did you know Mr. Holmes when he lived there?"

"No. He was fourteen years old when we met at school."

"The homestead is a pitiable wreck," continued Ida. "'A lonely tree and a desolated hearth!' he said. Those mournful words will haunt me."

"His is a sad story. His parents died within a month of each other—one by the hand of violence, the other of a broken heart. He had lost a sister previously; a year later his brother went to sea, and ship nor passengers reached the port. It is now three years since the death of a younger sister, a lovely girl, of consumption. This train of misfortunes hangs upon Lynn's mind and heart. He will have it that he belongs to a doomed race. But for his warm social sympathies, and devotion to his art, the superstition would become a monomania."

"You say his father died by violence; was he murdered?"

"In cold blood."

"Horrible! And the assassin?"

"Walks the earth, an *honourable* man! The sword of justice has no point for the duellist."

"This heathenish practice is a disgraceful stain upon the escutcheon of our State," said Ida.

"The laws are not in fault; popular prejudice does not sustain them."

"If they would make me autocrat for one year I would pledge myself to abolish this system of double murdering," returned he.

"How?"

"Hang the survivor—"

"What naughty words are you saying?" questioned Lynn, from Ida's elbow.

"A slip of the tongue, which Miss Ida would not have noticed, but for your officiousness," answered Charley. "Did I tell you of Art.'s professional call last night? We were awakened by an uproarious hallooing at the gate.

"'Who's there?' hailed Arthur.

"'O doctor! for massy's sake, come to see my old woman! she's dyin'—I'm Jeemes Stiger—make haste—I reckon she's most done dead by this time;' and the poor fellow blubbered out.

"'I'll be there in a minute,' said Art. 'Don't wait.'

"In three minutes and a half his horse's hoofs were clattering down the road, as though Tam O'Shanter's witch were upon the crupper. I had confidence in his skill, and did not doubt he would try whatever could relieve 'Mrs. Jeemes Stiger,' but it was a ticklish case; the entire contents of his saddle-bags could not rescue her from the jaws of death, if he had indeed clamped her. I had resolved to postpone compassion for the bereaved husband, to the morning, and was forgetting everything in a doze, when the trampling of a horse aroused me. I threw up the window. It was Art. in as hot haste as when he set out. 'What is to pay?' said I, as he came in. 'Forgotten any thing—or is the woman dead?'

"'Confound her!'

"I knew he must be pretty 'tall' to say that.

"'Never be a doctor, Charley.'

"'I wont, my dear boy; but what is the matter?'

"'Why nothing—just nothing!' beginning to laugh. 'I galloped two miles like a race-rider, and ran into the house, expecting a scene of distress—perhaps of death. 'Mrs. Jeemes' was sitting up, rocking herself back and forth. I felt her pulse and inquired her symptoms.'

"'You see,' stuttered Stiger, 'she's been sort o' poorly and droopy for three weeks, and better. I've been 'lotting to go for you, but thought maybe she mought be able to pick up after awhile. To-night I was so hungry myself that I didn't notice her at supper. She was mighty poking all the evenin', and jest now, she waked me. 'Jeemes,' says she, 'when folks' appetites gives out, they dies—don't they?'

"'Yes, honey,' says I.

"'Then farewell,' says she; 'I'm a-goin'. I wouldn't say nothin' about it at first, but I couldn't die without tellin' you I was a-departin'.'

"'O, Susan!' says I; 'how come you to think you are dyin'.

"'Jeemes,' says she, solemn as could be; 'I couldn't eat no supper, 'cept one herring and a pone of bread, and one cup of coffee.'

"'Doctor! you think she'll live 'till day? Oh! if I had a-gone for you three weeks ago!'"[1]

[1] Fact.

"'When shall we all meet again?'"

said Lynn that night, at the hour for separation.

"At Christmas, probably—next summer, certainly," replied Arthur's cheerful voice.

"We have been too happy together to hope for a repetition of the pleasure," said Ida. "Two such summers would be more than falls to the share of most mortals."

"If we never meet again in this life, we shall see each other somewhere at the end of the turnpike," observed Charley.

Sad as were the feelings of the little company, they smiled at his tone and action.

"Hush, Charley! I am petitioning Ida for a song," said Carry. "One of your own, my dear. We like no other so well. Just one more, that I may fancy I hear whenever I enter this room."

"A parting lay from our Improvisatrice," entreated Dr. Carleton.

Her voice was uncertain and low, but she sang the simple ballad with a pathos, that brought the moisture to the eyes of more than one of her auditors.

"Away with thoughts of sadness, love!
I will be gay to-night!
I would awhile indulge the hopes,
To-morrow's sun will blight.
Oh! once again, our favorite songs,
Together let us sing;
And thus forget the wailing strain
To-morrow's eve will bring.
Away with thoughts of sadness, love!
I must be gay to-night!

"Alas! 'tis vain! we who have loved
So long and well, must part!
The smile has faded from my cheek
The gladness from my heart.
And since at this, our sad farewell,
For months, perchance, for years,
We cannot join in blithesome lay,
Oh! let us mingle tears!
Away with thoughts of gladness, love!
For I must weep to-night!"

CHAPTER XI

"I'm very lonely now, Carry! and weary, and wakeful and home-sick. You and your home have spoiled me; my heart has been enlarged, only to aggravate the old empty feeling; you have disabled me for the life I must lead here. 'Discouraged already!' I hear you say. 'Did you not promise to be good and patient?' I am not like you, I cannot love, unless I am beloved; and had I your warm, open heart, it would be but attempting to heat Nova Zembla with a foot-stove. Hear, before you reproach. Our journey was pleasant. The children behaved à merveille; your sister was—as she always is—tender and motherly, (you know what that last means from me!) and the conduct of our gallant outriders was above praise. Leaving Mrs. Dana at her door, Lynn and Charley escorted me up-town. With their 'good nights,' and promises to see me again soon, connection with Poplar-grove was severed. My former self—I told you how it would be!—was waiting for me inside the hall-door. I was as little changed in the eyes of Mr. Read and his daughter, as they were in mine. The first-named was upon his etiquette stilts; and Josephine's fingers, as I touched them, were as limp and warm as the digits of a frozen frog. (Vide Charley.) I remembered you and my promise, and made a tremendous effort. 'You are looking so well, that I will not inquire whether your trip was as delightful as you anticipated;' to the daughter.

"'We spent our time agreeably;' dryly.

"'Were the waters of Saratoga beneficial to you, sir?' to the father.

"'My health required no improvement;' stiffly, and with a smack of offended dignity. But this is wrong, Carry! The air of this house must warp my sense of right. While under their roof, I should not ridicule them. There was pleasure in the sadness of last night—last night! it seems a century since! There is no bright thread in the sombre web I am weaving now! I look forward with a sinking spirit. This winter will bring me trials which you may not appreciate. Josephine and myself will ever remain antagonistic;—not that I am quarrelsome; I detest strife. I am sick of this eternal sparring and heartburning; but I am no dissembler; and I foresee many contests; perhaps as many defeats, for cool audacity is more than a match for hot blood like mine. Our characters will come into play upon a wider stage than heretofore, and should we close in combat there, the struggle will be fearful. I am willing,—thanks to you!—to sacrifice prejudice,—not principle or self-respect. Three long, dreary months before I can hope to see you! I fear to think how wicked I may become in that time. Richmond is, to me, a Sahara, whose single fountain of sweet waters springs up within your sister's home. Those, who, within a few months, were unknown, are nearer than acquaintances of years' standing. Poor Rachel stands by, waiting to undress me, her face as long as mine. 'Ah! Miss Ida! this ain't Dr. Carleton's!' She does not realise how painfully conscious I am of that fact. I can hardly say why I have written this incoherent note; except, that I am dispirited, and thirst to talk to you. Forgive my unhappy egotism! I cannot ask you to respond to emotions which never swell your gentle bosom. To your best of fathers, present my warmest regards. I owe him a debt I cannot repay. And to him, dear Carry, whose image blends with yours, in my dreams of the future; the only man I know, to whom I could willingly resign you, give a sister's love. The strongest proof of my affection is, that I am not jealous. Good night! and a blessing, my dearest! If your rest will be the sweeter for knowing that to another, than *him*, you make life lovely, believe it!

As ever, yours,
IDA."

"I saw Mr. Lacy upon the street, to-day," remarked Mr. Read, the next evening at supper.

"Ah!" said Josephine, delightedly. "Did you speak with him?"

"Yes; he stopped me to apologise for having delayed calling until this time. He is studying law with Mr. L., and has little leisure for visiting—so he says."

"Did you inquire after his sister's health?"

"No. You had better do so, if he calls this evening. He asked whether you would be at home."

Josephine coloured with pleasure; and Ida was curious to see one who had inspired them with such respect and admiration; for through Mr. Read's assumed carelessness, it was easy to discover that he was flattered by the promised visit. She gathered from their conversation that they had met Mr. Lacy at the Springs, whither he had gone with an invalid sister. As Virginians, they attached themselves to the Read party,—"*the* party of the season," so Josephine unblushingly asserted.

Too proud to go into the drawing-room, without an invitation, Ida went to her chamber, to spend the hours between supper and bed-time, in reading.

"Miss Josephine must 'spect her beau; she's mightily fined off," commented Rachel, when she came up from her meal. "I said so! that's the door-bell I Ain't you going down, Miss Ida?"

"No;"—not withdrawing her eyes from her book.

"You ain't a school-girl now, Miss Ida," Rachel remonstrated.

"Well—and if I am not?"

"Why, young ladies ought to see company. I can't bear for you to be hiding up here, just like you was an ediot or *per*formed; and Miss Josephine, who ain't nigh so pretty, nor good, for that matter, is stealing all the beaux."

"In other words, my good Rachel, you want me to get married."

"Yes ma'am," said Rachel boldly; "If you come across any body to suit you, I'd a heap rather you'd be his wife, than to stay here to be pecked at and worried."

"I am not easily worried; I am my own mistress, and restrained by no one."

"Your own mistis', Miss Ida! Don't I see you sittin' at table, and in the parlor, never opening your mouth to say nothin'; and ain't you cooped up here in this chamber, because Miss Josephine ain't got politeness enough to ask you down? and after they've been making as much of you at Dr. Carleton's as if you had been the Queen of Sheby! Miss Carry is a lady worth talking about, and so is Miss Jenny—none of your turned up nose, poor white folksy sort. I wish you could get into the fam'ly," she added, slyly.

Ida read on in silence.

"The bell agin!" muttered Rachel, fretfully. "I don't know what they're coming for. If they knowed as much as we servants, they'd as soon jam their fingers into a steel-trap. What do you want?" she said, snappishly to the footman who knocked at the door.

"Two gentlemen to see Miss Ross—Mr. Dana and Mr. Holmes."

"I'll tell her;" she returned, greatly mollified. "Now, Miss Ida, don't scare them off with no solemn looks and talk. Do just like you did at Miss Carry's; and 'bove all things, don't let Miss Josephine cut you out!"

We trust to the reader's good-nature to excuse the unfair use which Rachel made of the back parlor window. The affectionate curiosity that prompted her to "peep at Miss Ida, as she made her manners," was gratified by seeing her receive her visitors with as much affability as if Carry, instead of Miss Read, were present. As Rachel surmised, the latter had a beau; and Ida's hasty survey excited a feeling of surprise. He looked and moved the gentleman; but although he arose with the others, and remained standing, Josephine did not introduce him.

Charley's presence of mind prevented embarrassment.

"I beg pardon, Morton; I thought you knew Miss Ross—-Miss Ida, my friend, Mr. Lacy."

This assumption of the duties of host at a first call would have been inexcusable in most cases. Josephine understood it, as it was meant, as a severe rebuke for her negligence or ill-breeding.

The "my friend," too, nettled her. Mr. Lacy had presented the gentlemen to her when they came in, and had spoken to Charley as an old acquaintance, but what right had this stranger to insinuate, that, as his friend, Ida had a title to her "property?" She almost forgave him, however, when she found that, for the present, he was not disposed to push his advantage. He left her to the most delightful tête-à-tête; turned his back quite upon her, and addressed himself to Ida. She would have pocketed a dozen insults an evening to sit upon the same sofa with Morton Lacy, to read devotion in his speaking eyes, and hear love's music in every cadence of his voice. She was in Elysium—with but one drawback upon her felicity. The group across the room were maliciously unobservant of the tableau—her highborn looking suitor, so lover-like as he bent his proud head to catch the words that melted like honey-dew upon her lips; and herself—with falling lids, as though she feared he might see more in the modest eyes than maiden coyness would have him know—they *must* notice them, and seeing, Ida must be expiring with envy, and the gentlemen regret, while they envied, that they were too late to compete for the prize. It is not often that the truth is as sweet as the darling fictions we dream to ourselves, and on this occasion, assuredly, the reality would have rendered wormwood palatable in comparison; for the trio of friends were unaffectedly engrossed with each other, and stupidly ignorant of the duett played near them.

"Jenny sent her love to you," said Charley; "she will call shortly. She complains of being tired out with the labor of rectifying the disorders of John's bachelor establishment. She treated us, at tea, to a summary of his domestic economy. Half of the time, he forgot to go to market, and wondered at the want of variety in the fare. The cook was consulted, and hinted at the cause. The ensuing day, he laid in provisions for a week, particularly of such commodities as frugal housewives do not care to have on hand in hot weather. He bought a pair of parlor lamps. 'You wished to surprise me by this handsome present, I suppose,' said Jenny.

"'Why no—I should not have purchased them if the old ones had not been worn out,' said he.

"'Worn out! when we have not had them six months!'

"'Yes!' answered he, positively. 'They would not burn—went out as fast as I lighted them; and worse than that, the new ones have got into the same way. I complained to W——, and he said they were the best he had.'

"'Very odd!' said Jenny, 'unscrewing one of the lamps. Why, Mr. Dana! there is no oil in it! Have they been filled regularly?'

"'Never thought of it once!' exclaimed John, foolishly.

"See how useless marrying makes a man!"

"Rather, how comfortless he is without a wife;" responded Ida. "As respects order and management in household matters, I have an idea that you bachelors are not much superior to the Tartars."

"Say on a par with the Hottentots, and you will be nearer the truth;" said Lynn. "Nothing can be well-done that is unnatural. Not one man in a hundred has a talent for housekeeping; some acquire a smattering of the science, and make themselves ridiculous by an offensive display of it. Their wives should rig them in kitchen aprons, set them to rolling out piecrust, and officiate as their substitutes in the shop, office, or counting-room. There is a loud hue and cry after 'strong-minded women;' who says any thing about weak-minded men?"

"You do not consider that the feebler intellect belongs of necessity, to the feebler body, do you?" asked Charley.

"Not I! Do away with this absurd antipathy to clever women; give them our advantages of education, and they will outshine us mentally, as they do morally. The mind of a woman is a wonderful thing; like the scimetar of Saladin, it cuts through, at a single stroke what our clumsy blades have hacked at in vain. Light, graceful, delicate—it does not lack power because it has beauty."

"It is very pleasant to listen to agreeable speeches, even when we know them to be flattery," said Ida; "I acquit you of insincerity, Mr. Holmes—I perceive that Mr. Dana sides with you—but permit me to say, that I know more of the mental calibre of my sex than either of you. To a certain point, we can rival you successfully—like the hare and tortoise—we run well for a time, and laugh at your plodding; but we have not the taste or ability to bear you company to the goal. As well compare the bounding flight of the lark to the heaven-ward sweep of the eagle. We cannot reason—we are persuaded because we *feel* that a truth exists—for our lives, we could not tell you why we believe."

"And this is an argument to establish your inferiority!" exclaimed Lynn. "Where is the use of reasoning? I would trust a true woman's intuition in preference to all the systems of logic and induction, the blundering, lumbering brain of man has built. Do not depreciate this angelic faculty, Miss Ida; you hold it in common with higher intelligences."

"Yes!—I doubt if Gabriel bothers his head with syllogisms or logarithms," said Charley. "Two to one—Miss Ida—give up!"

"Men are inconsistent creatures," said she. "They will have it we are their superiors,—exhaust dictionaries and their imaginations to load us with exalted epithets; and behave, as though we were children, to be coaxed with sugar-plums. An angel in theory, the corporeal woman is soundly rated if dinner is late, or a room unswept. We are 'akin to higher intelligences,'—but let one presume to measure lances with a lord of creation in a conflict of minds, and how quickly is she assailed by the hoots of her professed adorers! You will allege that she has stepped out of her sphere. Granted—but according to your belief, she has stooped to your level, and you should be grateful for the grace. Is it so? 'The ladith are divine, tho long ath they don't meddle with thubjects above their comprehenthion;' lisps the dandy whose organs of speech serve to distinguish him from a marmoset;—and wise doctors of law and medicine and divinity, read us homilies upon the modesty, the humility, the submissiveness of the softer sex, and recommend St. Paul to our diligent perusal. We are not cherubim,—nor yet slaves;—not your superiors; and in mind are far from being your equals; but we *do* hold that we are, or ought to be qualified for your companions; and that your happiness and ours would be enhanced if you would throw sentimental nonsense overboard, and take this practical, every day view of the case."

"Let a lady alone for making her side good!" said Charley. "We'll call it square, and quit—which Lynn will inform you, is a cowardly way of acknowledging ourselves beaten. I never argued with one of you yet, that I was not glad to sneak off in five minutes after the first broadside."

"Their right makes their might;" observed Lynn, gallantly.

"And their invincible obstinacy," returned Charley. "That is not just the word—it is a certain never-give-up-able-ness, vexatiously delightful, which precipitates one into a rage and love, at the same time—he is divided between his disposition to kneel to, and to shoot her!"

"Are you tempted to murder me?" inquired Ida.

"Not at all. It is a peculiarity in the female disposition,—she can't help it—to cry 'scissors' to the last."

"I do not comprehend."

"Did you never hear the 'tailor's wife and scissors?'"

"A story of your own coinage!" asked Lynn.

"No—an authentic narrative. A tailor having amassed a fortune by his trade, cut the shop and removed to the country, to live in dignified leisure. His wife was a bit of a shrew, and apt, as all wives are,—to find out her husband's weak points. One of these was a shame of his former occupation, and she harped upon the jarring string, until the poor wretch was nearly beside himself. Her touch-word, 'scissors,' spoiled his finest bon mots, and embittered his grandest entertainment—it was flame to tow. He stormed and wheedled, threatened and bribed; the obnoxious instrument was constantly brandished before his eyes. They were walking, one day, on the bank of a river, bounding his grounds,—'I have displayed extraordinary taste in the selection of this estate,' remarked he, 'Its owner should have judgment, as well as wealth. You observe the Delta formed by the fork of the river. Its beauty decided me to close the contract.'

"Very probable, my dear,—it reminds one so much of an open pair of scissors!'

"One push—and she was struggling in the water.

"'I will pull you out, if you promise never to say that word again!' halloed the still foaming husband.

"'Scissors!' screeched she, and down she went.

"'Scissors!' as she arose again. The third time, she came to the surface, too far gone to speak—but as the waters closed over her, she threw up her arms, crossing her fore fingers—thus—and disappeared."

Ida laughed—her rich, musical laugh, which awoke strange echoes in those formal rooms. Mr. Read's portrait frowned down from its niche, and Josephine raised her brows with an air of astonishment, which would have been contempt, had she not been upon the amiable at the time. Another started too, but with a different expression. Few who saw Morton Lacy smile, forgot it. It was not a superficial illumination, but a flashing through of an inward light, as might play upon the surface of a gem-bedded stream, could the sun strike upon its concealed wealth.

"We seldom hear a sound like that, in this age of affectation;" said he, to Josephine.

"She will learn better;" she replied. "She is just from her books, and rather eccentric in some of her ways and notions. I rally her daily upon her little oddities, but she is wilful, as spoiled children will be,—and being older, and more clever than myself, out-argues me. The main point of disagreement is that she is fond of liberty of speech and action, declares Die Vernon her beau ideal of a woman, and I am prudish in my reserve."

"Not prudish—feminine!" he answered, emphatically. "Is she a relative?"

"No: a ward of my father's."

"An orphan!" with a remorseful pity, for which Josephine could have blasted Ida as she sat.

"She does not feel her situation so keenly as a sensitive person would. Those are happiest whose wounds heal soonest,—to whom a life-time grief is unknown. I am thankful that Ida's temperament is mercurial—she is spared much suffering;" and her voice trembled admirably, as she lifted her eyes to a portrait above the mantel. Another adroit hit! the base brought out the ring of the genuine metal.

"There are, indeed, losses, which, in an earthly sense, are irreparable, and although I know nothing personally of such a bereavement, I can understand that the shadow of a mother's tomb grows darker and longer, as the child walks on in the path her care would have smoothed."

"Especially to an orphaned girl; each day has wants and exigencies she had not thought of before. Yet who knows the pains of her lot?" said Josephine, sighing.

"'Few are the hearts whence one same touch,
Bids the sweet fountains flow!'"

repeated Mr. Lacy. "Have you learned that song, according to promise?"

"I always keep my promises."

"May I demand the proof that this one was remembered."

The piece in question lay suspiciously near the top of the portfolio, although she protested that she had "only played it over once, and a fortnight ago."

"It is set as a duett; will not your friend sing with you?"

"I don't know;" shaking her head, smilingly. "She is chary of her favors—all good singers are. Perhaps she will not refuse you—ask her, please! It will be such an improvement!"

Thus importuned, Mr. Lacy went up to Ida, and preferred his request.

"Excuse me, sir, I am not familiar with the music;" said she, surprised that Josephine had despatched him upon such an embassy, when her jealousy of Ida's superiority as a vocalist, had been the cause of innumerable slights and petty meannesses from herself and father.

"Now! be obliging, Ida!" she interposed, "you sing at sight better than I do, after a year's practising."

"I am sorry to appear disobliging, Mr. Lacy;" pursued Ida; and she spoke sincerely, as she met his smile; "but you would not thank me for ruining your song."

"Oh! how can you say so!" exclaimed Josephine. "Mr. Dermott called you a second Malibran; or was it Sappho?"

To Mr. Lacy, this was coaxingly playful; but the fiery spot came to Ida's cheek, at words, which had been piped over, and distorted, until malice itself must be weary of repeating them.

"I beg you to consider my refusal as final and positive;" she said, haughtily. Mr. Lacy bowed, with dignity, and returned to Josephine.

"Am I, also, to be refused?" asked Lynn, as Josephine picked out a third song. "You will not suspect me of empty compliments."

"Not for you, will I sing now and *here*!" said Ida. "Be sure I have my reasons for objecting to give you pleasure."

"Be quiet, Lynn! she means what she says;" interrupted Charley, as his friend persisted. Lynn obeyed, but his black eyes went from the face of the speaker, to Ida's compressed lips, until they darted an angry light upon Josephine, showing that he had an inkling of the truth.

"This is the beginning!" said Ida, as she knelt at her window to gain tranquillity from the cool and stillness of the night. The moon neared the horizon; the roof-tops contrasted brightly with the shade of the street; and one lofty spire pointed a snowy finger upward, the golden trumpet upon its taper extremity silvered by the pale rays. It was a "sweet south" that bore up the lullaby our beautiful river sings nightly to her myriads of sleeping children; but as the girl gazed and listened, inquietude, instead of peace, had possession of her—the nameless longing that makes mortals weep and strive, and die! that burning craving for something—they cannot tell what—except that earth does not bestow it, and the spirit will not rest without it. It may be, angel-teachers are with us, awakening a desire for, rather than imparting knowledge, which is their food, and can alone satisfy our immortal minds—or our young souls are fluttering their unfledged wings, restless for the flight, instinct tells them is before them—we know not—only that the thirst is fierce—maddening! and there is but one fountain which quenches it. The river's song should have summoned up the vision of those living waters, and their wooing, "Let him that is athirst come!" and the white spire—had its silent gesture no significance?

Ida's thoughts did not rise. A painful truth had that night obtruded itself upon her, that the love of those she esteemed most, had not strengthened her to bear the trials incident to her position. With Carry at her side, to defend and console, many a shaft would have fallen harmless, perchance, unremarked; in her absence, the certainty of her affection did not render Josephine's malevolence innocuous, or her society endurable.

"I was not born for this life! I do not breathe in the penthouse in which they would immure my soul. I cannot escape! I am virtually a prisoner in body and spirit—with energies, which must not act—affections, which must not flow! I thirst for liberty and love!"

Lower and lower dipped the moon—and higher mounted the shade upon the steeple—the golden trumpet was glistenless as the rest, and the stars only kept guard over the slumbering city, and the watcher knelt still—dreaming now love-dreams of appreciation and devotion—trances, almost realities in their passionate idealization; and then, as they cloyed by their very sweetness—or the real and the present would burst upon her, crying in anguished accents, "I thirst!"

CHAPTER XII

Josephine Read gave a party—her first, and the first of the season; an onerous undertaking for a young, and comparatively inexperienced housekeeper; but she went about it bravely and confidently. She did not overrate her capacity; if she had a talent for anything, it was for housewifery—"driving" included. If her domestic machinery did not work well, it was not for lack of scolding; and, it was rumored, not because more stringent measures were not employed by her own fair hands.

"Miss Josephine flies about the kitchen like a pea 'pon a hot shovel;" said Rachel, the day before that for which the rest of the week was made. "It's 'sprising how much spring she's got in that little body of hern, and how much spite too, if you'll 'low me to say it, Miss Ida."

"I certainly shall not," said Ida, severely. "I do not care to hear your remarks upon her now, or at any time. They are neither respectful or becoming."

"Law! Miss Ida! you know Miss Josephine as well as I do; what harm does my talking do? I was goin' to tell you, that I thought I should a' died laughin' to see how mad she was, when Joe dropped the big cake she sent to the confectionaries to have iced. Her face turned red as them curtains, and soon as she could move, she pulled off her shoe, and gave him such a lick 'pon the side of his head, I'll bound he seed stars!"

"Are your preparations concluded?" asked Mr. Read, that night.

"I believe so, sir."

"'You believe so!' why can't you give a direct answer? I hate this mincing you women think so pretty. Are you ready!"

"The table is not set," said Josephine, provokingly, "and the jellies and creams are not turned into the dishes yet."

"What will this tomfoolery cost?" barked her father.

"I don't know, sir—what other people's parties do."

"You are wonderfully independent, young woman! you intend to foot the bills I hope."

No answer, except a bar of a popular air, hummed, while trying on a head-dress.

"Whom have you invited?"

"There is the list—you can read it."

He looked at it surlily. "How many rooms do you open?"

"The parlors and dining room;—unless you prefer to have the dressing-rooms in the third story, and give up your chamber to the dancers."

"Have the goodness to leave me out of the scrape. I shall go to bed directly after supper. You two may do your husband hunting without my help. I pity the man who gets either of you."

"Since you are so much opposed to this party, I will recall my invitations to-morrow morning," retorted Josephine, irritated by his peevish vulgarity, to take a high stand herself.

"You will *not*, Miss! Carry out what you have commenced—much joy may you have of it!"

What pleasure or benefit could arise from this snarling contradiction, would have defied a wiser brain than Ida's to determine. She once imagined it a part of Mr. Read's schooling; that he sought to inure his pupil to the treatment she would receive from the world; but this impression was corrected by observing that the effrontery he had taught her angered him beyond measure, when exhibited towards himself. Variance appeared to be necessary to their existence; a safety-valve, for the ill humors they could not throw out upon others. It was a curious fact that their going into company, at home or abroad, was invariably preceded by this moral phlebotomizing, and in proportion to the extent of the depletion, was the subsequent affability. It was therefore to be expected that they should appear in the drawing-room on the evening of the party, looking their best;—she, deferentially respectful to "Papa," and he, marking "my daughter, sir's," motions with paternal pride. A large party usually belongs to one of two classes—the stiffly regular, or the noisily irregular. At the former, there is considerably less sociability and ease than is prevalent among a corps of raw recruits upon parade, under the eye of a martinet drilled serjeant. As many as can obtain seats, seize them; a vacant chair is rushed for, as in the game of "budge-all," and the hapless standers are awkwardly alive to the circumstance of being, not men, but hands, legs and feet; white kid gloves are at a premium, a bouquet is a godsend;—the pulling off and on of the first, and the criticism of the latter, are engrossing subjects of reflection and entertainment. There are knots of men in the entry, and in the corners, and behind doors; and rows of ladies against the wall, and stretched out transversely and longitudinally through the room. Supper over, watches are slyly consulted, yawns dexterously swallowed, and presently the crowd is thinner, though no one goes. Then come whispered adieux;—

"*so* sorry to quit your charming party at this early hour,—but papa charged me to be home by twelve, and he is *so* particular;" and "my dear Mrs. Heavyaslead, I must tear myself away—mamma was not well to-night; I am quite uneasy about her;"—and there are headaches and sideaches, and toothaches, until the poor hostess wonders that she never suspected before what an unhealthy circle of acquaintances she has.

At a gathering of the second class, everybody knows everybody else, or gets acquainted off-hand, with or without an introduction. The company are, to a man, in favor of a standing army. Except a small number of chairs, over which are carefully trained the confirmed wall-flowers, seats are voted in the way;—each joke is capital;—each laugh a scream. Girls rattle and coquet, and gentlemen bow and flatter; you stumble upon a flirtation at every step, and cannot tread upon a boot or corn without cutting a gallant speech in the middle; time pieces are put back two or three hours, and ostentatiously showed around, to prove that "there is time enough yet." Morning breaks, ere the revellers unwillingly depart, and Mr. and Mrs. Cricketspry hear, for six months after, of the "splendid time we had at your party."

Miss Read's soiree promised to be of the first-named order.—A large proportion of her guests were strangers to each other, and she had not the tact to amalgamate the mixture. A hostess must be impartial; the safest course is to ignore the object of her preference, even at the risk of being misunderstood; better offend one, than an hundred. Josephine made no such heroic sacrifice. She had invited Mr. Lacy; the rest were there to see, and they were not backward to discern this. She had twice made the circuit of the rooms upon his arm, and stood for half an hour between the folding-doors, in conversation, that, so far as her efforts went, was confidential, when her father touched her shoulder. "Are we to have no dancing, Josey?"

"If my friends desire it—certainly! Mr. Pemberton"—as that individual frisked by,—"Do me the favor to act as master of ceremonies, and form a set."

"With pleasure, Miss Josephine, provided I am honored by your hand—for the dance—I mean;" tickled to excess by his witty clause.

The hateful puppy! but there was no retreat. Had Mr. Lacy been out of earshot, she would have pleaded an engagement, so certain was she that he would ask her, but she could not utter so palpable a falsehood in his hearing. She did hope that he would interfere, and with the inimitable self-possession which distinguished him, open an avenue of escape by implying, if not asserting his right of priority; but he was silent, and she yielded an ungracious assent. Mr. Pemberton was a boasted adept in the art of "cutting out"—a system of counter-plotting, too well understood to need explanation here; and as he bustled around, officious and fussy, he circulated, as the latest and best joke, an account of his cunning in "heading off that chap, Lacy."

"Are you fond of this amusement?" inquired the latter of Josephine.

"Passionately!" said she, brightening up at this, as she thought, prefatory remark. The next was still more promising.

"You will not stop at a single set then?"

"Oh, no! I often keep the floor for hours. It is a healthful and innocent exercise. I had rather dance than spend the evening in gossiping after the fashion of the strait-laced sort, who are conscientiously opposed to 'wordly follies.'"

Mr. Lacy smiled, a little queerly. It was evident that he agreed with her, in her estimate of these over-scrupulous worthies. Still, the coveted request did not arrive, and she tossed out a desperate feeler.

"You do not think it undignified to dance, do you?"

"Perhaps if I were to state why I never participate in the pastime you laud so warmly, you would accuse me of an unmanly fondness for a dish of scandal."

What did he say? What did it mean? His amusement increased with her bewilderment, and before an explanation could be asked or given, Mr. Pemberton took her hand.

Ida had, thus far, passed the dullest of dull evenings. Lynn and Charley, who never let her suffer for attention when they were by, had a business engagement which would detain them until late; it was even doubtful if they could come at all. She talked at a moustached, be-whiskered, and be-imperialed youth who solicited an introduction, because he had heard that she was "smart," and hoped she could appreciate him; his conversational talents compensating in quality for their deficiency in quantity; anybody could talk, but who could dress, and stand, and look as he did? She tried to draw him out by encouraging smiles, and well put queries—he tugged at his waistcoat—she rallied him upon his abstraction—he stroked his left whisker—she pretended offence at one of his milk-and-water responses—he performed the like kindly office to the right—and she gave up in despair.

Mr. De Langue was next. He was "smart" himself, and therefore could appreciate *her*, and to prove this, he rolled forth volume after volume of French compliments, unanswerable, because so highly polished that one could not, as it were, take hold of them;—edified her by disquisitions upon subjects of which she was profoundly ignorant, and information respecting others, of which she knew more than himself. After much manoeuvring she sought refuge in a corner, fatigued, disgusted and misanthropical. "I have thought that I might shine in general company, where feeling never enters, and flaring flippancy passes for wit; it seemed easy to manufacture small-talk, but I was mistaken. This is 'rational recreation!' the pleasure of mingling in 'the best society,' as Josephine says. I envy St. Simon in his twenty years' solitude upon his stone pillar."

"Compton, my dear fellow, can you make room for me to pass?" said a voice near her. "If I were a lady, I would faint, and let you extricate me, as I am not, I must fight my way out."

The gentleman addressed exerted his powers of compression, and Mr. Lacy edged by him. His course was towards the door, but he stopped as he espied Ida "Miss Ross, have you a welcome in your 'Retreat' for a storm-tossed wanderer? Your quiet nook is most inviting."

Ida looked up mischievously. "I will not hinder your flight, Mr. Lacy. Your envy of my corner is wasted upon one who heard you singing a moment since, like the melancholy starling, 'I can't get out! I can't get out!'"

"I plead guilty—but if a mightier temptation has mastered my desire for liberty? There are birds that will not fly after the cage door is unfastened."

"They do not merit freedom," said she.

"Be it so—this is my prison," rejoined the gentleman, seating himself upon an ottoman which Josephine, to get out of the way, had wedged behind the door, thinking as she did so, that it might prevent the pressure of the crowd from breaking the hinges, with not a presentiment that she was furnishing a hiding-place for the last one of all the world whom she would have concealed.

"Now," continued he, "as I can see but one, I recognise but one jailor, and you will be merciful, remembering my voluntary incarceration. And as a starting-point to the conversation, why are you not in the other room?"

"For the simple reason that no one has invited me to dance."

He looked surprised, yet pleased at her frankness. "You would go, if you received an invitation?"

"That would depend upon circumstances. I should assuredly decline one from you."

"And why?"

"I would not accept of anything offered in obedience to what the one who tendered it considered a hint. How I might act if I were a devotee of Terpsichore, I do not know, but a conversazione is more attractive to me than a ball."

"We shall not quarrel there, and it is well that we agree in disagreeing with the general sentiment. Taught by the experience gained in our short acquaintance, I should prefer a petition with a quaking heart."

"You need not apprehend a refusal, provided your demand is reasonable and properly timed," answered Ida.

"Which of these provisoes was wanting to ensure the success of the suit you negatived, upon the evening of our introduction?"

"Both," she returned, laughing. "You insisted that I should sing, at sight, a song already dear to you, and I declined to spoil the music, and wreck my musical reputation with a stranger, from whose mind I might never have an opportunity of removing the unfortunate opinion."

"In contrariety to these considerations, were the wish to oblige me, and a dislike to wound the feelings of your friend, Miss Josephine, and this scale kicked the beam?" said Mr. Lacy, interrogatively.

"No; Josephine was out of the question; she did not expect me to comply. We never sing together—or very rarely. My voice is not a contralto, nor does it accord with her's. You will have to be content with my explanation; I speak truth in the smallest matters."

"The false in trifles are seldom reliable in things of greater moment," replied the other. "There is less deliberate, malicious falsehood in the world than we suppose. Men are oftener liars from habit, than from necessity or temptation."

"But to this habit there must be a beginning. Is there no sin in the earliest deviation from the right way?"

"I did not say that there is not sin in every violation of truth. Each one is a stain upon the soul—blots, that too frequently deface it forever; but I do not subscribe to the casuistry that gauges the guilt of a lie entirely by its effects upon others—which smiles upon, as a harmless simpleton, him who 'fibs' or 'yarns' or 'embroiders' in cowardice or vanity, and empties the vials of wrath upon the Pariah, who seeks, by one heaven-daring falsehood, to save what he holds most dear. One destroys the mirror by gradually damaging its bright surface, the other shivers it at one reckless blow."

"This has often struck me," said Ida. "It appears to me that the slower process deadens the conscience most surely, and the insensibility of those who practice it, betrays a more diseased state of the moral system than the pangs of remorse."

"Undoubtedly; and this should make us doubly watchful against any infringement of veracity. The straightest, the only safe road is 'the truth—the whole truth—and nothing but the truth.'"

"And who adheres to this rule?" asked Ida. "How much truth, do you imagine, is being uttered now in these rooms?"

"We are discoursing very philosophically, and will be charitable enough to believe that numerous couples are similarly engaged."

"Do you recollect Talleyrand's definition of speech?" inquired Ida.

"'A faculty whereby we conceal our thoughts'—yes—a sentence worthy of its author. What a life this would be if we were all Talleyrands!"

"We are—according to our capacities," said Ida.

"A singular sentiment for one of your age and sex!" replied Mr. Lacy, with a searching look. "Has the world served you so unkindly, that you condemn your kind without reservation?"

"There was a mental reservation; yet my observation was true in a general sense. Men live for themselves;—it is humiliating to see how this principle regulates feeling and action. We love our friends because they are ours;—the pronoun 'my' expresses a nearness and sweetness which causes us to idolize the thing we appropriate;—'my own' is the most endearing of appellations—what is the delight it inspires, but the grossest vanity and selfishness?"

"Pardon me, that I differ with you. Our love is won by the qualities of its object;—there would be no pleasure in appropriation were not our affections enlisted;—no thrill of joy in identifying with ourselves, the unknown or unlovely;—if forced upon us, dislike would ensue. We become attached to our dear ones for their own sakes; although it cannot be denied, that a knowledge of a reciprocation of affection is an auxiliary to the growth of that fondness."

"And do you honestly credit the disinterestedness of human nature?"

"I do—in many instances, and so do you. Look at the benefactors of mankind—a Howard, preferring the noisome prison-cell to competence and home;—a Wilberforce, spending and spent in the great work;—the missionaries of the cross, at this moment scattered in all lands, cut off from friends and civilization, without prospect of emolument or renown; forgotten, it may be, by all but Him, in whose strength they labor; where is the self-interest in this?"

"Your last is a puzzling case. The theory I have advanced, perhaps too boldly, was not of my own choosing. I was compelled to its adoption by evidence which seemed incontestable, and I retain it because it solves more riddles in the complex machinery of society than any other I have heard. But it has its difficulties, and the main one is such conduct as you allude to. There is a key to the enigma, I suppose, if I could only find it."

"There is," said Mr. Lacy, feelingly. "There is a love which purifies the rest, a peace we would have all men know. They err, who say that devotion to God weans the heart from our friends. Our Divine Master has left us a new commandment—'that we love one another,' and with the increase of our love for Him, our souls enlarge, until the arms of brotherly kindness embrace the universal family of mankind. There is no such being as a selfish Christian."

Ida listened in amazement. This language was uncommon at any time and place out of the pulpit, but from an elegant and popular young man, it was novel in the extreme.

"I can hardly understand the workings of a principle, which is itself a mystery," she said. "Time was when religion was a household word to me, but exposure to adverse influences has erased from my mind all knowledge of this kind, if I ever had any understanding of its meaning."

"You have the instruction of the immortal spirit within you. Is that satisfied with its fare? Are you content with yourself and your mode of life?"

"Content!" The tone was a sufficient reply.

"Will you allow me to use the freedom of a friend, Miss Ross, and show you that in neglecting this subject you shut your eyes to the only true happiness? I know that the lot which appears brightest is checkered with vicissitudes—inward struggles, more trying than many visible afflictions. Against these, neither the spirits of youth nor the reasonings of philosophy can always prevail. I know how the lip smiles and the heart bleeds, although the anguish within does not drown the gay words upon the tongue. We may—we do conceal, but the sting rankles the same. Our Father never designed that we should be happy away from Him. These misgivings, this discontent with ourselves, and pinings for something better and higher, are voices beseeching us to partake of his love; they are the homesickness of a child, who has strayed, and has forgotten in new scenes the parent he has deserted, and the sight of a flower, a breath of warm air, a song he used to love, calls up the remembrance of that father, and a gush of shame and longing he is too proud to confess. Thus much all feel, but upon some fall heavier trials. Earth has no cure for the woes which a residence here entails upon us. Young as you are you may know this?"

"I do!"

"Is what I am saying disagreeable to you?"

"No, sir;—go on, if you please!"

"Then, if we are told of One, who cannot only comfort, but convert distress into blessing; of whose loving protection nothing can deprive us; who will make this life tolerable—nay, pleasant, and assure us of an eternity of bliss to be shared with Him,—is it not the maddest folly to refuse the pledge He asks in return—a child's love and trust?"

"I do not feel that I have acted thus!" said Ida, suddenly. "My reason assents to what you have said, but my conscience is dumb. The thought of a God—Almighty and Holy—overwhelms me with awe—sometimes-with terror. As Ruler and Judge, I pay him homage, and obey, when I can, the letter of His law;—but He does not care particularly for me—one of the most obscure of His countless subjects. I believe that He is a tender Father to the favored ones who have tasted His grace, and they ought to adore and love. I thank Him, from afar off, for preservation—not for creation—and he does not call me nearer. You think me very wicked, Mr. Lacy;—but as I said, if I speak at all, I speak candidly."

"I like your truthfulness. You express what others secretly feel; this distant respect is the natural tone of an enlightened mind, wedded to an unregenerate heart; and in your remarks, I detect the bitterness which is its concomitant,—amounting, in some, to deadly enmity against their Maker and Redeemer. Do you read the Bible—may I ask?"

"Yes—occasionally."

"From what motive?"

"I read it as a curiosity in literature—but that is not the principal reason"—

"Excuse me,—I had no right to put the question. I wished to know if you had noticed one or two passages—such as—'All day long I have stretched forth my hands unto a disobedient and gainsaying people.' 'When I called ye did not answer—when I spake, ye did not hear.' 'O Israel! thou hast destroyed thyself, but in me is thy hope!' There is scarcely a page which does not bear some moving expostulation or entreaty; and the disciple who knew Him best, condenses in one celestial drop the stream of revelation,'GOD is LOVE!'

Not a word of Power or Justice! We cannot exaggerate these attributes, but we may dwell upon them, to the exclusion of His long-suffering and loving kindness."

"You have a strange way of speaking of these matters;" said Ida. "I am acquainted with a number of excellent Christians, who never refer to the name by which they are called, but at long intervals, in set terms, and in a tone which frightens the 'sinners' to whom they address their exhortations. I have been troubled whether to question their sincerity, or the Faith, which they assert, controls them."

"Doubt neither. Ascribe their silence to diffidence, or a fear of giving offence; their unhappy manner, to ignorance of the proper method of managing hearts. It is to be regretted that the one Reality upon the globe should be banished from familiar conversation. If a man is sleeping upon the sea-shore, the big waves washing his pillow at each surge, am I censurable if I end his happy slumbers? Or, to employ an illustration which suits me better—I have a dear friend, to whom you are a stranger. With my esteem for you, will not my desire to bring you together, grow stronger? When I discover traits in you which he would approve, will not I tell you of him, and use every means to facilitate an acquaintance, so pleasant and profitable? Especially, if a time is certainly coming, when you will require his assistance;—an emergency is to overtake you, when all help but his will be vain—does it not become my imperative duty to implore you to accept the friendship he stands ready to bestow?"

"Do not the Scriptures speak of the veil that is upon their hearts?" said Ida.

"Yes—but it is the veil of unbelief. If we do not of ourselves endeavour to tear it away, the light which streams upon us, at its removal, may be too late. God does not need, but He demands our co-operation in His schemes for our salvation. There is our friend, Charley Dana; he is late for a gentleman of his punctual habits."

The conversation changed. Ida would gladly have heard more of a topic, so unusual, and previously so unpleasing, but he dropped it, and she did not oppose him. The manner, more than the matter of his language, took her fancy. He did not arrogate superiority of sense or goodness, and had none of the stereotyped cant she dreaded; he did not preach, but talked, easily and quietly; most of the time, with the smile she thought so beautiful, and she observed his avoidance of "you" and "I,"—substituting, when it could be done—"we" and "us," as if to lay a platform of perfect equality. If he had intended to leave the room, when he fell in with her, he altered his purpose. Charley and Lynn paid their respects, chatted awhile, and went their ways;—the former to dance and jest with divers merry belles, who hailed his approach, a relief from the very minor flats, upon which they had been playing, during the tedious hours in the halls, which were *not* "halls of mirth." Lynn sought Ellen Morris; and if Ida had seen the scarlet stain that suffused her cheeks, as she perceived him, she would have had "confirmation strong" of a suspicion entertained from the first time she had beheld them together. Mr. Lacy withstood his jailor's offers of liberation. "If she were inclined to change her place, or to promenade, he was at her service, but no alteration could better his condition;" and Ida's fears of detaining him, being dissipated by this straight-forward avowal, she abandoned herself to the enjoyment of communion with a noble intellect and finely-attuned spirit. The announcement of supper, the tocsin of liberty to a majority of the company, interrupted their lively dialogue.

Long before this, Josephine's eyes had raked the parlours from wall to wall, and she was fully satisfied, or *dis*-satisfied that her polar star was missing.

In the sickness of the disappointment, she hated the show of pleasure going on about her: the most fagged-out of the chaperon wall-flowers did not wish for the hour of separation more ardently than did she. There was one streak of light upon the cloud;—no society could recompense him for parting with hers, and he had departed in consequence: but she could have bitten her tongue off, as she deplored her injudicious declaration (untrue too!) of devotion to an amusement, for which she cared nothing. Was ever girl so impolitic? What if he were himself one of this "religious sort?" the bare supposition was distracting! she had committed the unpardonable sin!

"What have you done with Mr. Lacy?" queried one and another, and a ready untruth answered, "He had an engagement, which obliged him to go early." Charley overheard one repetition of this excuse; but although his eyes wandered, with a comical roll, towards the retreat of the recusant, he kept his own counsel. By supper-time, she was so convinced of the truth of her fabrication, that she neglected to institute a search which would have showed her Mr. Lacy and Ida, at the farthest end of the table. Twice again, she could have been blessed by a sight of him. Charley having invited Ida to a promenade in the hall, Mr. Lacy bethought him of his fair and partial hostess; but she was not to be found. She was lying upon the bed in her chamber, fretting over her "foolishness," and the "stupidity and worry" of all parties,—hers in particular. Smoothing her face and ringlets, she regained the parlor by one door, as Morton left it by another. He encountered Ida and Charley, and walked with them until the carriages came to the door. Josephine accompanied several of her most fashionable guests to the dressing-room; and Mr. Lacy, seeing there was no one to receive his congé, made none.

The day after! Mr. Read was growling and headachy;—Josephine in her worst humor, and itching to vent it. The breakfast hour was enlivened by a continual peppering of small shot from her, varied by a big gun from her father. He sneered at her arrangements and company, saying much that was cuttingly true, more, really, than he was aware of; and she pecked at him and the servants. In spite of her dislike, Ida pitied her, as she surveyed the heaps of unwashed dishes and glasses; the carpets, spotted with wine,—cake and jelly trampled into their velvet; and the forlorn disorder that reigned over all. She was on the point of offering her assistance, when Josephine brushed by her, with a peremptory order to "folks who were cluttering up the room, to be off, if they did not mean to work!" Herself, the cat and the footman, who was collecting the remains of the feast, comprising the auditory, Ida thought herself justifiable in taking a share of the hint.

She sent Rachel down in her place, enjoining upon her, as a prudential measure, not to speak, unless when asked a direct question.

As to Ida, the close of her evening had more than compensated for the ennui of the beginning; she had no foiled stratagems, no tangled snares to lament; yet the dissipation produced a nervous languor, tempting, yet dissuading her from action. She read—and the letters danced cotillions and waltzes over the page. The piano was in the parlor—but so was Josephine. She essayed to sew, and stitched up a seam wrong side out, and ran the point of the needle under her finger nail.

"I must walk—I have it! Mrs. Dana will like to hear about the party, and there is Elle's doll's hat."

Her gloves were in a bureau drawer, and near them lay a velvet case, enclosing the miniature of her parents—excellent likenesses, but owing to some oversight in mixing, or in the quality of the colors, they were fading already. She had signified to Mr. Read her intention to have them copied, before they should be so much defaced as to render it impracticable; why not give them to Lynn? His ability was uncontrovertible—it would be a kindness to him now, in the outset of his professional career; and she had the vanity to believe that he would bestow double pains upon what she so valued. She would carry them to Mrs. Dana, and ask her advice.

That lady was in her nursery, which was one of Ida's accustomed haunts. She was at home at once; tossing the babe, and joining her voice to its chuckling laugh, until the room rang again; Charley hanging upon her dress to entreat her praises of his hobby-horse; and Elle waiting patiently to kiss her for the "sweet bonnet that just fitted Dolly."

"You have come to stay a good long time with me, I know," said Mrs. Dana. "Here is a note I was about to send to you, requesting the pleasure of your company to dinner. I thought you had rather be out of the way while Miss Josephine is 'cleaning up,' and to be candid, Mr. Dana has invited two or three gentlemen to dine with us, and I am too bashful to face them unsupported. I did not write this, lest you should have scruples on the subject, but you must stay for my sake and John's. He made it a point that you should be asked. Do you know I am getting jealous?"

"But indeed, my dear madam"—

"But indeed, my dear miss, you will remove your bonnet immediately."

Resistance was useless; nor would Ida have offered it, had she been sure of meeting only the family; for the sun shone more brightly into this home-nest of cheerful peace, than into the abode she had lately quitted. The Danas knew enough of Mr. Read and Josephine, to make them solicitous to withdraw Ida as much from their influence as was consistent with her duty as a ward. She never complained, except to Carry, but they respected her the more for her prudence.

"You will spoil me," said she, as Mrs. Dana untied her bonnet.

"No danger," replied the lady, kissing her forehead—Carry's caress—and as other lips did, years ago. Tears stood in the orphan's eyes, but they did not fall. Elle wondered why cousin Ida could not see her doll's cloak without holding her head so near to it.

Mrs. Dana approved entirely of her project.

"Will you take them to him this morning?" inquired she.

"I certainly had such a notion, but I do not like to go without you, and as you are expecting company"—

"No time like the present, my dear. My dinner is in the hands of the cook; I shall not be wanted here for two hours. It is a lovely day, and I am glad of an errand that affords an excuse to go out."

As they were passing "Dana & Co.'s" she halted.

"Had we not better ask Mr. Dana to pilot us? I am uncertain of the exact locality of this same studio."

Mr. Dana could not go; he was waiting upon a country customer with a memorandum as long as his arm; but he conducted the ladies into the counting-room. Charley was there, at a tall desk, buried in ledgers and filed bills; and so business-like, that Ida hung back upon the threshold—a fear, of which she was ashamed, as he extended both hands to her, thanked them for their visit, and offered to escort them. He unlocked his bachelor's pantry of crackers, cheese and choice Madeira, hospitality which they civilly declined. Mr. Dana left the counter "to hope that he should see Miss Ida at dinner;" a courtesy which was a a sign of esteem and favor from one of his reticent disposition.

Lynn's studio was a small, but exquisitely appointed room. It was a minute before the eyes, used to the out-door light, could penetrate the claro-obscuro of its twilight.

Ida knew Lynn by his voice, and pressure of her hand, then a taller figure was developed to her vision, and she recognised Mr. Lacy.

"Are you engaged, Mr. Holmes?" asked Mrs. Dana.

"No, madam; Mr. Lacy has just concluded a sitting—the last. Your coming is opportune, you can criticise his portrait."

The voice was unanimous. It was a masterly painting, and faithful to life.

"A personable individual too, Morton—considering—" said Charley. "Did you have it painted for a sign-board? 'Morton Lacy, attorney at law,—For recommendations, see heading of this article.' What a multitude of lady-clients you would have!"

"It is for a lady who will not part with it, even to procure me a press of clients—for my mother," returned Mr. Lacy. "She will feel herself to be under great obligations to you, Mr. Holmes, for so truthful a transcript of her 'absent boy.'"

Ida looked at the original instead of the picture. It was, then, the handsomer of the two. With a complimentary observation of the workmanship, he dismissed the subject, and directed Ida to a genuine Claude, Lynn's pride and boast. She slipped her case into Mrs. Dana's hand, and followed him. Lynn presently approached.

"It would be an idle form to say that I am honoured by your application," said he. "Your heart will tell you how I esteem this proof of your friendship. It is a sacred trust, and as such I will fulfil it."

"I feared you would discourage me," replied Ida. "Is it not difficult to take a picture, the size of life, from a miniature?"

"It requires care, and a just regard to proportions; but I have an assurance of success in my willingness to attempt the work. I hope—I *know* I shall not fail. Now, what shall I do to entertain you? I am so unused to morning calls from ladies—and such ladies! that I am at a loss how to bear my honors."

"Where are those long-promised portfolios?" said Ida. "We could not desire a more acceptable treat."

The hour consumed in the examination of the artist's pictured treasures, was, to Ida, one of unalloyed delight. There might yet be diamonds in the pebbly sands of Richmond. Coke loomed up threateningly before Mr. Lacy; and Charley and Mrs. Dana felt some conscience-prickings, at the thought of Daybooks and desserts; but they did not offer to stir until Lynn affirmed that he had nothing more to show.

"There are good points in this working-day life of ours, are there not?" said Charley, as they went down the steps.

"Just my sentiments!" answered Mr. Lacy. "Yet Mr. Holmes is a dangerous citizen. He has beguiled an unsuspecting youth out of two hours of study. This is my apology for leaving pleasant company;—it is a consolation to a benevolent-minded person like myself, to know that I, and not they, will suffer from the separation. Adieu!"

"'Till dinner-time," said Mrs. Dana.

Mr. Dana convened a circle of friends to meet a young Northerner, the bearer of an introductory letter from his New York partner; and it was apparent that his ideas of the boundaries of civilization—'North by Cape Cod—South by Sandy Hook'—were seriously shaken by this peep at Virginia life. Mrs. Dana was, Charley maintained, a 'star housekeeper'; and her laurels did not wilt to-day. A perfect understanding existed between her and her head-waiter, 'Uncle Abraham.' She did not issue an order; and in emulation of her quiet manner, his instructions to his satellites were inaudible to the guests. Mr. Lacy,

Lynn, Mr. Brigham, (the stranger,) Mr. Villet, a French gentleman, whose amiability and politeness would have been his passport in any kingdom and clime, Mr. Thornton, recently admitted to the bar, and a fair sample of the educated Southerner; with the two Danas, and the ladies, made up the company.

Mr. Thornton sat by Ida; Mr. Lacy opposite. His quick look of pleasure, as he was shown his place, indicated his satisfaction; and although he did not interfere with her brilliant neighbor by addressing her in words, he did so frequently by his eye and smile. The conversation streamed on in a glittering tide;—Mr. Thornton, always ready with fun or sense, and Charley, whose creed interdicted flagging chit-chat leading—then Lynn, warming, dashed in; pursued, very cautiously, by Mr. Brigham. Mr. Villet cheered them on by his gusto of every repartee; and John Dana set his seal of confirmation upon each profound remark. Mr. Lacy said comparatively little; he seemed to prefer looking on; but his intelligent countenance spoke so eloquently for him, that his silence did not obstruct the hilarious current. There was another listener, who entered heartily into the spirit of the hour;—never imagining that the speakers gathered animation from her beaming face. She was oblivious of the fact of her bodily presence, until brought to the knowledge by the host's,

"Mr. Lacy,—Miss Ross will take a glass of wine with you."

Mr. Lacy spoke a word to the servant who stood prepared to fill his glass; and bowing with graceful composure to his vis-à-vis—

"Miss Ross will not forbid my pledging her health and happiness in a purer draught," he said, and raised a tumbler of water to his lips.

Temperance societies were not much in vogue in those days; and were not in such odor as now; and this movement astounded all present. Mr. Thornton, who had the common infirmity of wits, who have not learned the inadequacy of this one talent,—rare 'though it be,—to supply the loss of everything else: and whose greatest fault was, that he ran his trenchant blade as often into the breast of a friend, as foe, assailed his professional brother on the spot. He was parried with immovable good humour; and the others came to his aid; some with arguments, some with questions. Even Mr. Villet could not refrain from a cut of polite ridicule. The assailed maintained his ground manfully; neither staggered nor dismayed by the odds against him. He knew every foot of the field, having fought upon it more times than any of them. Charley laid down his arms first—'silenced if not convinced' he owned; Mr. Thornton was 'floored' by a thrust equal to his last blow;—the fate of the battle was to be determined by single combat; Lynn being unvanquished. He was an expert fencer; and changing his tactics, stood upon the defensive. Once and again, was he forced into a corner, from which retreat appeared impossible; and as often was he seen the next moment, fighting in the open plain, with unbattered crest. His opponent proposed a suspension of hostilities, but the auditors vetoed it peremptorily. They were alike amused and interested; and Mr. Lacy observed, with a smile, that the ruby poison, the engenderer of the strife, was untouched during the discussion. Mrs. Dana made a feint of withdrawal, and was solicited to remain, 'to be in at the death,' Charley said. He had a double motive in supporting the request; he foresaw defeat for Lynn; and although the admirable temper of the argument was likely to continue to the end, he judged it best to keep his gallantry in play, as a balance-wheel to his impetuosity. The event did not disappoint his expectation. Lynn was game to the last, but surrender or not, he was indubitably beaten. Mr. Lacy covered his enemy's rout by a flattering tribute to his argumentative abilities, and the two laughingly shook hands, as they arose from the board.

In the parlor, their undisputed court, the ladies received the attention which had been diverted from them by the wordy war.

"To show that I bear no malice for old scores, I repeat the petition that met with so obstinate a refusal," said Mr. Lacy, giving Ida his arm. "Will you sing for me?"

"'Say, what shall my song be to-night,
And the strain at your bidding shall flow,'"

she replied, running her fingers over the keys.

"That I leave to you. I do not know what suits your voice or taste."

"'The Last Rose of Summer,'" prompted Charley; "afterwards, the 'Captive Knight.'"

Mr. Lacy laughed; supposing he intended a satire upon the "miscellaneous" songsters, he had also thought of, when he objected to making a selection; and Ida, slightly piqued at his want of confidence in her powers of vocalization, sang both with inimitable skill and expression. The gentlemen pressed around to ask, each, for his favorite song. She complied readily and patiently. The natural compass and strength of her voice had been increased by diligent practice, yet music was with her, more a passion than an art; her songs, spirit-utterances instead of the compositions of others, learned by rote.

"She is actually beautiful!" said Mr. Dana, aside to his brother.

"Something above the order of puppets, nicknamed young ladies, with which people ornament their parlors now-a-days," was the reply.

Removed from the gnome-like regards of Josephine, she was, indeed, a different being. The presence of this girl was a mental extinguisher—smothering the flame of feeling in fetid smoke—the kindliness of the Danas, the generous oil feeding the exhausted lamp. Years afterwards, when the purple flush had faded from life's morning, the scene preceding her departure upon this evening, would recur, as one of the proudest and happiest moments of her existence—John Dana, standing in front of her, his grave features relaxed into a smile of fatherly fondness, as he heard her defence of herself against an accusation of Mr. Thornton's—Mrs. Dana, her hand upon her husband's shoulder, listening and enjoying—Charley and Lynn, her allies and counsellors, waiting to add their testimony—Mr. Lacy sitting beside her, and drinking in her words with an avidity that brought the blood tingling to her cheeks, and excited the meaning smiles of the spectators. She was in her proper sphere; the centre and idol of a home-circle. The praises lavished upon her were honestly won—too much would have satiated, not spoiled—the utter absence of reward soured her.

"I have had a happy, happy day, dear Mrs. Dana!" whispered she, at going. "I shall write to Carry to-morrow, to apprise her how well you fill her place."

Mr. Lacy attended her home. Curiosity had set for him the study of her character. Her mien bespoke no ordinary soul; and the inuendoes of Josephine, meant to deter him from prosecuting it, stimulated his desire. They had been together repeatedly, previous to the party, but always in the company of the Extinguisher. Her arch glance and rejoinder to his thoughtless remark, while recalling Josephine's insinuation of her hoydenish propensities, nevertheless fascinated him. From being amused, he grew interested; he was working a mine of thought, and unless the clue was false, there was a substratum of feeling. The friendship of the Danas convinced him that the heart was warm and true. He saw the frank girl amidst the friends in the studio, and the accomplished woman in the coterie of the evening; and could not say which was most attractive. "So much intelligence and so little affectation are seldom seen in the same person;" he meditated. "She has the materials for a noble character." Did he think to mould it!

CHAPTER XIII

Our youthful débutantes were plunged into the maelstrôm of a fashionable season; a whirl which, in its outermost circles, was as gratifying to the feverish energy of Ida as to the vanity of her more grovelling-minded associate. The rapidly shortening days seemed longer instead, so uneventful and wearisome were they. Life commenced when the evening's thousand lamps were lit. The mingling perfumes; the crush and flutter; the wave-like roar of the assembly-room, were delicious excitement to the emancipated school-girl; and to the astonishment of those who had known her then, the reserved student bloomed into the dashing wit and belle; beauties and heiresses sitting, uncourted by, while "eligibles" contended for the honor of her preference. Her newness was a part of the secret. The spectacle of a wild Zingara, unreined, and glorying in the fullness of its freedom, scorning bit and spur, amongst a pack of jaded hackneys, who have been trotted and paced and galloped, year after year, until their factitious animation and oft-repeated gambols create pity and contempt, would cause a sensation akin to that awakened by her appearance. Her lightest words were jeux d'esprit; her laugh, a chime of silver wedding-bells; (things by the way, of which every body talks, but nobody we have questioned, ever heard,) her singing seraphic; her ballads lyric gems; herself a Corinne. Josephine was latest to perceive, first to resent this sudden accession of popularity. Rivalry from this source was as unexpected as unbearable. Her glass showed her a form, airy as a summer cloud; a set of features more delicate and regular than Ida's characteristic-physiognomy; and in dress, she certainly bore off the palm; her maid being invariably rung up an hour and a half before Rachel's services were demanded. She fought, as long as she could, with the conviction that this pre-eminence was as though it had not been to the world; and when it made a violent entrance into her circumscribed intellect, how was the milk of her nature curdled to vinegar! And how like nitre to vinegar, were the happily-chosen congratulations of her attendant beaux, upon her good fortune in inhabiting the same house with "her charming friend, Miss Ross;" or, "Miss Ida even surpasses herself to-night;" "A remarkable girl! such vivacity! and I hear, quite as much profundity of mind; is this so, Miss Read?" And the writhing dissembler had to assent, and corroborate, and smile, while the yeasty waves frothed and bubbled furiously in their confinement. To expose her envy would damage her prospects, hinged as they were, in part, upon her sweetness of disposition.

It might have been a salvo to her wounded vanity had she guessed by what a length of time her jealousy outlived the triumph which aroused it; how the feast of adulation, so daintily spread, ceased to tempt, then nauseated; how, from the jewelled robe of society the gloss wore away, and threadbare tatters were all that remained of what was cloth of gold; how prevarications and oaths refused longer to shelter falsehood; and the garlands withered and shrank from manacles which heated with the wearing; how the earth itself was a thin, hollow ball, that one could puff away with a breath; how, ere the fire the revel had infused into her veins cooled, the coronal was plucked from the brow, the costly attire crushed petulantly, a worthless rag! And at that window, the freezing air not chilling her heated blood—the envied one wept blistering tears of self-abhorrence and despondency—and the night-wind sighed to the moan—"Not this! not this!" and the old prayer for "liberty and love!" We say, had she known this, she might have felt avenged; but the public, nor she, saw any alteration in its fondling and her detestation. It was the middle of December. Balls, concerts, and soirées had been given in breathless succession, and Ellen Morris issued tickets for yet another. The appointed hour saw the house overflowing. Ida was near the centre of the front parlor, radiant and flattered as usual. One gentleman, with an air of easy assurance, was inspecting her bouquet; a second, pushing a mock flirtation with all his might; a third, a callow youngster, afraid to speak to the "bright particular," he had so panted to behold, staring into her face in sheepish agony; and a fourth peered over the shoulder of number one.

"The camelia, Miss Ida, what is its emblem?" asked the bouquet holder.

"Beauty without wit;" rejoined she, but half hearing him, and then finishing a sentence to No. 2.

"Without amiability, you mean," corrected No. 4.

"Without wit!" said Ida. "I relish an active perfume, which can be detected without effort of mine, and do not prize a flower that must be bruised to extract its sweetness; amiability is, at best, a passive virtue."

"But what is a beautiful woman without softness, tenderness, effeminacy?" said No. 2, whose stock of words exceeded that of ideas. "She wins us by her yielding submissiveness, her gentle mildness. Destitute and devoid of these, she is to me without charm or attraction. Do not understand me, however, as depreciating or undervaluing wit in *your* presence!" recollecting himself, with a salaam.

"No apologies are necessary. We all agree that such depreciation would come with a bad grace from Mr. Talbot," said Ida, pointedly, returning a still deeper curtsey.

No. 1 nodded, as he laughed, to some one beside her. "Good evening," said Mr. Lacy, as she looked around.

"And he has overheard this nonsensical stuff!" thought she, with inward disturbance. "When did you come in?" she inquired.

"About ten minutes since; most of which time has been spent in a search for Mrs. or Miss Morris."

"I am glad to hear it."

"Glad—how?"

"I feared you had occupied your present position some time."

He understood her. "There are more people here than I expected to see," he said, after some general conversation.

"Almost too many," replied Ida; "I am getting tired of these great parties."

"The heat is oppressive. Have you a liking for this stand?"

"No—my being here is accidental. It requires some effort to stand, or walk upright, in the heart of this crowd."

"I noticed, as I came through, that the music room was more thinly-populated—will you rest there?"

This was a mere boudoir compared with others of the suite, and the prepossessions of the company were for music of a different kind. The violin was discoursing its enchanting strains in the farther apartment, and there were not above a dozen persons in the one, where slumbered the piano and guitar.

"Are you indisposed, Miss Ross?" asked Mr. Brigham, who was fanning a fragile-looking girl, reclining in an easy chair.

"No—only tired. You have acted wisely in shunning the press and bustle, Miss Moore. I am happy to see you able to venture out in the evening."

"Your climate is doing wonderful things for me," answered Miss Moore, smiling.

"How dreadful to be deprived of health, and the hope of a long life!" said Ida, when they were seated.

"And especially mournful in this instance, if I am not deceived!" replied Mr. Lacy. "I pity that man! he will not believe that bereavement is inevitable; and if death was ever branded upon human brow, it is upon hers."

"I honor his constancy and devotion," said Ida. "The object of his visit in the fall, was to acquaint himself with the advantages our city possesses for invalids; then he went back for her mother and herself. He is both brother and lover. Who would have expected this from a man of his phlegmatic constitution?"

"Another warning of the folly of judging by appearances. It is possible, too, that we who are pitying her are as much in want of compassion. The highest happiness is unaffected by extraneous influences."

"Happiness!" echoed Ida, "It is a myth."

"So says the sage of eighteen—gay, gifted and caressed! You will not entrap me into a sermon;" said Mr. Lacy, sportively. "No! no! Miss Ida! you will regard me as a lineal descendant of Bunyan's Mr. Law—a Giant Grim, who frequents places of amusement to corner children, and relate scary stories to them."

"A monster who does not exhibit himself often;" returned Ida. "This is but the second large party at which I have seen you. Are you principled against them?"

"No, and yes. I do not disapprove of social pleasures. They make light, yet firm, the bands that cement our species. Their suppression would convert the most benevolent into a morose eremite; but I do see incipient evil in the frequency of these scenes. Setting aside the waste of time, which may belong to matters of importance, sooner or later they produce a disrelish for domestic duties, and an enervation, physical and mental, like the languorous sobriety of a toper. There is nothing nourishing to the immortal mind, in a ceaseless round of gaiety."

"How do you know, by personal experience?"

"Even so. I once drank pretty deeply of Pleasure's cup—did not drain it to the lees—but drew off the clear wine, and was beginning to taste the bitter, before I would let go. I was in Mr. Holmes' studio, yesterday, and missed your portraits. You have them?"

"I have."

"Are you pleased?"

"Entirely. I do not remember my father, but Mr. Read says the likeness is good. The other could not be improved."

"Mr. Holmes is a painter of exalted abilities, and an enthusiast in his art. I did not know him well until our passage at arms at Mr. Dana's, the day we dined there. We have been friends ever since. My sister writes that his portrait of myself is a solace in the loneliness of her sick chamber. She has the kindest of mothers and friends, but there are times when they are unavoidably absent, and she is childish enough to talk to the dumb semblance of one who is not worthy of her love, and imagine that it looks back its answers."

"Have you but one sister?"

"But one at home—three are married. Annie seems nearer to me; she is next me in age, and until a year ago was my inseparable companion."

His eye rested upon Miss Moore. "We were speaking of happiness in affliction. If skeptical on this head, you should know her. She is never free from pain and never impatient; her sunny, loving temper, makes her room the resort of the neighborhood—but this does not interest you."

"Not interest me!" said Ida, reproachfully. "Do you then think me the heartless creature I appear? I am not wholly absorbed in self. We have never conversed as strangers; do not let us retrograde now. True, I have no sister, but I have a friend who is more to me, so I may listen."

"Thank you," said he sincerely. "I have feared you might deem my informal address presumptuous; but I seem to have known you for years, not months. I cannot wear my company manners when talking to you."

"Perhaps we have met before, in an anterior state of existence," replied Ida; "and lurking memories of introductions, and compliments, and staid courtesies, render these preliminaries odious now. I could be sure, sometimes, that my spirit had lived in this world before it tenanted its present body."

"These are fascinating, yet dangerous speculations," he answered. "I am tormented by them myself, but I shun them as unprofitable."

"Why so? The soul, as our nobler part, merits most study, its mysteries are yet undiscovered. What a field expands to our contemplation! over which the mind may rove and exult for ages, and leave unimpoverished. I would not barter one hour of such thoughts—chimerical though they may be—for ten years of this vapid, surface life. I had rather dive into the ocean, to bring up nothing but valueless shells, than drift, like dead sea-weed, upon the top of the sleepy waves."

"May I describe another mode of life and action?"

"Certainly—so you do not laugh at me."

"Do you apprehend that I shall?" fixing his clear eye upon hers. "I would remind you of the humble mariner, steering his vessel boldly, but carefully, through the waters, thankful in sunshine, courageous in tempest, with one port in view, rowing past the Fairy islands that stud the deep; keeping a straight path in a trackless waste, for he looks to the eternal heavens for guidance."

"I must sport among the islets," said Ida. "You do not quite comprehend me, Mr. Lacy. I have told you more than once that life has thus far been a disappointment to me, but it is not that I have sucked the orange dry, and would cast the tasteless pulp away. Mine has been so acid I must hope that time and the sun of prosperity will ripen it to lusciousness. Others tell of unknown depths of happiness I have capacity to enjoy—am I unreasonable in trusting that my turn will come? Have I tasted all of earth's delights at eighteen?"

"Could you quaff them at one draught, your thirst would not be appeased. You are no nearer to contentment now than you were three years since. The drink-offering of popular award is growing dull and stale; you sigh at what would have chased gloom a month ago, and this is the hey-day of pleasure. Nay," continued he, dropping his earnest tone, and bending to look into her face, "I shall not forgive myself if I mar your evening's entertainment by my croaking. Messrs. Talbot & Co.'s anathemas against my impertinent monopoly do not occasion me a hundredth part of the disquiet your very sober face does. Mr. Thornton is coming to ask you to dance. Will you go?"

"Fatigued!" exclaimed the barrister, to her excuse. "I should as soon admit the plea of a star for ceasing to shine upon the pretext that it was too troublesome to continue its light."

"Has there never been such a disappearance?" questioned Mr. Lacy.

"I have seen eclipses," retorted the other. "The sun is invisible, when the leaden moon comes between it and us. This music is too inspiriting, Miss Ross; am I reduced to the necessity of seeking another partner?"

"I am sorry I can't say 'no,'" said she, laughingly.

Mr. Lacy was bent upon expelling the regrets reflection might beget; and wiled into confidence by his gentle endeavors to induce a trust in him as a friend, Ida spoke freely, though not unguardedly, of feelings and thoughts which had been so long hushed, that their speech was slow and imperfect; but he interpreted and prized their stammered story. As the night wore on, exhausted couples dropped in, and there was an end to connected conversation. It was as well, for both were forgetting where they were. Morton relinquished his chair to Ellen, and stood by her, and Lynn sank, playfully, upon one knee before Ida.

"Take care!" was his whisper. "Serpents coil in rose-thickets."

"What do you mean?" inquired she, struck and chilled.

"That we are the most tenacious of that to which we have the most meagre title."

"A masculine Sphinx! speak out!" she demanded.

"Miss Read could enact Oedipus to this riddle. Seriously, Ida, beware of that woman! She courts Lacy's society. I do not know what the ladies' verdict is—to us it is as plain as that he does not like her half as well as he does you. Do not avoid him; he deserves your favor; but do nothing to uncover her eyes—blindfolded by her egregious conceit."

"Lynn! you confound me! What have I to do with Mr. Lacy! I have no interests which would war with hers, were they ever so strong. Having nothing to lose, I have nothing to fear. I am obliged to you for your brotherly cares," she added, roguishly. "A fellow-feeling makes us wondrous kind."

"You know it, then!" exclaimed he, his large eyes splendid in their flash of intelligence and rapture.

"I am not insensible or indifferent, where the happiness of my friends is concerned," she rejoined, in the same confidential tone.

Another gleam thanked her.

Ellen Morris was what is termed, a "taking girl." The high, gay spirit, which had distinguished her among her comrades at Mr. Purcell's won her distinction in a world willing to be amused. She had objectionable traits, but there was also much that was admirable and loveable about her. If her over-weening fondness for merriment offended, it was easy to forgive one, whose lively sense of the comic was inbred and irresistible. Still, it was a marvel that the impassioned Lynn should recognise in her the embodiment of his poetic dream of woman. They met before he went to Europe, and the tricksy sprite of a school-girl was not dislodged from his memory by the lures that tried him there. He came back to find a blooming maiden preserving the fresh, joyous grace which had captivated him in the child—and loved! as men seldom love—as women often do—with an abandon of affection, an upyielding of every faculty and thought to the dominion of one sentiment— a love that brings gladness to few hearts, and breaks many! many!

Had he asked Ida, with the disinterested equanimity, some suitors we wot of, display, what course she would advise in this momentous matter, she would have responded with a sister's candor, "she does not suit you—rid yourself of your entanglement;" but it was too late;—she must hope with, and for him. In payment for his cautionary remark, she hinted, that, situated as they were, misconstruction and jealousy might be formidable foes to his peace of mind:—that neither smiles nor frowns were unerring indices of a girl's heart. He scouted the implied suspicion.

"Jealous of these popinjays!" glancing disdainfully at the black coats and white vests in attendance, as if he thought they contained wound-up automata.

"The danger does not appear imminent;" said she. "See that you retain this satisfied state of mind."

Her countenance fell, and he heard Josephine say, simperingly—

"How dramatic! pray, Mr. Holmes, is this a rehearsal, or a real performance?"

"Most ladies are so versed in love affairs, as to understand the symptoms at a glance;—is not your eye sufficiently practiced?" asked he, with a curling lip.

"No, sir. I regret to say that the gentlemen of my acquaintance are not sentimental or politic enough, to get up such scenes."

"I have no doubt you *do* deplore it."

"Why, Mr. Holmes!" ejaculated Ellen, with her gleeful laugh; "how ungallant!"

"You mistake. It was a skilful combination of veracity and politeness. I must coincide with her, and am pleased that it can be done without violence to my conscience. I wish I could propose a cure for the evil you lament, Miss Read, but I am afraid it is irremediable. Men are obstinate animals."

Ida, alarmed, touched his foot; and the lynx eyes saw the slight movement. A deadly light glowed there for an instant, and was extinguished in softness, as she assailed Mr. Lacy.

"'In what far distant region of the *hall*.'

have you kept yourself all the evening, Sir Truant?"

"Polyhymnia and Melpomene!" muttered Lynn.

"I have been a fixture in this room most of the time;" replied Morton.

"How selfish! had you no sense of duty? could you not sacrifice your ease to secure the enjoyment of your friends?"

"It would argue ridiculous vanity in me, to suppose that my absence has detracted from the pleasures of the assembly; and from the aspirants for the smile of the reigning belles, so unimportant a personage is not missed."

"Can he like her?" thought Ida. "There is still an air unlike other men, but he does not act or speak as he did to me. He looks amused but very careless. Oh! why must we have two faces?"

"Why did you stop me just now?" queried Lynn, pettishly. "I do not fear her; I am rather anxious she should know the extent of my dislike."

"How will that benefit either of you!" inquired Ida.

"Don't play the saint! much consideration you owe her! I am a good hater:—I cannot fawn and smile upon one,—woman though she is—beggared in principle and heart. She is capable of anything. Mean and tyrannical—those who deal with her, must be tools or enemies,—I choose the latter alternative. I will not hear any justification. Don't I know— cannot everybody see, that she is the trouble of your life,—that she would murder you, but for the cowardly dread of detection!"

"You will counsel me next, to sleep with pistols under my pillow;" said she. "What an array of horrors you are manufacturing?"

"It is as true as Gospel. Why disclaim it? Charley told me of the vixen before I saw her; he can be civil—I cannot—and what is more—*will* not!"

"He sees, perhaps, that animosity to my friends may be an engine to inflict suffering upon me;" answered Ida, thinking of Mr. Dermott.

Lynn coloured. "He intimated as much. I have not his self-command; he is a better, because a more unselfish friend than I."

"I have no fault to find with you;" was the reply. "It is a comfort to feel, that come what may, I have two brothers to depend upon."

Charley was leaning upon the back of her chair, and this remark was made partly to him. Lynn pressed her hand, as he recovered himself from his lowly posture, but there was as much meaning in the kind gaze of his undemonstrative friend. Their affection was a rill of pure water, stealing through a region of artificial light and bloom; and people pretended to, or did misinterpret it. Josephine credited, doubted, and was impatient by turns. One of them was the lover;—they were too friendly to be bound upon the same errand. Lynn's manner was most unequivocal—but his attentions to Ellen! Charley was not a marrying man—that was settled—everybody said; but the tender respect he paid Ida; the watchfulness that protected her from impertinence and neglect, were weighty offsets to this popular decision;—and again, opposed to these, were his disinterestedness in surrendering his post to Lynn, or any agreeable companion, who sought it, and the absence of uneasiness in his observation of her belleship.

Ida laughed at her mystification, as did those who effected it,—frequently concerting some manoeuvre, by which to lead her further into the labyrinth. If Charley made one of the family in the evening, the morrow brought Lynn to drive or walk. Charley lent her books, and imported a writing-desk from Paris, upon hearing Mrs. Dana say that Ida had made a fruitless search through the city, for one of a particular description;—Lynn appeared to have laid down the brush for the spade and pruning knife, so abundant were the bouquets, left with Mr. Holmes' compliments; and the walls of her chamber were adorned with pictures, from subjects proposed or approved by her. But amidst the frolicsome action of this drama, was collecting matter for another, to be closed only with Life,—to be remembered, perchance, with Eternity; and the chief actor danced and sang and sported, unaware of the importance of the dawning era. All her life a dreamer, she did not observe that the enshrined ideal was shaping itself into the real;—that the far-off future, her hopes had sprung forward to greet, as if to meet it half-way would hasten its lagging pace, was merging into the brightening present. She had expected the summer to burst upon her, with fragrance and music and sunshine, and took no note of the swelling buds and violet perfume of Spring. And here, let not him, who is wearied by the labors of Autumn, or numbed by the frosts of Winter, close our humble story, with a lofty scorn, or scathing displeasure at the prospect of a "love-tale." Rather let him unfold his shut-up heart, and read there of his own glad May, its dancing shadows, fairer than the oblique sun-rays that fall open his beaten track;—of the rosy June, the redemption of its young sister's promise:—and looking sadly upon its dust-eaten blossoms, think, with loving pity, of flower-cups which hold the dew-drop now,—soon to fade and shrivel as these have done!

CHAPTER XIV

It had been predicted from the premature beginning of the winter's gaieties, that an ebb would occur before the Southern carnival, Christmas, and the party-goers resolved to falsify the prophecy.

Mrs. Dana called on the afternoon of the 24th to invite Ida and Josephine to dine with her. "You will see only ourselves and Mr. Holmes, who is Charley's shadow."

"A stupid set," was Josephine's reflection. "How pleasant," Ida's; and their answers corresponded. The former, "very sorry, papa would always dine at home, Christmas-day; he held it to be a religious duty she verily believed," laughing affectedly, "and he could not eat unless she were there."

Ida said, "I will come with pleasure, thank you," and lost all but the main purport of Miss Read's apology, in an eager whisper from Elle, who was with her mother.

"I don't hear, will I 'please come to what?'" lifting her to her lap.

Elle put her arms around her neck, and her mouth to her ear.

"To your molasses stew!" said Ida, "indeed I will. When is it to be?"

Another important whisper.

"Josephine, are we engaged for to-morrow evening?"

"I do not know," she replied, shortly.

"I hope not," said Mrs. Dana. "Elle's head is full of her frolic. I was describing to her the molasses stew I had every Christmas, when I was a child, and nothing would do but I must promise her one for 'being a good girl.'"

"She deserves it, I know," said Ida, fondly. "I will come, Elle, if I leave fifty grown people's parties."

"Will you, too?" asked the child, going up to Josephine. Mrs. Dana pressed the invitation.

"I am not certain, but I have engaged to go somewhere else," said Josephine, smiling heartlessly into the pure little face. "If I can, I will do myself the honor, Miss Dana."

The wretched attempt at playfulness actually frightened Elle, who shrunk again to the side of her friend.

"Are you serious in promising to go to this babyish fal-lal?" snapped Josephine, the minute Mrs. Dana was gone.

"I am."

"Did not you hear that Anna Talbot is to receive company to-morrow night?"

"Yes; and I am rejoiced that Elle's invitation was earliest. There are Anna and Ellen Morris."

"I haven't time to stay," exclaimed the young lady, throwing herself upon the sofa. "You both must spend a sociable evening with me—a Christmas jubilee—egg-nogg, country-dances, etc. We are to have a high time. You are disengaged?"

"I am," said Josephine, promptly, "and if I were not, I could not resist the temptation to send a 'regret,' and go to your house."

"Thank you—and you, Ida—may I count upon you both?" drawing up her cloak. Ida declined courteously;—"she was engaged to Mrs. Dana."

"Oh!" began Anna, disappointed.

"Is it not too silly!" interposed Josephine. "It is a child's party—a molasses stew—think of it!"

"You are joking, Ida," said Ellen, "excuse yourself to Elle—we want you!"

"Not as much as my little cousin does. I cannot break my word to her."

"Little cousin!" smiled Anna. "I thought the relationship was closer. I will not give up the hope of persuading you. The nicest beaux in town are to be there—Mr. Thornton, Mr. Russell, and Mr. Villet, and Mr. Lacy, and a score more—*do* come!'"

"I cannot!" said Ida, with a pang.

"Papa will not be pleased with our going out separately;" said Josephine, that night.

"He does not object to my going to Mr. Dana's alone;" was the response.

"Thinking of number one, as usual, my amiable lady! I tell you what! I shall not demean myself, by playing puss-in-the-corner, and smearing my hands with treacle, when I might be at Mr. Talbot's, in decent company."

"As you like. If you represent the character of the company to your father, he will probably insist upon your mixing with them."

"He! he!" tittered Rachel, who was in waiting. Josephine flounced out of the room.

"Christmas gift, Miss Ida!" Her maid stood at her bedside, in the grey morning light. "Christmas gift!" called out the passers-by, as they encountered each other in the street "Hurrah for Christmas!" shouted squads of boys, at the corner, to a brilliant accompaniment of pop-crackers.

Ida heard it all, with a spirit out of tune with mirth. No gifts were prepared for her; the Thanksgiving-day was one of mourning to the homeless. She had anticipated a visit from Carry, during the holidays; but her last letter had dashed the hope. "Mammy" was recovering from a severe fit of sickness, and she would not leave her. Ida wished she were not to dine at Mr. Dana's; she was not fit for society, and sad enough, without the sight of joys, which reminded her of her losses and wants. In this discontented mood, she went down stairs. No Christmas yet! Mr. Read grunted to her formal bow, and Josephine said "the coffee was cold—it had been on the table so long." Mr. Read finished his second cup, and pulled out his pocket-book.

"People will be asking if I made you a present. Thank goodness! Christmas comes but once a year. Two would break a man. There!" fillipping a roll of notes to his daughter. "Don't waste it upon gimcracks and finery. If women had to earn money, they wouldn't be so crazy to spend it. You must have some, I suppose:" and he laid a smaller bundle upon Ida's plate.

"No, sir! I have money of my—" but he did not wait to hear her through. As she quitted the table, Josephine pointed to the untouched "present."

"Take it, if you choose!" said Ida, contemptuously. "I am not a dependant or a beggar!"

Josephine loved money, and pocketed it. "And the old curmudgeon is none the wiser!" chuckled the dutiful daughter.

Ida stretched herself upon a lounge, and set seriously about reasoning herself out of her despondency. She thought of Carry, and Lynn and Charley; but they came reluctantly, with selfishly happy faces; with their schemes and amusements and dearer friends. Mr. and Mrs. Dana pitied her;—this was the spring of their kindness! and her haughty soul winced at the idea. Hope and Fancy crept, with trailing wings, into hiding-places until the sun should shine out—she sullenly hugged her misery. What visionary who reads this, but has suffered from these morbose fits?

"Well?" said she, tartly, as Rachel tiptoed across the floor.

"I thought you was asleep;" replied the sable damsel.

"I am awake—do you want anything?"

Rachel rubbed her chin, gave her turban a twitch, and fumbled in her pocket "Law! I *ain't* lost it, I *know*! It must be in my bosom!"

Ida, awakened by her movements, watched her as she produced a tiny packet from the last-mentioned receptacle. With an odd compound of awkwardness and affection, she slipped a ring upon her mistress' finger.

"Thar! it fits! don't it?" intensely complacent.

"But where did you get it, Rachel? is it for me?"

"For you, and nobody else, Miss Ida. I was determined your nose should not be made a bridge of by everybody; so I've been a savin' my spare coppers—(and no servant of yours wants for 'em,) and when you was admirin' that ar ring of Miss Josephine's, I says to myself—'She shall have one!' and when I'd cleaned up your room, I took off down town to the jewellerers—and thar 'tis—wishin' you a Merry Christmas, and an ever-lastin' Happy New Year, ma'am!" stepping back with a flourishing courtesy. Ida tried to smile at her peroration, and failing, burst into tears. Rachel was transfixed. She was not used to hysterics, and had never seen her mistress weep before. Her consternation was a speedy restorative; and Ida finally made her sensible that she was not grieved or displeased, but overjoyed at her gift. Then the voluble Abigail recollected "somethin' else" she had to communicate.

"Ain't that tall gentleman, with black whiskers, that visits here so constant, named Mr. Lacy?"

"Yes."

"I thought so. When I went into the jewellerer's he was a standin' at the counter, buyin' a pair of gold spectacles—for his mother—I reckon. I heard him say they was for a lady. I asked for the rings, and the shop-boy gave me a string of brassy, ugly things—and says I— 'I want a handsome one, sir, for my mistis.'

"'Your mistis!' says he. 'Them's plenty good for her!'

"'Are these the best you have?' says Mr. Lacy, sort o' frownin' and talkin' like he was his master fifty times over.

"'No, sir—would you like to see some?' says the boy, turnin' white.

"'Bring them!' says Mr. Lacy; and when they come, he told me, with the sweetest smile, and so respectful! 'These cost a great deal of money—do you know it?' So I showed him what I had, and he said 'twould do. Bimeby, I picked out two, and could not tell which was the prettiest. I kept a-lookin' at one, and then at 'tother, and says he, 'Can't you choose between them?'

"'No, sir,' says I.

"'I think that the handsomest;' says he, pintin' to one, and that's it you've got on your finger, this minute, Miss Ida. He seed that low-lived boy give me the right change, and when I curchyed and said, 'I'm mightily obliged to you, sir;' he said, 'You are welcome,' just like I'd been the Governor! We colored folks know a gentleman when we see him, and *he* is a real born one."

The ring was very elegant, and the blood mounted to Ida's temple's, as she toyed with it.

"Perhaps, it was not Mr. Lacy?" said she, in a tone of extreme indifference. "Where had you met him, that you know him?"

"I never met him nowhar. I seed him one Sunday, when he walked home with you from church, and I was at the up-stairs window, and once through the dinin'-room door when he was here to supper, and once—through the parlor window."

"Peeping! Rachel! If he had seen you, he would not think as highly of your manners, as you do of his."

"Peeping! Law! Miss Ida, them was sly glimpses, permiscuous-like, you know. He warn't a-gwine to catch me."

A longer inspection of the ring. There was no blush this time, but the smile was happier. The motive was then as pure as the action was generous. The little shower had purified the murky atmosphere. This token of remembrance, at a moment when she believed herself forgotten, was none the less dear that the donor was a poor slave. It was the fruit of self-denying affection; and had no sooner clasped her finger, than it acted as the Open Sesame to a store-house of untold riches. "It has taught me more than one lesson," she murmured.

Rachel was garrulously happy.

"I do-clar, Miss Ida, you've been gettin' prettier ever since I come in;" said she, standing off to survey the effect of her toilette. "I hope thar'll be a crowd at Mars' John's. Is it a dinin'-day?"

"No—a family party."

"That's a pity! I 'spect that's another present! It never rains but it pours."

The footman said Mr. Dana was below. Charley waited to escort her to his brother's; and Ida began to realise, as he paid the compliments of the season, in a style, eminently "Charleyish,"—that Christmas had indeed come.

"Christmas gift! Christmas gift! cousin Ida," shouted two infantine voices; and Charley the less, and Elle scampered down the porch-steps to salute her. "Now mamma! now for the tree! She is here!"

"Oh! Mrs. Dana! have not they seen their tree? What suspense for the dear creatures!"

"It was their wish; and their father would not consent that the door should be unlocked until the family were assembled."

"Here is the last straggler!" exclaimed Lynn, springing into the group, shaking hands with his friends, and kissing the children. "We are all here!"

At a given signal, the door of the mysterious room was unfolded, and revealed the tree; its precious load glittering and gay in the clear winter day. Headed by "papa," and closed by the nurse and baby, the procession performed a circuit, and then formed a ring. Uncle Charley was distributor; accompanying each gift by an appropriate remark. For Ida, there were a pair of ear-rings from John Dana; a bracelet of fair hair, which did not require the simple "Carry" upon the chased clasp, to signify from whose brow it had been shorn; a handsomely-bound edition of Shelly's works—Lynn's taste; Charley gave a card case, a Chinese curiosity, and evaded her thanks and praises by pointing out a resemblance in the most grotesque figure, carved thereupon, to himself, a circumstance, which he protested, induced him to select it. Among the white buds of a perpetual rose-tree, hung a card—"Elle and Charley to their dear cousin;" and Mrs. Dana finished the list with a rose-wood work-box, supplied with every implement of female industry.

"Is this being friendless?" asked Ida, inly, looking at her acquisitions. "For the rest of the day, I will be grateful and contented."

The morning was spent in the nursery. On Christmas day, its door could not bar intruders; there were no men or women; all were children, Charley whipped his namesake's top; rocked the cradle; and instructed Elle in domestic economy, as he helped arrange her baby-house. The dinner-bell, rung an hour earlier than usual, on account of the wee ones taking that meal with the "big folks," was faintly heard in the din of a famous game of romps. The afternoon was less noisy; the children fell asleep, wearied with frolic; the gentlemen walked out; Mrs. Dana was busy; and so it was, that Ida sat alone in the drawing-room, at nightfall, watching the passing of the pink light from the clouds, and thinking—"Everything to gladden me, and yet ill at ease! murmuring soul, be still!" And then she wished for the society of a calmer mind, that should speak peace to the heavings of her unquiet spirit; for the comprehensive charity, the benign philosophy, which hoped for the best, and argued for the right—this was her version of the outgoing of the woman's heart—"Would *he* were here!"

But Elle's friends came early, and she had no time for higher thoughts than filling small mouths with bread and butter—"run-the-thimble," the vexed question of "how many miles to Babylon;" and "Chicken-me-chicken-me-craney-crow;" pastimes, whoso barbarous names cause the refined juveniles of this precocious '54, to join their gloved hands in thanksgiving, that their lot was not cast in those times! As the dignified master of the house deigned to participate in the ceremonies, we trust our heroine will not suffer a very grievous letting-down in the opinion of these formidable critics, for the prominent parts she assumed. A circle was ordered for "Fox and goose." Charley played Reynard, and Ida, goose the first. The children enjoyed, without fully understanding the game, and she had to keep the character longer than the laws prescribed. Round and round they flew—circling and doubling—the spectators screaming their applause—and she ran directly against a gentlemen who was entering. Her impetus was such that she would have fallen, but for his extended arm. A laughing voice said something, unintelligible in her confusion.

"Oh! Mr. Lacy!" cried Elle. "I was *so* afraid you wouldn't come!"

"I promised—did I not?" said he, stooping to kiss her.

"Yes, sir, but I thought maybe you'd rather go to Miss Anna Talbot's party, like Miss—"

"Elle! Elle! no, no!" whispered Ida, in time to suppress the name.

"You see I had rather be at yours;" he returned, without noticing the unfinished sentence. "What are you playing?"

"'Did you ever see a wild goose
Sailing on the ocean?'"

sang Charley.

"'The wild goose's motion
Was a mighty funny notion.'"

he added, aside to Ida.

No forced spirits now! The innocent fun—the converse of the social circle, after the little ones had gone—the walk home, beneath the tremulous stars—the "good night" and pressure, whose thrill lingered in her fingers 'till sleep sealed her eyes—all were sources of unutterable pleasure—pleasures born from one influence—flowing from one presence.

A month later, Josephine returned from an evening concert, with a violent toothache, the consequence of the sudden transition from the steaming hall to the ice-cold air without. She tossed and groaned in agony through the night; by morning the pain abated, a relief for which she was wickedly ungrateful, when she beheld reflected in the mirror, a tumefaction of the cheek, nearly closing one eye, and otherwise marring the symmetry of her features.

The pain came back at intervals during the day; and with fretfulness, threw her into a fever. Dr. Ballard was sent for. It was late in the evening when she awoke from the slumber, gained by the anodyne he administered. The rain was plashing against the window; there was no other sound except a subdued murmur of distant voices. There were visitors in the parlor—who had ventured through the storm? Her sharpened senses caught manly tones—tones she thought she recognised; and then Ida's rippling, joyous laugh smote her unwilling ear. The conversation became lower and more serious; and she could endure no more. Unmindful of health and prudence, she hurried on a dressing-gown, wrapped a shawl about her head, and glided down stairs, as stealthily as a cat. The front room only was warmed and lighted, but the folding-doors were ajar. Mr. Lacy stood by the mantel, hat in hand, yet in no hurry to depart. He was playing with a rosebud he had plucked from a vase near, but as unconscious of its beauty as of the lateness of the hour. The expression with which he regarded the earnest speaker before him was not to be mistaken. It even seemed that he would have it understood, for a proud smile trembled over his mouth, as her eye avoided his.

Josephine felt turned to stone. By a singular fatality, she had, up to this time, remained ignorant of the growing intimacy between these two. We have seen that many of their interviews were unknown to her, although some of them occurred in her very presence; and Ida, in obedience to Lynn's caution, had guarded against any appearance of rivalship. Now, jealousy and perception awoke together—at one sweeping glance backward, she saw herself slighted—foiled—duped! and she grew faint at the sight of the frightful results of her lack of vigilance, which rushed overwhelmingly upon her mind. Her native shrewdness soon came to her aid. Matters were not so desperate. There was no word of love;—she breathed more freely. "Not yet! not yet!" she hissed, under her breath;—and the small hands clenched in passionate resolve, as she added—"never!" The leave-taking was full of feeling, but friends parted as kindly. The outer door clanged to; and Ida sank into her chair. Buried in the cushions, she sat, looking into the blaze, a smile of ineffable tenderness illumining her face; her cheeks bright with unwonted scarlet. The patter of the rain upon the panes but lulled her into deeper reverie. And in contrast to a foreground so rich and warm, in its glowing colors and balmy air, and dreams of love and hope—was the dark, chill background, with its shape of evil, hideous in her distorted features and glowering hatred. Ida stooped suddenly. It was to pick up the bruised bud Morton had dropped. She looked around hurriedly, and with a more vivid blush, raised it to her lips, and hid it in her bosom.

"Rose-buds are not the only things which are played with for a time, then trampled under foot, as you shall learn ere long, my love-lorn damsel!" said the wily schemer, stealing back to her chamber.

"With us, now, it is war to the death!"

CHAPTER XV

Nothing appeared less likely, at this period, than the fulfilment of Lynn's prognostications of his destiny. He collected encouragement and praise at every turn. A Bayard in society—a Raphael at the easel, he bore a distinguished part in the lionization of the day. He sped well, too, in his wooing. A quick fancy and impressible heart could hardly resist the attractions of his person and genius; and the spice of coquetry, generally predominant in Ellen's disposition, lay dormant, as she hearkened to the voice of love. She made but one reservation in pledging him her troth—that their engagement should be secret. He would have had it proclaimed through the land—he so joyed in the bliss he had won; but he bowed to the scarcely uttered wish, respecting the maiden modesty that dictated the request. To Ida and Charley it was divulged. He would not accept a happiness they wore forbidden to share. For a few brief weeks this knew no shade or diminution; but a change came. Ida discovered it; but he was silent, and she would not extort confidence. It was a trial to see his clouded countenance and fitful spirits; yet she knew his peculiarly sensitive organization, and hoped the evil was magnified by its medium. In this hope she finally persuaded him to speak.

They met at a Fancy Fair. Ida was in an embowered recess, Mr. Lacy for a companion, and Charley hanging around to play propriety. Lynn entered alone, and did not attach himself to any person or party. He marched from end to end of the room, with folded arms, and a dogged look, too foreign to him, not to impress one unpleasantly. He perceived Ida after awhile, and acknowledged her presence by touching his hat, with no loss of gloominess. Ida was *distrait*; even Mr. Lacy failed to charm; and he was aware of it He guessed, too, from the direction of her eyes, the working of her thoughts, and proposed a visit to the refreshment table, which stood in the path of the promenaders. Lynn could not brush by without speaking. The first tone of Ida's voice affected him. The dull black of his eyes became lustrous, and the long lashes fell over them to conceal the momentary weakness. She would not let him go. She asked him questions without number or meaning, not waiting for answers, until she had eaten her ice; when she gave her glass to Mr. Lacy, and with an apology, his eye said was unnecessary, took Lynn's arm. He confessed all, as she had determined he should. It was a common tale; the scrupulousness of a love, made up of delicacy and truth, and the thoughtless trifling of a girl who felt her power;—so she explained it, but the young lover mourned the death of his first-born hope.

"I would as soon speak lightly of my dead sister, as tamper with *her* affection," said he. "Your excuse that she does these things to try mine—if you are right—proves that she never loved me."

"But why did I say she applied the test? In girlish caprice—foolish enough—but harmless as to intention. Have you forgotten what women are in their 'hour of ease?' if danger or sorrow menaced you, she would stand by you to the last. She loves you, Lynn,—I am assured of this."

"Not so am I. I called there this evening. She had promised to accompany me hither, but she was 'engaged with company!' Those addlepates, Pemberton and Talbot were there, doling out their senseless prattle; and she was gracious to them, repellant to me. If Pemberton were not a puppy, I would not sleep before I crossed swords with him. She waltzed with him last night. I had told her that I would not invite any lady, whom I respected, to engage in that most disgusting of dances. Conceive of my feelings, when, within the hour, I saw her whirling down the hall in his arms! And the coxcomb's insufferable impudence! if he thwarts me again, I will cane him!"

"You will *not*! Go and see Ellen to-morrow, when there is no one to annoy you, by preventing a private interview. Set before her the unkindness, the want of generosity apparent in her conduct; assert your rights with dignity, and your resolution to uphold them."

"I would not pain her, Ida. She has chosen the easiest method of undeceiving me; better this, than a life-time of misery to both. She said, the other day, to a gentle reproach for an open slight, which would have offended a vainer man, mortally, that she did it to mislead others. 'A young lady,' she remarked, 'sinks into a cypher, if it is suspected that she is betrothed. I have not had my lawful amount of admiration yet.'

"'Ellen!' said I, 'I have loved you as man never loved woman before; have believed you pure and high-minded. If I thought that the despicable coquetry you insinuate, caused you to insist upon the concealment of our engagement, I would trumpet it to the world, and then break it myself!'"

"Lynn, remember where you are! You are too harsh; it was a jest."

"The manner displeased me most, and to-night, when I saw those fops—could I be patient?" Their conversation and saunter were prolonged.

"Are you going home to-night?" asked Josephine, gaily, hailing them in one of their rounds. "They are extinguishing the lamps."

Ida changed color as she saw that she had Mr. Lacy's arm. Lynn observed it, and waited for her.

"You are fast walkers—go on," said Josephine, at the door. As they passed, Ida had a view of Mr. Lacy's features. They were so pale and rigid, that she started. He answered her look of apprehension with one that froze her blood.

What had she done to draw down that stern, yet sorrowful rebuke?

"The look you wear
A heart may heal or break."

Her pillow was damp that night.

Mr. Thornton had obtained a signal victory in his first important cause. Already, his legal acumen and oratorical powers marked him in the public eye for usefulness and fame; and on the evening after the delivery of the verdict, he called together a band of select spirits to rejoice with him. The banquet was well ordered; comprising the rarities of the season, and a variety of wines, varied by the introduction of agreeable non-intoxicants, coffee, tea, iced sherbet, etc. These unwonted accompaniments of a bachelor supper were looked upon with an evil eye by some of the guests. They were jealous of innovations which might end in puritanical abstinence; and their fears were further excited that three of their small number preferred the less stimulating beverages. That Mr. Lacy's example should be copied by Mr. Compton, a fellow-student, was not surprising, as they were intimate, and known as members of the same church; but at Charles Dana's rejection of the social glass, there was a hum of exclamations and inquiries, which was calmed by his imperturbability, and the polite tact of the host. Morton could not unriddle the conduct of his friend, for he knew that his most trivial action was not meaningless. "Not a convert, Charley?" he said, when the rest were in full cry after some inspiring subject.

"Unfortunately, no. It is from a motive of expediency that I abstain to-night."

They sat together, and as he spoke, Mr. Lacy chanced to remark Lynn, who was opposite. He drank deeply, but his potations had not had time to ignite the fire that burned in his eyes and checks. His talk was a volcanic eloquence, reckless as to course and consequence; and his laugh had the peal of a maniac's yell. In real alarm, Morton turned to his neighbor. Charley was on the alert; not outwardly—he might have been more grave and taciturn than common, but there were no evidences of anxiety. Morton divined his feelings, by a glance he saw exchanged between him and his heated friend; a look of warning and appeal on one side,—of anguish, scornful in its bitterness, on the other,—and the torrent rolled on as before.

During the giving of toasts, Mr. Lacy and Charley fell into a quiet chat, only pausing to lift their glasses in courtesy to the authors, ignorant, most of the time, of the sentiment proposed. Lynn was more sedate; from delirium he was relapsing into a comatose state, when he was brought to his feet by a toast to his art, coupled with a neatly turned compliment to himself, from Mr. Thornton. His unpremeditated reply was beautiful and touching. He was under the very spur of genius; rich metaphors, apt classical allusions, and delicate pathos poured from his lips, as thoughts from his brain; his rapt hearers scarcely conscious that he employed the machinery of words. The applause that succeeded the last musical echo was deafening. For a moment, the wild glare that had distressed Morton, disappeared, and with a happy, grateful smile, he bowed his thanks for this spontaneous tribute of approbation and regard.

"Egad!" said Pemberton, "you have mistaken your calling, Holmes—you had better burn up your canvass, and take to stump-speaking, you'd make more money by it."

Angry frowns and rebuking eyes were directed to the drunken speaker.

"If stumps and blockheads claim kindred, I shall not need to go far to exercise my vocation," said Lynn, hotly.

"Ha! ha!" laughed the other, with a violent affectation of derision.

"Don't be frightened, gentlemen! Mr. Holmes and myself have wrestled upon another battle-field, and I can afford to forgive him, from the soreness of his defeat. Your friend and instructress, that loud-tongued virago, Ida Ross, could not have uttered—"

Like a wounded panther, Lynn cleared the table at a bound, and grasped his throat. A general rush was made to the spot, and they were parted before either sustained serious injury. Pemberton had drawn a dirk at the attack, but it was wrested from him by Mr. Lacy. Reconciliation was impossible in the excited state of the combatants. Charley prudently withdrew his friend, relying upon time and reflection to prepare the mind of each for overtures and concessions. Lynn did not speak until they reached his room; then, extricating his arm from Charley's hold, he demanded in a high tone, what had been his object in terminating the conflict. "If not finished there, you know it must be somewhere."

"I do not see the necessity," was the reply. "It is a drunken broil, of which you will be ashamed to-morrow. No man in his senses would have noticed him as you did. He shall have a cow-hiding for his last speech; I would not disgrace a more honorable weapon by using it against him. I am mortified, Lynn—I hoped you were learning to control those childish fits of passion."

"Am I to be crossed and bullied forever by a meddling fool? Is it not enough that he has helped to wreck my peace, but he must taunt me with it?" cried Lynn passionately. "He ought not to live, and I do not care to!"

"You certainly are not fit to die." said Charley composedly, "or you would not rave so like a madman. Be sane for five minutes; by what means has your happiness been put in his power?"

Lynn was a humored, wayward child, and this cold severity did more to quiet him than an hour's rhetorical pleading. Charley listened with knitting brows, to a rehearsal of his story to Ida, and an account of that day's interview with Ellen. She was dressed for a ride with

Mr. Pemberton, and exasperated by this new example of her disrespect to him in encouraging a man he despised—Lynn had spoke hastily—angrily. She retorted with equal warmth, and after a turbulent scene they parted. Pemberton arrived as he was leaving, and his malicious twinkle told that he comprehended and enjoyed the state of affairs. Like Ida, Charley had never heartily approved of this match; but his indignation towards Ellen was none the less on this account. He saw, in her behaviour, the most culpable flirting, and he said so to Lynn. He shook his head sadly.

"Convince me of that and you destroy my faith in woman. No! I believe she once fancied she loved me; but I have become obnoxious to her. It is my fate. The last dream of hope is over—I have nothing to live for now."

He covered his face with his hands. Charley remained with him all night, an uninvited visitor. His host neglected him entirely, never speaking, and seemingly unmindful of his presence. Whenever Charley awoke, he heard him pacing the floor, or saw the outline of his figure, dark and still, at the window, gazing into the black night.

"You will not do anything in the settlement of this nonsensical matter until you confer with me?" requested Charley, on saying "Good bye."

"I shall not move in the affair," was the laconic rejoinder.

"You will acquaint me with Pemberton's proposals?"

"If I think proper—yes—you shall know in good time."

Charley was going out, and did not catch the exact import of these words. He proceeded with the business of the day, comparatively at ease. Knowing Pemberton to be an arrant coward at heart, bully as he was, he did not fear a renewal of the subject from him.

Ida was alone that evening. Mr. Read was in the country; and Josephine, having waited until visiting hours were over, went off to bed. Ida liked to sit up late, but she usually preferred the snug comfort of her room to the parlors. To-night she lingered over a book, reading and musing, with a tincture of gloom in her thought-pictures. She was pondering upon the instability of earthly plans and hopes. "How true that the brightest light produces the deepest shadows!" The words arose unexpectedly to her lips. In the loosely-linked chain of reverie, she did not know that they had their origin in the memory of a slighter circumstance than a word—in a look.

Rachel was coming to see after her, and hearing a ring as she tripped by the front door, opened it. A man handed her a package saying, briefly, "For Miss Ross," and instantly vanished. Ida saw Lynn's hand in the superscription of the bulky parcel, and broke the seal. Two letters were within it; one directed to Ellen Morris; the other,—enclosing a miniature—to herself.

"My best, truest friend!" she read, "I cannot trust myself to speak the farewell my heart indites to one who has been a loving and faithful sister to me. It would unman me, and I have occasion for all my manliness at this juncture. I have no regret in the prospect of leaving a world where my horoscope was cast in clouds and storm;—I cannot undergo the pangs of seeing your grief. Destiny will be accomplished, Ida, however insignificant the instrument with which it works. Charley will inform you of the baseness of that which has severed the one shining thread of my existence. Heaven grant you may never know the hatefulness of life, when that for which you thought, toiled, lived, is torn from you! I have struck the reptile who trailed over my Eden-flowers, and reared his head insultingly amid the ruin he helped to effect, and in his unspent malice he would sting me to death. The sting of death is gone! there will be unintentional mercy in the stroke that releases me. I have been mad—I am calmer now. If I know my own heart, I wish him no evil; I shall not attempt his life—I will not imbrue my hands in the blood of the murdered.

"You will give the enclosed to my poor Ellen—'*my Ellen*!' she has forbidden me to call her by that name. It may be, she will pity, when no more, the wretch she could not love when living.

"My sister and friend! what can I say to you? Forgive my ingratitude in being willing to die before I have made some feeble return for your goodness! Will you wear or keep this image of him, by whom you were never forgotten—not in the death-agony? I have written to Charley, but he will not receive the letter until all is over. I was unwilling to risk this—its contents are too sacred. You are dreaming in your innocent slumbers, of years of peace and joy—I shall not close my eyes but in the sleep that knows no awakening to care and woe. 'The blessing of him who is ready to perish' be upon you!

     "LYNN."

Ida's impulse was to scream for help; but ere her palsied tongue did her bidding, the futility of all attempts to save him stared upon her; the hour—nearly midnight; the illness of their man-servant; Mr. Read's absence; her ignorance of Lynn's locality or plans beyond his suicidal intention—towered, frowning spectres, mountain-high, each with its sepulchral "Impossible!" Some women would have swooned—some sunk down to weep in impotent despair;—the shock over, her energetic spirit rallied to meet the emergency. He should be saved! at the peril of her life, if need be—what were personal convenience and safety?

Charley—the sagacious, collected friend—what mortal could do, he would—she must see him. Rachel had not spoken, terrified by her mistress' expression and manner. It was a relief to aid her in any way; she brought, without a second's parley, the cloak and hood Ida ordered, and equipped herself to attend her. "Take the key," said Ida, as they went out of the door; and they sped on their way. The night was dark, and for whole squares not a light was visible. Half of the distance to Mr. Dana's was traversed without encountering a single being, when they approached a lighted doorway, in which two gentlemen were standing. Fearing to attract their attention by her hurried gait, Ida slackened her pace, and pulled her hood over her face. She heard one say—"If the spasms do not return he may not want watchers to-morrow night;" and a feeling of security stole upon her. The friends of the suffering would not molest her, whose mission was one of mercy. A few squares further on, they were met by a watchman. Rachel made out his badge of office through the obscurity, and pressed to her mistress' side. The man stopped. His keen eye discerned her color.

"Your pass!" said he, confronting Rachel.

"Her mistress is with her," answered Ida, emboldened by the exigency.

He bowed respectfully, and pursued his beat. Ida's heart throbbed loudly, but she stifled her fears by a reconsideration of Lynn's extremity of danger,—"it was no time for nervous failings." Rachel did not possess such a tonic, and had seen every shadow, heard every rustle of the breeze.

Before their adventure with the dreaded "guard," she had known that one of the gentlemen above-mentioned had taken the same route with themselves; keeping, however, upon the other side of the street; and after Ida's ready response removed her apprehension of "the cage" and Mayor's court, she saw him still upon her track—worse! crossing towards them. Overcome with terror, she clutched her mistress' arm, and by a frantic gesture, directed her to the object of alarm. He was within six feet of them; and startled by his proximity, and the fright of her attendant, she stood still. A minute of breathless suspense, and the stranger was at her side.

"Miss Ross," he said, in a low but confident tone. "This is a strange hour for a lady to be in the street with such attendance!"

His stern, cold address could not repress her thrilling pleasure.

"Oh, Mr. Lacy!" she exclaimed, clinging to his arm, and giving way, for the first time, to tears. "Life and death depend upon my action—the life of one very dear to us both—you would not reproach me if you knew—"

"Ida! *dear* Ida!" said he, mindful only of her sorrow. "Can there be reason for this excessive grief? Your fears have misled you. Of whom do you speak?"

She could not speak quite yet, but her sobs were subsiding under his soothing.

"Will you not trust yourself and our friend to me, Ida?"

She looked up. "Yes," she said, simply.

He put her hand within his arm. "First, tell me where you are going."

"To Mr. Dana's."

"For what purpose?"

"I have something to tell Charley."

"I will be the bearer of your message. Let me see you home;—you shall give it to me on the way."

She obeyed submissively as a child.

"Now!" said he, as they turned back.

"I had a note from Lynn to-night. It is worded so ambiguously,—contains so many allusions I do not understand, that I can glean but this—he has quarrelled, and been challenged;—they fight to-morrow, where or when I do not know, nor the name of his opponent. It is all a horrible mystery."

It was more clear to him. He related the incident of the altercation at supper, suppressing Pemberton's use of her name.

"Oh! can it be! he will not stoop so low! And he will die! he declares his solemn determination not to resist the attack. His life is thrown away!"

"Not if man can prevent it—I promise you this much. When did you get this letter?"

"Not an hour since."

"Why did you not send to Charley or me?"

"Mr. Read is away, and John sick."

"What is the tone of the note? revengeful?"

"Oh, no! he says expressly—'If I know my own heart, I wish him no evil.' He writes, weary of life, and relieved at the thought of getting rid of it."

"'Getting rid' of the life God has bestowed!" repeated he, indignantly. "Forgive me, Ida! yet *you* cannot tolerate this sentiment! Does he believe in an hereafter? Does he allude to it?"

"No—but he does believe—I have thought, sometimes, with more than the intellect. Do not judge him hardly;—he has suffered much of late; more from morbid sensibility than actual troubles, but he imagined his woes too heavy to be borne. He is not fit to cope with sorrow."

"None of us are, 'till we have been taught the uses of affliction. This recklessness is, you think, more an impulse than a purpose?"

"I am sure of it."

"He will be more manageable then," he replied encouragingly.

The wind blew roughly, and he folded her cloak around her.

"I recognised you by this, and your walk, and fearing lest you might encounter rudeness in your nocturnal ramble, kept you in sight. I heard your voice at the watchman's challenge, and concluded to declare myself your protector. I have been sitting with a sick friend."

Ida did not know herself when they stopped at the door—her uneasiness all gone, and with it the unnatural strength that impelled her venturesome step—he had assumed the burden; and he was so strong and sanguine, it did not oppress him. With the mild authority which had checked her tears and reversed her design, he bade her "dismiss anxiety, and rest quietly until morning, when he would send her glad tidings." And with the same childlike docility she repaired to her chamber, and betook herself to slumber.

CHAPTER XVI

In the bosom of the forest, the tall oaks girdling it, like a band of mailed warriors, changed by the spell of beauty from assailants to a guard, lay a little glade, free from brush or sapling; its tender green carpet freshening in the March sun. The trees loved the dance of the shadows over that sylvan ball-room, and they revelled there all the day, and at evening, slept upon the turf in the moonlight. The clouds of the night had rolled away before a westerly breeze, and the forest was full of sweet and pleasant sounds. The oriole had come in advance of the season to look for his last year's nest; the woodpecker thrummed upon a hollow trunk; and the robins, too busy for more than an occasional note, flew about with sticks and mud in their bills. The teeming earth was quick with vitality; you could hear the unfurling of the grass-blades, the rustle of the leaf-buds as they broke ground.

An inharmonious sound interrupted the concert—the rattle of a carriage. It stopped; then another drove up; and six gentlemen, three from either side, entered the glade, saluting each other as they advanced. Lynn's friends were Mr. Thornton and Mr. Villet; Pemberton's Talbot and another of "the set," by the name of Watson. Without wasting time in irrelevant chat, the seconds walked apart for consultation. Pemberton, with a braggadocio air, offered his cigar-case to his companion; and nothing abashed by his dignified gesture of refusal, planted himself against a tree, and began to smoke. Lynn paced the little area in silence. He was haggard to ghastliness; the effect of a night of sleeplessness and racking thought. He was brave; his nerves did not tremble in the hour of peril; but the soul, forced, before its time, upon the verge of an unknown sea, shook with a nameless dread of the punishment of its temerity. Early teachings, and the convictions of later years weighed upon him. A tiny wild flower blossomed by his foot—he plucked it, and pressed its petals open with his finger. Whose hand had fashioned it? Whose sun kissed it into bloom? Whose goodness granted it this lovely home? It owed its little life to the Father, from whom he had derived his poet-soul; it had fulfilled the end of its creation;—he was about to hurl his gifts, a million times more precious, into the face of the Giver. He would gladly have courted other thoughts, but these would come; and long-forgotten texts floated before him; apparently without a cause to call them forth. One met him, wherever he looked—"Despisest thou the riches of his forbearance, and love and long-suffering?" And as he repeated, "despisest thou"—another—"Behold, ye despisers, and wonder and perish!" These words were upon his tongue, as Mr. Villet put the pistol into his hand, and motioned him into his place.

Pemberton had sent the challenge, with no thought of its being accepted, counting upon the interference of Lynn's friends. Mr. Thornton had waited upon him with his principal's answer, settling time, place and weapons; driving him into a corner, from whence he could only escape by following out his own proposition. A strained sense of honour was Lynn's birth-right. His father had died upon the field; and repudiation of the duellist's code involved censure of him. Thus they stood, face to face, upon this unclouded, fragrant spring morning, to wash out in blood the memory of a trifle which would have perished of itself in this time, but for the pains they had taken to perpetuate it. Oh, Virginia! most fondly loved of mothers! how often has thy soil drank the blood of sons, the tears of daughters, whose lives and weal have been sacrificed to this pitiless Moloch!

Mr. Talbot explained that the signal was to be the dropping of a handkerchief, after he should have counted three slowly. Mr. Villet held the handkerchief "One—two—" said Talbot, deliberately. Lynn had only time to see the murder in his antagonist's eye, when a report rang through the forest, and he felt a sharp pain in his breast and arm.

"Treachery!" shouted Thornton, excitedly. "Shoot him down, Holmes! he deserves a dog's death!"

Lynn's hot blood was up—he raised his arm. The loaded and discharged pistols were whirling in the air—and Charley Dana and Morton Lacy threw themselves between the combatants.

"At whose instance was this meeting brought about, gentlemen?" questioned the former, peremptorily, scanning the group.

"The challenge came from my principal," answered Watson, with a brazen look.

"Will you honour me by a minute's private conversation, sir?" asked Charley, facing Pemberton, with a sneer seen by him alone. "You need not be afraid," he pursued, not receiving an immediate reply, "*I* do not carry concealed weapons."

Pemberton went aside with him very reluctantly. He respected, because he feared Charley. Without a correct understanding of his character, he stood in awe of the keen ridicule and calm courage, for which his blustering was no match.

"You must be at a loss for something to do, that you covet such business as this;" began Charley. "I have no objection to your blowing your brains out—and any coroner in the country would decide that an inquest would be 'much-ado about nothing;' but it is another matter when you try, in cold blood, to take the life of one, who has some pretensions to the name of man. You are a cowardly poltroon! If you are on the look-out for insults, there is one, if truth can insult. Two policemen are at a little distance. The law will have a more serious job than I anticipated. There are five witnesses to the fact, that you fired in advance of the time. Join this to your provocation of the other night, and your having sent the challenge; and it will not require a Philadelphia lawyer to make out a case, which will put a stop to your murderous propensities for awhile. Now, sir, what do you propose to do?"

The bully shook visibly. "Really, Mr. Dana, this is an extraordinary procedure. You and I have no quarrel."

"I beg your pardon—men of honour do not pass over such remarks as I have indulged in. You did not hear me, perhaps; I said, and say now, you are a pitiful poltroon! shaking in your shoes, this minute, at the prospect of the penitentiary, and the loss of your soap-locks. But before I give you into the keeping of your lawful guardians, I have a proposal to make on my own account. I came here with the intention of giving you a castigation for your impertinent mention of a lady. I will not fight a duel with you, but if you resist, I will take care you do not shoot *me*. I meant to horse-whip you, and I will—within an inch of your life, if you do not make an ample apology. You cannot bully or blarney me, Pemberton. We know each other."

In abject terms, he declared that he had the highest veneration for Mr. Dana's friend, Miss Ross; he was in wine at the time spoken of, and was unaware, until told of it, that he had mentioned her—

"That will do!" interposed Charley. "Are you ready to rejoin your friends?"

"You will not do me this great injury, Mr. Dana! think of the exposure—the disgrace! A duel is an honourable affair, if carried out; but when it takes a turn like this, you will admit it looks confoundedly mean."

Charley could not but smile at his ludicrously pathetic tone.

"Will you bind yourself to behave better to your superiors—Mr. Holmes included—if I help you out of the scrape?"

The pledge was eagerly given.

"Your best plan will be to state to the company that, in consequence of explanations made by me, you retract the challenge, and likewise the offensive remark that provoked Mr. Holmes to assault you. Offer your hand to him, with the best grace you can muster; jump into your carriage—and you shall not be pursued."

The seconds were huddled together, talking of the novel phase of the affair; Lynn and Morton walking to and fro; the latter speaking earnestly, while Lynn's averted face showed he was not unmoved. Pemberton obeyed instructions to the letter; and with a trepidation and hurry which nearly betrayed Charley into a disgrace of the dignity of the occasion. After a grasp at Lynn's hand, he bowed hastily, summoned his attendants, and disappeared among the trees. The crack of the driver's whip proclaimed his departure. Thornton and Villet were profuse in their inquiries, but they were little wiser for Charley's replies. An exclamation from Morton interrupted them.

"You are wounded!" said he, pointing to Lynn's arm, from which the blood was oozing.

"Only a scratch," replied he.

Charley ripped up his sleeve; uncovering a flesh wound of no great depth. The ball had passed between his side and arm, grazing both;—its aim was the heart.

"If I had seen this sooner!" said Charley, involuntarily.

"What if you had?" inquired Lynn.

He made no reply, but proceeded to bind up the wound. "Gentlemen!" said he, when he had done;—"your carriage and breakfast are waiting. I take it, you have nothing more on hand this morning."

Thornton and Villet bowed, half-offended; Lynn lingered. "How are you going back?" he asked of Morton, but looking at Charley.

"Our horses are not far off," answered the former, kindly. "We will see you again in an hour or two."

"Coming!" responded Lynn, to his friends' impatient call. He looked again to Charley's grave face, beseechingly and timidly; but could not summon courage to break the silence.

"Do not punish him too severely, Charley," said Morton. He turned from him without speaking. He had never seen him so affected before. They were alone in the glade; and the birds, silenced for a time by human voices, were heard again twittering in the boughs. Charley spoke at length.

"I have been deceived, Lacy. I thought I knew men, and was prepared for any inconsistency; but if I had been told that the man, cherished for years as a brother, would mislead me purposely in a matter of vital importance to us both, I would not have credited it. I had his promise, or what amounted to a promise, that he would not stir without consulting me. What weakness!" he continued, more agitated, "to abandon fame and friends and life, because of a fancied slight from a woman!"

"Yet are we guiltless of similar failings?" said Morton, impressively. "Have there not been times when we too were impatient—despairing—for no more weighty cause? My dear Charley, let us judge leniently errors into which we might have fallen, but for greater strength or less powerful temptation. Disapproval and forgiveness are not incompatible."

"You have witnessed the one—will you be the bearer of the other!" asked Charley, trying to smile. "I will not oblige him to ask it. He has had humiliation enough for one day."

Mr. Lacy's first care, upon their return to the city, was to dispatch a note to Ida. It merely announced the success of their expedition; the means adopted to secure it, she gathered from Charley. They had gone together, first to Lynn's then to Pemberton's lodgings, when Charley had been informed of the projected meeting. They were reported "not at home." They then hit upon the unpromising expedient of going to every hackstand in the city, to ascertain, if possible, at what time the party was to start in the morning, and its route. They failed, in two or three cases to arouse the keepers; and from others received unimportant and early replies. Charley had just asked, "Do you mean to give it up?" and been answered by a firm "Never!" when a negro bustled by them. Morton seized him by the shoulder, and led him to an apothecary's lamp.

"I thought so!"

"I've got a pass. Let me go!" said the fellow, struggling.

"Not until I know where you have been. You are Mr. Talbot's servant—you may gain something, and shall not lose, by answering me civilly. What were you sent for!"

By smooth and harsh words, he was brought to acknowledge that his "young master" having had company all the evening, had forgotten, until late, to send him to a livery-stable to engage a carriage for five o'clock next morning.

"Who is with him, besides Mr. Pemberton?" inquired Mr. Lacy.

"Mr. Watson, sir."

"How far are they to go, after crossing the river?"

"Lor! Massa! how you reckon I know?"

"No trifling, sir! If I wanted to create mischief, you have said enough. Tell me everything, or I will go at once to your master!"

The man instantly named their destination, which his master had let slip in his hearing; and added that they were "fixing pistols." The information was corroborated by a call upon the liveryman, and they acted upon it. The delay, which was so near being fatal, arose from their ignorance of a newer and shorter road than they chose.

"How Lacy guessed their intentions, I cannot imagine," said Charley. "He would not entrust to me the name of his informant; and Lynn is as much in the dark. He brought your letter to the door after he was sure you had retired and mine was left upon his desk. But Lacy is discreet from principle, not from caprice."

"He is," said Ida with heightened color. "If any stigma attaches to the informer, it must rest upon me."

"Just like him, noble-hearted and faithful!" exclaimed Charley, when her story was ended. "Shall you tell Lynn?"

"Yes—if only to show him how his friends love him. He may view it as a breach of confidence, but I had rather he should reproach me, than suspect the innocent."

Whether he reproached her or not, the revelation did not diminish his regard for her. Except at their first agitating interview, he never adverted to the unfinished duel; but he seemed drawn to her by a new tie, in the recollection of her readiness to adventure so much in his behalf. Ellen Morris had left town for a visit to Petersburg, the day after the rupture:—left without a message or line of penitence or conciliation. Lynn did not complain, but his moodiness subsided into a pensiveness, illumined by the flashes of his former animation, like the sparkle of smouldering embers.

It was during one of these gleams that he spent the evening at the rendezvous of what Josephine styled the "Dana clique." John Dana and his amiable wife were great favorites of his and Mr. Lacy's. Their friendly calls may have been more frequent because it was Ida's chief visiting place. Mr. Dana was in New York, and she had dined and taken tea with her friend.

Lynn came in with Charley, and the latter, excusing himself for an hour after supper, left Ida and the young artist together.

"I have been thinking lately, how sublime a thing is philanthropy," said Lynn, throwing himself with boyish abandon, upon the rug at her feet. "I welcome this train of thought as a sign, that I am growing less selfish, for I have been sadly, sinfully selfish, Ida—madly intent upon my schemes, my happiness—forgetting that God placed me in the world to benefit others. Lacy was in my studio to-day, and we had a talk upon this subject. He says there is always a reflex tide of the happiness we send forth to those around us; a purer, truer joy than self-gratification. 'In this respect,' he observed, 'we can best imitate the example of our Supreme Benefactor.' Imitate our Creator, Ida! that is something worth living for."

"You have much besides, to make life precious, Lynn. I remember when it seemed worthless to me; when I thought I had tasted all the sweetness it possessed—I have changed my opinion since."

"Ah! but you have never bowed soul and spirit to an idol, and 'found it clay;' never realised in the dread hour that saw its demolition, that the fairest growth of heart and mind—the plants which you flattered yourself were climbing heavenward, had only twined themselves with strengthening tendrils about the altar of that one love! I know the meaning of the expression, 'broken cisterns, which can hold no water.' I have felt for some time past as if my heart were a stagnant marsh, flooded by wasted affections. To-day I have been happier, more hopeful. I will begin life anew, and strive for my art and for my kind."

"I have often told you that you have rare qualifications for usefulness," rejoined Ida. "Your besetting fault is unsteadiness of purpose; the best resolutions avail nothing if they are not adhered to."

"I know it. I dare not say now, that I will keep my present frame of mind until to-morrow; but I do feel as if a broad field were spread before me, and a bright, bright heaven over-arched it. I can think and speak of Ellen; I comfort myself by imagining that our separation is for our mutual good—our characters required discipline, and dimly in the future I see visions of reconciliation and re-union." Poor boy! the idol was not gone yet! He sat in an attitude of careless grace, his hand supporting his cheek, and the light falling upon his upturned face. "Yes," he continued, thoughtfully. "I am convinced that my life has been spared for some important end, and I will work it out, whenever Providence designates the ways and means of its accomplishment. I do not overlaud my ability; for youth, and health, and energy, are almost omnipotent, and I am young, and strong, and willing."

"You will not be offended if I aid you in the work?" asked Ida.

"No; and I anticipate your warning. You would say that self-conquest lies at the base of all other victories. Ah! you will yet be ashamed of your incredulity as to my regeneration. That is Charley's voice, he has brought Lacy, too! I am glad!"

Ida was more than glad. She had seen him since their midnight walk, but Josephine's presence had debarred her from even a look of acknowledgment.

Mrs. Dana came down stairs, and completed the fireside group.

"What have you two been prosing about?" asked Charley, presently.

"I have been talking—Miss Ida listening," said Lynn. "She has no faith in my determination to play 'good boy,' and as she knows me better than I do myself, I am uneasy for the durability of my excellent resolve. Do say something encouraging, Lacy."

"What is this reformation? of mind or manner?" inquired Morton.

"Mind, manner, heart and will. I have been a wilful troublesome child all my life; I mean, from this time forward, to be a *man*."

"And how are you setting about it?"

"Oh! I am theorising now. I have no distinct object, except to do the best I can; to mortify evil passions, to uproot selfish desires, to foster the germs of good in myself and others."

Mr. Lacy smiled, a little sadly. "You have undertaken a Sisyphus task, if you heave the stone up the hill in your own strength."

Lynn looked dismayed. "Yet it is our duty to do all this. The Scriptures, for whose infallibility you contend, set a higher standard of faith and practice than I have done."

"But they tell as in so many words, 'Ye can of yourselves do nothing.' Who can say, 'I have made my heart clean—I am pure from my sin?'"

"You do not agree with the fanatics who denounce morality, I hope," said Charley. "I heard one hold forth last Sabbath. He told us 'our righteousness was as filthy rags.' I had read my Bible, and knew that; but he heated Gehenna seven times hotter for 'ye miserable moralists' than for the vilest outcast that ever dishonored the image in which he was made. I make no pretensions to piety, but I endeavour to do my duty to my fellow-men; to hate none, and help all. I go to church because I think it right, if only for the example I set to others; I don't expect my good works to be a passport to heaven; but I thought, as I listened to him, that his orthodoxy and zeal, without charity, would profit him nothing."

"You were probably nearer right than he;" said Mr. Lacy. I do not decry morality. Reason teaches us that the benevolent citizen, the honest tradesman, the kind parent and husband, find more favour in the eyes of a righteous judge than the rioter, the cheat, the debauchee and tyrant. Much injury is done to religion by the mistaken zeal of its advocates. This was not the spirit of its Founder. To me, the history of the young ruler, who came to Christ, is one of the most affecting in the New Testament. He was not driven away by disheartening rebukes; but 'Jesus, looking on him, *loved* him.' How tenderly must he have uttered—'But one thing thou lackest!'"

"But how unnatural is the finale!" said Lynn. "'And he went away sorrowful, for he had great possessions.' He let his lucre outweigh his soul!"

"Take care how you condemn!" said Charley. "There are 'possessions' besides silver and gold, which clog a man's steps. Love of pleasure has ruined more souls than love of gain."

"And procrastination more than both together;" added Morton.

Ida looked at Charley. "Do you remember our conversation after the protracted meeting, last summer?" asked she. "I felt, when you spoke of Death and Eternity, that I could never close my eyes again in peace; but the impression wore off; and we are here, to-night, it may be, no better prepared for our inevitable change than we were then."

"Yet we are content to hunt for the motives of this inconsistency of belief and action, instead of rectifying it!" said Mr. Lacy, seriously.

"You predestinarians may excuse us upon the ground that we are waiting the 'set time;'" remarked Charley.

"God's time is '*now*;'" answered his friend. "'To-morrow' comes with a note of warning—'Boast not thyself of to-morrow;' 'To-day is—to-morrow is cast into the oven.'"

"You have battered my scaffolding, and not provided me with another;" cried Lynn. "You say I am helpless, yet cry, 'the night cometh!'"

Mr. Lacy took a Bible from the table, and handing it to Ida, requested her to read aloud the passages he pointed out.

"'Then said they unto him; What shall we do that we might work the works of God? Jesus answered, and said unto them: this is the work of God that ye believe on him whom he hath sent;' and 'Knowing that a man is not justified by the works of the law, but by the faith of Jesus Christ, even we have believed in Jesus Christ, that we might be justified by the faith of Christ, and not by the works of the law.'"

"Thank you," said Lynn. "Then I am to do nothing?"

"Nothing as yet, but believe and trust. Having enlisted in the service, you will not be left idle. But I am overstaying my time; I engaged to meet a friend at half-past nine, and it is nearly ten. I had rather stay here, but good night, nevertheless."

"And I have not thanked him!" thought Ida, disappointed—but—

"Miss Ida!" called Charley, from the porch. "Come, see this cloud!"

A pile of snow-clouds was heaving up towards the moon, which fringed their jagged outlines with silver, unearthly bright from the blackness below.

"You would say, 'gloomily beautiful;'" said Mr. Lacy.

He was close beside her, and approachable as ever; and Charley held Mrs. Dana and Lynn in conversation. In one sentence, she expressed her sense of obligation, and her regret that he had had so much trouble in executing her commission. His face was in the shade, but she *felt* his look.

"Nothing is a trouble to me, that promotes your happiness."

She went back to the parlor, with a tumultuous joy at heart. The full significance of his words she did not understand till long afterwards.

"Mr. Lacy should study for the ministry;" said Mrs. Dana.

"He does more good as he is;" replied Charley, stoutly. "If all Christians performed their duty as well, you and I would live to see the Millennium. He can reach men, who would fly at the glimpse of a white cravat. There is some charm about the man; his religion is a part of himself; and he carries it everywhere he goes. I have seen the wildest fellows I know, cluster around him, and introduce the subject, for the pleasure of hearing him talk. He knows when to begin, and when to leave off. He says plain things to me; I might knock down another man who took the liberty; I thank him, and am sincere in so doing."

"I love to listen to him; but he makes me very uncomfortable;" said Mrs. Dana.

"It is so with me;" responded Lynn. "Our conferences always leave me out of humour with myself, and envious of him."

"I think the secret of his influence lies in his humility and charity;" remarked Ida; "in his not holding himself so far above us 'deluded worldlings,' as certain of his brethren. He believes there is good in all; not that he is all-good."

"These all-good people are too apt to slam the door of Heaven, as soon as they are on the safe side, themselves;" answered Charley. "Lacy would be willing to see the whole human race saved."

"Who would not?" laughed Ida.

"'Who would not!' why, I honestly thought, before I knew him, that many professors of religion,—those of his denomination, especially—would be sorely chagrined at an event so opposite to their calculations."

"I wish I were as certainly 'predestinated' as he is;" said Lynn, with a smile and a sigh.

"I cannot quite subscribe to your 'election' principles; but if I were altogether such an one as he seems to be, I should consider my chance pretty safe;" returned Charley.

"You are not going, Ida!" remonstrated Mrs. Dana. "Stay all night with me."

"I cannot. We shall have a snow storm to-morrow, and I might be detained several days."

"No great harm if you are!" said Charley.

"Not if I have duties which call me home? I will come again shortly, but I must go now."

Charley, as host pro tempore, got his hat; and Lynn followed them into the street, with, "I hope I don't intrude!" The tempest was near at hand; the gust that buffeted them at the corners made them stagger. Lynn forced Ida to take his arm also, and in this style they breasted the storm, gaily. Ida looked out after them, before she closed the door. They hurried along, arm in arm, their merry voices borne back to her by the wind, after the darkness swallowed up their forms.

The snow fell steadily all the next day, and the next.

Josephine was "blue;" her name for ill-humor—"bad weather always made her blue," Mr. Read had a twinge of the rheumatism, and was amiable accordingly. Ida wrote a long letter to Carry; read Charley's last budget of books; and watched the snow-flakes; enjoying the perfect quiet, and freedom from interruption. Upon each evening, she sat by her window, until she could not distinguish the boundary between the leaden sky and the white earth; and the snow, she had been brushing off all day, banked up against the glass. "Heigho! we dreamers have some pleasures more sensible people know nothing about;" said she, as the tea-bell sounded the second night. "It will seem so dark and dreary below after the society that has cheered my sanctum!"

The ice was breaking up below, in a hail-storm, which had all the sharpness of a conjugal "difference," without the stinging politeness genteel people throw into their wrangles. Ida listened and sickened and sighed. A pealing ring checked the disputants. Ida's heart fluttered, and Josephine looked up anxiously at the footman's entrance.

"Mr. Dana, to see Miss Ross."

"Of course then, I shall not go out;" said Josephine, haughtily.

Ida ran into the drawing-room. "Oh! I am so glad to see you!"—but his look stopped her short. "You have bad news! Carry!" she articulated, sinking into a chair.

"No: Carry and Jenny are well; but I am come for you. Our poor friend Lynn, is very ill."

"Ill!" said she, incredulously.

His lips quivered. "VERY ill!"

"Lynn! brother!" A mist fell over her sight—then cleared, as one long choking sob relieved her burdened breast. Charley raised her.

"There is no time to lose."

"I am ready."

Mr. Read and Josephine came into the hall at the bustle.

"Miss Ross! may I presume to ask whither you are going, on such a night?"

"To see a sick friend, sir!" returned Charley, as dictatorially.

"Whom sir, and where?"

"*My* friend, and she is under *my* protection;" said he, impatient at the detention. A carriage was waiting. Ida asked one question—"When was he attacked?"

"Within three hours after we parted from you. He stayed with me at John's that night; complained before retiring, of thirst and chilliness; and awoke with a raging fever. The doctors pronounce the disease inflammation of the lungs, of the most virulent nature. He had a lucid interval this evening, and asked for you."

She did not say, "Is there hope?" She knew there was none.

Charley exchanged a word with the servant who opened the door, and led the way directly to the sick-chamber. Mrs. Dana met her with a tearful embrace; she saw no one else, but the figure upon the bed. But for the dark circles about the eyes and mouth, the unmistakeable signet of Death, he might have seemed in perfect health. He appeared to be asleep, until she stood at his pillow; then opened his eyes upon her horror-stricken face, and made an effort to smile.

"Ida!"

"*Dear* Lynn!"

His breath was short "I am almost gone. Give my farewell to Ellen,—I forgave and loved her to the last. Bury her miniature with me. I have done with earth."

He closed his eyes. They brought a cordial. His wistful glance ran around the room, and returned to her.

"What is it, dear Lynn?"

Oh! the mournful intensity of that look! and the clammy fingers clasped hers. "*I did not think I should die so soon!* Is Lacy here?"

He came forward at her sign.

"I am dying—I have not time to search for myself—see if there is any promise for me!"

"Him that cometh unto me, I will in no wise cast out;'" repeated Mr. Lacy, instantly. "'He is able also, to save unto the uttermost all them, who come unto God by Him,—seeing He ever liveth to make intercession for them.'"

The fading eyes were re-lit with eagerness.

"Is *that* there? did He say so, or did you?"

"He said it, who declares, moreover, that He is not willing for 'any to perish but that all should turn and live.'"

His dying gaze was upward, and his lips moved in prayer.

"To the uttermost—the uttermost!" he whispered. "'Lord! remember—me,—when Thou comest—into—Thy—'"

He sank into a stupor; and the physician administered another stimulant. He had besought them not to permit him to sleep while reason lasted. One and another had come in, on hearing of his danger, and the room was nearly filled; but there was not a word or loud breath, to distract the meditations of the parting soul.

Charley and Mrs. Dana were nearest him on one side, Ida and Mr. Lacy, on the other. He looked at them fondly.

"Friends! *dear* friends! 'There is a friend—'" to Lacy.

He finished the sentence—"That sticketh closer than a brother."

"Yes:—I remember—who is able to save—to—the—utter most—" his voice died away. When next his eyes moved, it was slowly and painfully; but their restless light was not extinct. The stiffening mouth contracted.

"He says 'Pray!'" said Ida to Morton.

Every head was bowed; and the opening sentence of the prayer brought a deeper quiet to every heart.

"'Lord! Thou hast been our dwelling-place in all generations!'"

The language was simple, scriptural and fervent,—the pleading of a son, in behalf of a brother, with an indulgent Parent. As he repeated the text, Lynn had dwelt upon, Ida felt the feeble pressure of his hand;—he was alive and conscious then. The rest arose at the "Amen." She had not knelt; but she did not raise her head from the pillow;—her soul had caught the farewell of his, as it flew away upon its long journey! There was a movement through the room—a breathless pause—a solemn voice said "He is gone!" and tears and sobbings broke forth.

His hand still held hers; and the other was folded over them in supplication;—the eyes still looked heavenward—but they were fixed.

Dead! dead! in his glorious beauty—in the flush of youth! deaf to the recall of mourning hearts—and the awakening echoes of the fame his genius had won! If *he* could die, who was sure of an hour of life.

CHAPTER XVII

Ellen Morris accepted an invitation to Petersburg, ere the angry pique, aroused by Lynn's reproaches, passed off. The promise was hardly given, when she would have revoked it, had not pride held her to her word. Her friends were solicitous, that the far-famed hospitality of their city should not seem to the Richmond beauty, to have been vaunted too highly; and she appreciated their efforts; but the fortnight she had named as the period of her stay, crept slowly by. She hoped confidently to see her lover again at her feet, when the heat of passion was over; yet she was wretched in the recollection of her trifling, and the misery it had inflicted upon his high-toned spirit. Twice she prepared to write to him, and end a suspense torturing to both,—and twice dashed down the pen in shame and pride. The wished-for hour of departure arrived. The morning was bleak; the snow had ceased falling, but the clouds were low and threatening. Her entertainers begged her to wait but a day longer.

"If it were a matter of life and death, you could not be more obstinate," said her hostess, fretted at her unreasonableness.

"And how do you know that it is not?" answered she, jestingly.

"It is no joking matter, Miss Ellen," said a young man, gravely. "They have not cleared the snow from the track as it ought to be done. You would feel badly to have your neck broken."

"That is a trifle compared with a broken heart;" and she laughed lightly.

The train started, and the shivering passengers resigned themselves to a comfortless ride. Ellen's escort, an elderly gentleman, lost no time in settling his chin and ears down in the collar of his great coat, and the rest of his body in a corner, to sleep. She was wide-awake; and her spirits, raised by the near prospect of the meeting, her hopes had fed upon, for weary days and nights, found amusement in the uncouth figures, seen by the struggling light. She did not suffer from the cold or damp; her pulses bounded warmly; and when tired of being a solitary looker-on, she closed her eyes, and beguiled the time by fancies of home and *him*; whether he too were repentant; if he did not show it, rather than lose him, she could humble herself to lure him back;—she could not be happy without the assurance of his love. She would tell him how miserable their parting had made her; and imagination revelled in the anticipation of the refreshing flood, her thirsting heart would receive in return. There were pictures of days, which should fleet by like a dream;—when doubts and fears should be lost in perfect beatitude; the dingy, smoky cars were metamorphosed into their cottage home, with its music and flowers and birds, and its atmosphere of love;—and the votaries of his divine art thronged to offer incense to him—her peerless one!

The halting of the laboring engine startled her. The drowsy travellers gathered themselves up; and elbowing and grumbling, rushed out. She lifted the window. They were at the Depot. Half-frozen officials stamped their toes and blew their fingers; hackmen swore at their horses and the porters;—now and then, a pair of watery eyes peered into the cars, in quest of some expected one; but the form she looked for was not there. "Pshaw! how could he know when she was coming? how silly not to recollect this!"

"There is no one here to meet you, Miss Ellen," said her companion, re-entering.

"I hardly expected it, sir; if you will be so kind as to get a carriage for me, I will not trouble you further."

Her smile thawed the old man's churlishness. He volunteered, his foot upon the step "to see her all the way home;" but she would not consent.

"I am not afraid; this kind 'uncle' will carry me safely."

The driver scraped and grinned, although his woolly whiskers were hoary with rime. "Pity *all* women can't be agreeable!" said the escort, trudging through the drifts, to his hack. That a gentleman of his temperament was ever otherwise, even on a raw morning, did not occur to him.

An omnibus blocked up the street;—Ellen's carriage was behind it, and the driver's objurgative eloquence retarded, instead of quickening the movements of its proprietor, who was stowing away baggage upon the roof.

"Hallo!" cried a young man, to another, who was knocking the snow from his boots against the curb-stone. "When did you get in?"

"Just now. Horrid weather for March!—isn't it? Any news going?"

"Not a bit—all frozen up—ah! yes! Lynn Holmes is dead."

"What! not the artist! when did it happen? I saw him on the street a week ago—another duel?"

"No—lung fever. He died night before last, after forty-eight hours' illness."

"Shocking!"

"Ellen! you are white as a sheet!" was Mrs. Morris' greeting. "My dear child—are you sick?"

"No ma'am—only cold—oh! *so* cold!"

"Come to the fire."

"I think I will lie down awhile—I am chilled to the heart!"

The servant, who carried her breakfast, reported her asleep, and the careful mother would not let them waken her. Later in the day, she took a cup of hot coffee up to her. She was motionless; her head covered.

"My daughter!" said Mrs. Morris, softly, drawing down the coverlet.

She looked at her, but did not speak.

"How do you feel now?"

"I don't know, ma'am."

"You are not quite awake yet, I believe," said her mother, smiling. "Here, drink this—it will do you good."

She took it.

"By the way, my dear," continued Mrs Morris, busying herself with the folds of a curtain, which did not hang to suit her. "I have melancholy news for you. Our friend, Mr. Holmes, died suddenly, night before last. I never was more astonished and grieved in my life. He was such a handsome, promising young man, and so attached to us! I said directly how sorry you would be to hear it. You were so much together—where are the pins? oh! here they are! His disease was a rapid inflammation of the lungs. The funeral will take place at the church this afternoon;—some of us must go, if the weather *is* bad. Do you think you will be well enough?"

"Yes ma'am."

"Well—I hope so; and now I will go down and keep the children still, so that you can sleep."

The thunder of a thousand cannon would not have disturbed her. She heard and saw all that passed; but in place of heart and sense, was a dead vacuity, empty and soundless, although it had engulphed thought and feeling. She went to the funeral. Prudent, appearance-loving Mrs. Morris, dexterously flung a veil before the stony eyes, whose tearlessness people might observe, and wonder aloud, as she did mentally, at "Ellen's want of feeling;" but her daughter quietly raised it. The church was crowded. The untimely end of one so gifted and popular, thrilled the community, as the breast of one man. All was as still as the grave; the roar of the busy city-life deadened by the heavy atmosphere and cushioned earth. The wail of a clarion stirred the air;—nearer and nearer it sounded; and the plaintive breathing of other instruments; and at long intervals, a single roll of the drum;—nearer and nearer—they ceased, and the procession moved up the aisle. First walked Charles Dana and his sister-in-law, clad in deep mourning as for a brother; then Morton Lacy, pale and sorrowful, and on his arm another black-robed figure, (such privilege had Friendship above Love!) then a small band of fellow-artists; and the coffin! borne and followed by the Masonic fraternity, of which he was a member. It was set down in front of the pulpit; "the Book," with its drapery of black crape, laid reverently upon it; and the service proceeded. There were prayers and hymns and a sermon; she heard none;—the coffin lay in her sight—*his* coffin! It was *not!* Where then was the vigorous life which moved the still form within it?

where the soul of splendid imaginings and lofty aspirations? where the heart, with its wealth of feeling? they could not die! He lived still—and living, loved her. That narrow coffin was a horrible mockery. And so, when the cover was removed, and those, who from curiosity or affection, desired to look for the last time upon his face, filed slowly by it, she arose too. He was there! royally beautiful, even in his prison-house; the rich black locks swept back from the marble temples; and a smile resting upon the lips. Oh! what power bears woman up in a moment like this! Her life—her world was shut in with the replacing of that lid; but she saw each screw returned to its place, without a tear or a shudder;—herself, proposed to her mother, that they should follow the corpse to its home; and watched them heap the snow and clods upon it. And through that and many succeeding nights, she stood in the attic, in cold and darkness, straining her eyes towards where the gleaming tomb-stones were visible in the day, and fancying she could tell which shadowed an unsodded mound.

Charley was his friend's executor. In the fulfilment of his trust, he found a casket marked—"To be given, at my death, to E.—M." He thought of sealing it up, and sending it to her with a note from himself; but decided upon further deliberation, to entrust it to Ida. It was a painful duty. She was not able yet to speak of Lynn without distressing emotion. His decease was so sudden, so awful,—snatched, as he was, from her very side, with the barest intimation of his danger, after months of intimate intercourse. She mourned for him as sisters and friends seldom weep. Charley did not command. "She was the more proper person," he said; "but he would not grieve her by enforcing the request."

"I cannot meet her!" said she. "He was so dear to us—how can I endure the sight of her indifference? They say she was calm and careless while they were burying him."

"Calm—she certainly was; but the glance I had at her face assured me not careless. I am much mistaken if she was not the greatest sufferer by that grave. I was angry with her, previously; I believe now that she merits our compassion."

Yet it was an unwilling heart that Ida carried to the interview. Ellen sent for her to come to her room. "I am busy, you see," said she, with the ghost of a smile. Ida held the precious legacy more tightly, as she noticed her occupation. A ball-dress was spread upon the bed, and she was fastening roses upon the skirt. Her cheek was white, as Ida glanced at her own sad-colored dress.

"You are going to the party to-night, then?" said the latter.

"Yes—will Josephine attend?"

"I have not heard her say—have not inquired—have not thought of it."

Despairing of broaching the subject in any other way, she took the casket from under her shawl, and laid it upon the dress.

"The living forget sooner than the dead, Ellen!" was all she said.

The unhappy girl recoiled at the familiar characters upon the lid, and stretched out her arms with an imploring cry. Ida reached her as she fell. She had fainted. Charley's words were verified, and Ida blamed herself severely for her cruel abruptness. Her tears ran fast, as she strove to restore consciousness "Oh! Ida—Lynn!" groaned Ellen, reviving. Reserve, pride, self-control were borne down;—they wept in each other's arms. With the casket pressed to her bosom, Ellen heard his last message, and the hopeful words he had spoken of the future, he was not to know upon earth.

"I did love him! Heaven is my witness—I did love him!" she cried, anguishedly. "He did not condemn me; but I can never forgive myself! If I could have seen him once more to tell him so! Dead! oh! that I were in the grave beside him!"

This was grief without a glimmer of hope. Ida had no word of comfort.

Ellen's eye fell upon the gossamer robe.—she threw it upon the floor, and trampled it "I hate it! and myself, and everything else! I am a hypocrite! a lying hypocrite! with my hollow smiles and broken heart. Leave me! go! or I shall hate *you!*"

Ida left her thus—writhing under the scorpion-lash of remorse, and rejecting consolation. She met Josephine, a square or two from home, and upon the door-step, Mr. Lacy. Admitting him, she ran up stairs to efface the marks of her recent agitation. Her pallor and swollen eyes remained, however, and did not escape him. He did not begin, as many would have done, in his place, to speak of topics entirely foreign to what was in their thoughts; he wished to apply a curative, not an anodyne.

"Charley tells me you are going to the country, before long;" he said. "I do not regret it, as I should if I were to stay here myself. After the first of April, I shall study at home, until autumn. You are to pay your friend Carry a visit, are you not?"

"Yes."

"She is the 'sister' I have heard so much of?"

"The same—I wish you knew her."

"I think I do. Her cheerful society is what you need. While it is neither possible, nor desirable to forget that we have been bereaved, we should beware how we indulge in a luxury of woe. Our duty to those we have lost, does not oblige us to neglect the friends who are spared to us."

"Very few remain to me," said Ida, tremulously.

"You are wrong. You may never find one who will fill his place; but the rest love you the more, that you are afflicted. Charley is a true brother."

"He is—and of late he is more unreserved, more affectionate than he used to be; his sympathy is very sweet. I must speak of yourself, also, Mr. Lacy, although I have no language to thank you for your kindness. I fear I have been wearisome at times; but you seem to understand why this was no common bereavement to me."

"So far from being wearied, I am grateful for your confidence. No act of mine shall cause you to repent it."

"Charley has given me some lines which he thinks were written recently," said Ida. "They were among some loose sheets in a portfolio of drawings. I wept over them, but they comforted me. I have been wishing that you had them. This is a rough copy, you observe; and probably not read after being penned."

Mr. Lacy's eyes filled, as he read at the top of the page, "11-1/2 P.M., after a visit from M. L."

"ALL IN CHRIST.

Jesus, Saviour! from Thy dwelling,
High all stars and thrones above,
Hear my faltering accents, telling
Of weak faith and smouldering love.

Poor love for Thee, the only worthy—
Dull faith In Thee, the only wise—
While to all things base and earthy,
How madly cling my wistful eyes!

I am blind! in rough paths groping,
With outstretched hands and sightless eyes;
Through gloom so dense, I scarce am hoping
That dawn will ever gild the skies.
Black, grisly spectres hover o'er me,
Filling my quaking soul with fright;
Thou—of all worlds the sun and glory,
Radiant Redeemer! be my light.

I am lonely! often keeping
Sad vigils o'er affections dead;
Some in the grave's strait chamber sleeping—
Some like bursting bubbles fled!
Yet for full love my deep soul longeth—
Gently each seeking tendril bend
To Thee—to whom that soul belongeth;—
Loving Redeemer! be my friend.
I am guilty! oh how sinning!
Against my kind—against my God;—
Hell and corruption ever winning
My soul into the downward road.
Insanely gloating on pollution—
Quaffing thick lees for pleasures pure—
Rend thou away each fell delusion,
Holy Redeemer! be my cure!"

"Do you recollect the visit to which he refers?" inquired Ida.

"1 was with him until late, one night, a week before his death," was the reply; "and our conversation may have inspired the thoughts he has expressed here; but I cannot say with certainty, that it did. If this temper of spirit and heart was habitual to him, what may we not hope?"

"If!" exclaimed Ida, sadly. "Doubt is agonizing. It is not consistent with God's mercy that he should be consigned to never ending misery; he whose faults made us love him better; the soul of honor and integrity! I will not believe that so much that was pure and good is quenched in eternal darkness. This thought is with me night and day. What authority have men, his inferiors by nature—hardly his equals in the practice of virtue, to doom him, and hope a happier fate for the themselves?"

"Who has done this?" asked Mr. Lacy, sternly.

"More than one, in my hearing; and Charley was exasperated to insult a man, a church member, who exhorted him not 'to imitate his example, and thereby meet the same awful punishment.' Charley regrets now, that he spoke rudely to one his senior, and whom he had hitherto respected, but says he, 'a Christian should not forget that he is a man!'"

"Nor does he," replied Morton. "From some who cross the river of Death we hear the 'All's Well,' when their feet touch the solid ground; then we may rejoice in the confident assurance that we shall meet them again. As many pass over in timid, as in despairing silence;—timidity, exchanged for rapture, on the bright shore beyond. God only knows the heart—only knows when the doomed oversteps the bounds He has appointed for his mercy; and as we hope for it ourselves, we should tremble at the thought of limiting it by our finite judgments. In this immeasurable love and pity is our trust, Ida; doubts and fearings cannot solve the mystery; we know this, however—'He doth not afflict willingly,' and 'remembereth our feeble frame.' Who pardons a child's faults more than a parent? and 'Our Father' is also *his*. Yet," continued he, "Charley erred in repulsing the warning, kindly, if injudiciously extended. The suffering we experience in our uncertainty as to his condition, should teach us to make our salvation sure, so that when our hour shall come—if a call at midnight, we may not leave those who love us, comfortless."

"His death has caused a heart-rending void," said Ida. "I start whenever the door opens at the hours he was accustomed to visit us. At Mr. Dana's, I am listening all the time for his step or voice. Oh! why do nonentities, cumberers of the earth, spin out a tiresome life, and the loved and useful perish?"

"Perhaps they are taken away from the evil to come. You would not rebel if you believed this? At best, what are the short years of toil and change we pass below, compared with the never-ending life of our heavenly home?"

"You forget that I have no portion in that home, Mr. Lacy."

"No portion! You do not mean to refuse an inheritance so graciously offered! It may be long before we have another opportunity to speak of these things; will you make me a promise?"

"If I can perform it," answered she.

"It is that you will every day, ask yourself, 'What happiness does my soul desire that Christ cannot, and will not bestow?' Will you do this?"

She promised.

"It seems impossible," he pursued, "that a sorer trial than that which you are now undergoing, can befall you; yet there may be such in reserve, and then, I would have you recollect, that as He is the only happiness, He is also the only comfort. Willingly—gladly as I would suffer in your stead, I would not save you a pang, if I thought it was His means to bring you to Himself."

He spoke with emotion, as if possessed with the conviction that the event he adverted to would assuredly take place; and that this was his sole chance of preparing her for it. He arose—she gave him her hand—it was taken as silently, and held for a long minute.

"This is not our parting," said he; "if we both live, I shall see you again soon, but to provide against contingencies, I will ask you now to write to me; I mean, of course, in answer to my letters, as you would to Charley—to a brother,—will you?"

"Yes, if your letters are as frank as your speech, and I am granted a like indulgence."

True to his promise, he called upon the eve of her departure, but the presence of the family and other visitors prevented private conversation; and Charley's manoeuvres, skilful and unsuspected as they were, failed to effect a diversion of Josephine's watchfulness. Yet as they said "farewell" Ida felt a card slipped into her hand. Upon it was pencilled, "Remember your promise. Mizpah."

CHAPTER XVIII

Life at Poplar-grove was much as it had been, the previous summer; still and bright. The mornings were spent in Carry's pleasant sewing-room, from which male visitors were rigorously excluded; in the afternoon, were the siesta, and ride or walk; at night, music and social chat. Carry feared that this monotony, while it suited her wishes and employments, might be less agreeable to her friend; that she would miss the gay whirl, the intoxicating incense of her city career. But Ida was contented, even happy. Beloved and caressed by the whole household, in the home of kindred tastes and feeling; and above all, with the firm hope that her life-long search was at last ended; her wild cravings laid to rest beneath the waves, which welling from the unsealed fountain, had risen higher and higher, until her soul was overflowing with love and rapture;—she revelled in the quiet hours of friendly communion, and the sweeter seasons of witching reverie. Carry knew nothing of the spring of her happiness. She saw that her mind had acquired a more healthy tone;—that her affections had expanded, and attributed it to the influence of friendship;—to a strength of mind, which had determined the world should be what it chose to have it;—to anything but the true cause,—an idolatry that left no room for suspicion or discontent. Once Carry alluded to the twilight promenade, when Ida had told her of her forebodings of the wane of their love, after the nuptials, which were now fast approaching; and was answered by a warm embrace and smile, which said those fears were quelled, and might have betrayed to more prying eyes, the enchantment that had exorcised them. Her evening improvisations entranced, not only the parlor-circle, but drew to the windows a larger audience from without, spellbound by her heart-melodies. All her delight was not in memory. Letters came and went;—from Charley and Mrs. Dana; and gossiping notes from Anna Talbot and other of "the girls." These, Carry enjoyed with her, and asked no questions about those which she did not see. Morton's were what he engaged they should be; sincere and friendly, without a hint that could alarm her delicacy. They were tinctured with a sadness, she did not comprehend, until she noticed his many references to his sister's sufferings, and his anxiety on her account. It was her turn to console; and her most valued treasure was the letter, in which he thanked and blessed her.

Carry was to be married the last of July. The middle of June brought Mrs. Dana and the children, under Charley's protection. For the week of his stay, he was the life of the house. One cloud was upon the spirits of all;—Lynn was missed and mourned, and by none, with more sorrowful tenderness, than by his vivacious friend; but he was unselfish even in this. Ida could win him to speak of their loss; to the others, he never mentioned it of his own accord. She was correct in saying that he had grown more communicative and affectionate. He seemed to have transferred to her the watchful love that had been Lynn's safeguard and solace.

"Nothing changes you, Mars' Charley?" said Uncle Ike, the plantation patriarch, halting at the piazza steps one afternoon, when he had crawled out into the sunshine.

"I should like to say the same for you, Uncle Ike; time and sickness have not treated you as well as you deserve."

"Better'n I desarve, Mars' Charles!—heap better'n I desarve! Time for me to be packed and shoed for my journey. I'se lived in these low-grounds of sorrow, nigh 'pon ninety years, and many' the young folks I've seen step down into the grave before me. When I heard that poor, handsome Mars' Lynn had gone too, 'pears-like I was ready to grumble 'cause 'twant me—but 'twas the Almighty's will, Mars' Charles,—'twas his will. It 'joices me to see you so well and lively—jest like you used to be. You don't take trouble, I reckon, Marster."

"No; it's against my principles;—beside, we'll have a plenty given to us."

"Fact, Marster! You ain't knowed much yet; but 'the evil days will come, when you shall say, I have no pleasure in them!'"

Charley kept his seat upon the step for some time after the old man had gone:—once he sighed heavily. Ida was in the parlor, and longed to go out to him, for she guessed the tenor of his thoughts, but doubted the propriety of intruding upon them. He got up, presently, and began to walk the porch, whistling an opera air. Spying her through the window, he came in. "You are ruining your eyes and health with this eternal stitching;" said he. "As I live, you are boring holes in that piece of cloth, for the pleasure of sewing them up again! No wonder woman's work is never ended! What are you making?"

"A handkerchief." She displayed the corner, in which she was embroidering, "Carry Carleton."

"Where are the others?" he inquired.

"Mrs. Dana is in the nursery; Carry asleep; Dr. Carleton and Arthur abroad."

"Come, walk with me!" requested he. "Any handkerchief,—a wedding mouchoir—can wait an hour."

Their course was along the brink of a deep ravine; overshadowed by large old trees; and bridged by fallen trunks. The sides were grass-grown, and at the bottom rolled the rivulet, which had fretted out the gorge; blending its complainings with the low rush of the wind through the forest.

"So one feeling often wears away the soul!" remarked Charley, reflectively. "Man is but clay after all!"

"You! the champion of your species—turning against them!" exclaimed Ida.

"No. I am still an unbeliever in the total corruption of our nature; a doctrine so opposed to reason and experience, that I will never assent to it, if it is preached at me until doomsday. But this is a miserably unsatisfactory life!"

"Yet the world says you enjoy it."

"And do you, an adept in concealment, credit a man's outward show!"

"At least, I do not practise this accomplishment upon my friends;" replied Ida, piqued.

"Did I say that you did? I am not sure that I could not prove this point, too;—but we will let it pass for the present. I believe you to be what you appear to me. Carry would never forgive one who impugned your sincerity;—and what would Mr. Germaine say?"

This was a gentleman of the neighbourhood, whose marked attentions to Ida subjected her to the raillery of the Poplar-grove household.

"Nonsense!" said she, laughing. "He has never been beyond the outermost court of my heart."

"I own his does not appear likely to be the hand to unlock the penetralia. This is the spot I wanted to show you. Is it not a fairy nook?"

It was a mossy bank at the foot of a venerable sycamore, from whose branches the trailing vines touched their heads. A spring of the clearest crystal bubbled among its roots.

"Oh! for a fairy goblet!" said Ida.

"It is easily made, if these leaves are large enough," answered Charley. He gathered some, but they were too irregularly-shaped to suit his purpose. "It is a simple process," said he, as he failed, after several trials, to convey a thimbleful of water to his amused companion; "but as the man said who tried to fly and couldn't—'there is every thing in knowing how to do it.' I never like to be outdone, even in trifles. I saw some leaves as we came along that I know will do—excuse me a moment, and I will get them."

He was gone before she could object; and she strolled idly around the giant trunk of the sycamore, admiring the al fresco boudoir, of which it was the centre ornament. She set her foot upon something harder than the soft carpet—it was a small morocco case, which she picked up, with an ejaculation of surprise, and without a thought of who had dropped it, opened. She had nearly let it fall, as Carry's lovely face smiled at her from within. "Arthur has been here," was her comment, but a glossy curl untwined itself from an envelope labelled in Charley's hand—"*The seat under the honeysuckle. May 1st*, 18—," a date four years back. There was no impropriety in his having Carry's likenesss;—they had long been in feeling what they were shortly to become in name—brother and sister; but her heart beat so with indefinable terror that she could not stand;—it was as though, instead of the senseless case, another heart, its every throbbing revealed, lay in her hand.

"You are tired waiting, I suppose, but I had a longer search than—"

The glow of a stormy sunset rushed to his face as he saw the miniature she did not attempt to conceal. She had never conceived of the dormant passion which now awoke in his eye and form; but she did not quail.

"I found this over there, and opened it thoughtlessly, not suspecting what it was or to whom it belonged. I am very sorry."

The storm passed while she was speaking. The man's wonderful self-command was master. He dipped up the water with a careful hand; the leafy cup did not quiver.

"Do you like it? is it cool?"

"Yes—thank you."

He drank draught after draught himself, threw away the leaves, and resumed his seat upon the bank.

"There is no help for it, Ida! you must hear what I did not intend you ever should; not that I disdain your sympathy, but it is a rule with me not to disturb my friends with troubles, which they cannot alleviate. I do not know what suspicions have been forced upon you, if they are of the honor and affection I owe my brother, or of *her* fidelity to him, they are groundless. That picture was painted for me before I had any intimation that his was the prize I foolishly hoped to secure. I relinquished her; but this is the amulet which has saved me in many temptations. Although hope was no more, memory remained; and vice could not mate with the visions of purity that memory recalled. There has not been a time since I first saw her, a laughing babe, just liberated from her nurse's arms, when I have not loved her more than any other earthly being. As boy and man I have thought, studied, labored for her alone. When I quitted home to seek my fortune, she was still a child, who clung weepingly to me, and kissed me as fondly as she did her father. It was the last time! At my next visit she was away at school;—at the second I obtained that curl. She was then fifteen; innocent and loving, full of jesting surprise at 'Charley's mannish ways,' and hurt that I would not call her 'sister.' She did not ask this the ensuing summer. Lynn was with me; and in the confidence of a hope that saw no cloud ahead, I imparted to him my dreams and desires, and engaged him to take her portrait secretly. I went back to New York, and wrote to her father, asking his sanction of the proposal I could not delay. The letter was upon my desk, ready for the post, when one arrived from Arthur. He was not to blame for his silence; I had been as reserved to him; but he entreated my forgiveness for hiding this, his only secret, from me. She knew it now;—her father's only objection was their youth—a 'fault,' he remarked, jocosely, 'which will mend with time.' In place of the letter to my guardian, I forwarded one to my brother, congratulating him upon his happy engagement to the woman I idolized. He is worthy of her, if a mortal can be. I can see that it is best. He has talents and energy, and loves her as she should be loved—I am rough and eccentric, caring and striving for nothing, now that my guiding star has set."

"Charley! Charley! you shall not so defame yourself!" cried Ida bursting into tears. "You—the kindest—most generous of men! you *are* worthy of her! Oh! I wish it could be!"

"Hush! hush! I would not have it otherwise. I came home last summer, and saw them together without a pang of selfish regret; and gloried in my subjugation of a passion their betrothal made sinful, until our ride to 'the Castle.' My arm saved her from mutilation or death, and instead of thanksgiving, sprang up a horrible envy, that I had rescued her for *him*. It was momentary, but the repentance was bitter. I abhor myself when I think of it. I have never fancied since that I did not love her. I know it as well now that another month will make her his bride, as I did when hope was highest. Poor Lynn! it grieved him to his dying day!"

Silence and tears was a fitting reply to this narration. It came to Ida, like sudden death to a festival; producing not only sorrow and dismay, but a trembling insecurity—an awful whisper—"Who next?" Did human love, then, always terminate in misery? Was there no remedy? She wanted Charley to speak again, and say that he had some source of comfort; or at least, strength for the last, greatest trial. His words put this hope to flight.

"I have borne as much as I can;—if it be cowardly to avert further suffering, I am not brave. I have business in the West next month, which could, but shall not be postponed. John will not know of it in time to provide a substitute. Arthur will be disappointed; I would spare him this trifling pain, if I were certain that I should not give him more by remaining. I shall not wear this after the marriage—I may become a castaway without it, for aught I know. When Lynn died, I said, 'My secret is buried with him.' I have committed what the Machiavelis of the day would call an unwise act," added he, smiling; "'consigned it to the keeping of a woman'—but I have no fears for its safety with you. Do not let it prey upon your spirits. I would not caution a less sympathetic nature. Be happy, Ida,—it is your manifest destiny; and I am still disinterested enough to 'rejoice with those who do rejoice.' The sun is setting—you shall not go to the house with that woe-begone face. Smile! or I don't stir."

He laughed at her attempt. "Rather hysterical,—with that sob treading upon its heels; but it will do. Come, sister!"

Ida could have cried more heartily at an expression and tone, that reminded her of Lynn; but he was resolute in not allowing it.

Carry was upon the piazza. "My dear friends!" cried she, running to meet them. "Where *have* you been! here's a house full of company, and I have sent scouts in every direction. Did not you hear or see them?"

"'I heard the owls scream, and the crickets cry;'" said Charley. "Who is here, that we can prefer to each other's society?"

"Your forest ramble has taught you gallantry. You'll find him but a dull scholar, Ida—why, there are Messrs. Faulkner, Euston and Germaine, impatiently waiting the belle's appearance."

"Irresistible—more irresistible—most irresistible! Are you going off to beautify, Miss Ida? Don't hurry—I will tell them we got lost or drowned in the woods."

When the girls went down, it was candle-light; and the "Irresistibles" were laughing themselves black in the face, over the piano, and the "funniest of fellows," who was entertaining them by an original parody upon "Oh no! I never mention her!"

CHAPTER XIX

Charley departed, and for several days, Ida disregarded his injunction of cheerfulness. She liked the warm-hearted, reliable Arthur; but she was unjust in her vexation at his happiness, when she pictured the lonely brother, who had sacrificed his, to preserve it unabated. Her conscience reproached her for a display of this impatience, while they were watching the receding form of their visitor. Arthur linked her arm in his, saying playfully, "Come, cousin Ida, tell us what made you and my rattling brother so sober this morning. You parted as if you did not expect to meet again in this world. Is there any hope of my claiming nearer kinship?"

With a quick, fretful gesture she broke from him; and although she recovered herself immediately, and answered pleasantly, he was amazed and wounded, and never repeated the familiarity. A letter from Mr. Lacy came opportunely to brighten the current of thought. She wished Charley could read it; but as this was not to be, she embodied its sentiments in her reply to a communication she had received from him. She was in the habit of moralising speculatively; and he had no clue to betray from what quarter this practical strain had emanated.

John arrived a week before the marriage, with intelligence that set the house in a turmoil; Charley had started to Missouri that morning. He "was the bearer of his excuses and the bridal gift." Carry wept; and Arthur was indignant; Dr. Carleton proposed a postponement, which was unanimously voted for by the servants. "Twouldn't be no wedding wuth talking about, 'thout Mars' Charles was thar!" The motion was strenuously opposed by a minority of three—John, Ida and Arthur; John asserting, in his business way, that the ceremony could be performed as well without the absentee; and that his example of punctuality in keeping engagements should be improved. The two others deprecated a change, without distinctly stating their reasons. They carried the day. Poplar-grove was visible for miles around, on the moonless night of the bridal. Lights blazed in every window; starry festoons depended from the trees; and in the garden, the glow-worm fairies might have been celebrating the royal birth-night. In doors, the scene was one of bewildering beauty. Fairies of mortal mould flitted through the summer bowers, at whose decoration, Flora must have presided in person. Carry was too modest to covet display; but Dr. Carleton was wealthy and liberal; and Ida and Mrs. Dana, who were both fond of splendor and excitement, had his hearty concurrence in their designs. The former planned everything. It was a new business to her; but she struck out boldly, copying a gorgeous conception of her fertile brain, guided solely by her eye and judgment. Her subordinates marvelled at first; but had too much faith in her to rebel; and as the idea was developed, their industry and delight surpassed her expectations. When completed, the effect was so novel and pleasing, they were ready to fall down and worship her; and more cultivated taste did not derogate from their eulogistic approbation. Dr. Carleton thanked her with moistened eyes; Arthur laughingly wondered—"what talent next? her versatile genius kept him in a state of perpetual wonderment;" but Carry's silent kiss was dearer praise than all. As first bridesmaid, and an inmate of the mansion, Ida was virtually mistress of the ceremonies; Mrs. Dana confining her attention to the arrangement of the banquet, dressing-rooms and chambers. Carry had invited all of her schoolmates who were within reach; among those who came, were Anna Talbot, Emma Glenn, Ellen Morris, who was staying at Mr. Truman's, and our old friend Celestia;—"cousin Lucindy" being again conveniently remembered. The three first named, were bridesmaids. Ida walked with Mr. Euston; and as the train formed, she thought of the two who would have taken precedence of him; of the chilly sleep of the pulseless heart, and the desolation of the living one; while the irrevocable words were said, she heard, like the echo of a knell—"caring for nothing, striving for nothing—now that my guiding star has set;" and the sigh, which contended with her smile of salutation to the bride, was "poor Charley!"

Ellen Morris, too, may have had her reminiscences; this event could not but revive the recollection of her sister's bridal, not a year before; but the sparkling hazel orbs were unshadowed as then; her manner as charmingly coquettish. Celestia had not forgotten Mr. Euston; and seized an early opportunity to renew their flirtation. The gentleman was not so willing; he was not exactly in love with his partner; but was not insensible to her attractions, and that in his position he was envied by most of the single men present—cordially hated by one. Ida knew not that he was taxing every energy to achieve fascination. She felt the nervousness of a youthful hostess that things should "go off" well; the company be pleased with their reception and themselves; conscious, that although the praise or censure might not be put upon her, yet in reality the result depended upon her exertions. Solicitude yielded to triumphant satisfaction, as the electric sympathy spread, leaping from tongue to tongue; and evolving, in dazzling coruscations, from kindling eyes. She did not seek her reward then, but she had it. Few were so blind and ungrateful, as not to recognise her hand in the pleasures offered to them. The girls, the most fastidious of the various classes for whose whims a party-giver has to cater, forgave her magnet influence upon the choicest beaux, as they were themselves well-supplied notwithstanding; the old people were charmed with her respectful affability; and of her immediate attendants, there was not one who was not convinced that he contributed most to her amusement.

Ill-nature is indigenous to all soils, and spite creates its own food; and she did not escape wholly unscathed. She overheard the epithets, "flirt," and "dashing," in the same breath with her name; but she laughed at the silly shot. If she flirted, no one was offended or injured; if she dashed, she did it with a grace her maligners tried vainly to copy. As she left the supper-room, a glance at the hall-mirror showed that her head-dress was disordered; and she repaired to the dressing-room to rectify it. She paused before the glass there, in unfeigned wonder at the reflected figure. It was the first time a spark of personal vanity had ever inflamed her mind. She knew that she was admired; she believed, because she amused people by her sprightly repartee; compliments upon her appearance were forgotten as soon as heard, leaving, as their only trace, contempt for their author. To-night, the thoughtful eyes were alive with light; the cheeks, usually colorless, as rosy as Carry's; and the wreathing smile imparted a wondrous beauty to the proud lips. A softer, sweeter happiness succeeded the girlish exultation—pardonable since it was short-lived—she turned from the mirror, with indifference, as she murmured—

"Young, loving and beloved!
These are brief words, but—"

An exclamation interrupted the quotation. She snatched up a letter from the table. "It must have come this afternoon, and they forgot to give it me. How unkind!" This was too public a place, there was constant passing in and out; but she could not be debarred its perusal until the guests' departure. A closet opened beyond the chamber; she carried a lamp in thither, and bolted the door. He wrote kindly, but more constrainedly than formerly; and the sense of some phrases was confused, as if he had commenced them, meaning to say one thing, and changed his mind ere the conclusion. His sister had been very ill, he said, but was now out of danger; and his statement of this simple fact appeared embarrassed. She read two pages in perplexity whether to chide his ambiguity, or her unsettled thoughts; "And now, my dear friend," so ran the third, "I have to solicit indulgence for my egotism, while I speak of an event of incomparable importance—and than which, nothing was more remote from my thoughts, four months ago. Annie has another nurse besides myself this summer; an early playmate of ours, a gentle girl, who, I think, must resemble your friend Carry, in character and person. She visited Annie early in April; and an angel of healing she has proved to our beloved sufferer. It is an affecting sight—one so young and fair, deserting the society she would adorn, for the wearisome offices of a sick-room. I have said that she is gentle, and in disposition and deportment essentially feminine;—add to these, the intelligence and accomplishments of a strong and thoroughly-trained mind; and you will not be surprised that she has gained our hearts;—will not accuse me of precipitancy, when you hear that I have sought and obtained her promise to return to us, united by a dearer tie than the bonds of friendship. I do not merit this gift at the hands of Providence; for I have rebelled, in times past, at the strokes I knew were just, but could not acknowledge were merciful. There is nothing earthly which can compare with the love of a true-hearted woman.—If I ever needed an incentive to industry I have it in this. Months—years, perhaps—must elapse before our union. It may be said, I have not acted prudently in forming an engagement, whose consummation is so distant; but I have obeyed the voice of my heart and conscience."

Aye! crumple the sheet in your grasp, and sink to the earth—a crushed thing! struck down from the zenith of your pride and bliss—crushed and mangled—but living and *feeling!* Grief does not always stun—it seldom kills—you must live, although each lacerated heart-string is crying out for death! Say not that it came without warning! Was there no voice in your early bereavement—in the stern lessons of your girlhood—in the frustration of an hundred cherished purposes—in Lynn's suicidal madness—in Ellen's remorse—in Charley's withered heart? Why were you made to feel, see, know these, if not to teach you, that they who lean upon mortal's love trust to the weakest of rotten reeds—they "who sow the wind, must reap the whirl wind"—black, bitter, scorching!

CHAPTER XX

"I never thought you unreasonable before, Ida."

"I am sorry you should now, Carry."

"How can I help it, when after travelling with us for weeks you suddenly resolve to return to Eastern Virginia by yourself; and to that lonesome place in the country, which you have not visited for years!"

"I have an escort; a gentleman who is on his way to Richmond, and will take charge of me."

"But why this notion, just as we decided to go north? Has your curiosity to behold Niagara diminished since your sight of 'the Bridge?'"

"Frankly and truly, I do not care to see it. I would not ride to the House Mountain yonder, if Mont Blanc, the Lake of Como, and the Great Fall were to be seen from the other side."

"Do you hear that, Arthur?" said Carry, despairingly, to her husband, who was reading.

"No—what is it?"

"This obstinate young lady is about to deprive us of the honour of her company. She is going back to Staunton to-morrow."

"To the Lunatic Hospital?" inquired Arthur, putting aside his book. "You are not in earnest, Ida? Are you tired of us; or do you dislike our sketched route? If the last, we will alter it."

"And if the first, we will alter ourselves," interposed Carry, laughingly.

"I would have you and your plans remain as they are. I am not well, and require rest—not change. My desire to see old Sunnybank is not a caprice, as Carry supposes; I have had it in contemplation for a long time. Mr. Read deterred me from it by representations of the discomfort I would encounter; the only white man left on the plantation being the overseer. This summer he has been removed, and his place given to a former tenant of mother's; a man of family; and the accommodations, which serve for them, will keep me from hardship."

"She is sick," said Carry, when Ida retired. "She has not been herself lately. Were it not that she is used to dissipation, I should think that the round of parties, after our wedding, overtasked her strength. Yet, she enjoyed them."

"Her malady may be of the mind," said Dr. Dana, thoughtfully. "Do you consider this probable?"

"Oh, no! she was well and happy when she came to us; and what can have occurred since to affect her?"

"You are right, I dare say;" returned he, absently. He was pondering upon her behaviour after Charley's departure.

Argument did not dissuade, and conjecture was baffled in the effort to explain this unexpected movement. They parted in Lexington—Ida to recross the mountains eastward; they, to travel north by way of Harper's Ferry.

If there is an enjoyment, which is purely of the intellect, its usurpation is man's high prerogative; the sticklers for woman's "equal rights" will never establish her title to it. The mind masculine may be nourished and exercised, and attain its full size, while the heart is dwarfed and sickly;—as with twin children, one sometimes grows to man's stature, healthy and strong; and the other pines and dies in childhood. In woman, intellect and the affections are united from their birth;—like the Siamese brothers, one refuses food, which is denied its companion; and who dare peril the life of both by severing the ligament which joins them?

Ida's route was through the garden-spot of our State—the magnificent Valley, with its heaven-bathed, impregnable eyries, among which our country's Father selected a resting-place for Freedom's standard—America's Thermopylæ, should the invader's power drive him from every other hold;—where one may travel for days, encircled by the Briarean arms, the sister ridges stretch, in amity, towards each other—each rolling its streams and clouds down to the verdant plains between;—where morning and evening, the sun marshals his crimson and gold-colored array upon the purple heights, which are coeval with him and Time; and flings shadows and hues athwart them, in his day's march, he never vouchsafes to Lowland countries;—and this region was traversed with not a thought beyond a feverish wish to be at her journey's end and rest. She stopped in Richmond but one night. Mr. Read and his daughter were out of town, and she went to a hotel. At dawn she was upon the road, with no attendant but the driver of her hack. Rachel had gone to Sunnybank a month before, to see her relations, little expecting her mistress to come for her. Ida's spirits and health declined alarmingly, now that the necessity of eluding suspicion was over. She had never been sick a day in her life; but she began to feel that mental ills may be aggravated by bodily disease. The unnatural tension had been maintained too long. When Sunnybank appeared, she was unable to raise her head to look at it. The negroes flocked out at the phenomenon of a travelling carriage in the disused avenue; and loud were their astonishment and compassion, as they recognised its occupant.

"I have come home to die, mother," said she, as they lifted her out, and fainted in their arms. In the midst of their consternation, the family pride of the faithful underlings was stubborn. "Their young mistress should not be carried to the overseer's;" and Aunt Judy, the keeper of the keys, hurried off to unlock the house doors. Ida had a cloudy remembrance of awakening in her mother's chamber, and of a gleaming fancy, that she was once more a child, aroused from a horrid, horrid dream, then her senses forsook her, and there was a wide hiatus in memory. It was night when she awoke again; she was in the same room;—a fire burned in the chimney, and cast fantastic shapes upon the ceiling. Crouched in the corner of the fire-place, was a dusky figure, whose audible breathing sounded loudly through the apartment. Her slumbers were not very profound, however, for she sprang up at the feeble call—"Rachel!"

"Miss Ida! honey! what do you want?"

"How long have I slept? my head feels so strange!"

"That's because you've been sick, honey."

"What is the matter with me?"

"Fever, dear—you caught it in them dreadful mountains, and have been laid up for four weeks. But you'll git well, now—you were out of your head 'most all the time—and the doctor says you mustn't talk."

Ida desisted, too weak to disobey. With vague curiosity, she followed her with her eyes, as she smoothed the counterpane, pushed up the bed on one side, and patted it down on the other; then she put the "chunks" together upon the hearth, and there was the clinking of spoons and glasses at a table.

"Here's your drink, Miss Ida," she said, lifting her head with a care that proved her a practised nurse. It was cool and palatable, and the heavy lids sank in natural slumber.

Mr. Grant (the overseer) and his wife had not been remiss in their duty to the sick girl. She had the best medical attendance the county afforded; and Mr. Read was written to at the commencement of the attack; the letter was unanswered—probably not received. Rachel was "sure Miss Jenny or Miss Carry would come in a minute, if they knew she was sick;" but was ignorant of the address of either. Their nursing might have been more skilful, but it could not have exceeded hers in tenderness. She took turns with Mrs. Grant in watching, but she never left the room except for her meals. She was amply repaid for her labor of love by the improvement which henceforward was apparent in her patient. Her raptures awoke no responsive harmony in Ida's bosom.

Her physician was a son of Mr. Hall, the old minister, who had gone to his rest.

"You must exert yourself, Miss Ida," said he. "Have you walked yet?"

"No, sir."

"Cannot you do it?"

"I don't know, indeed, sir."

"But, my dear child, nature cannot do everything; we must aid her. It is as binding upon us to save our own lives, as those of others."

"When they are worth saving."

"You want more powerful tonics than any I have;" said the doctor, eyeing her curiously. "I must think your case over. I *command* you to walk across the room twice to-day, three times to-morrow, and so on. See that she minds me, Rachel!"

Rachel gave her no peace, until she consented to sit up awhile in the easy-chair, by the window. Sunnybank was sadly changed. The buildings and enclosures were in good repair, and the fields cultivated; but the walks and shrubbery were neglected; and the garden, into which Ida was looking, overgrown with high weeds. Here and there a rose-tree struggled for a foothold, a scanty growth of yellow leaves clinging to the mossy stems; the sweetbrier still hung over the window, its long, bare arms rattling in the cold wind like fleshless bones; the tangled grass in the yard had run to seed, and piles of dead leaves were heaped against the palings. She could not see the grave-yard; she knew, though, that the willows were leafless, and how the sprays were waving in their melancholy dance, and whispering their old song—"Alone!" If alone then, how now? sick—dying, perhaps! where were those who had proudly borne the name of friend? where the sister, in whose bosom she had lain for months, and eased her sorrows and heightened her joys? the brother, she had averred, was "all kindness and truth?" and oh! where he, who had filled her heart to the brim with the rich, red wine of life, to change, in a moment, to fiery, deadly poison! She felt no resentment against him; she was too utterly broken-hearted, she thought, even if she had cause; and she had not. Her wilful self-deception had been her snare; instead of studying his heart, she had judged it by her own. Were his candor—his undisguised interest in her welfare, tokens of love, that ever seeks concealment? No! he had tried to lead her, a wayward child, to the paths of happiness; and she had seen nought but the hand which pointed the way. There was prophetic meaning in Lynn's eye, when he spoke of "the finest growth of heart and soul, which you flattered yourself were climbing heavenward, twining with strengthening tendrils around the altar of that one love!" She had been impious enough to imagine that she was imbibing a fondness for holy things; her heart had burned within her, as he talked of the loved theme; she had read the Scriptures, and prayed, in words, for light and guidance. And by the fierce rebellion which fired her breast—rebellion against—hatred of the Being, this lip service had blasphemed, she knew that she had never bowed in soul to Him; and her heart—broken, though she said it was,—trusting still—adoring still the mortal, through the great love she bore him—yet reared itself in angry defiance, saying to the Chastener,—"I will not submit!" What had she done, to be left desolate—

comfortless in the spring-time of life! "He is, they tell me, merciful and all-powerful;—let Him give me back my love, and I will believe in Him." And as day by day passed, and there were no tidings of Carry or the Danas, she felt a morose complacency in the confirmation of her hard thoughts of them, and in repeating, "I am not humbled yet!"

"Uncle Will wants to know if he can come in to see you, Miss Ida," said Rachel, one Sabbath afternoon.

Ida was dressed, and rocking herself listlessly before the fire. "Let him come," she replied, languidly.

This man was her mother's steward and factotum; a hale, fine-looking negro; better educated than the generality of his caste, and devotedly pious. He brushed off a tear with the back of his hand, as his mistress greeted him. He had not seen her since she was grown, and was moved by her likeness to her mother.

"You would not have known me,—would you, uncle Will?" she asked.

"Yes ma'am; you are your mother's own child."

"Indeed! I am called like my father."

"You're like *her*, ma'am—in body, and like her in spirit, too I hope."

"No, Uncle Will, you cannot expect that;—she was an angel."

"Better than that, Mistis—she was a Christian!"

"And how is that better?" said Ida, surprised at the reply. "She is an angel now—is she not?"

"No ma'am; she is one of the spirits of the just made perfect; and according to my notion, that's better than to be a born seraph. Angels may praise and glorify the Lamb, but they haven't so much to be thankful for as we."

"I do not understand you. They have been happy from all Eternity; and those who have lived in this world, have had sorrow and pain and sin—'mourning all their days.'"

"They needn't, ma'am—

'Why should the children of a King
Go mourning all their days!'"

said Will readily—"He holds us up under whatever trouble we have; unless we bring it upon ourselves by our transgressions, and He will deliver us then, if we call to Him. The Saviour is the Christian's glory and song—He didn't die for angels."

Ida mused. "There is a question I wish to ask you," said she. "God can do as He pleases;—can He not?"

"Certainly, Mistis—'He worketh according to the counsel of His own will.'"

"And He is very pitiful and gracious?" she continued.

"Like as a father pitieth his children, Mistis."

"Then when He knows that we are miserable and sinful and helpless, why does not He take pity on us, and make us good and happy?"

"He will, ma'am."

"But He does not. He only waits for us to love anything, before He robs us of it. So far from liking to see us happy, it would seem that He grudged us the poor crumbs we picked up of ourselves."

"Because they ain't good for us, Mistis."

"Why did He allow us to take them, then? why wait, until we have tasted and found them sweet, before He snatches them away?"

"I remember, Mistis, when you were a little thing, no higher than my knee, you were mightily taken with some red peppers growing in the garden. Your mother called you away from the bed, four or five times, and ordered you not to touch them. By and by I spied you running down the walk towards them, when you thought she didn't see you; and I was starting in a hurry to fetch you back, but she stopped me. 'No, Will!' says she, 'the punishment sin brings with it, is remembered longer than a hundred warnings. She will have a useful lesson.' I was loath to have you hurt; but I had to mind her. Your lesson was right hard; for your mouth and face and hands were swelled and burning for hours. But you didn't go near the pepper-bed again. And it seems to me, ma'am, that the Almighty treats us just so. We run crazy after things, that are like the red peppers,—pretty outside, but hot as fire when we get to playing with them. He doesn't push us towards them—*He lets us alone*; and we are mighty apt to run to Him, after we've got a fair taste. You didn't know but your mother would whip you for disobeying her; but you went straight to her when you felt the smart."

"This does not follow, of course, uncle Will. I have tasted some hot peppers since those days; and I cannot see any mercy or use in the lesson."

"Maybe you haven't asked an explanation, ma'am."

"From whom? from you?"

"No ma'am! From Him, unto whom belong the deep things of the Almighty. And if He doesn't show you their meaning now—He will, sometime. Children are often puzzled at their parents' dealings."

As he was leaving, she observed his wistful look.

"Have you any requests to make, uncle Will? you will not ask anything unreasonable, I know."

"I hope not, ma'am. You see—we've been in the habit of holding our Sunday night prayer-meetings in the basement-room, under this. We used to meet there in your mother's time. She had the room fixed on purpose for us. When it's clear weather, in summer, we meet out-doors;—it's getting cool now—"

"And you are afraid of disturbing me; is that it?"

"Yes ma'am," said he, relieved.

"You may be quite easy as regards that. Has that room been ceiled yet?"

"No ma'am—'twould have been if—you all had stayed here."

"I am glad that it is not. I can hear your hymns—how I used to love those old tunes! Have your meeting. I wish I had no other disturbance!"

He had got into the entry, when she recalled him; and with the sad smile she had worn during their conversation, said, "Uncle Will! if you think I have not done hankering after forbidden fruit, you may pray, that I may be cured."

"I will, Mistis! God bless you!"

She had forgotten, and Will did not know, that all the services could be heard through the floor. The worshippers assembled so quietly, that she was not aware of this, until Will's tones startled her with the idea that he was in the room. He commenced the exercises by reading the fourteenth chapter of John's gospel. "Let not your hearts be troubled; ye believe in God, believe also in me." He offered neither comment nor explanation. He was a believer in what he called "the pure Word;" "if I can't comprehend one part," he was wont to say, "I comfort myself by thinking that there is so much that is plain even to my weak understanding." The quavering voice of an aged man led in prayer; and in spite of its verbiage and incorrect grammar, Ida listened, for it was sincere. They sang in the sweet voices for which the race is so remarkable,

"There is a land of pure delight,"

with a wild, beautiful chorus, repeated each time with more emphasis and fervor—

"Oh sing to me of Heaven!
In Heaven alone, no sin is known,
And there's no parting there!"

Ida shut her eyes and lay motionless, lest she should lose a note. Forgetful of her unholy enmity to her God—her distrust of her kind—borne upon the melody her soul arose to Pisgah's top, and looked yearningly upon the "sweet fields beyond the swelling flood," heard the jubilant song of the redeemed—

"In Heaven alone, no sin is known,
And there's no parting there!"

A solemn hush followed; and Will said, "Let us pray." His deliberate accents quickened into animation, with the unfolding of his petitions; spurning the fetters of his imperfect speech, his thoughts clothed themselves in the language of the Divine Word; coming to a King, be adopted unconsciously the vernacular of princes. In speaking of Ida, his manner was earnestly affectionate. "We beseech Thee, O Father, to deal gently with thine handmaid, whom thou hast set over us in worldly things. Thou hast seen fit that she should bear the yoke in her youth, hast made her to possess wearisome nights, and days of vanity; hast mingled her bread with tears, and her drink with weeping; Thou hast taken from her father and mother,—the hope of her soul, and the desire of her eyes; it is the Lord's doings, and it is marvellous in our eyes and in hers. Lighten her eyes, Our Father! though weeping has endured for a night, Thou hast promised that joy shall come in the morning; tell her, that no affliction for the present seemeth joyous, but grievous; but that Thou wilt make it work out for her an eternal weight of glory; that whom Thou lovest Thou chasteneth, and upon Thy Blessed Son Thou didst lay the afflictions and iniquities of us all. May her hungry soul run to Him, from the far country in which she has been living, and may He heal her broken bones, give her the oil of gladness for mourning—the garment of praise for the spirit of heaviness."

The hot, dry channel was broken up, and tears flowed in plenteous measure. From the softening soul sprang her first real prayer. "Oh! be my Father and Comforter!"

When Rachel awoke in the morning, she saw that her mistress had unbarred the shutters of the window by her bed, and was reading. Her face had a still deeper shade of gloom; but the attached girl drew a favorable augury from this mark of interest in anything, except her own thoughts. The book was a mother's gift—a Bible; she had read it with tolerable regularity for the giver's sake, but she found herself now lamentably ignorant of its contents. She read of the unapproachable purity of the Immaculate, of judgment and justice;

denunciation of the wicked, and the "fearful looking for of vengeance" that remained to rebellious children; in vain she searched it for a message to her—a promise she could apply. Her alarm augmented, as the fruitlessness of her endeavors became apparent. The life she had lightly esteemed was inestimably dear, as she realised what eternity was; and her heart was still with fear at the thought of the uncertain tenure by which she held it. In times past she would have blushed at these shakings of spirit; now she could not banish them. She would not be left alone an instant; she was afraid to sleep, lest she should not awake in time. She had said, "what evil have I done?" she saw now that she had committed evil, and that continually; as she beheld "idolatry, hatred, variance, emulation, wrath, envyings" in the same enumeration with monstrous vices—a catalogue which brings to our ears the warring clash of Pandemonium, rendered more horribly discordant by contrast with the gentle music of "Love, joy, peace, long-suffering."

In angry despair she threw the volume aside; but tortured conscience drove her to it again. "I *will* be a Christian," was her primal resolve,—as the terrors of the law flamed before her—"I *must* be!" and a week of labor and agony ended in a total sinking of hope, and an exhausted cry, "I cannot!"

It was a calm Sabbath in the Indian Summer, and her chair was wheeled to the door. The "summer's late, repentant smile" shone fondly upon the landscape; the russet fields, the dismantled forests, the swift-rolling river.

She had seen it look just so, often; when the breeze played among the child's curls, and lent a quicker bound to a light heart—but faded in body—prematurely old in spirit—she saw no beauty in earth—had no treasure in heaven. Her Bible was upon her knees; she turned the pages indolently, and was saying, for the hundredth time, "No hope!" when a passage appeared to start up from the page. Could it have been there while she sought it carefully and with tears? "The Lord hath called thee as a woman, forsaken and grieved in spirit; and as a wife of youth, when thou wast refused, saith my God. For a small moment have I forsaken thee, but with great mercies will I gather thee; in a little wrath I hid my face from thee for a moment, but with everlasting kindness will I have mercy upon thee, saith the Lord, thy Redeemer. * * * * Oh! thou afflicted, tossed with tempests, and not comforted! behold, I will lay thy stones with fair colors, and lay thy foundations with sapphires!"

As Will passed under the window on his way to Church, he was arrested by an unusual sound. No one was visible, but his heart and eyes ran over, as he recognised the voice that sang softly—

"Other refuge have I none,
Hangs my helpless soul on Thee;
Leave, oh! leave me not alone,
Still support and comfort me.
All my trust on Thee is stayed,
All my help from Thee I bring;
Cover my defenceless head
With the shadow of Thy wing."

CHAPTER XXI

The trembling which mingled with her transport, was so foreign to Ida's ardent temperament, that she doubted sometimes, if she had indeed found peace. But as her filial love and trust strengthened with time, she rejoiced with more hope. Much of the old leaven was left; her imperious temper still chafed at restraint, and she was disheartened at the discovery, that the loveliest of the "Blessed Three" graces was most difficult to practise. She leaned upon a Saviour's arm, and was willing to walk in the ways of His appointment, but the weak heart pleaded that He would not send her back into the world. Sweet Sunnybank, rich in associations;—with its peaceful duties and holy enjoyments, must be more favorable to the advancement of her new life;—she hoped against hope, that she might be permitted to remain. A letter from her guardian settled the point. With laconic terseness, he declared the thing "impossible. By her father's will, the estate was hers, when she was of age; until then, no preparatory step could be taken." Her scheme had been to invite a sister of Mrs. Grant, an excellent woman, now dependent upon her brother-in-law, to reside with her, in the capacity of housekeeper and companion; and leaving the control of her finances in Mr. Read's hands, to devote herself to the improvement of her servants and poor neighbors. It was a praiseworthy enterprise, and it cost her a sharp pang to resign it, and prepare for the return, her guardian pressed, "as desirable and proper." Her trunks were packed; and she had come in from a tour of the negro cabins, and a visit to her mother's grave, to spend the last twilight in the room in which she was born—in which her mother had died. The November blast howled in the chimney;—here it was the music of early days;—in Richmond, it would be so dreary!

She was not gloomy, although the firelight glistened upon cheeks wet with tears;—she was not going away, as she had come—alone; still she was sad at quitting her retreat, and in the prospect of the temptations awaiting her. There would be trials, too—trials of faith and patience and charity—and trials of feeling—what if she should be found wanting! But a whisper tranquilised her—"Fear not—*I* am with thee!" Mrs. Grant opened the door. She held a lamp whose rays blinded Ida's tender eyes.

"A gentleman to see you, Miss Ida,—and as there was no fire in the drawing-room, I've asked him into the dining-room;" announced the dame, who was remarkable rather for sterling goodness, than for grace and discretion. The door of communication was wide open, and Ida had no alternative but to walk directly into the adjoining apartment. Charley Dana met her, ere she had advanced three steps beyond the doorway. He was so shocked at her altered appearance that he could not speak at once, but stood, pressing her hands in his, and gazing into her face with inexpressible solicitude and tenderness. She must make an exertion.

"This is kind, Charley! Am I to flatter myself that you have turned out of your way to see me?"

"No. I have looked neither to the right nor to the left. I came by the most direct route from Richmond. Sit down—you are not able to stand—and give an account of yourself. What in the name of all that is ridiculous and outrageous, brought you here alone, and has kept you here until the middle of the winter?"

"Not so bad as that, Charley! It is only the last month of Autumn. I came, because I did not want to go North, and was pining for a sight of the old place; and have been sick ever since. But tell me of yourself. When did you return, and why have not you written to me?"

"That is what I call 'iced!'" said Charley, with a laugh that sounded like former times. "Haven't I sent letters to every post-office in the Union, and not received a line in answer, since you parted company with Arthur and Carry? I arrived at home, ten days ago. Mr. Read 'presumed' you were 'yet in the country, and would be back when you were ready:' John and Jenny were in the dark; had written and inquired to no purpose: daily dispatches were pouring in from Arthur, certifying that Carry was nearly deranged with anxiety. Yesterday, I met Mr. Read, who told me you had been 'indisposed,' but would be down shortly. I asked your address, and here I am!"

"You could not be more welcome anywhere; but how unaccountable that your letters miscarried!"

"Easily explained! I stopped down the road, at a house, half-tavern, half-store, where I espied 'Post Office,' painted upon a shingle, hung out of a dirty window; and inquired the name of the place. 'Thompsonburg;' said the P.M. 'Burg,' indeed! 'I thought there was an office in this neighborhood, called 'Oakland;'" said I.

"'Oh! that's discontinued more than a year ago;' answered he. "Twas at the Cross-roads below.'"

Simple solution of a mystery which had led her to doubt her best earthly friends! Charley looked at her intently.

"'Indisposition,' forsooth! Why, I'll be hanged—"

"No you wont, Charley! Don't say so."

"Shot, then! if I am sure that I am not talking to a spirit! You've been to Death's door. What made you sick?"

"Oh! a variety of causes."

"Which means, it's no business of mine to inquire. All I have to say is, that your friends would not have treated you, as you have them. If I had died in Missouri, I would have left 'good-bye,' and a lock of my hair for you. You might have departed this life twenty times, and we been none the wiser."

"How quarrelsome you are! I'll never do so again, if you'll forgive me this once."

"Forgive! I have nothing to forgive—you were privileged to do as you pleased;—only, if you had said adieu to the land of the living, it would have been a gratification to us to know it."

Ida laughed out so merrily that Mrs. Grant, who was superintending the setting of the tea-table, raised her spectacles to look at her, and smiled gratifiedly. She and her husband sat at the table, and the guest's "sociable ways" ingratiated him with them, before the meal was half over. They retired with the waiters, and Charley, dropping his bantering tone, established himself for a "quiet coze." It was strange that he should be the first confidant of Ida's change of heart;—he, whom men styled careless—sometimes "scoffer."

He did not scoff now;—he paid diligent heed to her recital, and when it was finished— "From my soul, I congratulate you!" he exclaimed. "Would to Heaven, that I too believed!"

"You may;" said Ida, timidly.

"You do not know the thickness of the crust around my heart, Ida;—the unbelief, and ingratitude and worldliness. I can battle with men, and wear a bravado mask; but I do not forget that I have a soul, and that it must be attended to. Whether I will ever do it, I cannot say. I think I must be the most hardened of sinners;—Lynn's death would have subdued a less obdurate heart;—and do you know that, while thoroughly persuaded that it was a judgment aimed full at me—for he was my dearest friend, and I felt his loss, most of all who mourned him—I hated the Power which had dealt the blow, and scorned angrily the presumption, that I could be forced into measures!"

"You were not more wicked than I was. There is not a truer sentence in the Bible, than that the 'carnal mind is enmity against God.' Ah! Charley! if we loved holy things more! It is so mortifying to find our thoughts straying away from these subjects, when we are most desirous of contemplating them!"

"That is the fault of Old Adam—the 'body of death,' Paul writes of;" replied he. "I am not much of a Bible scholar, but it strikes me he says something in the next verse of a Deliverer, 'who giveth us the victory.' Why are Christians ever low-spirited, I wonder."

And poor Ida upbraided herself with the same query, many times within the next few days. She bore the partings and the journey better than Charley had feared she would. He did his best to save her pain and fatigue, but he saw, with secret reverence, that she was supported by a stronger Friend.

"We are almost there!" said he, letting down the carriage-window, upon the afternoon of their second day's travel.

Ida leaned out, and beheld the spires and roofs of the city. She was unprepared for the effect the sight had upon her. Recollections of her years of loneliness; the trials of her home-life; the one friendship of her school days; a brother's fondness, and his doom; her love and its blight—rushed upon her with overwhelming force—she fell back upon the cushions, and wept aloud. She had not entirely recovered her composure, when they stopped at Mr. Read's door. Josephine hardly knew the wasted figure, Charley carried, rather than led into the house; and Mr. Read was, for once, shocked out of his dignity.

"Why! Mr. Dana! Miss Ida! bless my soul and body!" was his *un*characteristic exclamation.

Charley was in no humour for trifling, or he would have said, "Amen!"

"Miss Ida's indisposition was not so unimportant as you supposed, you see, sir;" said he sarcastically. "Thanks to the kind attentions of her *country* friends, she is now convalescent."

"Hush, Charley! *please*!" said a distressed whisper from the sofa, where he had laid her. "Mr. Grant wrote to you, Mr. Read;" said she, aloud; "but as you were travelling, we doubted whether you received the letter."

"I did *not*;" he answered, the flush going off from his brow.

"I was so carefully nursed, I did not require other attention;" she continued. "I should have regretted it, if your summer's enjoyment had been interrupted needlessly. Dr. Hall, and Mr. and Mrs. Grant were untiring in their kindness; and Rachel here, ought to have a diploma to practice medicine."

It was a maxim with Mr. Read, that for every mischance, blame must rest somewhere; and Ida, having exculpated him, he could not do less than return the compliment, by pitching it back upon her.

"I do not presume to lecture you, Miss Ross; but you will admit that this freak of yours was one of unsurpassed imprudence. You left my roof under the protection of those, whom I considered fit guardians for a young lady." Charley made a movement to speak; but Ida's imploring glance restrained him. "I hear nothing of you for a long time; and you write, at last, from an uninhabited country-house, begging permission to take up your abode there. I refuse the preposterous request, and you are brought home reduced and weakened by a severe illness, of which I have not been informed. I cannot be responsible for what the world will say to all this, Miss Ross!"

The rack could not have silenced Charley now. "I will tell you what the world's opinion is, sir; and hold you responsible for your own words. 'The world' has said, in my hearing, that the guardian, who loses sight of a ward—a member of his family—for six months, without being apprised of, or inquiring into her locality and welfare, is unworthy of his trust. And if I describe his reception of an invalid, who might have perished through neglect, for all he knew or cared—'the world,' sir, will declare indignantly, that he is a disgrace to society and mankind! I have nothing more to say at present. If you take exception to my liberty of speech, you can call on me, and relieve your mind. Miss Ida, let me recommend to you to retire; Mr. Read will finish his lecture to *me*—good afternoon, Miss Read. Sir, I have the honor to bid you good-day!"

Josephine burst forth with a torrent of invective: which Ida did not stay to hear; nor did she see either of them again for two days. She was not well enough to go below; and they avoided her chamber.

Mrs. Dana called that evening. Ida was preparing for bed; and she supplanted Rachel as maid and nurse. Her softest, most nimble of hands undressed the tired, dispirited girl; smoothed the pillows; and gave her a composing draught; and with her kiss warm upon her lips, her pitying eyes watching over her, and a prayer of thankfulness at her heart, Ida fell asleep.

She learned to expect a daily visit from this dear friend; and rarely looked in vain. At her third coming she brought a note from Charley. "He was happy to state;" he said; "that the skirmish which had excited her uneasiness, had arrived at a bloodless issue. Mr. Read and himself had had an interview; he had apologised for using language to him, in his own house, which he considered himself justifiable in employing anywhere else; and Mr. Read excused his harshness to her, by representing the excitement of surprise and alarm, under which he was laboring at the time. It was agreed the matter should stop there—that is;" wrote Charley; "that his bugbear, the world, shall not get hold of it."

Josephine had received her orders; for she carried her work into Ida's chamber, that day, and sat one hour, to a minute, never opening her lips, save in monosyllables to the questions Ida forced herself to ask. Abandoning seclusion so soon as she had sufficient strength, the latter joined the family at meals, and remained longer in their society than she was wont to do formerly; and if her hope of eventually conquering their dislike did not increase, her meekness and patience did. She had occasion for it all. Josephine was quick to discover that she was happier in her affliction and debility, than she was in health and prosperity; and when the truth came to light, her natural malignity to the cause, and her hatred of its humble professor triumphed in the fiendish anticipation of how she could, by deriding one, wound the other. She would have descried soil upon an angel's robe. Ida was a young Christian, contending with the manifold disadvantages of temper, habit and irreligious associates; and her wily assailant was not passive long for lack of weapons and opportunity for her warfare. Any symptom of a convalescent's irritability; the utterance of a taste or opinion, which did not tally with her standard of consistency, was marked and laid by for use; and no complaisance or concession on Ida's part, moved her purpose. Mr. Read paid his pew-rent, went to church once every fine Sunday, and had a pleasant impression that by so doing, he was "keeping along;" paying interest as it were, upon the debt, sanguine that when the distant pay-day arrived, he would be able, by one prodigious effort, to discharge the principal. He "hated cant, because it was silly and useless" and if he did not chime in his daughter's slurs upon religion, and the conduct of Christians, he never rebuked her by word or sign. Watchfully, prayerfully, Ida strove to keep her feet in the path, and by no misstep or fall, to cast obloquy upon the name she loved.

Anna Talbot, a friendly, good-natured girl—her brother's superior in sense and feeling, was a near neighbor; and she ran in directly after breakfast one morning, full of a ball to which she was invited. Josephine had a ticket also, and was wishing for her—she must consult her about her dress.

"Ma has bought me a lovely white silk," said Anna. "I am to wear sprigged illusion over it—but oh! I was so disappointed! I wanted silver-sprigged, you know, like that Miss What's-her-name, from Philadelphia, wore to Mrs. Porter's party—but although I ransacked every store in the city, I could not find a piece. What will you get, Josey?"

"I have not quite determined."

"Do let us dress alike! There is another pattern of silk at P——'s."

"Well! I will look at it. What head-dress?" inquired Josephine.

"Oh! that's another novelty! I saw two darling little loves of wreaths down town—rose-buds and lilies-of-the-valley—pure white. I asked Mrs. V—— to lay them aside until to-day. I thought of you."

The "darling little loves" were pronounced *au fait*.

"What ornaments?" said Josephine, who was in her element.

Anna made a gesture of despair. "There's the trouble! I have nothing but those rubies, and they will not do at all. I dislike to go without any; but it cannot be helped."

"Pearls would correspond well with your dress," observed Ida.

"Ah, yes! my dear! and if I had a pearl fishery, I would draw upon my divers forthwith;—unfortunately I have not."

"Are you certain?" returned Ida, smiling. "Imagine me a diver. I have a neat set, which is at your service, if you will honor me by wearing it."

"Oh! you dearest of girls!" exclaimed Anna. "But you want them yourself—I beg your pardon—I forgot you were in mourning;—but your black is not too deep for ornaments."

"But her odor of sanctity is too strong," said Josephine. "She has renounced the pomps and vanities you and I love, Anna, and 'put on the ornament of a meek and quiet spirit.' How do you reconcile it with your conscience, to let your pearls attend a ball, Ida? How much scouring and praying will cleanse them again for your use?"

"Oh! I will get you or Anna to air them for me, once in a while, and trust to time to purify them," said Ida, willing to pass it off as a joke.

"Do you really think it sinful to go to balls?" asked Anna, wonderingly.

"I could not do it innocently," replied Ida.

"Why not? you used to like them as well as the rest of us."

"For pity's sake! no sermonising!" rudely interrupted Josephine. "I can show you the root of her piety in two words. Don't you remember a certain gentleman, whose handsome face and saintly smile set off his religion so well?"

"Oh!" laughed Anna; "but I thought he liked her very well as she was."

"Nothing like making assurance doubly sure!" answered the other. "Pity he did not return to town this winter. Love's labor is lost."

"Why, Ida! what a flirt you are!" cried Anna. "When everybody says you are engaged to Mr. Dana!"

"Everybody is wrong, then," said Ida, calmly.

"Everybody is *right*!" contradicted Josephine. "She reads in her Bible, that she 'must love all men;' and her being in mourning for one beau, and dying with love for another, are no impediments to her engagement with a third. This is Platonism with a vengeance."

"Fie! Josephine!" said Anna, perceiving by Ida's face, that the pleasantry, as she still thought it, was going too far. "You know, as well as I do, that Mr. Holmes was only a friend. Mrs. Dana is in black for him too—it is as reasonable to say that she was in love with him."

"She may have been, for anything I know to the contrary;" retorted Josephine, growing more and more insolent. "I don't pretend to understand the morals of 'the clique.'"

"I am going up stairs, Anna," said Ida, "and will send you the pearls. If they please you, you are welcome to them, whenever you wish them."

Anna pulled her down. "Don't go! I want to talk with you. You must not regard Josephine's nonsense—it is only a foolish jest."

"One, which must not be repeated!" said Ida. "I may not notice an insult to myself, but if my friends are slandered, I must defend them."

"Defend them, as long and loud as you choose;" replied Josephine, retaining her disagreeable smile and tone. "Recriminate too, if you like. It is but politic in you to fight for your patrons. Aha! that flash of the eye was Christian-like! Did you never observe, Anna, that when the 'brethren' are wrought up to the belligerent point, they are the fiercest of combatants?"

Ida hurried up stairs—threw herself upon the bed, and cried bitterly; unobservant of Rachel's presence.

"Oh! Father! pity me! I am so weak and wicked!" she prayed.

Rachel went out boiling with rage.

"More of that Evil's work! Hope I may be forgiven for saying sech a word, but if she didn't come from the bottomless ditch, I should jist like to be *re*formed whar she was made! I know mighty well whar she'll go. I ain't a goin' to stand it! Miss Ida shan't be terrified forever and ever. I'll speak my mind to Miss Jenny, before I'm a day older; maybe Mars' John can get her away from this dreadful place. Miss Ida'd never forgive me; but she needn't know nothin' about my tellin'!"

"Miss Jenny" heard her with indignant astonishment; but giving her no encouragement to proceed with her tale, or to hope for an amelioration of her mistress' condition, merely said she was sorry she could do nothing for her; and advised her to imitate Ida's prudence and silence; counsel which confirmed Rachel's skepticism in "white folks' friendship." Ida thought Charley kinder than ever, that evening. If he had known the severity of her day's discipline, he could not have been more tender and consolatory. His inattention to Josephine, who also had visitors, troubled her somewhat; but she had the comforting reflection that she was not to blame for it. The day of the ball, he took her and Mrs. Dana to ride. They called at the residence of a country friend, to whose green-house Charley had the *entrée*; and he improved his privilege by culling a bouquet of Camelias, tea-roses and orange blossoms "for the belle of the ball;" he told his hostess. When they were again in the carriage, he handed them to Ida, with a laugh. "I have no idea of going to the ball, and you would be the belle, if you were to attend; so there was no fibbing, was there?" The flowers were beautiful, and at this season, very rare; and Ida bore them home carefully, and put them in water in her room. They were sweet company; she could only watch, and pet, and talk to them the rest of the day.

Mr. Read was uncommonly jocose at supper time.

"Make yourself pretty, Josey," said he, lighting his lamp; "you don't have me to escort you every evening."

Josephine looked after him with a sneer. "A mighty honor! If he had a spark of generosity or politeness, he would have bought me a bouquet, if they do ask such enormous prices. I have a good mind not to go, I shall feel so mean without one."

Ida said she regretted it; and she did feel for her. She knew, that to party-goers, these little things are no trifles; she had seen a girl dull or sulky for an entire evening, because of a deficiency of this sort.

"I wish I could help her," she was saying to herself, as she returned to her apartment. The aroma that stole upon her senses said, "you can." She was no heroine, for she stood over her flowers, and doubted and pondered for a good half hour, before her wavering mind rested upon its pivot; and then a tear bedewed a Camelia's spotless bosom, as she emptied the vase, and saying aloud, "If thine enemy thirst, give him drink," set about arranging them anew. Her Christmas rose-tree was hanging with buds, which, on the morrow, would be blossoms, but she despoiled it of its nodding pearls; and adding geraniums and citronaloes, completed as tasteful a bouquet, as ever bloomed under the fingers of a fashionable florist. She gave it to Josephine, when she came into the parlor to survey her full-length figure in the tall glass.

"Oh! how lovely!" she exclaimed involuntarily; then recovering herself, said coldly, "They are pretty;" and returned them.

"They are for you," said Ida.

"Who sent them?"

"They were presented to me; and as their beauty is wasted upon the 'desert air' of my chamber, I shall be obliged to you to display them."

Josephine would have rejected the generous offer, if there had been the remotest chance of another; but it was late, and she could not go bouquetless.

"Who gave them to you?" she asked.

Ida paused, then replied, "Mr. Dana."

"He will know them; I had rather go without any."

"No danger of that! he will not be there." Her patience was nearly spent. Josephine accepted the gift with a very bad grace; she was awkward and embarrassed, and what appears more improbable, a little ashamed. Mr. Read was attired with scrupulous neatness and elegance, and looked ten years younger than he really was. Ida "presumed" to tell him so, and was recompensed by a bland smile. She had done her duty, perhaps more, and she did not repent of her self-denial; but something of the desolate feeling of "lang-syne" fell upon her, as she was left, sole tenant of the parlor and the house. Weak and weary, she sighed for human society and affection. It was a darkened hour; clouded by self-doubtings, mournful memories and forebodings. The piano was open; she had not touched it since her arrival at home; but she went to it now; only plaintive tunes came to her fingers; she played fitfully, as her mood disposed her; the music was the voice of her thoughts; and she sang to a rambling, irregular measure—

"I am alone—the last light tread
And laugh have died upon my ear;
And I may weep unchecked—nor dread
The scorn, that forces back the tear.
I turn to Thee! oh! when the strings,
The trustful heart has fondly thrown,
Wound closely round its best-loved things—
Are, by one stroke, asunder torn,
And bleeding, crushed, uncared for, lie—
When Hope's gay smile no joy can throw,
And the soul breathes but one wish—to die!
To whom else can the suffering go?
Thou—Thou dost look within, and read
How I have sought for love, and found
Reproach instead—how in its need
My spirit bowed it to the ground,—
E'en to the dust—and deemed it nought
Bore patiently, when pained and wronged
And smiled on sorrow, if it brought
The priceless boon for which it longed.
In vain! in vain! and now I come—
As to her nest the dove doth flee;
Give Thou my wandering heart a home—
And bind its shattered chords to Thee!"

"My poor child! are you then so sad?"
She knew the hand upon her drooping head before he spoke; and with a prayer for support, that calmed her fluttering heart, arose to greet him.
"Am I forgiven for my intrusion?" said he, leading her to a chair. "The front door was ajar, and hearing your music, I entered without ringing."
"Freely pardoned! Have you been in town long?"
"Since five o'clock this afternoon. I am on my way to the south with Annie. She is ordered to winter in Florida. Go with us—will you not? Charley supped with us; and Annie proposed this plan on hearing of your feeble health. She will wait until you are ready if you comply."
"I am very grateful for her kindness; but I cannot avail myself of it."
"Are there any 'propriety scruples?'" inquired he, smiling. "You will be her companion; and the most fastidious cannot object to the escort of a brother, and—an engaged man."
She was fortified against even this. Her arch glance hid the heart-pang faithfully. "Where is *she?*" she questioned.
"Lelia? at her father's house in S——. Here is her counterfeit." He unclasped a locket.

"It *is* like Carry!" said Ida; then she scanned it long and earnestly. She was very beautiful; with large, blue eyes; and a cherry mouth, just parted in a smile; and shining hair, folded above the smooth forehead—fair enough for *him*! and as she raised her eyes to say how lovely she was, she beheld herself in the glass opposite—wan, hollow-eyed and sallow—and felt how presumptuous—how reckless in its folly, her dream had been! He shut the spring, without looking at it himself, (it was delicate and considerate to avoid the comparison!) and making no reply to her praises of his betrothed, began to speak of the bond of fellowship, formed between themselves, since their parting. She had been discouraged by her inability to talk of what was ever in her mind; had distrusted the genuineness of her faith, because her tongue faltered in telling of the love which had redeemed her. He entered fully into her feelings; and she surprised herself by the freedom the consciousness of this afforded her. He told her of his difficulties and temptations and conflicts, often anticipating what she would have related of her own experience. So well did his counsels and comfort meet the inquiries and wants of her spirit, that she debated within herself whether he were not sent by heaven—a special messenger in her hour of trial.

"Say on!" said he, encouragingly, as he caught her eye.

"I was about to ask if you believed in what are termed minute or particular Providences."

"As in my existence! even to the numbering of the hairs of any head. You have not been troubling your brain with quibblings upon this subject, I hope?"

"No; but I have heard it disputed by very good people, who confuse me by their 'free agency,' and 'accountability,' and 'decrees.'"

"Discard theories, and eschew arguments. Let your Bible and your common sense be your teachers. As a machinist fashions the minutest cog of the smallest wheel, as carefully as the mighty lever, the main power,—so the Supreme Governor looks to the balance of the tiniest atom in His universe."

"Then," said Ida; "I do not commit presumption when I trace my Father's hand in every-day events; when I lift up my soul in thankfulness for a pleasant, or ennobling thought, a visit, a gift, an act of friendship, which has made me better or happier—or say 'Thy will be done?' in the petty trials, which annoy, rather than afflict us!"

"It is your privilege and duty. The introductory sentence of the Lord's Prayer is sufficient to inculcate this truth. 'Our Father—' is not a father's care constant? He says moreover—'we must become as little children.' Who relies more than a child? 'As thy day is, so shall thy strength be;—' no matter where, or how we are placed, God will give us the requisite strength; and as our positions are changing every moment, does not this say that He will be with us every moment, and order the success of whatever we attempt, by the amount of strength He imparts? And again, 'not a sparrow falls to the ground without your Father.' Nothing which God does is *small*, and He 'orders all things according to the counsel of His own will.' Then nothing is insignificant, because God orders everything. Our actions may appear trivial; but do they not assume a terrible importance, when we learn that even our fleeting words are to be the data of our judgment, at the last day? A few good people doubt the doctrine of 'special Providences;' but is it not better for us to believe what God says of his character, than to determine what character he ought to have? If He says He is the God of 'the hairs of our heads—' of 'sparrows' and lilies of the field—all we have to do, is to take His word for truth, and act accordingly. His attention to small things is as conclusive a proof of His Divinity, as to great ones. It has been well said, that 'man cannot comprehend the Infinitely great, nor the Infinitely small.' But I weary you."

"You do not—I am interested and instructed. I am but a babe in leading-strings; so weak and ignorant, it terrifies me to think of the possibility that I will be obliged to take a single step without holding my Father's hand."

"That is what none of us are called upon to do, Ida. 'I will never leave thee, nor forsake thee.' 'Even there shall thy hand lead me, and Thy right hand shall hold me.' We could not stand alone an instant, were this 'right hand' withdrawn."

"Charley, who strews many pearls among the rubbish he scatters abroad, once set me to thinking seriously—I hope, not unprofitably, by wondering why Christians were ever low-spirited," said Ida. "It seems to me that they would not be, if their confidence in God were implicit and abiding; but I am often sad—almost desponding."

"To-night, for instance," said Mr. Lacy, cheerfully. "'This kind goeth not out, but by prayer;' and you must not be cast down, that you cannot, in a month, overcome a habit of years. Humanly speaking, you have had much to embitter your lot;—but as we can, in reviewing our past lives, see many events which, Janus-like, approached us frowningly, now changed to smiles of blessing, ought we not, with this attestation of experience to the truth of His promises, to trust Him in the dark ways we now tread?"

"Poor Lynn!" her full eyes overflowed. "How frequently I am reminded of his—

'I am blind! in rough paths groping
With outstretched hand! and flightless eyes!'"

"Let us hope that the Everlasting arms received him," said Mr. Lacy. "I feared to speak of him to you, Ida; knowing, as I do, that upon a heart like yours, such a blow must have left indelible traces. You have not—you never will forget him, but can you not believe that this, too, was intended for your good?"

"I do—although at the time, it seemed very hard that from my meagre list of friends, one so necessary to my happiness, should be stricken. I may never meet another, who will give me affection so fond, yet so disinterested."

"Disinterested! that is a term not generally applied to love which leads to betrothal."

"Mr. Lacy!" ejaculated Ida, astonished. "But no! you knew us too well? did Lynn never tell you—" she stopped.

"No, I first heard of your engagement from a third person; you confirmed it, subsequently."

"What *do* you mean? you are under a strange misapprehension. I never was betrothed to Lynn; he never thought of me but as a friend."

"Ida!" his tone was stern. "What are you saying? Have you forgotten the night you left my side for his, upon seeing his dejection—the long promenade, and his reproaches for what he deemed—wrongfully, as I am now assured—was coquetry in you? I was told then, what I had heard, without heeding before, that you were plighted lovers. So confirmed was I in my disbelief that I would have declared it, in defiance of the proofs presented to me, had I not overheard by accident a portion of your conversation. He said—(I remember it well!)— 'I have loved you as man never loved woman before—have believed you pure and high-minded. If I thought that the despicable coquetry you hint at, had caused you to insist upon the concealment of our engagement—' I lost the rest. Is not this enough? must I harrow your feelings by recurring to your appeal to me to save him from crime and death for your sake;—or to the awful hour when you were summoned to receive his last sigh? Oh! Ida! Ida! I have trusted in your truth—do not shake my faith now!"

There was bewilderment, but not falsehood in the eyes that sustained his rebuking glance. "I have spoken the truth. The sentence which misled you, was the repetition of a remark made to another;—the whisper in his dying hour, a message to the same. To me—I repeat— he was a brother, devoted and true to the last—but nothing more."

His lips were ashy white;—his self-command had utterly deserted him.

"I have been *terribly* deceived!" he said, rising and pacing the floor. "Ida!" he resumed, coming back to her side, "we have spoken of the mysterious dealings of Providence. I did not think my trust would be tested so soon. You have unwittingly awakened a pain, I thought was stilled forever, and justice to you, and to myself, requires me to endure it yet awhile longer. We are friends—we can never be anything nearer—but if I were the husband, instead of the betrothed of another, I should feel bound to clear my honor from the aspersion my conduct has cast upon it. My actions—my language, must have convinced you that I loved you;—you were ignorant of the mistake into which I had fallen—what interpretation have you put upon my course, since? You did not misconstrue my attentions then—tell me—am I a knave—a hypocrite in your sight?"

"Never!" said she, lifting a face, as pale as his own. "My confidence in your friendship and integrity has not swerved, and there lives not one who will pray for your happiness with more sincerity; who is more thankful for your noble renunciation of personal feeling to advance her welfare. We *are* friends! we will forget everything but this."

She was standing before him; and while speaking, laid her hand in his. He gazed silently into the countenance, so elevated in its look of heroic self-devotion.

"You have chosen one far more worthy of you than I could ever have been;—you will be very happy together. I hope to meet her some day, and love her, as all must love the beautiful and good. There is a consolation those friends have at parting, whose home is not here;—that, although we walk in different pathways on earth, they all lead to our abiding-place—Heaven." With an uncontrollable impulse, he drew her to him, and pressed his lips to her brow! He was gone! and the poor human heart bled from the slow torture to which it had been put. He had not dreamed of it,—had not suspected, when her steady, sweet tones told him of their separate pathways, that her soul was reaching, in intense yearnings, towards the lightsome way, where flowers sprang beneath his steps, and shuddering at the tomb-like chill of that which echoed her lonely foot-fall. He was gone! and the weeping eyes which sought Heaven, showed from whence she had derived the supernatural strength which had borne her through the trying interview;—and with the cry of unspeakable sorrow that succeeded his departure, arose a petition for larger supplies. It was granted. She wept still; but not in wretchedness. Solemn, pure resolutions were growing up beneath the waves of grief. The destruction of this hope—-the dearest in a woman's heart, was the fall of a proud plant,—the garden's pride—in its matured beauty. Buds and blooms wilt and perish upon the stalk, but from the laden seed-vessels are showered far and wide germs that shall rejoice many hearts with the sweetness and loveliness their parent garnered for one.

CHAPTER XXII

It was so cold and damp in the morning, that Rachel, in virtue of her nursely prerogatives, forbade her mistress' rising before breakfast. Ida was not averse to keeping her room. She wished to achieve another victory over herself before meeting Josephine. A suspicion of her agency in Mr. Lacy's deception ripened, upon reflection, into a certainty, her love of justice prompted her to banish. But a hundred incidents occurred to her memory. Especially, she recollected that Josephine had accosted him, directly after she had taken Lynn's arm in the Fair-room, that she was still with him at the close of the evening, and that he had looked sorrowfully—reproachfully at her. She had no just conception of the girl's total destitution of principle, nor of her envy of herself; but she knew her to be weak, vain and spiteful; and against her will, she had to credit a conclusion, she judged uncharitable. She did not desire to ascertain its truth; it could make no difference at this late date. Another perplexity assailed her;—should she tell Josephine of the visit she had had? Should she hear of it from some other source, or by a direct inquiry of herself, whether she had spent the evening alone—what conjectures might not be formed as to the motive of her silence? She was deliberating thus, when the door flew back, and Josephine walked in. Ida, nervously excitable, started from her pillow; and clasped her hands in speechless alarm at the suddenness and disorder of her appearance. She was frightfully pallid, and her eyes were inflamed with weeping and rage.

Locking the door, she advanced to the foot of the bed, and grasped the post tightly, as if to brace herself for some desperate act. Ida could not stir, and the two regarded each other for a moment without a word. Josephine was torn by some fearful conflict: Ida had never seen her eyes dimmed by a tear; and when the struggle for language ended in a tempestuous burst of weeping, the thought flashed over her, that she was bereft of reason.

"Josephine! what has happened?" she could scarcely utter.

Josephine dashed off the thick-coming drops.

"Happened! yes! it will not matter to you, who can leave this abominable place in two years—or to-morrow, if you choose to have your own way. *I* am to stay, and be pushed about, and lectured and ruled by a hideous vixen! I could kill her, and him too!"

"Are you raving? Who is it?"

"His wife! the dotard! the foolish old greybeard!"

"Josephine! you cannot mean your father!"

"I do mean him; and he *is* a doting fool, to be playing the sighing lover at his age—and to whom? A baby-faced chit, just out of her teens! a spoiled doll of a thing whose prattle and tricks have addled his brains—if he ever had any. I won't stay here! I will beg my bread in the street first!"

"But he is not married yet; you may be mistaken. How did your hear it?"

"From himself, on our way to that detestable ball. I wish he, and she, and it, were at the bottom of the Dead Sea! He commenced 'Josey, my dear!'—Oh, the deceitful villain!"

"Josephine!" said Ida, shuddering.

"He is! and I will say it! 'Josey'—said he, simpering and giggling like a shame-faced school-boy.—'Can you guess why I consented to your having that dress?"

"Because I liked it—I suppose, sir."

"'No, my dear;—I had my reasons for wishing you to look well to-night. I expect to meet a friend at the ball, to whom I shall introduce you.'

"Who is it, sir? may I ask?" said I.

"He giggled and winked—oh! so disgustingly! 'Did you imagine that I was idle all the time I was in the country? You were flirting at the Springs, and I concluded to try my hand. You have too much care upon you, for so young a person; what do you say to my engaging a 'help?''

"A housekeeper *would* be a convenience;" answered I.

"'A ball is a proper place to hunt up housekeepers!' said he, blazing out. 'No airs, miss! you understand me! I am to be married in a fortnight, and you may as well take it quietly—or it will be worse for you.'

"It is too late for him to brow-beat me, and so I said: and that I would worry his and her life out, as surely as she crossed this threshold—that he had made himself the laughing-stock of the city—had been taken in by a designing creature who wanted his money—for he had lost his good looks and his senses too, it appeared—"

"'If you say another word,' said he, griping my arm—there! you see the bruise! 'I will put you out of the carriage, and you may die before I will give you a cent to save you from starvation. You will see this lady to-night, and if you do not treat her with becoming politeness, you don't go home with me, nor after me, either!'

"You never saw such a tiger! When we were there, I scowled at every dried-up old maid, who looked as if she were husband-hunting. I had picked out one, with a skinny neck and corkscrew curls, when up steps our youthful lover, with a lady hanging on his arm;—he, all honey and smiles—she, cool and bold. 'Miss Copeland—let me make you acquainted with my daughter!' I wanted to strike her in the face, but his eye was too threatening;—so I choked myself with a pretty speech, and she bowed condescendingly. I gave her one look, though, when he did not see—and she glared back at me. I'll warrant there'll be no love lost!"

"But what is she like? She may be an agreeable companion," said Ida.

"Ida Ross! I didn't come to you for canting consolation! I was too full to keep my fury to myself—and I hate her rather more than I do you. This is why I have told you about the wretch. 'Companion!' I'll be company for her! She had better be burned alive, than come here. She will wish she had been, or my name is not Read!"

"But you can escape by marriage;" suggested Ida, who perceived that the girl was suffering, and pitied her, while she trembled at her frenzy.

"Say that again, and I will murder you!" retorted Josephine, in the white heat of concentrated passion. "You will make me remember that our old scores are not quite settled yet."

"I have no scores against you;" said Ida, firmly. "The past cannot return—why refer to it?" Josephine regarded her fixedly. "You are wise!" she said, presently, breaking into a contemptuous laugh. "To another, you would preach repentance—you know I never repent!" and with this strange speech, she quitted her.

Now that he had broken the matter to his daughter, the bridegroom used the utmost celerity in the despatch of preliminaries. The house was filled with workmen, upholsterers and cooks, whose din destroyed the quiet of Ida's chamber, the only one left unaltered. Josephine adhered to her resolution not to move a finger in the preparations for the detested intruder's reception. She would not go to the marriage, which took place at the bride's father's, in the country. Mr. Read did not insist; he was secretly pleased to be free for this evening—conscious that he could acquit himself more creditably, if her eyes were not upon him. The wedding party was to be at his house, the next night but one. The supper was in the hands of the profession; Mr. Read being too prudent to risk the probability of a grievous mortification, by entrusting the most trifling arrangement to his filial mar-plot.

It was dark when the bridal party arrived. The girls were dressed, and in the drawing-room. Ida's picture of the bride, drawn from Josephine's representment, was of an overdressed, forward country girl, who had wheedled and flattered a man of treble her age, into an offer of his hand and fortune; and she was puzzled by the elaborate toilette of the step-daughter. If her aim was to outshine the creature she had described, she had certainly over-estimated the labor its accomplishment required. She swept into the apartment with a hauteur, that made her diminutive form appear two inches taller; her jetty hair, almost an incumbrance from its length and profusion, dressed partly in ringlets, partly in braids—instead of, as she usually wore it at parties, and as her father liked to see it—in natural curls floating upon her shoulders. This style gave her a juvenile air, pleasing, heretofore—discarded by the full-fledged woman she acted to-night. Her robe was of white satin; the falling shoulders and proud swell of the throat exhibited to fine advantage by the low bodice. Ida was dressed in a silver-grey silk, with a berthe of rich black lace; the throat-latch and cuffs of black velvet and jet, making her extreme paleness more striking. Her figure and expression of repose had its opposite in the impersonation of splendid inquietude, which trod the rooms impatiently, rustling and gleaming in the blaze of the chandeliers.

"They have come!" said Ida, with a pitying accent, she could not repress, as Josephine turned deadly pale at the sound of wheels. "We *must* meet them," and she took her hand. Hers was fiercely thrown off. Repellant, defiant, she disdained support. The bride's brother and bridemaids had accompanied her; but Ida scarcely remarked their muffled-up figures, as "Miss Murray—" "Miss Arnold"—were named. Her eyes and thoughts were for the new Mrs. Read. Josephine's aversion had hood-winked her. Ida subscribed to her "cool and bold," as the solitary clause of the description that had the slightest resemblance to the reality; and "bold" was too coarse an epithet for the polished indifference of a woman of the world. She was not more than three-and-twenty, handsome, even in her travelling apparel—not "baby-faced"—and went through the introductions with a nonchalant grace; touching Josephine's cheek with her lips; extending to Ida, the tips of her fingers,—and bestowing a fashionable nod upon the group of servants in the hall; then, escorted by her husband, led the way, up-stairs. Josephine's face was balefully dark, as she resumed her walk. It was a part of her retribution, although she would not see it,—that as she had slighted, and thrust aside others, whose rights were equal with hers,—she was to take a secondary place where she had ruled so long.

The company were assembled, before the happy pair made their entry. Charley was with Ida—he was seldom far off—"November and June!" exclaimed he, aside. "Its enough to cause a man to forswear your sex, to see such a being a voluntary victim upon the altar of mammon."

Ida caught his arm; and seeing that she was fainting, he seized a bottle of cologne-water from the mantel, and dashed a handful into her face, so quickly and dexterously, that his nearest neighbors did not understand the movement. The powerful perfume recalled her scattering senses. Charley put her in the corner of a sofa; and placed himself in front of her, to screen her from observation, until her agitation should subside. It was quickly over; and only remarking—"You cannot get through the crowd just yet—sit still!" he continued fanning her, and chatting, as if her illness were the most natural thing imaginable,—a matter of no moment. His eyes were as busy as his tongue; and in their apparently aimless rovings, no group escaped scrutiny. He was fairly at fault; and opposed as the conclusion was to the premises he had assumed, was compelled to refer her attack to physical causes. Once, he fancied he saw an imploring agony in her eye, which entreated for help or comfort; but while he looked, it disappeared, leaving a serenity that rebuked his suspicions.

"Who is this Mr. Read is convoying this way?" he inquired. "I ought to know him."

"He is a stranger to me," replied Ida.

"Miss Ross, Mr. Copeland fears you will not recognise him, without a second introduction," said the host.

"And Mr. Copeland's fears were not groundless," said that gentleman, when his brother-in-law was out of hearing. "A less modest individual than myself might be dubious of the durability of an impression, made under such circumstances, as our briefest of brief interviews,—when I could have been, at best, but a fourth-rate attraction. Mr. Dana—I believe! I need not excuse myself for not observing you before. This is a brilliant assembly, Miss Ross. I have been rating my excellent brother-in-law"—there was the least curl of scorn upon his handsome mouth as he pronounced these words—"for deserting this galaxy of beauty to seek a mate in our gloomier regions."

"Isolated stars often dispense more light than the millions composing the galaxy," answered Ida.

"I have thought the same since I reached this corner," he returned, gallantly. "I parted with a friend of yours, yesterday, who would not have granted me time to say a word for myself, if I had engaged to deliver a quarter of the messages he charged me with."

"Ah! who was so unreasonable?"

"Mr. Germaine," he replied, smiling, as the blood rose to her cheek. "He enacted Telemachus last summer, with a difference in the object of his search."

"But with a like termination," said Charley, who seemed to understand the allusion.

"Yes—as it proved; but he did not know it at that time. He called by to see me on his way home. He was in a deplorable state of mind; but I am happy to say that the consolations of friendship were not unavailing. I have succeeded in inoculating him with hopes of more fortunate chances in future. Yesterday, he was ready to swear with Barnadine, that he 'would not die that day for any man's persuasion.'"

"Had he been long absent from his own neighborhood?" asked Ida. "Did he speak of Dr. Carleton's family?"

"Frequently. They are in their usual health, I believe, although he was not explicit upon this point; all ideas connected with Poplar-grove having a marked proclivity backward. 'Last summer' was the starting-point and terminus of his discourse to me. I am going to say something rude, Miss Ross. Is the lady by the pier-table your cousin-german?"

"What if she were my sister?"

"I should say, with all frankness, that I could not detect the family likeness. As she is not related by consanguinity or affinity, we will hope, benevolently, that her attendant is not constituted like my sister, who faints at passing a freshly-painted house; and furthermore award her praise for her liberality. You have heard of the clay that lived with roses—do you think that gentleman would appreciate the apologue?"

Ida and Charley laughed, although the remark might have been considered ill-natured. The pure red and white of the lady's face remained intact, but the gentleman's coat-sleeve had received a bountiful donation of flour or chalk from the snowy arm resting upon it.

"Is not that your friend, Miss Read?" pursued Mr. Copeland. "A pretty casket, but how frail to enshrine the spirit that speaks in those orbs! There is stirring music there, or I am mistaken. Hear me, Miss Ross, before you annihilate me by a second look of reproof. We simple yeomen do not get away from our farms often; and not above once in a lifetime happen upon such a godsend as this is, for adding to our slender stock of information. I am a boy of an inquiring mind, and my venerable and respected father's parting injunction was to keep my eyes and ears open. You believe every word I am saying—I see it in your countenance. *You* do not fear to accept my arm for a promenade? Mr. Dana—*au revoir*."

"I am afraid you have chosen an indifferent cicerone," said Ida.

"How unjust! I repel the insinuation, and to prove my innocence, will not ask a question concerning any one but yourself."

"I will answer those upon any other subject more readily."

"I had not expected to find you one who would shirk inquiry into her character and actions. Luckily I am not deputed to institute it. You do not flirt, I understand, Miss Ross?"

"Never. Why the question?"

"It is the principal amusement here, I observe; and that reminded me of my curiosity to behold you, when I heard that you were, in this respect, an anomaly in your sex."

"Is your judgment so unsparing?" said Ida. "I know many, whose sentiments and practices coincide with mine; but before we dispute, let us have a clear sense of each other's meaning. What is your definition of flirting?"

"With men, it signifies paying attentions that warrant the expectation of courtship:—a formal declaration, or expressions which are tantamount to it, when we have no inclination or intention to fulfil an engagement of marriage. The man who does this, incurs the opprobrium of the community, unless the lady is as great an adept in the art as himself. Then, it is a harmless sham fight; no mischief done, and nobody to blame. On the other side, the hapless wight, who is worsted by a coquette, has to bear ridicule, in addition to his bruises. She may beckon her victim on by smiles and blushes and half-uttered fondness, actually give him the pledges, and admit him to the privileges of an accepted lover; and then laugh in the face of the fond fool, whose peace she has wilfully destroyed;—and this sensible, charitable world claps its hands, and shouts 'bravo! for a clever woman!'"

"No *woman* will acknowledge the truthfulness of this sketch," rejoined Ida. "I have seen unthinking girls act thus; but we are cognizant of the crime—not its punishment, which is inevitable and severe."

"They settle down generally, like their neighbors, to a home and a husband," said Mr. Copeland.

"This is their outward lot; who knows their inner life?"

"The inner life of a woman! who, indeed! what a tissue of contradictions it must be! Follow my eye, Miss Ross. Do you see that Peri with cerulean eyes, who is bowing to that gentleman's petition for 'the pleasure of her hand?'" Again, that blanching cheek, as she murmured 'yes.'

"It is Lelia Arnold—my sister's bridesmaid. She is the loveliest and gayest girl in the room; you would say that she could not exist, but in this hot-house of flattery and pleasure. Last spring she went on a visit to a sick friend, and for four months we lost sight of her. She resides about six miles from, us; and we were notified of her return by her driving over, one day, attended by a handsome fellow, brother to the 'dear Annie' with whom she had been staying. The truth was out! The parade the family made of her disinterestedness and attachment to the invalid deceived my sister, but not me. She aims at universal fascination; this Lacy has prepossessing manners and appearance, talent,—and it may be, money. Her four months' nursing was a judicious outlay. Helen—Mrs. Read, declares there is no engagement; but I retain my opinion. She is, to-night, *la reine du bal*; on Sunday, she will kneel, in Church, the most angelic vision that ever was vouchsafed to a Catholic's prayers; relate a tale of woe, and the eyes now dancing in mirth, will be dewy with tears; if you are worth winning, she is the tender, love-beseeching girl. I am the only one who quarrels with her. The first time, I was ready to blow my brains out, for my brutality. I think now I shall wait for a more convenient season. She is

'A perfect woman, nobly planned.
To warn, to comfort, to command,'

—minus a heart!"

"Are you well advised of this?" Her voice was very low.

"I wish I were as sure of a diadem! and if I had it, I will not be my own security, that she could not coax it from me, in five minutes after it came into my possession. Do not imagine this a digression from the subject. I could tell you of an exile from his native land, driven thence by her falsehood; of one, with high intellect and gigantic energies, paralyzed by his fall from the dizzy height, to which her promises had raised him;—and the snow, this winter night, enwraps another pierced heart, as cold as that which moves her fleecy drapery. What do you say now, Miss Ross? Does the world heap no honors, lavish no applause upon her?"

"I do not know how to believe you!" said Ida, putting her hand confusedly to her forehead.

"It is no private scandal;—I do not retail such,—the facts are notorious. Yet ask Helen—ask any woman who 'knows society,' and she will certify to the frequency of these occurrences—'crimes' you called them—and the impunity with which they are committed."

"It is a crime!" said Ida, wildly;—"an atrocious crime!"

"My dear Miss Ross! one would think you were reprobating a highway murderer! Recover yourself—the perpetrators are your acquaintances and friends. Another set, Helen! does Mr. Read take the floor, too!" he said to his sister, with the mocking smile Ida had noticed once before.

"I do not know;" she replied, carelessly. "He can take care of himself—"

"Having nearly arrived at years of discretion;" he concluded the sentence.

Ida did not like the unnecessary taunt, nor the smile with which he turned to her.

"Your naive abhorrence of flirtation, emboldens me to ask another question. Has disinterested affection an abode upon earth?"

"Are you infidel there also?" said Ida, lightly.

"You evade. I ask no reply but that. You are a believer; and while I was telling my story, your mind was running through the details of conduct, diametrically opposed to our fair friend's yonder."

It was a random shot; but that it told, he was assured by the nervous tremor of her arm; and kindly violating his promise not to be inquisitive about his fellow-guests, returned to his jesting strain.

It was well that he did. She was fearfully tried. At Miss Arnold's entrance, she had known the original of "Leila's" miniature; but cowering at the unexpected ordeal she must undergo, while she was beneath the same roof with herself, took refuge in the hope that she was deceived by an accidental resemblance. Mr. Copeland had torn down this frail shelter, and added a new sorrow to the burden that was crushing her. Why was she made to hear this recital? Was there a "special Providence" in his being Mr. Germaine's friend, and singling her out among a hundred strangers? What directed his mind into the channel it took? what pointed his finger to Lelia Arnold, and thereby probed her heart to its core? She had taught herself to think of, and pray for *his* wife—the good and beautiful, but not for this heartless coquette—"not for her! oh! my Father! I could have borne anything but this!" she cried, in bitterness of spirit. It was an experience which smites many with sore amazement—that it is easier to learn resignation for ourselves, than for those we love. She had begun her uninviting journey meekly; but rebelled that a cloud lowered over him.

Night, morning passed—the afternoon was upon the wane, ere she gained fortitude of body and spirit, for a re-encounter with the formidable stranger. A prop to her resolution was applied by Rachel, who "thought them young ladies must be having a mighty dull time. Mrs. Read nor Miss Josephine didn't leave their rooms from breakfast to dinner; and looks like they meaned to stay thar, till plump night; and Miss Murray and Miss Arnold are wandering about, like lost sheep. I wish you was well enough to sit with them awhile, Miss Ida."

Matters were much as she had represented. Miss Arnold was watching the passers-by, with an *ennuyée* air, and Miss Murray lounging in an easy chair, with a book. The latter arose with a cordial air.

"I am glad you are able to be with us again. You seem feeble, and we were uneasy lest fatigue might have made you sick."

Miss Arnold bowed distantly, and held herself aloof, during the dialogue that ensued. Ida gathered courage as she witnessed her uninterested attitude, which could hardly have been feigned. She had not recognised her; or as she reflected, in her humility, was more probable, had never heard of her. The thought was unflattering, but there was relief in it. Miss Murray was affable and unaffected; her features only redeemed from plainness by their agreeable expression. They talked of the distinctive traits of town and country life. She "had never resided in the city," Miss Murray said, "but had attended Mr. Purcell's school one session." Ida inquired "when?" and heard that they were there together, but in different classes.

"I do not remember seeing you," said she.

"But *I* knew your face, yesterday afternoon;" was Miss Murray's reply.

"Carry Carleton was your desk-mate, and Anna Talbot sat before you."

They were at no loss for topics now; and "Alice" and "Ida" superseded the formal "Miss."

"I read of Carry's marriage in the papers, but the name of her *caro sposo* has slipped my memory;" said Miss Murray.

"Dr. Dana,—he is an excellent young man; handsome, amiable, and has a high reputation as an intelligent man, and skilful physician."

"Dana! was there a gentleman of that name here last night?" asked Alice.

"Yes—his brother."

"He was introduced to me;"—and she laughed. "He is an original. I was highly entertained by his humorous sayings."

She was interested in Ida's graphic limning of his character.

"He is an intimate friend of yours, then?"

"One of the best I have;—the kindest of brothers."

"I knew he was as good as funny, from his face. You saw him, Lelia?"

"Whom?" asked she, without moving.

"Mr. Dana, the humorous gentleman, I talked to so long, by the piano."

"I saw him, but heard no humor. I thought him very stupid."

Miss Murray reddened. "Why, Lelia! but you are not a fair judge. If he had talked to you, you would not say so."

"He 'bored' me for what seemed an eternity, but which, Mr. Copeland, who released me, said was only ten minutes," said she, carelessly.

Miss Murray was content she should be silent, after this mal-apropos observation. Ida said "one must be well acquainted with him to appreciate him." Miss Arnold measured her from head to foot, and saying coldly, "I rarely err in a first opinion;" turned her blue eyes to the window again.

The others were forgetting her in the deepening stream of chat, when she came to the fire-place. "I am chilly!" she said, and throwing one of the sofa-pillows at Alice's feet, seated herself, and leaned her elbow upon her friend's lap. She was bewitchingly lovely—Ida owned; and so may have thought Richard Copeland, who *happened* to enter, just as she was settled.

"Rehearsing tableaux, young ladies!" said he. "Miss Ross—Miss Alice—good evening. You play humility, I perceive, Miss Lelia."

She did not offer to rise. "Do not I become the character?" she inquired.

"The character becomes you, at any rate. How have you wiled away the day, Miss Alice?" Her sunshiny face made him as frank as herself, when he addressed her.

"Oh!" said she. "In sleeping, reading and eating, I contrived to dispose of all but the past hour or two, of which Miss Ross has kindly relieved me."

"I can testify to her adroitness in this particular," he replied. "She did a little time-lifting for me last evening. Have you finished your official returns of 'killed, wounded and missing,' Miss Ross?"

"I suspect my bulletins would comprise most of the latter," said Ida.

"And mine!" echoed Alice.

"There is one exception, at least," he returned, bowing. "Decide between yourselves to whom the captive belongs."

"May I be umpire?" asked Miss Arnold, her cheeks dimpling mischievously.

"When I was a boy, Miss Lelia, I read in an old spelling-book, of two cats, who came to the scratch over a piece of cheese, and agreed to refer its division to the monkey's arbitration. You have read it too, and recollect the catastrophe."

He appeared to take pleasure in being as rude to her as the letter of politeness allowed; and she bore it patiently, without relaxing her efforts to please and attract.

"Where are Helen and Miss Read?" he asked of Alice. "Do all the duties of hospitality devolve upon Miss Ross?"

"They are resting, I suppose, to be blooming at the party to-night," replied she.

"Your roses, then, are not so precious. Is this so?"

"Say instead, that they are perpetual," said Ida.

Alice blushed and laughed.

"Are we to be favored with your company, Miss Ross?" inquired Mr. Copeland.

"No, I do not keep late hours until my health is confirmed."

"What a pity!" exclaimed Alice. "Do go! I shall feel so strange, so lonely!"

"Mr. Copeland will prevent that; and I make over to you my interest in my friend, Mr. Dana, for one evening."

"Are you in the market for the first bidder?" said Miss Arnold, with pretty archness, to the former gentleman.

"If Miss Ross pleases. I intended to ask permission to remain in my present quarters until the hour at which we ultra-fashionables go to routs; but if she banishes me sooner, I am proud to do her bidding, hard as it is."

The lamps were lighted; and Mrs. Read conferred the further illumination of her presence. "Where's your liege-lord, my lady?" asked her brother; and she replied, as she did, whenever she could, to inquiries concerning him—"Indeed, I do not know," and sank indolently upon a divan. The large, slumberous eyes did not brighten at his step in the hall; and when she drew her dress aside to make room for him, it was with more thought for the costly fabric, than desire to have him near. Josephine came in, as the bell sounded for supper. It was a cheerful meal, in spite of her haughty silence, and Ida's inward conflicts. Alice Murray's even spirits had an equalising effect upon the varied temperaments around her; Miss Arnold was witty and charming. Ida could not deny her eyes the luxury of watching her animated countenance. They feasted upon its beauty, until every thought was merged in admiration; and this, while, Mr. Copeland's sallies were exclusively for herself. Mrs. Read aroused from her proud languor, and manifested a keen relish for the ridiculous, and satirical powers, not inferior to her brother's. There was a veiled acrimony in their manner to each other, which impressed Ida with the belief of some unsettled feud, never lost sight of by either; and which she could not reconcile with Alice's assertion, that he was Mrs. Read's best-beloved brother. Their personal resemblance was marked; but gay and caustic as he was, there were scintillations of feeling in his dark eyes, which had burnt out, or were smothered in hers. "And how else could it be?" she said to herself, as she looked at her dignified guardian, transformed for the nonce, into the uxorious husband; and marvelled, for the thousandth time—"What made her marry him?"

They were incredulous when Mr. Read said it was time to dress for Mrs. Talbot's.

"You go with us, Richard?" said his sister.

"I will meet you there; I must go to my hotel awhile first."

There could be no reason for this, yet Ida thought Miss Arnold's brow clouded.

"Your hair was prettily arranged last night, Ida," said Alice. "Will you give me a few hints as to my *coiffure*?"

"With pleasure. I was about to ask if I could assist you in any way?"

So, instead of going off to her "sanctum," she busied herself in the dressing-room. Alice laughed and talked incessantly; Miss Arnold was grave and mute, except when her maid paused for directions. She objected, in the mildest of tones, that there was not light enough upon her table, and thanked "dear, obliging Alice," who sent a candle from hers, without fearing she could not spare it.

"I never looked so well in all my life!" said Alice, clasping her hands in pretended rapture. "I am all impatience to try the effect of my beauty. You have won me one admirer, Ida— myself."

"Add me to the number," said Miss Arnold, and gliding up, she kissed the rosy cheek.

"O Lelia! my darling!" screamed Alice. "My darling! you are an angel! Ida! is she not lovely?"

"Very!" said Ida, and she *felt* it. Alice said an affectionate—the rest a polite farewell;—they drove off;—and she went very quietly to her chamber—quietly—though her hand was pressed hard upon her heart; and her throat ached, as if iron fingers were tightened around it;—and while they were dancing, she was kneeling before that precious Bible, forgetting sorrow and self in its sublime teachings;—hours before their return, she slept, peacefully, happily—such sleep as even in this life "He giveth His beloved."

CHAPTER XXIII

Sunday was rainy, and Ida was deprived of the opportunity of judging whether Miss Arnold's church behaviour was as Mr. Copeland had portrayed it. But she was to learn how just to life another part of his description was.

The morning, yawned through in the other apartments, passed swiftly in hers, in reading, study, and blessed communion with her Heavenly Friend.

A low tap was heard at the door, and her "come in," answered by Miss Arnold.

"Pray, keep your seat," said she, closing the door with a shiver, as the cold draught from the passage blew over her; "I have ransacked the parlor book-case in vain for Sabbath reading, and Alice said you could probably supply me."

"My little library is at your service," said Ida, parting the curtains before a handsome set of shelves.

"You have quite an extensive collection;" remarked Miss Arnold, patronisingly. She did not ask her to help her in the selection, and Ida returned to her chair. Miss Arnold pulled out one and another slowly, so as to consume as much time as possible in the occupation. Ida glanced up from time to time, to see what choice she made. A modest volume, presented by Mr. Lacy, stood near the centre of the top shelf; and she looked up once as Miss Arnold was in the act of taking it down. She watched her with suspended breath. She read the title and title-page, and shutting it, raised her arm to replace it; but a look of recollection flitted over her brow, and she re-opened it—at the fly-leaf. Ida dropped her eyes instantly to the page before her, yet she saw as plainly as with her bodily organs of vision, that after reading what was written there,—"Miss Ida Ross, with the regards of M. L.," a gaze of keen inquisition rested upon herself, that the inscription was thoughtfully examined,—then the subject matter of the book, which was afterwards restored to its place, and with another, selected at hazard, her visitor moved gracefully towards her. "You have been so kind to me—to us—during our stay here, that I am encouraged to beg an additional favor."

Her silvery voice had a new tone, and it was as if a malicious spirit repeated to Ida,—"If you are worth winning, she is the tender, love-beseeching girl." Hitherto, her conduct had afforded decisive evidence that she was *not* worth the trouble. She drove the whisperer away and answered politely,

"I shall be happy to oblige you."

"Then may I stay with you awhile? This is such a dear, home-like nook, and it is so dreary out of doors, and not much better down stairs, for Alice is drowsy, and Helen invisible."

Ida would have acceded to almost any other proposition more readily, but she submitted with forced complaisance.

"Go on with your reading. I shall retire if I interrupt you;" continued Miss Arnold.

"I have been reading all the morning;" said Ida, seeing that the other's book was untouched.

"And won't my talking annoy you?" cried Miss Arnold with childish pleasure. "I have *so* longed to know you better—to get nearer to you! Bear with me while I say it; you are so— not exactly stern to me—but so distant! That it was not your nature, I discovered from your demeanor to Alice. I could not but love you for your goodness to her; and—child that I am—I would have entreated you to care for me a little in return—but you froze the words upon my lips. I have cried over it after I went to bed at night. Will you not tell me truly why you dislike me?"

The violet eyes were sparkling through tears.

"I was not aware that I was so frightful," replied Ida, smiling. "My coldness was imaginary, or unintentional on my part, Miss Arnold."

"There!" said the beauty reproachfully; "it was 'Alice' before you had known her a day."

"Because we were old schoolmates."

"Strangers, nevertheless. Come, *Ida*—be my friend—will you not?"

Could a false flirt copy Carry's look and tone so faithfully? and she kneeled upon the rug, as she had done on that November night, when she said, "Love me, Ida!" She could not resist the temptation to lay her lips against the snowy forehead, beneath which those matchless eyes beamed with love and gratitude. She would have recoiled as that satiric whisper again hissed through her heart; but the soft arms were around her—the beautiful head upon her shoulder.

"I am not the butterfly I seem, Ida; nor is the ephemera gaiety, in which you see me floating, my proper sphere. I have not your unwavering principle—your independence; I cannot of myself say to the world,—'I hate your vain pageantry, and pine for a nobler life!' Often, often I feel when the din of pleasure is loudest, that I am bound to a wheel whose revolutions I cannot control. Show me how to be happy."

"There is but one happiness which cannot die," said Ida, with an effort. "You do not require that I should point you to that!"

Her look of sorrowful deprecation was touching. "I know what you mean," she replied, subduedly. "You would intimate, that professing as I do, to be trying to lead a Christian's life, I ought to be as familiar with the path as yourself; but I am a child—too much the toy of impulse and fancy. I have been a pet from my infancy; have leaned upon the judgment— abided by the decision of those I love; and you cannot conceive of the difficulty I have in acting for myself, and in opposition to their wishes."

This was plausible. Ida wished from her inmost soul, that she had never heard Richard Copeland's story, which, after all, might have been coloured, if not sketched by prejudice, or revenge for some slight to himself. She would have taken this young girl, *his* betrothed, to her bosom, and soothed her fears, and stimulated her failing resolves. But the conviction of her heartlessness was too strong upon her; and her upright nature forbade the assumption of an appearance of confidence she did not feel. She spoke, indeed, as freely as she could of the love which pities and forgives our infirmities and backslidings; but Lelia shook her head dejectedly. She "had not reached her case. I thank you, though, and love you!" She drew her cheek down to her lips. "Have you had much sorrow?"

"Not more than falls to the lot of many, more deserving of exemption.—Why?"

"Your serenity is so remarkable; you seem never to have suffered."

"The ocean is calm sometimes," said Ida, unconsciously.

"That is not your emblem," rejoined Lelia. "It is mine; ruffled by every breath—dark in storms—flashing and laughing in sunshine—always changing, yet always the same—and, ah! who believes that there are treasures under the waters which are worth the seeking?"

"The ocean is constant in nothing except change," said Ida.

"That is the surface!" she spoke exultingly—

"The water is calm and still below;
For the winds and waves are absent there,—
And the sands are bright as the stars that glow
In the motionless fields of upper air."

"Those are fine lines!" said Ida. They were recited with a purity of tone and emphasis that lent them an additional charm.

"They are Percival's," was the reply. "I love poetry, if I have not, like one of my friends, received the poetic afflatus. Ah! Improvisatrice! did you think me ignorant of your glorious gift?"

"You honour my petty talent by a higher name than it aspires to earn. Your informant was given to exaggeration."

"You do not ask who it was!" cried Lelia, peeping into her face. "Ah! that blush! you surmise. Now my demure darling, how will you excuse yourself for not having breathed his name in my hearing, when you knew how deep my interest is in all relating to him or his connections?"

This query was ably turned; but Ida's habitual self-control saved her from the pitfall. She would know and confess nothing.

"And you dare look in my eyes and deny one of your best friends?" said Lelia.

"I deny no one. The merest acquaintance may have imparted this information."

"It was not a casual acquaintance. Shall I name him?"

"If you choose," said Ida, with quickened pulsation.

"Then it was Mr.—look at me!—Mr. Germaine!"

The blood flowed regularly again. Miss Arnold's *ruse*, if such was intended, failed signally; and Ida shortly had cause to congratulate herself upon the equanimity she had maintained through the interview.

Leila's friendliness continued without abatement; and her predilection for her society was openly manifested. She invited her to walk on Monday afternoon, and was inconsolable for her refusal until Richard Copeland offered himself as a substitute. Alice rode out with Mrs. Read and Josephine; and Ida lay down at dusk upon a sofa, within a recess of the parlor. She soon dropped into a light slumber; and thought that she was dreaming still, when she heard voices, and saw, 'twixt sleeping and waking, two figures, dimly visible in the fire-light.

"You are cruelly unjust, Richard. Why seize upon every pretext to attack and wound one who never had an unkind thought of you?"

"Because I have no respect for you, Lelia," was the cool rejoinder. "Your trifling is disgraceful—inhuman!"

"I never trifled with you."

"For the best of reasons—you never had the chance. You will affirm too, that you did not design to coquet with Hilton or Sheppard."

"Their unhappiness was the fruit of their own blind folly."

"'Blind folly' it was to love a heartless woman! And this Lacy—are you retaining him as a *corps de reserve*?"

"He is nothing to me—."

An ejaculation of extreme disgust interrupted her. "Now this is too much! Do you think then that a solitary manoeuvre has been unnoticed by me? that I have not divined even the motive of your altered behaviour to Miss Ross? You have either guessed or heard what has been told me within a day or two—that he was her lover last winter—either discarded, or engaged to her now. Have a care! you may be foiled with your own weapons! Adieu!" His mocking laugh rang through the room. Lelia remained where he left her; the ruddy glare lighting up features contorted by anger or grief. "Can it be?" she said—"But, no!" she smiled, contemptuously. "A made-up tale to work upon my jealousy! *That* matters not at present—but this—yet I am not discouraged—he is the only one!" and muttering over— "He is the only one!" she lifted her bonnet and shawl, and carried them from the apartment. Astonishment had chained Ida's limbs and tongue after she realised that she was awake. She grew weak and sick at the accomplished duplicity of one so youthful, so faultless in seeming;—the windings of her arms about her neck—her kisses were like the coil and sting of a serpent. She detected the artfulness of her pretended confidence; her lures to inveigle her into some embarrassment or admission which would betray her acquaintance with Mr. Lacy. She had suspected her then; the change of manner followed too soon upon the recognition of the handwriting. She rejoiced that the house was to be freed of her on the morrow. If *he* could be warned! but this was a prohibited subject to thought as to words, and she was learning how to govern both. There was a soirée that evening, and Ida had never been more happy to see company. Alice and Lelia came together to her room to say farewell, for they were both to start early in the morning. She tried to treat them alike, but her regrets at losing them were addressed to Alice; and if they were heartfelt, the sigh of relief, with which she turned the bolt after them, was equally sincere.

The bridal festivities were not over until after Christmas, but Ida avoided further participation in them by spending holiday week at Mr. Dana's. She was invited expressly to meet Carry and Arthur, and, although the precedence belonged to them, as more unfrequent visitors, she was installed in the seat of honour as chief guest. Carry inveighed against Mr. Read's marriage, and was anxious to learn whether it would render her position more unpleasant. Ida thought not:—her heart said this could hardly be, but she spoke hopefully of the wholesome check Mrs. Read's elegant propriety would be upon Josephine's brusqueness. "They will not agree at first, for Mrs. Read, if she does appear too fond of her ease to contend, is not deficient in resolution; yet the end may be mutual endurance and forbearance. In any event I shall remain neutral. Who knows, Carry, but, unpromising as the field is, I may do as well as suffer, even there?"

They were alone in Carry's room. "There is one subject, upon which I wish to speak to you;" said the latter, seriously. "Has Arthur said anything to you of himself?"

"No—not particularly."

"He was always too good for me," pursued Carry. "You need not hold up your finger so threateningly—but for a year past, I felt that he was growing better, while I made no progress. After we were married, I discovered that he was in the habit of the daily study of his Bible, and secret prayer. I did not hint that I knew it, for it was too sacred a matter for me to touch. Ida! I suffered! he had a care which I could not share—was ill at ease, and I must not cheer him. When you wrote, recounting the alteration of your views and prospects, he unsealed his heart to me. He had long sought peace, without finding it; but latterly, had experienced a glimmering hope he feared to divulge, so faint was it—that he was a child of God. I wept for joy and grief—joy, for I was sure, although he was not, that he was a Christian;—and grief at my own hardness of heart. His light has burned brighter and brighter every day; and he is prepared now to avow it to his friends and the world. He says your fearlessness, in declaring your principles, filled him with shame, and urged him to emulate your example."

Here was one sheaf—an earnest of whitening harvest. The barrenness of opportunities for serving and honouring her Redeemer, was a troublesome stumbling-block. Her sphere of usefulness was so limited; and she had talents, which might be deployed to some purpose in a larger arena. The glowing zeal of a young convert called for action. In a moment of discontent with herself, and perhaps with her situation, she had expressed this to Charley, who silenced her with one line—

"'They also serve, who only stand and wait.'"

The intelligence of Arthur's conversion was an unlooked-for and refreshing element in her week's felicity. "Now, Charley, one thing more!" she said, when they were talking it over. She seldom made a pointed appeal, although he always took it kindly. He did not reflect her smile—he only said, gravely;—"You cannot desire it more than I do, Ida."

Invigorated in soul and body, and with a bounteous store of loving memories heaped up for the time of famine, she sought her uncongenial home. "Ah, well! it's allers been my experience that molasses and water is mighty apt to sour, if it's kept; and it don't deceive me now," remarked the oracular Rachel, with the decline of the honeymoon. The metaphor was apt. Mr. Read's fondness was the saccharine that qualified the insipidity of his wife's apathy. He had been elevated to the seventh heaven of ecstacy, at his triumph over a host of rivals, younger than himself. Her evident preference had incited him to the contest, and he had no misgivings of its reality. She was "a splendid woman!" He delighted in exhibiting her; and hearing this from all sides, with compliments and congratulations to himself. But this renewal of youth was evanescent. He had counted more than half a century—she, not a quarter; and outraged nature revenged herself for his infatuation in striving to overleap this mighty gap. She was a "splendid woman!" that was unquestionable; but as he mounted guard, from ten at night to two or three o'clock in the morning against the wall of the assembly-room, waiting for her to despatch the list of partners that covered both sides of her tablets—he tired and moped, and stupidly wondering if the radiant creature, whose laugh came to him with each whirl of the interminable waltz, were in truth married, and *his* wife! it *is* problematical if he derived permanent consolation from the well-timed praises of his old friends, who facetiously inquired if he were not "jealous of his pretty bird"—or felt greatly flattered by the fine things, comparative strangers were saying about "his daughter." She *was* a "splendid woman!" and she shone most at the largest party of the winter, where everybody danced (she most sylph-like of all) except the papas and mammas, and the "past-worthy" chaperons. The rooms were hot:—the dancers must have air—the windows were robbed of their sashes. Mr. Read was in a draught—what of that? the reflection of his wife's splendor should have warmed him. *She* was not uncomfortable;—so she glided and pirouetted and swam by in the polka, and he shook as if he were afflicted with a dance of quite another name. An attack of inflammatory rheumatism was the finale. His life was in danger for awhile; and to his wife's credit, be it said, she nursed him dutifully, if not affectionately, until he entered upon his convalescence.

A few mornings after the doctors announced his safety, Ida observed, at breakfast, that Mrs. Read was looking badly.

"Confinement in a sick-room does not agree with you, I fear," said she, with interest. "We must not let you fall ill, too. Will you not delegate one of us to represent you this forenoon, while you take a ride?"

"Constant attendance is unnecessary," she replied. "Hereafter, I shall not stay in doors as I have been doing. I thank you for your offer, however. If I can avail myself of it, I will do so."

"Why did he not come down to breakfast?" asked Josephine, ironically.

"He cannot leave his bed;" was the calm reply.

"Nor turn himself in it, I believe, madam?"

"You are right."

"It must cost you a pang to surrender to another the privilege of allaying his pains, and paying those endearing little attentions, to which affection imparts such sweetness. How can you think of it?"

"I do not consider my health unimportant."

"Not in comparison with his?" continued Josephine, provokingly.

"The duty is not rendered less imperative by any comparison."

"The pursuit of pleasure and ease is included in this prudent care of yourself, I presume, madam?"

"In that, as in everything else, I shall consult my own inclinations."

"I did not know that a woman had a will of her own after she married," retorted Josephine.

"I am not conscious of having lost my volition or free agency."

"And acting upon this unbiassed volition, you will occupy your box at the theatre to-night. I saw a ticket upon the table in the parlor."

"I shall be there; but there will be room for you, and whatever friend you honor by accompanying."

"And this is conjugal devotion!" the suppressed wrath boiling over,—"After cajoling a feeble old man into marrying you, you desert him upon a bed of languishing, where he is laid by your follies, to flirt with your train of gallants in the most public place in the city!"

"If you have more remarks of like import to make, I will hear them in your father's presence, Miss Read," answered the unruffled step-mother. "Miss Ida, please excuse my withdrawing before you have finished your breakfast."

Josephine had emphatically picked this quarrel. She had received no provocation, and combined with this disadvantage, that of loss of temper. Chafing with anxiety to commence the warfare she had declared, she was too eager to wait for a pretext; and had plunged into a rash conflict, before estimating the strength of the enemy's forces. Ida said nothing, until she was ready to leave the room. She deemed it her duty to speak.

"Josephine," said she, mildly, "it is not my place to dictate to you; but as a well-wisher, I warn you not to carry this further. Constant dissension will be the only result. She is inclined to live peaceably with you; and she will be a dangerous, a powerful enemy."

"Have I asked your advice?" said Josephine. Her scowl dissuaded Ida from a second remonstrance. In reckless audacity, she proceeded straight to her father's chamber. It was pitiable to see that gray-haired man—helpless as infancy with disease, and remember that his frayed thread of life was entwisted with the golden cord of hers, who had barely attained the meridian of her early womanhood.

Josephine's visits had been rare and brief, and his salutation was surly. "To what am I indebted for this superlative pleasure?" he inquired, stretching his upper lip across his teeth, as was his wont, when displeased.

"If I had supposed that my presence was conducive to your comfort, no consideration should have detained me from you sir," was the meaning rejoinder.

He did not answer, but moved uneasily, and asked his wife for water. The goblet was nearest Josephine, and she held it to him. "Lift my head!" he said, fretfully, "Ugh! you hurt me! this comes of your officiousness. Why couldn't you let *her* do it?"

"I regret, sir, that my unskilful touch is painful," said Josephine, "since you are to be dependent upon my cares."

"What the deuce are you talking about?" he demanded, sharply.

The slumberous eyes surveyed her listlessly over the couch.

"My speech is blunt, sir; I learned it from you, and I have an inconvenient practice of saying what I think. Old men, who have young and fashionable wives, should not indulge in the luxury of sickness. What woman, who has a right appreciation of her charms, can hesitate what course to pursue, when a decrepid husband is put in one scale—society and a score of beaux in the other?"

His glare of impotent fury was demoniacal—he was too weak to control it. The liquid eyes were dreamy and motionless still. The irascible old man jerked his head so that he could see her face—"Helen! what is that girl driving at?"

"She can best explain herself, sir."

"Speak!" he commanded, at the top of his tremulous voice.

"I hope you have made your will, sir;" said Josephine, deliberately.

"By my life, I *will* do it, and cut you off, without a copper, if you parley much more?"

"You virtually severed our connection two months ago, sir. A stranger has supplanted me in your heart and house; and up to this time, I have held my peace. This is my revenge. Your idol, having used you for her pleasure and advancement, does not mean that this sickness, caused by your doating indulgence, shall fetter her dainty limbs. On the contrary, it frees her from the restraint of your observation,—the incumbrance of your attentions."

She dropped each word slowly, purposely to aggravate his impatience, which was now frightful. Manacled, bound down by the fiery bands of his malady, he writhed, as upon a Procrustean bed.

"Helen! speak! tell her she lies!"

"I never reply to inuendoes, sir." The eyes were passionless as ever.

"She is gentleness and patience personified," said Josephine, "Ask whom she will accompany to the theatre to-night and pray her,—your faithful wife—to stay with you."

"The theatre!" he uttered. "Are you going, and with whom?"

"With Mr. and Miss Talbot;" and save that she fastened her gaze upon him, instead of her, she looked and spoke the same.

"The 'Miss,' is an adroit addenda," sneered Josephine.

Her father was silent. His selfishness was wounded. He was angered and mortified that his wife should consign him to the care of others and find enjoyment in gay recreations, while he lay crippled and racked; but he detected the spring of Josephine's interference, and pride cried loudly that her impertinent malice should be punished. A study of his wife's determined face settled the point. If they differed, the mischief-maker should not know it. "Hark you!" said he, with sudden composure. "I see your game, my lady, and you may as well throw up your cards. I am master in my house, and there is no law against turning you out of it. I thought I had taught you this already. I have a piece of advice, you will do well to bear in mind. Attend to your own business, and let your betters alone. Now, be off! and don't let me see you again until you can behave yourself."

"I obey you, sir. If you want my services, I trust you will send for me."

Mr. Read was awkwardly embarrassed, when left with his wife. Domineering and stubborn as he was, she awed him. Her haughty endurance of his foolish fondness gave him no lien upon her affections; and the sang-froid, she had preserved under Josephine's insolence, was a bad augury of the efficacy of reproaches. She consulted her watch, and informed him that it was the hour for his medicine; administered it, and shook up his pillow.

"Helen," said he, coaxingly, "are you in earnest about leaving me? What shall I do?"

"Sarah will wait upon you. I have the utmost confidence in her fidelity."

"But what is a servant's nursing, after yours?"

"It is a pity you entertain this repugnance to every one's attentions but mine. My health and spirits are injured by fatigue and want of rest. You are recovering, there is no absolute necessity for my remaining with you; and it *is* necessary that I should take care of myself. We had best suspend this discussion, Mr. Read. You have been too much excited this morning; and arguments are useless, as my plans are made."

And "my plans are made" became the law of the household,—Josephine excepted, who had her schemes also. There was an ominous calm. Mr. Read mended gradually. His daughter's resentment outlived his; but his pride was as inflexible as hers. She would not enter his chamber, and he would not recall her. His wife performed mechanically a routine of duties, self-enjoined, as covering all that could be required of her. The residue of her time was devoted to the world, out of which, she did not seem to *live*. She held her position as leader of the ton. She was the best-bred, best-dressed, and best-educated woman of her circle. No party was complete without her; and none vied with hers, in elegance and agreeableness. People gossipped, and prophecied, and pitied her "poor old husband"— courted and aped her. Ida had made a public profession of her faith, and was humbly "waiting." Her health did not now debar her from mingling in society; and she could discern neither wisdom nor piety in a hermit's life. Her re-appearance amongst them was hailed with acclamations by most of her acquaintances. Some were shy for a time, thanks to Josephine's exposition of her "strait-laced notions;" but her cheerful frankness banished their reserve; and if not so noisily admired, she was more beloved than in her palmy days. She was one evening at a "sociable" at Mrs. Morris', the cynosure of a group, the liveliest in the room, for it comprised Ellen, Mr. Thornton, Charley, Mr. Germaine, Mr. Villet, and Richard Copeland. Charley was relating an amusing story; and Ida's peculiarly contagious laugh created as much merriment as the anecdote.

"Miss Ross is ever happy," said Mr. Villet. "Your being *devoté* does not make you sad, morose—*comme à l'ordinaire*."

A glance of apprehension was exchanged by some of the circle; and Ida colored, as she replied, smiling, "I do not know why it should, Mr. Villet."

The Frenchman shrugged his shoulders: "Nor I! I do not comprehend these affairs myself, but it is usual, I believe, for the visible visage to elongate with the expansion of the—*qu'est ce que c'est?*—grace in the soul."

There was a laugh. Charley and Ida were grave; and Mr. Villet's politeness took the alarm. "I entreat your pardon, Miss Ross; I did not meditate an offence."

"You have given none," answered she. "You would not knowingly make sport of what you must respect. Religion is not gloomy, nor is it ridiculous."

"Its professors, with some honorable exceptions, are one or the other," said Richard.

"This is their misfortune or failing, not the fault of the system," returned Ida. "Mortal nature is fallible, Mr. Copeland."

"You admit it, then?" said Mr. Thornton. "The greatest objection I have to pious people is that they do not permit this indulgence to abused human nature. They wind themselves up in their impenetrable cloaks of sanctification and perfectionism, and send us—no matter where—for hankering after innocent amusements. And if one of their caste beats time to a merry tune, or shows his head inside of a theatre, he is run down as if he had the hydrophobia. Such sermons as they preach about the hand or foot offending! It would be a wise precaution, in my judgment, to make the amputation of the feet part of the ceremony of initiation into church membership. You are superior to such narrow-mindedness, I hope, Miss Ida?"

"If 'narrow-mindedness' signifies drawing a distinct line of demarcation between the church and the world, I shall come under your lash, Mr. Thornton."

"And do you, candid and liberal as you are, declare that there is sin—mind you! a 'want of conformity to, or transgression of the law of God'—in moving through a certain form of steps to the sound of music?" said he, indignantly.

"I do not profess to see sin in the mere act of dancing," replied Ida; "but—I do not wish to argue, Mr. Thornton. If nothing else forbade my joining in the amusement, it is prohibited by the church to which I belong."

"Worse and worse! Miss Ida, this is unworthy of you. It is the Papal doctrine of depositing one's conscience in the priest's pocket book. If your church commanded you to steal or kill, would you obey?"

"No; for a higher law forbids it. I am bound to follow the church only so far as it follows the Bible."

"But the Bible says there is a time to dance."

Ida smiled; "I am surprised," said she, "that sensible persons should quote that poor text so frequently, as authority for dancing. In the same connection we read, 'there is a time to kill;'—you would be loath to defend a murderer who justified his crime by an appeal to this passage. 'A time to die;'—who sees in this permission to shorten his days?"

"And you must turn pavier, Thornton, because 'there is a time to gather stones together,'" said Charley.

There was another laugh, in which Mr. Thornton joined good-humoredly. "Weak as my text is, I am consoled by the knowledge that you cannot produce one interdicting that which reason and observation teach is not reprehensible."

"Not an explicit prohibition, perhaps," answered she, hesitating.

"Well an implied one, then?"

Ida's cheeks flushed, painfully, but her voice was firm as she said, "I read, 'Be ye not conformed to the world;' and 'Whatsoever ye do, do all to the honor and glory of God,' and my conscience says I would be guilty of wilful disobedience to the written commandment, and dishonor my profession, if I disregarded the plain meaning of these words."

Charley had bided his time. She stood the test well, and he came in to the rescue. "She is right, Thornton. You and I know it—why dispute it? Only yesterday, you were laughing at the inconsistency of the 'dancing Christians' you frolicked with down the country."

"I commended their liberality, their freedom from superstition," interposed Thornton, still laughing.

"Humbug! you said—'they have found a road to the Celestial City, which our orthodox brethren about here do not patronise;—have graded and widened the strait and narrow way we read of, until it is as smooth as a ball-room floor; and dance up the shining route. I used to think some preparation was requisite, before I could be fitted for heaven; but I am comforted in spirit since meeting them. My chance is as good as theirs in the long run.' Those were your very words—deny them if you can, or that you were ridiculing them. You are, like myself, more than a Sabbath-day's journey from being a Christian; and you assert that they are not much better off. The plain English of which is, that you are consistent to your professions;—they say they believe one thing, and practise the opposite. Pretending to despise the vanities of this life, they pursue them more eagerly than the things which are unseen and eternal. If a man unites himself with the church, let him live as if he were changed. I go to the theatre, although I do not consider it the best school of morals one can frequent; but it *grieves* me to see, in my neighbor, a so-called pious man. I am ashamed for him—my respect for the reputation of his church is greater than his. I dance—and sleep afterwards with an easy conscience; but if you ever see me 'tripping on the light fantastic toe,' with an angelic creature who is a communicant in a Bible-reading sect, you may write it down as an immutable fact, that she asked me—not I her!"

Charley was lawless. Nobody criticised or was offended with him; and Ida was always certain of finding in him, an ally and advocate; but grateful as she was for his ready aid, upon occasions like the present, she prized more highly the counsels, which his knowledge of mankind, and his undeviating sense of rectitude qualified him to give. She had faults,—he pointed them out; she erred in judgment,—he corrected the evil as far as he could. The spectacle of his daily life was useful. He possessed almost boundless influence over his associates, and their attachment to him was close and strong. They understood, intuitively, the worth of the inner man,—never fully unveiled to the majority of them, and could not but admire and esteem. And Ida's constant thought of him was—"If he, calling himself unconverted, accomplishes so much—what ought not I—a Christian, to attempt?"

CHAPTER XXIV

Mr. Read was in his private sitting-room;—it adjoined his chamber, and his longest walk was from one apartment to the other. The sun beamed cheerfully through the damask curtains, and the fire blazed and crackled in the grate; but wrapped in his wadded dressing-gown, his feet sunk heavily into a cushion, and his face contracted into a fretful frown, he appeared to be enduring the extreme of cold and discomfort. He was a sorry picture of a three months' bridegroom. His surroundings were tasteful and luxurious,—books and papers and pictures and handsome furniture, and at his elbow stood a silver hand-bell, whose tongue would bring an obsequious servant, ready to perform his bidding; yet his sigh, as he fidgeted uneasily in his downy *fauteuil*, was a groan of repining.—"Like a jaded old hack! they won't knock him in the head, in consideration of past services; but he may die as soon as he can—the quicker the better!"

"The Northern papers have come, sir, and I thought you would like to see them;" said a gentle voice. It was his ward. A grunt and a gesture bade her put them upon the stand.

"Are you in pain this afternoon?" she asked, sympathizingly.

"I am always in pain!"

"Can I do anything for you?"

"No!" He reached for the papers; but a twinge in his shoulder forced him to drop them. Ida picked them up. The desolate old man excited her sincerest pity.

"It must weary you, holding those large sheets; and the print is fine. If you will designate the articles you wish read, I will do it for you with pleasure."

The offer was tempting, although its acceptance was ungracious. He pointed to a piece, and she removed her bonnet and seated herself near him. He did not inquire if she were going out, and she did not make her sacrifice meritorious in his eyes, by informing him that she gave up her walk to minister to his enjoyment. She read well;—her voice was exquisitely modulated; her enunciation perfect; Mr. Read forgot to be peevish, and his corrugated forehead lost half its wrinkles. When she ceased, he seemed to have been lulled by a strain of music. The article selected was an editorial leader on political economy, unintelligible and prosy to Ida; but she endeavored not to let this appear. He nodded, and stripped the envelope from another sheet. His eye gleamed, and with an approach to a smile, he showed her six columns of an oration;—a grand effort of the immortal sage of Marshfield. Ida was appalled at the superficies of the solid mass, but she said over to herself, a verse she had lisped at her mother's knee.

"Did I this day, for small or great,
My own pursuits forego,
To lighten, by a feather's weight,
The load of human woe?"

and began the terrible undertaking. The preamble over, she became insensibly interested. Her soul-lit face and ringing intonations supplied to the auditor, the actual presence of the orator; he looked and listened until the light failed; then rang for candles. Mrs. Read, returning from her airing, seated herself silently by the fire. It was the prettiest domestic scene that had ever been witnessed in that house; and how little reality was there in its air of home-happiness!

"Is that all?" asked Mr. Read, at supper-time.

"Almost, sir. I can soon finish it. I will not detain you Mrs. Read." But she waited to hear the conclusion. A gruff "Thank you," was Ida's only reward, besides the praise of her conscience; and her tired throat obliged her to refuse Charley his favorite song that night, but she did not repent. She volunteered her services whenever she knew that there were new books or journals, and at length, the latest intelligence was distasteful, unless it came through her lips. It was a selfish gratification; and she did not delude herself with illusions of personal attachment. She strove to live for the benefit and pleasure of her fellow-beings; to leave her interest and ease out of sight; and she could not have been in a better school. The woman's heart was not still. There were moments of weariness and longing, and passionate regrets. The soul, refusing the realities, which made up the sum of every-day duty, pined for the remembered "Dream Land;"—its retreat, and the scene of its holiday revels;—and when the aching and thirst were at their height, it was a trial to smile at a caress from Mrs. Dana, or a friendly act of Charley's—dear and thoughtful brother! when she could have rested her tired head upon the kind bosom, and wept her life away—but she *did* smile, and bore up bravely until God gave her strength to rise above the weakness.

The Sabbath was a season of delight. A band of little girls watched eagerly for her at Sabbath-school. Inclement indeed must the day be, that saw their form vacant; for she was always at her post, and regarded snow and rain as minor hindrances when her flock nestled closely to "dear Miss Ida." No class loved their teacher and their Bible so well as hers; her co-laborers said she had a secret spell, by which she won and governed them; and she had,—for she was ever mindful that she had another account to render than her report to the Superintendent, and prayed that it might be—"Those whom Thou gavest me, I have kept, and none of them is lost." She loved her pastor; but her acquaintance with him was slight. He visited her at stated times, and esteemed her an "amiable girl, with a creditable fund of general information;" he "could not know the exercises of all his members;" and that a woman whose life was so uncheckered, should have any difficulties and sorrows, but such as are incidental to the experience of every Christian, never crossed his brain. But he was a faithful expounder of the Scriptures; and if he did not remark the changeful light of the eyes, which never released him from the text to the "Amen" of his discourse;—she felt that consolations and advice so applicable, must be meant for her; and remembered him in her orisons, as a Shepherd who cared for his sheep, and selected for each, food convenient for him. She resolved repeatedly, to thank him for his fidelity; but her courage melted when the opportunity arrived; and she would rebuke the vanity that bred the desire. She read that in the primitive church, "those who loved the Lord, spake often to one another;" and imagined, in her simplicity, that such intercourse would be of mutual comfort and profit; yet a seal was upon her mouth, and she waited and wished in vain, for a word in the conversation of her brethren, which would dissolve it. It was strange that she could speak freely and heartily to Carry and to Charley, and be restrained by the presence of those, who had tasted like joys—were bound upon the same pilgrimage as herself.

There was an exception—a minister from another State, with whom she once dined at Mr. Dana's; a merry-hearted, whole-souled man, whose store of anecdote and pleasantry enlivened the company at table;—and after dinner, gathering from a passing remark, that she was a professing Christian, he sought her out; and while the rest were busy about other matters, they were talking of the "peace which passeth understanding," and the home in preparation for them;—not with austere gravity, but, easily and happily, as befitted a topic so inspiriting. They separated—not to meet again in time; and Ida went on her way, cheered and strengthened by the interview, and hoping to thank him in heaven, for the seed he had sowed by the wayside—*not* in the Scriptural sense of the term.

Mr. Read's disease assumed a chronic type. Some days well enough to transact business in person,—then relapsing, in consequence of trifling exposure or change of weather, his existence was a series of anxieties and sufferings. Ida did not know how she became his nurse; Josephine would not endure his petulance, and her retorts exasperated him; and his wife was too deep in the vortex of fashionable life to waste many minutes upon him; it was unjust and unfeeling to abandon him to the care of menials; and as with her reading, what was a favor, voluntarily offered, came to be regarded as a duty, expected and unrequited. The Danas objected to this thankless sacrifice; but she persisted. It was during one of his worst spells, that an incident occurred, which she did not heed at the time, but when recalled by subsequent events, was fraught with meaning. It was in the evening; and she was on her way to the dining-room, to order a cup of tea for the invalid, when the light streaming through a crack in the parlor-door suggested the probability that the servant she was in quest of, was lighting the lamps in there. She pushed the door open. Mrs. Read was in the middle of the room, her face averted, and her arm extended in repulsion or denial, towards a tall, dark man, who was speaking in a low, excited tone. "'Forget!' I do not forget that circumstances are not what they were then!" was all that Ida heard, as she retired hastily and unseen. As she passed through the entry, she caught a noise, like the rustle of drapery, but supposed it to be the waving of her dress in the wind. Mr. Read was in agony; and Ida sent to request Dr. Ballard's immediate presence. The messenger's steps were not cold upon the stairs, when the sick man tormented himself with impatience for the physician's arrival. "If the servant had a pass, it was not signed—if it was signed, he had lost it—if he had lost it, Ballard would wait to eat his supper, before he came. I wish he had this shooting fire through his limbs! It would put some speed into his lazy body! Ah! there he is!"

It was Mrs. Read, who meeting the servant with the tea, and hearing of her husband's state, had taken it from him. Ida, preoccupied as she was, noticed that she was pale and agitated. Her voice too, was tremulous, and had a cadence that might have been mistaken for tenderness.

"I grieve to see you so much worse. Drink this, it may relieve you," she said, slipping her hand under his pillow to raise his head. Ida sprang forward to arrest the movement. He was suffering excruciating pain in his neck; and frantic at its augmentation by this change of position, he dashed the cup to the floor, with a shocking oath.

"You want to kill me! I've seen that for a long time; and then you can flaunt to your heart's content. You can marry whom you please, and make him rich with my money, like the shameless wretch you are!" he yelled, distractedly.

The smothered fire leaped high—the dark eye blazed with wrath, but she uttered not a sound, as she turned from him. Ida had never seen such a look in mortal face, and wild with fear of, she know not what, darted after her, and overtook her in the dressing-room.

"Oh! do not! do not!" she exclaimed, flinging her arms around the stately form.

"Do not what?" said the lady, trying to unlock her fingers. Ida held her fast.

"Oh! the horrible thing that is in your thoughts! He is mad with pain—he did not mean—did not think what he did. He says as hard things to me, to every one—but he loves you! he *does* love you!" and dropping her head upon the lady's breast, she sobbed like a child.

The haughty woman stood irresolute—passive in the tenacious grasp of the over-excited girl.

"He drove me from him—struck me!" she said, in thick accents. "Why should I stay?"

It was rather a soliloquy than a question, and Ida reiterated, "He did not mean it! he loves you!"

"Do *you* love him?" inquired the lady, lifting her face, and gazing piercingly into it.

"I pity him," said Ida.

"Do you hate him?" she asked, more energetically.

"No, I hate no one."

"Yet you have cause."

"I try to forgive."

"You do not hate him!" repeated Mrs. Read; and again to herself, she added, "*I* do!"

Ida let her go. "I pity him!" she said, with mournful earnestness, "but I pity you more! doomed to a life of falsehood and misery! Heaven pity you as I do."

"Stay!" said Mrs. Read, as she would have gone back to the chamber. "Do you despise me utterly? Am I lost?"

"'Lost!' no—while life and reason last, there may be room for repentance."

Repentance! what had she, so queenly in her pride and beauty, to do with repentance? yet the words seemed to strike her. Mr. Read's querulous tones called "Ida!" "I must go," she said. "Will you come?"

"Not now—presently."

The patient was slumbering heavily under the influence of the medicine Dr. Ballard prescribed, when his wife rejoined her assistant nurse—lofty and unimpressible. She regarded the sleeper long and fixedly. His hair was nearly white, and his features pinched by sickness, but there was no softening of compassion in the rigid lines of her face. Setting her chair into the shade, she was speechless and motionless for hours. They watched him together all night; exchanging only brief remarks as to his situation, and the remedies to be employed. He rallied from this seizure, and Ida was as far from the brilliant worldling as before.

An unexpected event attracted her from the retirement in which her charitable functions had secluded her. Celestia Pratt was married! and to Ellen's chagrin, to a cousin of the Morris family. He was good-looking, ambitious and poor;—she susceptible a "Representative's" daughter, and rich. He wrote to his aunt that they would take Richmond in the wedding-tour; and she was obliged, *nolens volens*, to give them a party. Ida was disinclined to attend; but Ellen's solicitations conquered her reluctance. Mr. Cranleigh, the groom, was gentlemanly, even handsome, and accepted the customary greetings with as much complacency, as though his wife were not, as Ellen groaned to Ida—"Celestia, unmitigated Celestia!"

"A penny for your thoughts!" said Ida, tapping Charley's arm with her fan.

"I was thinking what falsehoods geologists tell us about the thickness of the crust of the earth, and how many years the mines of Peru have been worked."

"A profound subject for deep meditation, but I am at a loss—"

"Why, allowing a thousand brides a week in the civilized world, (and there are quadruple that number,) according to my rough computation, the miners ought to be within hail of the Chinese, or whatever nation is the antipodes of the Peruvians, by this time."

"Their kindred craft, the jewellers, have been called upon by the Celestia-ls," said Mr. Thornton.

"'Pon my word!" remarked Pemberton to Josephine, "I have heard of men who married 'for pretty,' but it's my opinion, Cranleigh married for ugly."

Josephine laughed, but her attention was absorbed by some object in another part of the room. "You know everybody," said she; "who is that gentleman talking with the bride?"

He knew everybody, and this must be nobody. He had certainly seen him somewhere before—it might have been at Newport—or perhaps in New Orleans, yet he could not call his name. Why did she inquire?

"A question by the way—she was not curious. He had a foreign air, and she fancied might be one of Mr. Pemberton's friends—he had so many abroad."

He had, and it would be awkward not to recollect him, if he should speak.

"There's Cranleigh! he knows!"

The stranger's name was Ashlin, an early acquaintance of Mrs. Cranleigh's, and later from the West Indies.

"Had he resided there long?" Miss Read asked.

"Two years—nearly three, indeed."

Mr. Ashlin was graceful and *distingué*, and Ida was attacked by an unaccountable curiosity. She interrogated the bride.

"What handsome man was that, you were conversing with, awhile ago, Celestia?"

Her face was broad with smiles. "Law! why Mr. Cranleigh, my husband, to be sure! Haven't you been introduced? Here! Mr. Cran—"

"Oh! don't!" said Ida. "I know him—don't interrupt him! I alluded to that tall gentleman by the folding-doors."

"That's Mr. Ashlin. He used to live close by Pa's; and then his uncle died out in Cuba or West India, I forget which—and he went off there, where he's been three years, rolling in money they say. He's mighty smart too—*I'm* 'most afraid of him. Don't he look like a-a-cannibal!" said Mrs. Cranleigh, some reminiscence of New Zealand history coming to her help.

"His is a dark beauty, certainly," replied Ida, hiding a smile. "I should say if he had not lived abroad, that I had seen his face somewhere else."

"You needn't be setting your cap!" retorted the bride, spitefully, "He won't be so easy caught as that Mr. Euston, you all think such an *Adolphus*. He's engaged."

"Ah! who is the fortunate lady?"

"A Miss Courtland,—or some such name;—that is—he was engaged once, but, seems to me, I've heard that he jilted her, and she married a rich old man for his 'tin.'"

"What did you call her? Speak lower!" said Ida.

"Law! you're scared! what ails you?"

"Nothing—nothing!" laughing. "You had as well be silent about this Mr. Ashlin,—he has quick ears, and gentleman do not admire gossiping ladies. You have a splendid bouquet—is this Mr. Cranleigh's taste?"

And while the history of the courtship, from their meeting at the "Sulphur Springs" to the present glorification, was pouring upon her tympanum, she was arguing away her unjustifiable suspicions. His general appearance was that of the gentleman she had a glimpse of in Mr. Read's parlor; and Mrs. Read's behaviour that evening was so extraordinary as to give colour to the story;—But Celestia always garbled the simplest narrations, murdering names and jumbling facts, until it was next to impossible to arrive at the truth. A three years' absence, too! How nonsensical she was! Her fears returned, however, with reinforcements, when he attached himself to Mrs. Read's cordon of admirers. These were not all young men. Elderly gentlemen, who had not lost their eye for fair faces, and taste for repartee, were recipients of as gracious welcomes as were apportioned to their youthful rivals; and sagacious damsels, of doubtful belleship and charms, crept beneath the wings of her popularity, large enough to shelter a female favorite or so. Mr. Ashlin entered the outmost precincts of this circle, and by imperceptible advances penetrated to the centre of attraction. Mrs. Read flushed slightly, with surprise or displeasure, as he established himself by her side; but nothing intimidated, he presently usurped the management of the conversation; holding up some to ridicule so cleverly that they had only themselves to blame, and did not suspect his agency; flattering others, until they dropped off like surfeited leeches; and angering some so openly, that Ida, who was near enough to get an inkling of what was transpiring, was assured that he was playing for a rich stake. His purpose was effected; he had a clear field; and with no alteration of manner, unless a shade of respect moderated his gay *insouciance*, he continued his attentions. No place is better for a confidential confabulation than a crowded room, if the parties understand how to conduct it. The initiated would have surmised from an occasional gleam of the eye, and the varying expression of that most uncontrollable of features, the mouth, that something more important than sugared nothings was upon the tapis; but to the purblind merrymakers, as a body, Mrs. Read was examining a portfolio of prints, and her companion, a travelled gentleman, descanting upon "High Art" in "the States," as contrasted with the love for poetry, painting and music, which, it was said, prevailed in gay, pleasure-loving Havana.

Ida was surprised that Mr. Ashlin requested a presentation to herself, and still more at the pertinacity with which he cultivated the acquaintance he must see she did not desire. He triumphed over her prejudice, inveterate as she had thought it. His air of deep interest—the admiration, too respectful to be conveyed in words, which spoke in every look and action, were dangerous flattery, and Ida was not invulnerable. But in reviewing the events of the evening, distrust obscured the pleasing recollection of his captivating address and the magic of his eloquence. Why was it bestowed upon her—a stranger, and so little attractive in her appearance? Why, especially, should he have asked permission to call? He knew Mrs. Read, and to her the application should, in etiquette, have been made. There was a vague apprehension hanging over her—a foreboding, for which she could assign no cause. He called, as he had promised, "at an early day." The family were collected in Mr. Read's room, when his card was brought to the lady of the house.

"Mr. Ashlin," she read. "Whom did he ask for, John?"

"The ladies, ma'am."

"Very well. Josephine, I will thank you and Miss Ida to receive him, and excuse me."

"Excuse *me*, if you please!" answered Josephine, bridling. "I scarcely know the gentleman, and do not covet the honour."

"Miss Ida?" said Mrs. Read, inquiringly.

"Why not go down with me, ma'am? Are you indisposed?"

"You need not say so—I am engaged. I really wish it," she added, for Ida was undecided.

"Then I will go," said she, with a sensation of infinite relief.

Josephine followed her out. "Beware, my lady-like Tartuffe!" hissed she, sneering in baffled malignity. "You are mixing yourself up in a scrape which will not reflect much credit upon the elect."

Her fiendish laugh was echoing after her, as Ida gained the parlor.

Mr. Ashlin did not appear abashed or disappointed, upon receipt of the apologies. He bowed, with a civil regret, and seemed to forget that there were other ladies in the house or in the world, than the one he was entertaining.

Ida's disagreeable oppression returned once, at his smile, when, in reply to his inquiry, she stated that the portrait in the niche opposite him, was Mr. Read's.

He got up to inspect it. To Ida, he was measuring himself with it, as he straightened his Apollo figure, and expanded his full chest.

"A good painting!" he observed. "How long since it was taken?"

"Two years."

"The pencil of time is the best test of the value of a picture—to some it is a destroyer,—it beautifies others. An excellent piece of work!"—still scanning it. "Is the likeness correct?"

"Uncommonly—or was, when it was painted. Mr. Read looks older and thinner now, that his health is impaired."

Again that sinister smile! but he said nothing more.

He called again, with a friend, an *habitué* of the house. It was evening, and Mrs. Read saw them. The length of his stay in Richmond was indefinite;—they were not sure but each visit was his last; and he, keeping up the uncertainty, came frequently, at the hours which suited him best. Josephine, succumbing seemingly, to the power of his wizard wand, freely declared her dread of his departure; Ida felt as much when with him, and revoked it, secretly, as soon as her eyes recovered from their dazzlement. Mrs. Read treated him, as she did her other visitors, and bore no part in the chorus of laudations chaunted in his absence. When Mr. Read was well enough to see company, he fell an easy conquest to the arts of the inimitable stranger. "He was"—he protested, "a better doctor than Ballard. An hour of his society was more beneficial to him, than the apothecary's entire stock of drugs."

His birth-day was near at hand, and he determined to invite his friends to rejoice with him, at his partial restoration to health. It was to be an unostentatious affair—a dinner, and no ladies but those belonging to the family. Mr. Read was as impatient as a child at its first tea-party.

"They are late, Helen! they are not coming!" he said every few minutes, while they were awaiting the guests. He was working himself into a passion, when the welcome ring appeased him.

"Mr. Copeland!" called the stentorian lungs of the footman; and Mrs. Read was as white, as if the hand of Death had smitten her.

"How are you all?" said Richard, in his joyous, rattling style. "Miss Ross, I am delighted to meet you—Miss Josephine, I will not disparage your blooming cheeks by asking after your health,—and you, Mr. Read, have been practicing upon our fears, by stories of illness—hasn't he, Helen—*you* are ill!" he said, brought to a full stop by her pallor.

"Ill! you are well—are you not?" said Mr. Read, in alarm.

"Well! yes! what notions you have, Richard!" and the color flowed back. "When did you come in?—down, I mean, and how are they at home?"

"'Home' is too bridish for a demure matron; but they are well, and sent love. I arrived this morning, and should have been in before, but for business."

"Don't leave the room, Helen. Somebody will come while you are out. Send John for what you want;" said Mr. Read.—She was slipping out through the back parlor.

"I will be gone but a second," she answered; and Mr. Read was still telling Richard how opportune his visit was when she returned. She was the collected, urbane hostess, only an eager glance at each arrival, betrayed nervousness or expectation. Mr. Read watched the door, also; and his displeasure at the tardiness of his favorite was audibly vented.

"Helen! why don't Mr. Ashlin come?" he said, in Ida's hearing. Ears less acute would not have distinguished his wife's reply.

"Hush! these people are jealous of your preference already. He will be here before long."

Ida had mislaid her handkerchief, or not brought it into the room; and Richard offered to favor her retreat by a journey into the next room, to look at some green-house plants. Leaving him bending over them, she ran up-stairs, found the missing article, and was hurrying down, when a ring arrested her upon the lower landing. Thinking to let the visitor enter before her, she stepped back out of sight.

"Mr. Ashlin, I beg your pardon, sir," said John, "my mistress told me to give you this before you went into the drawing-room, sir."

Mr. Ashlin paused—she judged, to read a note.

"All right!" said he. "Tell your mistress, I regret exceedingly that I am called into the country, on account of a friend's danger, and cannot comply with my engagement to Mr. Read this evening. Deliver the message as I have given it. This is for yourself, John. Good day."

"Thank you, sir. Good afternoon."

Ida's limbs shook beneath her. She had not time to unravel the mystery—for mystery she knew it to be;—Mrs. Read's fright at her brother's entrance; her incoherence and exit; the strangely worded message; the bribe to the servant—swam in a chaotic medley through her mind. She was sick with terror, until warned to conceal her emotions by Richard's saying that "Helen's queer symptoms had become epidemic." Partaker of the alarms of guilt, by her knowledge of the sin,—averse as she was to participation in its concealment, she was possessed with the idea, that to her was committed the work of blinding Richard. While her ears were alert to every sentence uttered around her, and she was quaking at the least approach to a mention of the absentee, she aimed to monopolize Mr. Copeland's sense and thoughts. She anticipated their quitting the table as a blessed change; then a cold agony came over her, at the remembrance that the gentlemen would remain. Discovery, in this case, was inevitable. His wife's caution would not restrain Mr. Read from pledging Mr. Ashlin's health. She thought of bantering Richard into withdrawing with the ladies;—it would be too bold—too forward. He would obey, but his respect for her would be diminished;—as a final alternative, she must venture it—but was there no other?

"Our patient does us credit, Miss Ida." Her next neighbor was Dr. Ballard.

"Does *you* credit, Doctor. I am only your custodian—a daring one, however, for I have a petition to submit. Will it not be imprudent for Mr. Read to remain long at table, after the cloth is removed? His system is still inflammatory." Her conscience reproved her for the deception, although she spoke the truth, but the case was desperate. The doctor's professional cap was on instantly.

"Unquestionably, my child!—unquestionably! well thought of, Miss Ida! We must guard against a relapse. How shall we get him into the parlor?"

Ida consulted Richard, who referred the case to Charley and returned her the reply, that if the ladies would delay their departure, a little longer than was customary,—not to startle those who loved to tarry at the wine, he would concert with most of the company to rise at the same time. Charley was at the helm, and Ida could safely have slept upon her watch. Mr. Read demurred at an infringement upon banquetting laws, but the seceders gallantly insisted upon attending their fair leaders; and the most disaffected had not courage to stand their ground. It was a weary, weary evening to Ida; she looked and felt wretchedly ill, after the guests dispersed. Richard looked in again, after saying "good night."

"I have purchased a buggy to-day," said he, to Ida; "and my pet horse is in town. Shall I have the pleasure of driving you out in the morning?"

She assented.

"At what hour?" he asked.

"I wonder what has happened, that Ashlin stayed away!" said Mr. Read.

Richard started violently. "Ashlin!" he echoed with a fiery look at his sister. "Ashlin— Ashlin;" he repeated, sensible of his imprudence. "I have heard the name—who is he?"

"An old friend of your sister's," replied Josephine.

Richard's face was profoundly meditative. "A small man—is he not? red-haired, stoops in the shoulders, and wears spectacles?"

Mr. Read spoke up indignantly. "A magnificent fellow! gentlemanly, intelligent, and one of the best hearts in the world."

"I do not know him then!" said Richard, emphatically. "Now I think of it, the red head's name may have been Ash*ton*. Say eleven o'clock,"—to Ida—"it will be pleasantly warm then."

"It will suit me," she rejoined, trembling before his gaze.

He was punctual to the hour. Mr. Read hobbled to the door to admire his "turn-out." To him, Richard was lively and friendly as usual, but he refused his sister's invitation to come in, and his bow, as his horse sprang off at the loosened rein, was to him. They left the city by the shortest route. Beyond the houses, Richard slackened their headlong speed.

"Miss Ross!" he said, abruptly facing her, "I have classed you among the limited number of your sex, who are upright and truthful. Within twelve hours past, I have doubted *you*. You are under no personal obligations to answer my questions;—but as a brother—for the honor of my family, I demand of you, all that you know of this Ashlin."

"Which is very little. I never saw him until Mr. Cranleigh's marriage, when he was introduced to me at Mrs. Morris'."

"By whom? by Helen?"

"By Mrs. Morris, herself. He made a party call, and has continued to visit the house."

"Artful as ever!" he said, through his shut teeth. "Does Mrs. Read see him?"

"Yes; and Mr. Read."

"The old blinkard! Does Helen receive him as your friend or as hers?"

"As the friend of the family."

"Tush! I might commend your diplomacy, Miss Ross, if I were not so thoroughly in earnest. It is clear you will not advance a step, without knowing why you are questioned. Having more confidence in you, than you have in me, I will set you an example of candor. Ashlin and my sister were betrothed when he was at college. We were 'chums.' He is ardent— generous in some of his impulses, but as I perceived, even with my boyishly irregular notions, lax in principle. Helen was not ignorant of my opinion, and with a woman's faith and perseverance, set herself to break it down. You do not know her as she was then— high-spirited, proud and passionate, but tractable as a child to the voice of affection. Her will was more ungovernable than mine, and she almost reconciled me to her choice. He had just completed his course at the University, when the death of an uncle put him in possession of a valuable estate in Cuba. The marriage, which was to have taken place immediately, was postponed for twelve months. Meantime, he was to visit his property, and prepare for a permanent residence in the West Indies. The year elapsed—he did not return—and suddenly his letters were suspended. Helen was insanely trustful; he might be ill or dead—dying, or in the grave, he was true! Her romantic independent disposition led her to the formation of a mad project—to search for him in person, since she could learn nothing in any other way. I could not dissuade her;—she made but one concession,—that I might accompany her. The object and direction of our expedition was known only to ourselves. We were ready—a day before that fixed for starting, a letter came! He was enamored of an Italian cantatrice; 'designed marrying her, if Helen would liberate him;— if not, he would redeem his early pledge to her.' She was ill for weeks; and upon what, I believed was her death-bed, she extorted from me a vow not to revenge her. She 'should have foreseen how it would end,' she said, 'blind, confiding dupe, that she was!' She arose— a hardened, I think, sometimes, a heartless woman of the world:—with her trust in him, had perished her faith in God and man; an unfeminine panting for wealth and distinction filling its place. Chance threw this gold-fish, Read, in her net; and she clutched him. I had sorrowed for, and commiserated her until then; but so sordid, so wickedly weak was this act, that I reproached her angrily. I said it sprang from wounded vanity, and a mean desire to glitter, a hollow-hearted, tinselled doll in the view of those who would gibe, while pretending to applaud;—that her conduct was as degrading to her, as mortifying to us,— and she bore my vituperations, without attempting to defend herself, 'Richard!' she said, when I had exhausted my indignation, 'better reason with a tornado, than a slighted woman!'

"You regard me as a chattering coxcomb, Miss Ida; but I solemnly declare that I could have gone to the block more resignedly, than I saw my beautiful sister sold to her hoary bridegroom. These were circumstances, with which I could not cope—but the diabolical schemes of this assassin of her peace shall not mature! This is the sad tale—is it quite new to you?"

"In its details;" and she related Celestia's version.

"Which furnished you with a key—you have a clear head, and a woman's wit—have you found no locks that it fitted?"

No reply.

"Did you divine the cause of Helen's embarrassment at my appearance, yesterday?"

"Not at the time."

"But afterwards. He was invited—did she warn him of my being there? If so, do not say it. I can bear your silence better than the truth."

"I can neither deny nor assert, Mr. Copeland. I have imagined many dreadful things, which may have no real existence. You may judge for yourself."

His brow was lighter, when he had heard her unvarnished relation.

"I thank you!" said he, heartily. "We may cicatrize this wound yet. I will see Helen to-night; she expects a reproof; and if she is not what she appears,—refined steel—I will make her feel. I dare not meet Ashlin—but I will write—and if he crosses my path again—." He resumed in a milder tone, "I would crave one more proof of your good-will, but that I fear a refusal."

"Ask it."

"If he renews his visits, will you inform me?"

"No, sir!" said Ida, positively. "The service savors too much of espionage."

"I was afraid you would see it in that light. Miss Read," he continued, scornfully, "would require no persuasion to play the spy. I was near committing myself last night. His name was a galvanic shock."

"I cannot but hope," said Ida, "that our fears have magnified shadows into spectres. We are so prone to shape events after the fashion of our inclinations or forebodings. Do not consider it an impertinent liberty, Mr. Copeland, if I recommend to you to be very gentle in your reprehension of your sister. Callous, self-dependent in semblance, think what her sufferings are, empaled by memory and conscience. Oh! if we had more charity for the tempted!"

"Temptation, sin, suffering! how naturally the words succeed each other!" mused Richard. "And they are an epitome of all human woe," said Ida "It is a doctrine of mine, that a small proportion of the great aggregate of crime is committed from actual love of sin."

She was gratified at his demeanor towards his sister upon their return. He dined with them, and was markedly attentive to her, combining so much brotherly kindness with a certain deference to her wishes and sentiments, that she struggled with the softness which menaced her proud composure. As they quitted the table, he passed his arm around her waist, and there were tears in the eyes upraised to his. No more auspicious time could occur for the contemplated conversation; and Ida enticed Mr. Read into his reading room, by the lure of an uncut periodical. The words fell from her mouth mechanically—her mind was upon the momentous interview. In the character and life delineated by Richard, she traced, with a thrill, a similarity to her own; the impetuous temper—unmanageable, save when the breath of love sighed over the heart; the blasted hope; the unworthiness of the object of adoration—ah! this bitterest ingredient in the cup of despair was spared her! but the prostration of soul and body; then the heaven-threatening billows of blasphemous misanthropy, and self-abandonment—the parallel was just here—to diverge how widely in the result of the ordeal! one, wilfully completing the ruin of her happiness by perjury—cauterizing her heart with corrodents, that eat away its fevered life; the other, dragging herself, wounded and weary, to the feet of the Good Physician, to be healed, and fed, and sustained by His loving mercy; and the language of Ida's thanksgiving was, "Lord! *Thou* hast made me to differ!"

CHAPTER XXV

The season of sunshine and roses had come, and Carry's demands for her friend's society were importunate.

"You would not fret your dear heart with harrowing doubts of my love for you and Poplar-grove, if you could peep in upon me this morning," wrote Ida. "Mr. Read is worse. I am unfamiliar with the diagnosis of this malady; but I fear his condition is very precarious. He is entirely disabled; cannot lift his hand to his mouth without extreme pain, and his nervous system is much deranged. I write now at the window farthest distant from his bed, and cautiously, that the scratching of my pen may not disturb him. I can see your hands and eyes go up, and hear the 'this is too much!' which signals the last throe of expiring patience as you picture me a nun-like figure, with serge gown and close cap; or more affecting, an attenuated damsel, such as we see upon tomb-stones, pressing a handkerchief to one eye; I imagine your multitudinous arguments, each unanswerable in its excellence, and which I know by heart. You allege that he is not entitled to my cares, inasmuch as there are no ties of blood between us; that he has never done me an ungrudged favor; that he is greedy and thankless for my services; that his wife and daughter should esteem it their duty and pleasure to tend him; and fifthly and lastly, that it is wrong to endanger my health, as your whimsical country doctors will have it I am doing. Putting the last first,—reassure yourself my dear—I am *well*. I do not prevaricate to allay your fears; I look well, eat well, and sleep well, and I may dismiss the remainder of your objections in one sentence—I am doing my duty, Carry! I am morally certain of this, more certain, than if you were my charge; for my love would be the mainspring of action then. I am upheld by the assurance, that I am fulfilling, in my humble way, the command, our Saviour appointed as the touchstone of piety to the end of time—'Do good to them that hate you, pray for them that despitefully use you.' I thank Him that He has vouchsafed to me this opportunity to examine myself by this criterion."

The sufferer moaned, and she laid down her pen. "You have had a refreshing sleep, have you not, sir?"

"No! there is no ease for me. Why is that window open? It does seem that you all have conspired that I shall die, whether or no. Where is Helen?"

"She was here awhile ago, and will be in again soon."

"Is she in the house?"

"I do not know, sir. Let me get what you want."

"I want *her*!"

She was not at home, and Ida renewed her offer.

"Gone out, hey!" he rambled on, peevishly. "How she walks! as if the ground were not good enough for her feet! ogling and coquetting! and I am *here*!" with an oath. "Where is Josephine?"

"Down stairs, sir."

"What is *she* about?"

"Anna Talbot is with her."

"More folly and vanity! ringlets and ribbons, and bonnets and beaux! The world is peopled with knaves and fools—women are knaves—men fools. You are a mixture."

Ida suppressed a smile. "Your lips are dry," she said "here is water."

He drank it. "You are!" he went on, obstinately, "I hated you from the minute you entered this house, and you repaid me with compound interest. Here you are, sitting up at night; waiting on me all day. I can't do without you, because you are handy and wakeful, but I don't like you. Do you hear?"

"Yes, sir."

"I *don't*! and therefore, I'm a fool to tolerate the sight of you. I'm a fool—*that's* proved! You are spoiling your eyes and complexion, and losing the time you might be catching a husband—mewed up here. You expect to be paid when my will is read—that's knavery—hypocritical knavery. I haven't left you a red cent; you are a fool to think of it, and *that's* proved!"

Pitiful driveller! It was not insensibility, but compassion, that closed Ida's month, although she knew this was the revelation of the inner chamber of thought, now that the veil of custom and policy was rent in twain.

"What time is it?"

"Twelve o'clock, sir."

"That's a lie! it's three, at least! Bring the witch to me. It has stopped! Hold it to my ear—you've put it back! Lay it down by me! I don't trust you again!"

The hands pointed to one when Mrs. Read appeared.

"Well, madam!" the form of each tooth was seen through the thin lips, stretched over them like yellow parchment. "And where have you been traipsing?"

"I walked down the street."

"And on Main street, too, I'll swear! spending more money than you'd sell for at auction! Why don't you answer me? Your tongue was more glib when you were passing compliments with that fellow who walked with you."

"I went out alone, and did not go on Main street."

"You would have been better employed in the kitchen—forever gadding! I don't want you in here—I'm sick of you and your brazen face!"

"What error to suppose that sickness softens, and predisposes the heart to repentance!" thought Ida. She went into the other room, and beckoned Mrs. Read. "The doctor was here this morning," she said; "and told me, privately, not to mind his irritability, nor to answer him, unless silence increased it. It is an ordinary symptom in neuralgic affections. We must be forbearing."

"There is a limit to everything," was Mrs. Read's response.

"True—but forbearance should last as long as the pain we would cure."

"That is your theory, Miss Ida. I am tired of the practice. You mean well, I have no doubt, but I am not a fit object for your charity."

The asperity was pointed at herself, rather than at her hearer, and Ida pondered upon her words and manner, often during the day.

"It did not agree with" Josephine "to sit up"—a constitutional weakness, loudly lamented, and encouraged, instead of overcome. Ida and Mrs. Read divided the vigil; the mulatto nurse, Sarah, sleeping in the apartment. Ida was to watch the latter part of the night. The patient was cross and restless, when she looked in upon him at bed-time—railing, and swearing and abusive.

"You want me dead!" he said to his wife; "but I won't die—to spite you. I shall live years, and years, and years, 'till you are a toothless hag, and walk with a crutch! Ha! ha!"

"He is delirious!" whispered Ida. "Let me stay with you!"

"He is *not*! I prefer your retiring. Sarah will call you at two."

"I shall not undress, to-night, Rachel," said Ida. "I have a presentiment I shall be wanted."

"Is he much worse?"

"No—but I may be called up. I shall sleep here, upon the lounge."

But sleep was coy to her wooing. If she had ever felt fear, she would have known that she was scared and excited. The south wind generally affected her unpleasantly, creating heat and nervousness; but to-night the breeze was from the north, and the moonbeams were spread in broad, white sheets upon the floor. "I must be sick!" she said, aloud. "I cannot ascribe this numb horror to anything else. They have a superstition that it is a precursor of death." Her mind rejected this explanation, but the utterance of that word had populated her soul with phantoms. Lynn's chill, damp hands again enfolded hers; and his glazed, upward look—still and fixed, moved not at her weeping; the clods rattled upon the coffin— frozen clods! and how warmly soever the sun smiled upon the swelling turf—down where he slept, it was frosty night still! Must he, the loved and gifted, rest there forever? would a tender mother's arms never more embrace her,—the dear lips, now turned to dust, never cling to hers, in speechless fondness? But the dead should rise! some to the resurrection of the just, some to everlasting shame and contempt. Oh! the unspeakable woe of a hopeless death! the dying strife of the finally impenitent! Was *his* end approaching? "My God! avert from him this doom!" His room was beneath hers. She could hear occasionally a groan, which she knew was an execration. He might be dying. She thrust her feet into a pair of felted slippers, and descended to his door. "Quiet—quiet *as death*!" "This is improper! irrational!" said she, severely, to herself. "I need repose and steadiness of nerve—there are watchers with him." But she would not go back to her room. She went, instead, to the parlor. The hall-lamp burned all night; and setting open a door, and unclosing a shutter, to dissipate the darkness, which suffocated her, as a thick pall, she stretched herself upon a sofa. She slumbered and dreamed—visions, like her waking fancies. She was in Mr. Read's chamber; writing to Carry, at her far window;—the door swung back, and his wife glided in. With a gesture of silence to her, she passed to his bedside, and poised a knife above his heart! Ida strove to scream—to move—but her mighty efforts only shifted the scene—did not awaken her. He was dead; and his friends had come to the funeral. They thronged the room where his corpse lay in its costly coffin; and the carriages, headed by the hearse, grated upon the pebbled gutter. The undertaker was tightening the silver screws—when, oh! horror! the lid was heaved up from within—crashing and splintering—and the dead sat upright! The distorted features were Mr. Ashlin's,—the yell, as he tossed his arms aloft,— Mr. Read's. "I will not die!" She was in the centre of the apartment; the cold beads dripping from her forehead, and her hair, dank and heavy, upon her face and neck. She put it back, and listened. The silence drove by her in waves—throbbed with the beatings of her heart. Hark! it was not all a dream! the pawing of hoofs rang upon the stones. The moon had set; and the lamp was brighter than the starlight. She had the presence of mind to creep to that side of the window hidden by the shutter, and looked out. A carriage was at the door—in appearance like the doctor's. He had been summoned—the sick man was worse. Something light and white sailed past her window, from overhead; as it fluttered to the ground, a tall figure stepped from the vehicle, and caught it to his bosom. The apparition of the Arch-Fiend himself would not have shaken Ida, as did that manly form. She was awake! A stealing step fell, softly as a snow-flake, upon the floor above—she heard it. With the speed of light, she flew to the front door—locked it—to that at the other extremity of the passage—hid both keys beneath the cushion of the hall-sofa, and back again to the street entrance, as Mrs. Read, dressed for travelling, had her foot upon the lowest stair. The fugitive leaned against the wall for support, faint with the terrors of detected guilt.

"Back!" said Ida—her cheek bloodless—her eyes flashing living fire. "False to your word! false to your sex! I will save you from public disgrace! Back! I say!"

"Not while I live!" was the answer.

"And you cross this threshold over my body!" cried the girl, passionately. "Oh! shame! shame! you—the pride and idol of your family and your husband! that you should break their hearts and disgrace his name!"

"It is not my name after I leave this—I shall forget and be forgotten. Let me go!"

"Forget! forgotten! you may! a false woman can forget the mother who reared her! but the stain upon them! your tears, nor *his* blood can cleanse it!"

"You are mad!" said Mrs. Read, regaining her composure. "You cannot stop me. My home is in another land. Why do you talk of disgrace? the brutal dotard I fly from, will unfasten my legal fetters, and then I shall *live*! the life for which my Creator destined me!"

"*You* speak your Creator's name! trampling upon His laws—His curse hanging over you! Oh! I entreat you, by a mother's prayers—for the sake of your old father, tottering upon the verge of the grave—in the name of your honorable and loving brother, not to expose your design! You shall not—you cannot go; the doors are locked—-call for assistance from those who are without, and I will alarm the household. To-morrow your name will be trumpeted at the corner of every street. Ha! that cry! they have discovered all! Too late! too late! but no!—" She tore off the cloak and bonnet, and threw them into a corner, as Sarah rushed down the steps.

"Mistress! Miss Ida! for the Lord's sake, come! Master is dying!"

A cry from Josephine pierced their ears. Ida forgot her companion, but she reached the chamber with her. Writhing, convulsed, screaming, he was wrestling with the Destroyer; the disease had grappled his heart. Mrs. Read sank upon her knees, as blasted by a thunderbolt; Josephine shrieked in helpless dismay; Ida was wrought up to too high a pitch, to think of self.

"Where is John?" she cried. "Here! run for Dr. Ballard! Mr. Read is *very* ill! Call for Mr. Talbot as you come back. Fly!"

He was down stairs while she was speaking. "Why, Miss Ida, the key is not here!"

She ran for it, unlocked the door, and pushed him out. A man stood in the shade of the porch, whom John did not perceive, in his rapid egress; but he seized Ida's hand, as she would have shut him out.

"Helen!"

"Mrs. Read's *husband* is dying, Mr. Ashlin!"

"Good heavens!"

The bolt had shot into its place, ere he could say more.

All the accompaniments of the last agony, of which Ida had ever heard, read or conceived, were realized in this struggle;—the blackening features, drenched with sweat, the starting eye, the twitching muscles, the death-rattle,—the soul was tearing through the clay receptacle: yet for two hours the awful conflict was protracted.

Morning! a sheet covered the rigid, motionless limbs and countenance, telling in death, of suffering; and there were solemn stoppings and stifled whispers through the house; and crape waved from the door, where the traitorous friend had waited, at night, for the dead man's wife.

Mrs. Read was borne to her chamber in hysteric convulsions, and continued raving and swooning all day—attacking, in tigress fury, every one who approached her, excepting Ida. Her she would not suffer to quit her sight. Holding her hands in a frantic grasp, she poured forth such tales as made her heart ache: of warm Spring evenings, when the air was laden with sweet-briar scent, and the young moon was swimming in the pale blue sky, and the star of love shone upon them—an eye of light—from the blushing west, and he sung to her—poetry ascending from his heart as perfume from the flowers—songs, upon whose memory she lived, in the winter of his absence. "But"—and the deep wells of her eyes were black with anguish, "her heart died, and dissolution came not to the body—would that it had! and the thought of the past was a yawning abyss, like the abode of the lost, from which arose hot, poisonous simooms and tormenting spirits. The world brought incense and gaudy offerings, and friends their best treasures, but it closed not—and she resolved, by self-immolation, to shut the chasm; by an irrevocable sacrifice, to seal it forever. The effort was idle—she sold soul and body for nought. He came, and turned her face to the Future. His heart had wavered, but returned to its allegiance. She was his, by an earlier, holier tie than her loathed tyrant's;—away in the sunny land of their youthful dreams, they would live, unmolested by memory or care. She clung to duty, until her husband drove her from him with a curse; to a brother's love,—and he painted that brother's hatred of him, and threatened to see her no more;—and by the specious names of "soul-dictates," and the "religion which enjoins truth, and condemns hypocrisy," gained her promise. The hand of the Almighty interfered!

Ida shut up her tears, and reasoned and plead with her; praying inwardly for her comfort, and that her own mind and nerves might not fail her. She rested the maniac's head upon her breast—bathed the beating temples, and pressed her cool lips to the parched ones, working with pain—beseeching her, with every endearing epithet, to rest and forget. But the lava crust was heaving; and the long-repressed flood spread over it in fast, soothing streams. The June twilight was on the earth—as she had described those of years agone; and in calming tones, she bade Ida "sing."

"What shall I sing?"

"Of love and faith and hope."

The exhausted girl rallied her strength, and the sweetest of written hymns seemed whispered to her spirit.

"'Oh! Thou, who driest the mourner's tear,
How dark this world would be,
If pierced by sins and sorrows here,
We could not fly to Thee!

'The friends, who in our sunshine live.
When winter comes, are flown;
And he, who has but tears to give,
Must weep those tears alone.

'But Thou wilt heal that broken heart,
Which, like the plants that throw
Their fragrance from the wounded part—
Breathes sweetness out of woe.
'When joy no longer soothes or cheers,
And e'en the hope that threw
A moment's sparkle o'er our tears,
Is dimmed and vanished too;—
Oh! who could bear life's stormy doom,
Did not thy wing of love,
Come, brightly waiting through the gloom,
Our peace-branch from above!
Then sorrow, touched by Thee, grows bright,
With more than rapture's ray,
As darkness shows us worlds of light
We never saw by day.'"

The head weighed upon her arm, she did not withdraw it Scarcely breathing herself, she listened to the regular respiration, that said the distempered brain was locked in forgetfulness. One—two—three hours—and a cold lifelessness succeeded to the smart and aching suspended circulation had first produced, a torpor, creeping to her shoulder—affecting her whole body; but she would not terminate that blessed slumber. A fleet step ascended the stairs,—it did not belong to any of the household, yet was not strange. A knock—which she could not answer—the bolt was cautiously drawn.

"Helen!" said her brother's voice.

The "hush-sh-sh!" silenced him, but he entered. The moon revealed the dark and white forms upon the bed.

"Your sister sleeps!" said Ida, under her breath. "I beg you to retire—she must not see you. Oh! go!" for she was awaking.

"Ida!" said Mrs. Read; "what am I doing here? Oh! mercy! I remember!"

"Peace! peace!" and with gentle violence, Ida forced her back to the pillow. "You are safe and well now."

She was still for a minute. "Whom were you speaking to when I awoke?"

"Some one opened the door, and I did not wish you disturbed."

"It was a servant, then? I dreamed Richard had come. Oh! if he should!"

"Do you want us to send for him?"

"Never!"

"But the fatigue of travelling rapidly over so great a distance will be too much for your parents. Some of your friends ought to be with you."

"But not Richard! any one else!"

Ida was perplexed. He would insist upon seeing her, as soon as he heard that she was awake;—they must meet in the morning, and the shock then might unfit her to endure the trials of the day; yet to tell her now, appeared cruel and unnecessary.

"You have not eaten to-day—you will take some nourishment if I bring it?"

"Don't leave me!"

"Only for a little while. Promise me to be good and quiet, until I can run down stairs and back."

"Only do not stay—I am afraid to be alone."

Richard was pacing the hall with a troubled air. "How is she?" he asked.

"More composed."

"May I go up?"

"It pains me to deny you, but she can see no one, at present."

"This is extraordinary, Miss Ida. We know that there is not ground for this excessive grief, and Helen has not miss-ish nerves. What ails her?"

His frown commanded her to reply, explicitly.

"You do not reflect how sudden Mr. Read's death was, Mr. Copeland. It was an alarming event to us all. After awhile, your sister will receive you. She does not know that you are here;—her mind has wandered all day; and I deemed it safest not to agitate her. Trust me to do all in my power for her and you."

"I do!"

Mrs. Read remained comparatively tranquil, saying little, except to supplicate Ida not to leave her.

"You are better—are you not?" inquired the latter, stroking her brow.

"Yes—easier, and more quiet."

"I find your brother has been sent for;" she pursued.

"He has come!" ejaculated Mrs. Read. "Oh! what shall I do? what shall I do?"

"It is unavoidable;—you must meet—why delay it?"

"Oh! he will kill him! he said he would, if he ever spoke to me again!"

More perplexity! Ida staggered under it. Her ingenuousness pointed to the straightest, as the best road. The guilty mind would never be unburdened without confession; but there was solid rock, underlying the foamy flow of Richard's character. When his distrust of Ashlin did not amount to a denned conviction, he had said, that he "dared not see him"— and she recalled his meaning,—"If he crosses my path again!" The dilemma was fearful— a life of concealment to one, murder to the other. Mrs. Read's consternation redoubled on perceiving hers. "What shall I do? oh! if I could die!" she moaned, tossing from side to side. Ida spoke in accents of command—representing the unhappiness she would experience in her intercourse with her deceived brother; the watchfulness, and subterfuges, and the misery of accepting a love she had forfeited; and on the other hand, the remorse of the murderess; the blood of another soul clogging hers; the public ignominy—but this was barely touched upon.

"Yet sin unconfessed to man, is not always unrepented of to God;" said she.

"Can you resign this base-hearted man, and devote your life to an endeavor to repair—you cannot of yourself, expiate your offences against your Maker and your fellow creatures?" And the haughty, hardened woman bent before the simple majesty of truth and feeling, and solemnly vowed herself ready for her work.

CHAPTER XXVI

Richard was to take his sister home; and Ida was busily assisting her to pack her trunks, the day after the funeral, when Josephine sent to request an audience. She ordered the servants out of the room as she came in, and without preamble, entered upon her subject.

"You two have been confederates in many amusing schemes. Wedded spirits at sight, you flattered yourselves that you counterfeited indifference successfully. But not to me—my fair intriguers! You, Miss Ross, were wilfully imprudent. I foiled your manoeuvres to entrap Morton Lacy, the man you loved;—you owe the disappointment, from which you will never recover, to me. You were unwary to oppose me a second time. And for you— lovely and inconsolable widow! your downfall was decreed from the moment we met. I poisoned that old man's mind against you. He weakly tried to repel doubt—to confide— the fool! in your love—but the venom was subtle—certain! *I* overheard your first interview with your recreant lover—marked, step by step, your reconciliation, and furthered it when I could:—*I* saw your trepidation when your brother's arrival menaced an *exposé*; and compelled John afterwards to a confession of the warning he transmitted, and the reply, 'on account of a friend's danger!' That 'friend' is in imminent danger now! The cessation of his visits did not mislead her, who dogged you in your walks, and saw him by your side. *I* was awake the elopement night,—saw your signal, and heard the theatrical dialogue in the hall, rehearsed for the benefit of eaves-droppers, to clear the skirts of your accomplice, when your flight should be discovered. Pah! a child could see through it! a remarkable coincidence that Miss Ross should select a parlor for a dormitory, and arouse, just in season to confront you at the door! It was a scene,—as the play-bills have it—'for one night only.' Your plan proved abortive; death has left you as free as a divorce would have done; and when the 'days of mourning are ended,' you think to marry, and the public be in blissful ignorance that this measure was in contemplation before your husband's decease. Idiot! is this the revenge I have worked for? Your swain is yet in town;—act out your plot. You need not go to Cuba—the laws of Virginia do not forbid the bans. If, however, your saint-like confidante reprobates 'indecent haste,' my game is nevertheless sure. I give you to-day and to-night for deliberation and escape. At the end of twenty-four hours, if you are in this house, your hot-blooded brother shall hear the interesting facts, of which I have presented a summary;—I have spoken, and *I never repent*!"

Her auditors had not moved hand or foot, since she began to speak; and after she had gone, they gazed at each other in the same dead silence. Mrs. Read's stony despair revived Ida's energies.

"I am lost!" she said, in a hollow tone. She put by the garment she held, and seated herself, with folded arms.

"You are not!"

"She '*never repents*!'"

"God grant she may, before it is too late!" said Ida, looking upward; "but I do not rely upon her relentings for your deliverance. We must consider. Bear up, and remember your vow!" But her own heart sank. Contrivance and expedient presented themselves,—all inadequate to the emergency.

"Are you willing to brave Richard's wrath, if it affects only yourself?" she asked.

"I am! to the shedding of *my* blood. Your face brightens! Is there any hope?"

"Iniquity defeats itself!" said Ida devoutly. "The Helper of the tempted will provide a means of escape. Have we not time, and the knowledge that he is in the city, and liberty to communicate with him? Write him a warning, and *final* farewell;—he must fly for his life—he will do it! The traitor is seldom brave!" she said inwardly.

Mrs. Read's nerveless fingers dropped the pen.

"I cannot!"

"You must!" said Ida, authoritatively. "His life—your peace, depend upon it. Write! I will dictate."

The note was short and imperative. If the hand quivered, the heart that indited did not.

"Take comfort!" said Ida, sealing it.

"How will you send it?" said Mrs. Read, whom grief and shame had robbed of mind and fortitude.

"I will carry it myself."

"Oh! not you! what will be said?"

"Trust me. If Josephine has emissaries, so have I. I will not compromise myself or you. I was cut out for a conspirator, and to keep up the character, you must disguise me. My appearance on the street so soon after the—yesterday, will excite remark. Ah! this thick veil, and that black mantle, will serve my purpose. Now, would you know me?"

"Never—but dear Ida—"

But repeating "Take comfort!" Ida kissed her, and went out. She tripped across the back yard, under shelter of the buildings, unlatched the gate, and was safely in an alley, bisecting the square, and parallel with the street upon which the house was built. She walked briskly, thinking over her plan. As in Lynn's case, Charley was her aim; but she was not so sure now of his co-operation. It was a delicate and dangerous matter;—would he be a blind tool? confidence was not to be thought of. With his nice notions of propriety, would he take a note from her to Mr. Ashlin, of whose character she had heard him speak disparagingly. "This is foolish!" she interrupted herself—"he must!" and she was conscious that this word from her, carried with it an authority few had the hardihood to resist.

John Dana was in the store, but he did not know her, and sent a clerk forward.

"I wish to see Mr. Dana, sir."

She raised her veil as he responded to the call.

"Ida! my dear child! I should never have recognised you!"

"I did not design you should. My errand is with Charley—is he in?"

"In the counting-room. What is the matter?"

"With me? Nothing, sir;—a state secret. He is my Vizier."

"Very well!" said he, smiling. "Walk this way." He pushed aside the baize door, and Ida thought she should faint, as Richard Copeland was discovered talking with Charley. John also retreated.

"He is not alone;" he said, "I will call him out."

"Not while Mr. Copeland is here!" she faltered. "Oh! I would not have him see me!"

"Ida!"

"He must *not* see me, Mr. Dana!"

"Then I will hide you—shall I?" He took her to the end of a counter, piled to the ceiling with goods; gave her a tall stool, and bade her "rest awhile."

Ida was ashamed of her perturbation, and heartsick of the feints and concealments her nature revolted at;—all the consequences of another's errors.

Charley and Richard entered the store. "You had better say you will go," said the latter. "It is insufferably stupid;—staying here this weather."

"I don't know whether I can get off;" answered Charley. "We'll see."

His brother directed him to Ida. He was astonished to see her.

"But you can never be unwelcome."

"*Cela dépend*;" said Ida, "I sue for a favor."

"Consider it granted."

"That will not do. Can you perform my bidding, without asking questions?"

"I am not inquisitive; and I depend upon your discretion."

"Then, will you deliver this letter immediately?"

His countenance changed. Ida lifted her finger.

"I have promised," he replied; "but Ida—if you were my sister, I would not be the bearer of this!"

"Charley!"

"I do not say it to hurt your feelings, but I know men, and this man, better than you do. This is not your handwriting. My fear is that you may be tampered with—not your integrity—but that designing people may impose upon your credulity."

"I thank you sincerely for your consideration, but I act with my eyes open, and conscientiously believe that what I demand is actually necessary. *I* dictated that note. Will you oblige me now?"

"Unhesitatingly."

"Be sure you give it, at once, to him. I cannot explain, I may never do it, perhaps. One thing more. Where does Mr. Copeland want you to go? and when?"

"To the country, to-morrow; a *tête-à-tête* drive out of town; a dinner at a tavern; and spend the day in the woods, gunning."

"Go, please! I have a special reason for asking it—and start early."

"More mysteries!"

"The last I shall ever annoy you with, Charley."

"Enough! if possible you shall be obeyed. I trust you, Ida—not one of the other parties concerned. By the way," he added, putting on his hat, "Lacy passed through the city yesterday; stopped but an hour, and left his regrets and respects for you. He would have called, but for the circumstances of the family."

"I should have been happy to see him," said Ida, very naturally. "Was his sister with him? how is her health?"

"Not improved. They contemplate a sea-voyage. I heard a queer report about him the other day." They were at the store-door, and Ida did not lower her veil, although the light was glaring. Charley was scrutinising her from the corners of his eyes, and she was aware of it. "I don't credit it;" he said. "They say he is engaged to be married to Miss Arnold."

Ida smiled. "Why do you discredit it?"

"Why I hear the girl is a flirt; she is pretty, but I don't relish the match. Besides, to be frank, I had a private opinion that—"

"That he was engaged to me!" finished Ida, laughingly. "Your shrewdness is at fault for once, Charley. I have known of his engagement ever since last summer—almost a year."

"How did you hear of it?"

"From himself."

"All right then, I suppose;" Charley reluctantly conceded "I'll be hanged if I don't believe it's all wrong!" he muttered, as he walked down the street. Ida did not mutter or sigh, on her way home. She cheered Mrs. Read's drooping spirits by reporting their case in excellent hands, and the happy Providence which appeared likely to befall them in Richard's projected jaunt. "A day is as precious to us, at this juncture, as if its minutes were diamonds," said she.

Withdrawing to her chamber, she wept long and sadly. "If I could only have seen him for one hour! one minute! Oh! I shall never be free—never forget! Can I censure poor Helen, when I am myself so weak? for it is sin to love him, the promised husband of another!"

An hour—and she was with her dejected charge, busy and cheerful—yet so thoughtful, so sympathetic, that the repentant wanderer blessed her as a heavenly messenger of compassion and goodness.

Ida was dressing in the morning, when she received a note from Charley.

"Mr. A—— decamped yesterday afternoon, servants and baggage—it is said not to revisit these parts shortly. I do not know whether this much discussed Hegira is, in any way, attributable to your billet, but write, in the supposition, that the fact may not be uninteresting. Mr. C—— and myself are on the point of starting upon our ride;—return to-night.

In haste, yours,
CHARLEY."

Ida smiled scornfully. "The caitiff! I said the false were seldom brave!"

She sent the note to Mrs. Read. Rachel brought up an answer. "You are my guardian angel," it said. "The God you love and serve, may reward you—I never can. I shall spend this day alone. Richard must hear the truth, and I should be his informant—not that miserable girl, who would gloat upon the sight of his grief and amazement. I shall write him everything. Pray for me!"

Towards evening, Rachel, as the only trustworthy bearer, was dispatched to Richard's hotel with the letter. Mrs. Read had expended her moral courage in the execution of this mortifying duty. She passed a wretched night—a prey to agonizing anticipations—imagining Mr. Ashlin's return; his being overtaken; the death of one or both; Richard's desertion of her, or that her family would disown her. Ida stayed with her, but her condolences and sanguine predictions were futile.

"You do not know Richard!" was Mrs. Read's invariable answer.

He appeared at the hour for departure, and without coming in, sent to inquire if she was ready. Ida supported the half-swooning woman down stairs. Richard was in the porch. He saluted her slightly—his sister, not at all;—his face so gloomy and stern, Ida dared not accost him. Josephine was less timorous, or had a stronger incentive. She walked boldly to the door.

"Mr. Copeland, can you spare me a minute of your valuable time? I have a word to say to you."

He wheeled upon her with a withering sneer. "I am admonished of the purport of your communication, Miss Read, and my regret is only second to yours, that the indulgence of your amiable penchant for bloodshed is inevitably postponed by the flight of our chivalrous friend. I give you credit for having acted in perfect consonance with the finest feelings of your soul. Permit me to express the hope that the consummation we mutually desire, is not very remote—that the "transgressor may be rewarded according to his works;"—and while this is the burden of your prayers, I would have you remember that I shall put up a like petition with regard to yourself!"

Mrs. Read strained Ida to her breast silently, and the hot tears fell fast upon her cheek. She tendered her hand to Josephine. It was disdainfully rejected.

"Farewell, Mr. Copeland;" said Ida, holding out her hand.

He clasped it, and inclined his head, as in adoration. "It is well," he said, in an under tone, "that I have met you. You have preserved me from total abnegation of female truth. Thank heaven that you have but a physical resemblance to your sex!" He closed the carriage-door upon his weeping sister, mounted his horse, bowed to his saddle-bow to the wave of Ida's handkerchief, and galloped off.

Anna Talbot was to stay with Josephine until the necessary legal formalities should leave her free to select a home; and Mrs. Dana claimed Ida. She needed rest and nursing. This week of agitation and wearing fatigue, was the forerunner of a fever, which might have resulted fatally, had she retained her old quarters. There was nothing at Mr. Dana's to quicken memory into action upon unpleasant subjects; no darkened chambers, or everburning tapers; no hurryings from room to room, with the suppressed bustle, that indicated a renewal of the patient's sufferings. These were sights and sounds painfully familiar to her of late. She lay in an airy apartment; the light tempered, not excluded; with books and flowers, and if she wished, the happy children to amuse her; and when she started from sleep, with a groan or shriek sounding through her head, her eye fell upon the placid face of her hostess, smiling tenderly to dispel her alarms; or Elle's cherry mouth said, in the flute-like accents, so like her aunt's, "You're just dreaming, cousin Ida!" She left her bed, but her tottering steps would not bear her far; and John Dana carried her in his strong arms every evening to the parlor, where was Charley, disposing, with the skill of an accomplished nurse, the pillows that heaped her sofa. She was thankful for the debility that made her the recipient of these tokens of true affection. They loved her; she no more doubted this, than she questioned her attachment to them. One day she appeared thoughtful, and Mrs. Dana remarked upon it in private to her coadjutors. She was afraid it arose from some saddening reminiscence, or mistrust of the future; "Charley must enliven her." And Charley, if he did not bring mirth, eliminated the caged troubler.

She "had heard," she said, "that the law required her to choose a guardian."

"True;" said Charley.

"Is there any specified time? has it expired?"

"A month hence will do; although Miss Read has made her choice."

"Ah! whom?"

"Mr. Talbot, the elder. Easy soul! he has not a thought of the pickle he is in."

Ida was more serious. "Will you say the same of my selected protector."

"Probably—you being a *fac-simile* of her."

"May I choose whom I please?"

"Undoubtedly."

"Will it be a very troublesome office?"

"Hum-m-m! I should say not. Some care—some responsibility—that is a mere song, though, as your schooling is done, and you are a moderately discreet young lady."

"Will you ask your brother to act? I prefer him above all other men in the universe."

"Why not do it yourself? he will not object."

"He might be influenced by my anxiety, and assume the task because it will make me happy—I want him to make an unprejudiced decision."

"I will look him up;" said Charley.

They re-entered together; and John bowed his tall form to kiss the flushing cheek. "You will not seem more like a daughter, when you are my ward, than you do now, Ida."

CHAPTER XXVII

It was chinquapen season; and a grove of "bushes" on the outskirts of the Poplar-grove plantation resounded with the jocund voices of a nutting party. The green beards rolled back their white lips, in a smile, saving as plainly as smile could say, for the shining brown treasure—"Come and take us!" As a loaded upper limb was roughly shaken, and screams of laughter and pretended fright arose from the group, upon whose heads the hurtling shower descended, our friend Charley might be seen, sauntering away, in suspicious unconcern;—Ellen Morris was weaving her gay-coloured meshes around Mr. Euston's susceptible heart, and Mary Truman, with Charley, as aid, was pioneer to a dozen children of assorted sizes. One couple had strayed to the edge of the grove, where, from the brow of a hill, they overlooked a wide expanse of landscape. The lady, whose bloom was heightened by exercise, or some other cause, was profoundly occupied in sifting chinquapens—taken, a handful at a time, from her basket—into the same again. Her cavalier was speaking low and impressively.

"You cannot argue indifference from my delay. I was ready for this declaration a year ago; but you were not; and while I left you in no doubt as to my intentions, I wished you to have ample time and opportunity for making up your mind. I have not the vanity to hope to allure by personal attractions or showy qualities; but if the disinterested love of a manly heart can win your regard, I may trust that my offering will not be scorned. I visited you last winter, and saw that you were not happily situated. A more hasty lover would have spoken then:—I would not have your discontent with one home, influence your decision in my offer of another—would not have you self-deceived; for your happiness is dearer to me than mine. But now, you are translated to a sphere, in which you are appreciated and beloved, your will is untrammelled by the restrictions of a stern guardian—free to move, without the goad of desire to escape a disagreeable lot. I have been very patient, Miss Ida."

He had—and she knew nothing of him but what was generous and honourable. His persevering attachment was guaranty of its depth. Pleasant as her life was now, the death of her guardian, or his widower-hood—(she thought of such chances, in these days of death and change—) would cast her out upon the world—alone and homeless as before. She had all the woman's longing to be paramount in one heart,—the sun and attraction of a home. She could give her suitor but a sisterly regard, at present; but she had been told that this culminated in a calm affection, lasting through life—mighty in death. The passionate idolatry of earlier days was conquered by religion;—she believed that it had subsided into friendship;—its hopelessness impelled her to forget it—how more effectually than in another love? Her colour fled, as it ever did, before powerful emotion, and the fingers, while they went on, burying themselves in the glossy brown heap, were icy cold. She must reply—she looked up—not in the intelligent face—handsome in its pure fervor of devotion—but beyond—to where the blue sweep of the hills lay, graceful and light, against the rosy horizon; and she gazed, until her dark eyes were dilated and moveless, and her companion, struck by their expression, looked to the same spot. He saw but the hills, and the heavens, spanning them in crimson glory—she verily thought, as she stood, rooted to the earth, in the dumb agony of memory, and recoiling at the fate, her tongue had almost sealed,—that she beheld—as if the folds of that glowing canopy were drawn aside—the form and features of her first—what she knew now, was to be her only love!—that looking back, from whatever height in life, she should see the remembered lineaments distinct, unaltered, stamped upon that part of the Past he had made radiant.

"Ida! do you never mean to marry?" inquired Charley, that night.

"You gentleman say every girl will as soon as she has a good offer;" was the rejoinder.

"Germaine is not an 'eligible' then?"

"Who said anything about him?"

"I did. I am unable, by any system of ratiocination with which I am acquainted, to establish why a sensible, fancy-free lady should refuse a man, who is unexceptionable in morals, behaviour, education, appearance and prospects."

"What an array of recommendations! what evidence have you that I have committed this egregious folly?"

"Your quibblings—if nothing else. Deign to enlighten me as to motive—the act being granted. Why did you discard him?"

"Because I did not love him, Charley."

"That is to the point! now—why didn't you love him?"

"Because I could not."

"Not so good. Why couldn't you?"

"Impertinent! is love made to order? As with a soda fount, have you but to twist a screw in the heart, and it bubbles up for any 'unexceptionable,' who prays for it in a flowery speech?"

"Jumping the question again! What is your ideal husband like?"

"He must be my master!" said Ida. "Mr. Germaine is kind and excellent—intelligent and gentlemanly; but my will would never yield to his. He would say—'Shall I?' and 'will you?' in matters where his interests, no less than mine, were involved. My ideal says, gently, but decidedly—'*I* think'—'*I* will?'"

"So our friend may ascribe his ill-success to his lack of Blue-Beardishness! Oh, woman! thy name is caprice!"

Ida had scanty faith in the reality of his wonder, but most of that expressed was genuine. "Such a fine young man! well-to-do in the world, and she so unprotected!" Carry had built many castles in the air, upon Ida's presupposed acceptance of her neighbor, and expostulated with her.

"Better a lonely, than a miserable life, dear Carry;" was the reply. "I have my Bible to direct me,—my Heavenly Father to lean upon. While I obey Him, He will not leave me friendless. As to the obloquy of old-maidism, I do not dread it."

At the fall of the leaf, the town Danas returned home, and Ida slipped into her place in the family, as though she had always constituted a part of it. The time winged happily and uneventfully along until Christmas. Dr. Carleton, Arthur and Carry were with them then, and another visitor, Ida's namesake, and the miraculous prodigy of Poplar-grove;—a lovely babe, four months old; with its father's hazel eyes, and the transparent skin, and bright flossy curls of its beautiful mother.

On New Year's eve, the older members of both families collected in the parlor, to greet the commencement of the new cycle. Ida occupied an ottoman, between her guardian and Charley; chatting, with girlish vivacity, to the latter. Mrs. Dana was in the opposite corner, in the shadow of the mantel, conversing with her father; but her voice shook at times, and her eyes wandered constantly to her young friend. Ida did not notice this, nor the sadness that tinged her guardian's fatherly look, as he smoothed her chestnut hair for a long time, musingly. She did not suspect he was thinking of her. He smiled, as she threw up her eyes to his face, and rested her head against the arm of his chair; but it was a fleeting light—the uncertain enjoyment of a pleasure, whose loss one anticipates. Finally he spoke.

"Ida! will you give your attention for a minute?"

"For an hour, if you wish it, sir. I am all ear."

"You must be mouth, too—for there are questions for you to answer. Yesterday, in examining certain papers of Mr. Read's, pertaining to the guardianship, I found a packet of letters, mostly from your mother—some from Mr. Grant, and one of yours—written after your illness at Sunnybank. You say therein, that it was your mother's wish for you to take her place, as mistress of the establishment there, so soon, as in his judgment, you should be possessed of the ability; that there were plans laid off, but unfinished by her, whose completion she bequeathed to you;—and you enclose a schedule, which surprised me by the sound sense and foresight displayed in its provisions and items. You conclude by declaring your prepossessions for a country life, and the binding character of the duty, which you conceived was resting upon you. I referred to your mother's letters. It is not for us to censure the dead, but it is amazing how Mr. Read could have slighted the desire, virtually conveyed in every one of them, viz.: that it should be optional with you, at what time after you had attained the age of eighteen, and remained single, you should return to a home, to which, she was assured conscience and affection would alike attract you. She describes your strength of mind and purpose, when a child, as remarkable; and says that she would not fear to entrust to you, the execution of any directions concerning the business she then superintended. My course is too plainly laid down for me to deliberate or waver. In a year, you will be of age; your judgment is as ripe now, as it will be then; you are competent to control yourself, and your subordinates. It is for you to say whether you still consider it obligatory upon you, to anticipate your legal majority."

There was a blank silence. Mrs. Dana alone, was not surprised, and she had most pending upon the verdict. Ida hid her face upon her guardian's arm.

"I would not trouble you needlessly, dear child;" he said, passing his hand over her dark locks; "else I would tell you how dear you were to us, before you lived with us;—how doubly dear you are now. If personal feeling were the arbiter in this case, I would never have made the statement you have heard to-night; and Jenny has not spoken, because foreseeing that her affection might outrun her discretion, I exacted a promise of non-interference. Your home is here, dear Ida, as long as you choose to make us happy by your presence. I repeat—the decision rests with you."

"I do not know what to say. Determine for me, dear Mr. Dana."

"I may not, my child."

"Carry! Charley! what ought I to do?"

Charley shook his head; but Carry was not so prudent. "Oh! Ida! your going will break sister's heart; a year cannot make much difference."

"If it is my duty at all, it is now, as much as then—is it not?" asked Ida, of Charley.

"I am afraid so;" said he, seriously.

"Charley! how can you!" exclaimed Carry. "One would think you were willing to lose her! You are young, Ida—there is no necessity for burying yourself alive, yet."

"Have a care, Carry! John is right—*she* must decide;" cautioned Arthur.

"One question, Ida," said Charley, kindly. "You have revolved this issue often in your mind, even since you have been with us—have you not?"

"Yes."

"You said, a year ago, you felt bound to fulfil your mother's wishes, and that your inclinations leaned the same way—how is it now? There is the case in a nut-shell."

"One hard to crack, nevertheless;" said Ida, with glistening eyes. "I love Sunnybank, and I have had misgivings that the indulgence I meet here, may spoil me for the active, self-denying life I must lead;—for I have always looked forward to a residence there, some time or other;—but I am so happy here. Still, Mr. Dana, I have a vast deal of surplus energy which ought to be employed. I am not working with all my might. Does this sound ungrateful?"

"Not a bit of it!" struck in Charley's assuring tones. "It is not that you love Caesar less, but Rome more."

"But it is so far!" objected Carry,—"and so out-of-the-way. Suppose you fall sick! O, brother John! it is heartless to send her off by herself!"

"She shall not go by herself, Carry. If she concludes to leave us, it must not be before Spring; then Jenny and I will go with her. If she is convinced, upon trial, that she is inadequate to the enterprise, or dislikes it, we shall be too glad to have her back. Grant is a respectable man, and an intelligent farmer; and she must secure a companion. You mentioned his sister-in-law, I think, Ida?"

"As to the distance," said Charley, "If those snail-like fellows continue the railroad, as they say they will—it will pass within six miles of Sunnybank."

This was a ray of comfort; yet Mrs. Dana burst into tears, and Carry threw her arms around Ida, sobbing bitterly, as she "feared she ought to go."

"Carry! Jenny! you must not!" said Charley. "She has done her duty—and should be encouraged. You are borrowing trouble upon interest. Who can tell what may happen before Spring? An earthquake, or the end of the world may stamp 'Finis' upon sublunary things, and you'll be ashamed of yourselves for having anticipated evil."

He succeeded in calling up a smile, and Carry unintentionally effected a further diversion. "Oh, Ida!" she sighed. "If you had married Mr. Germaine!"

"I am happier as it is, Carry."

"I move a postponement of the subject, *sine die*;" said Charley. "We must welcome in the year with a song. Come to the piano, Carry. Ida, Arthur—come! we want a quartette."

They learned to speak of the coming separation with composure; but its shadow was upon all hearts, longer and blacker as the time drew nearer. Ida sometimes debated with herself whether she could be called to sever a relationship which had taken such hold of her inmost soul. She was not supine or useless; for the love a Christian's virtues gain, is indirectly leading men to the Saviour; and every day she could animate some drooping spirit, or alleviate some woe, were it only a child's. Yet she was not performing labors commensurate with her talents and energies; she was upon the circumference of the wheel;—Nature designed her for the centre and motive power. There was a satisfaction in having the matter settled. She had not the courage to introduce it herself; but her guardian's straight-forward summing-up and appeal had convinced her, and the rest of his hearers. A scheme, so uncommon, had opposers and despisers in abundance. Some honestly lamented her departure; and many more insinuated at "family disagreements" and "high-spirited young ladies." She was "Quixotic" and "masculine," said others, boldly; and there were benevolent friends who thought it a pity so much eloquence should be wasted and carried faithful reports to the cause of the commotion. Among the busiest in promulgating scandal, was Josephine Read, until she was taught caution by a scathing rebuke from Charley, inflicted publicly, in response to a sneer, not meant for his ears; and of the opposite party, Ellen Morris' unobtrusive grief affected Ida sadly. They seldom spoke of Lynn; but there was a tacit understanding that his memory was the bond of their intimacy. Outwardly, Ellen was the same—only Ida knew that the spontaneity of her gaiety was no more, and that the most brilliant jets were forced up by a pressure, that would have destroyed the spring of most hearts. On the second anniversary of Lynn's death, she came to invite Ida to a walk—

showing a bouquet of spring flowers concealed in her veil. Divining their destination, Ida turned their steps, of her own accord, to the cemetery. The spring was forward; so it had been the year he died; but its young blossoms were killed by the frost and snow which should have belonged to winter—and he perished with them! The turf was green; the evergreen rose, creeping over the headstone, was full of glossy leaves and the violets upon his breast were budding. The girls knelt on either side of the grave; trimmed away the dead twigs of the rose, plucked the sere leaves of the violet, and clipped the ragged grass—talking softly, as over a sleeping babe. Besides themselves, there were no visitors in the grounds; and having deposited their offering upon the mound, they sat down. Ellen's arm was encircling Ida's waist, while one of the latter's rested on the grave.

"I may not do that," said Ellen, mournfully. "Although when it rains or snows at night, I weep to think how it beats upon him, and pine to shelter him with my arms,—when I am here—and I come often, Ida—secretly! I see him dead—perhaps murdered by me—and I no more dare embrace that clay, as you are doing, than the murderer would touch the body of his victim, lest it should bleed afresh."

"This is morbid regret, Ellen. I was his sister and confidante. You had nothing to do with his death; if you had never parted, the disease might have assailed him. The blight upon your heart is deadly enough, without increasing it by unmerited self-reproach. Everything is so calm and sweet here, this afternoon, and I have such a consoling surety that he is happy! The spirits of the loved return to earth—are hovering about us—present, although unseen. He may be with us."

"'Do they love there still?'" said Ellen.

"They do—with a love purged from selfishness and doubtings—perfect—pure! Oh! Ellen! the bliss and holiness of Heaven! why do we love this world so well?"

"They are loveless alike to me; I have no hope or rest in either. When he was here, I loved this earth, because he was upon it; its charm has gone—and can I thank, or revere Him who bereaved me?"

"My dear girl! He smites to heal. In my short life, I have studied His providences sufficiently to teach me that it is the wise Physician, as well as the Father, who takes away our hurtful delights, and rives our hearts. He waits now, Ellen, to infuse life—His life, into your fainting soul—to wind these severed cords about His loving heart. This patient, boundless love was our Lynn's dying hope; and you will never be comforted until you accept it."

"It is easy to talk!" said Ellen, fretfully. "You cannot understand a sorrow like mine."

"The heart knoweth its own bitterness, Ellen, and my life has not been all sunshine. There are griefs, piercing and drying up the spirit—never revealed to man."

"I know that. Is not my soul shrouded in sackcloth drinking wormwood and gall—when my body is bedizened in its finest array, and the sparkling wine reflecting the lying bloom, that says I am glad and gay! I envied you your mourning dress as long as you wore it; and when he was named by the hypocrites who fawned upon him in life, I had to seem as unconcerned as they; you had no need to stifle your sighs, for he was your friend. I had denied him as my lover, while we were betrothed; I cannot publish it now. There is but one restraint upon my despair. If, as you say, the spirits of beloved ones are with us, and he is among the blest, he must be grieved,—if they can grieve—that I contemn the Being he loves."

"Ellen! this language is evidence that your chastisement is not wanton injustice. Whether he hears you or not, you grieve and insult your Maker by your mad words, the Saviour, to whom you are indebted for being and comforts and friends—who has loved you from the beginning. You knelt to a creature He had made; He interposed the gate of death, to save you from the fate of the idolater, and you ask to spend your life in bewailing your affliction—in showing your adoration of perishable dust, and reviling your best Friend! Is this your gratitude?"

Ellen did not speak. Ida drew her closer. "My dearest girl!" she said, "I do not reprove you in my own name. I have been as guilty as yourself; and it is in remembrance of the retribution which followed, I warn you—in remembrance of the love that forgave me, and bestowed peace and joy, in place of disquiet and mourning, that I entreat you—come to Jesus!"

"I cannot! your pleadings are water upon a rock. I have been thinking, as you were speaking, whether I cared to go to Heaven—and I painted it, gloriously beautiful, as holy men tell us it is—but without the love, my foolish vanity tempted me to sport with, when it was mine—for which I would imperil my soul now—and the Creator of that heaven, and its angels, and fair sights and music were delightless. Rather misery with *him*, than every other joy without. Oh! if he had known how I loved him!"

Her head fell upon the tomb, and the tears rained upon the turf. Ida wept, too—but in pity. Ellen was perverse in her hopeless sorrow—her friend could only commit her to the tender mercy she had besought her to seek.

"If you knew how Our Father loves you both, dear Ellen!" she whispered, but there was no reply.

It was a trial to say farewell to that grave. She had visited it ere the sods joined over it; planted flowers there, and watered them with tears; had sat there at sunset, and watched the "long, bright pomp" he used to love; had learned there lessons of contentment and charity, and active usefulness, "while the day lasted." Next to one other green heap, where the willow shadows were dancing, this was the dearest spot on earth to her. She seemed brought so near to Lynn by the sight of it; and as she had kissed his white brow in death, she pressed her lips to the marble, with a murmur of regretful fondness—"Brother!"

CHAPTER XXVIII

John Dana, his wife and little ones, attended Ida to Sunnybank. They arrived late at night, tired and sleepy; but their sunrise matins were caroled by Ida, as she sang a lively hymn in the breakfast-room, under the guest-chamber. She roamed briskly to and fro, rummaging side-boards and peeping into closets.

"Jest like you used to do, Miss Ida!" said Aunt Judy. "Law me! this comes of faith. I allers said I should live to deliver up them keys into your hands. And you've come home for good, honey?"

"Yes, Aunt Judy—come to stay with, and take care of you. That's 'for good,' isn't it?"

"To be sure! It's a mighty 'sponsibility, honey!"

"She'll have strength given her to bear it!" said Will, behind her. "It's time your biscuits were baking, Aunt Judy, and you're talking about 'sponsibility!'"

"I shall depend upon you, Uncle Will," said Ida. "The servants were easily controlled while mother's influence was at work. How they will submit to one of my age and experience remains to be seen."

"Mr. Grant keeps them tolerably straight, ma'am. I can't say it's exactly as 'twas in her time, but they'll break in pretty easy, I reckon. An overseer, no matter how smart and good, ain't a marster or mistis. We get our victuals and clothes, and look just the same, but there's nobody to ride down from 'the house,' after planting, and hoeing, and harvesting's done, and say, well done, boys!' and at night, when we, whose quarters are in the yard, come up, it's so dark and lonesome, and still, and the doors and windows all shut, it makes us low-spirited—like 'twas no use to work—and Sunday—we feel it *then*!"

"So you are rather glad I am back again?"

"Glad! mistis! I couldn't be more pleased if you was my own child! We need you, ma'am; we need you!"

"Still, as Aunt Judy says, it's a great responsibility."

"You're one of the Lord's lambs, mistis. He will provide."

He went out, and Ida caught up his last words, and through the dark nooks and reverberating galleries of the old house, sounded the refrain—

"His call we obey, like Abram of old,
Not knowing our way, but faith makes us bold,
For 'though we are strangers, we have a good guide,
And trust in all dangers, the Lord will provide!'"

She met her guests with a kiss, and a jingle of the key-basket, and seating them at table, poured out the coffee; refuting Mr. Dana's objection that his was too sweet, by the Irish lady's answer to a similar complaint from General Washington—"Shure, and if 'twas all sugar, 'twouldn't be too good for yer Honor!"—piled the children's plates with buttered cakes—rattling all the while of her dignities, possessions and "'sponsibility." After finding a clean grass plat for the children's playground, she challenged Mrs. Dana to a stroll over the house and garden. It was an old-fashioned family mansion, rambling and picturesque; some rooms wainscotted to the ceiling, and lighted by rows of narrow windows, with surprisingly small panes. These were chambers: the lower story, the parlour, dining-room, and the apartments appropriated to her mother and herself, were light, large, and finished in a more modern style. Mrs. Dana preferred the antique. The massive furniture suited them so well, and it was interesting to think of the generations they had known—what stories they would relate if the panelled oak could speak.

"With a little variation, they would tell one of all," replied Ida. "They were born, suffered, joyed and died!" And she thought how she had gone through all, except the last, within these walls. The garden was ploughed up. There was no comeliness in it, but it was less desolate than when overgrown with weed.

"The soil is fertile," said Mr. Grant. "We shall have vegetables worth showing this summer, Miss Ida. Mr. Dana sends his respects, and will you step into the parlour? we would like to consult you."

Ida composed her face into a Malvolio expression of solemnity and conceit: pompously apologised to Mrs. Dana, and obeyed. But the account books were shut, and her guardian was luxuriating in an arm-chair and a cigar.

"Mr. Grant and myself have been investigating and comparing accounts, Ida," he said; "and the result is highly creditable to him and those in his service. Without wearying you with particulars, I have set down the sums total here. You perceive that the crops have met the expenditures of the plantation; and each year, the net profits have surpassed those of the preceding—a proof that your land is constantly improving. This, as I said, is to be attributed to Mr. Grant's judicious management. Your servants are well fed and clothed, and the doctor's bill trifling in its amount. Praise is also due to Mr. Read. I approve entirely of the investments he has made of the funds, left after the necessary disbursements for expenses. Your money is safe and not idle. You were fortunate in your stewards, and assume the control of an unincumbered estate, under most favorable auspices."

"I am indeed grateful to Providence, and to them, sir. It is not my wish, however, to release you from your guardianship. I cannot do it nominally, as yet, and after the law shall permit it, I shall still rely upon you for direction. A woman is not fitted to be a financier. It is a trespass upon your time and goodness, but I cannot endure that you should give me up."

"Nor I, my child. You will never ask advice or assistance from me in vain. If your measures are ill-advised, I shall oppose them, and forward your interest by every means in my power."

"Thank you, sir. I was unjust to question this for an instant. You feared to weary me with particulars;—you have no other objection to my looking into them?"

"None, certainly."

She pored over the columns attentively, and her guardian felt his respect for her rising still higher, as the deep thoughtfulness which had its home in the eyes and brow, slowly covered the face. It was no common mind speaking there—it was competent to its work. A gleam of pleasure shot across her countenance, as she concluded the examination. Dipping a pen into the standish, she sketched rapidly a calculation upon a sheet of paper, and spread it before Mr. Dana.

"I registered a vow, years ago, that my maiden enterprise, when I should come into office, should be the establishment of a charity school. You have there an estimate of the amount needed to put it into operation—not guess-work, but the actual sums I will have to expend for teacher's salary, books and furniture, repair of the room, and a small remainder for contingent expenses. This knowledge I have gained by inquiry of those familiar with these things. I am confounded at the paltry total—I interpret that arch of the eyebrows," she continued, laughing, "but before you cast any obstacle in my way, listen—dear Mr. Dana! I have kept an 'expense-book' ever since I can recollect. During the first winter and spring of my going into society in Richmond, I spent more than that in dresses and ornaments—the two summers I passed with Carry, previous to her marriage, as much more,—for it was a fashionable country neighborhood, and in such, the passion for show and ostentation is not a whit less than in the city. The price I should pay for board elsewhere, will meet my personal expenses here; I have no near relatives for whom to economise, and there are scores of children, growing up around me, destitute of education, except that bestowed gratis by poverty and vice."

"I commend your resolution, my daughter,"—this was his phrase of greatest endearment—"but it is a weighty undertaking for a young person, and a woman. If commenced, it must be prosecuted vigorously, or it will do more harm than good. One session will hardly suffice for a beginning. This appropriation, which is a liberal deduction from your income, small as you deem it, is not for this year alone. Hitherto your affairs have prospered, but you may have reverses. A failure of crops, which not unfrequently happens to others, would embarrass you considerably."

"I would draw upon my invested funds."

"And if stocks fall, or a bank breaks?"

"And what is more probable than that all these misfortunes will crowd upon me at once, I may die!" said Ida, with persuasive gravity, "and when my Heavenly Master demands the reckoning of my stewardship, I shall render in the plea, 'Lo! here is Thy talent, hid in a napkin!' He has given me—if not riches—more than a competency for my wants. It may not be worldly-wise, dear guardian, but it is Christian-like, to give of my present abundance, and trust that he will be as bountiful in time to come, as He has been until now."

"There's sense and religion in that!" commented Mr. Grant, admiringly.

"He that giveth to the poor, lendeth to the Lord," said Ida, smiling in her guardian's face. "What think you of the security, Mr. Dana?"

"That your faith shames my caution. Assuming that the plan is feasible and prudent in its main points, let us descend to the minutiæ—'Repairs of building'—where is the room?"

Ida pointed from the window to a house in the yard. "My father built it for an office—my mother used it as a lumber-room. The plastering has fallen, and the roof leaks, but Will tells me the plantation carpenter and bricklayer can put it in good order. They can make the desks and benches too."

"'Books'—this is the probable outlay, I suppose."

"It is computed from a list of prices, furnished by a book-seller."

"Now, last and most important—the teacher. Is it to be a girls' or a boys' school?"

"For girls, mainly; but small boys will be admitted. Large ones might be refractory to a lady."

"You will have an instructress, then? Where will she board?"

"Here. Shall I not have a spinster household?"

"With Miss Betsey to matronise you. You will be fastidious in your selection, as she is to be a member of your family. Your provident brain has not picked her out, surely?"

"You will laugh when I say that I have one in view; but I am hesitating as to the propriety of making her an offer. I have no false pride to prevent me from engaging in honest labor; but very sensible people, in other respects, are troubled with this weakness. Neither do I mean to term mine a 'charity school,' in consideration for pride of a more commendable kind, which the parents may have. The teacher will be my equal and companion. Without interfering with her government, I shall be as well known to the pupils as herself; if she is absent or sick, be her substitute; yet she may regard the situation as too humble. Did you ever see a school-fellow of Carry's named Emma Glenn, a modest, sweet-looking girl?"

"Glenn! I cannot recall her. She is your choice?"

"Yes, sir. She is, like myself, an orphan. Anna Talbot awakened my sympathies for her, by relating how and where she saw her last summer. She is dependent upon her own exertions, and for two years has taught in the family of an uncle, for the miserable stipend—think of it, sir! of fifty dollars a year! for instructing six children, two of whom, sleep in her chamber; and her position is uncomfortable from various other causes. She was universally beloved at school; and her standing for scholarship, unquestionable. Can it be more humiliating to labor as my colleague, than the despised beneficiary of a niggardly relative?"

"I imagine not," he rejoined, smiling. "What is your notion, Mr. Grant, of this hair-brained young lady?"

"That we should all be better, and I am not sure, but wiser too, for some of her spirit;" he replied.

"I am not, I hope, thoughtlessly sanguine, Mr. Dana;" pursued Ida. "I expect discouragement and difficulties, for I know the class I have to deal with. It is no girl's ambition to play lady patroness that spurs me on in this task. The idea originated with my mother, and was a darling scheme of hers and mine; but was laid low with many other benevolent plans—laid by, I should say—for my prayer and aim are to prove myself worthy of my parentage. Few females at my age are placed in my circumstances; and I do not court notoriety or responsibility, although some will have it so. Constant, stirring exercise is as indispensable to my mind as body. Forgive me, dear sir; but I have been distressed by an occasional misgiving, that you thought me unfeminine, regardless of public opinion. I love my friends as dearly, truly as any one; I have no relish for masculine pursuits; I would have woman move in her God-appointed sphere;—but if He has endowed me with talents and opportunity for extending my usefulness, I *fear* not to improve them. Do you understand me?"

"My daughter! must I say, that next to my wife, you are nearer to me than any woman living? and I respect and honor, as much as I love you. Where is the mammet of fashion I would consult and trust as I do you? You are honestly striving with a purpose, and hoping for no plaudit but 'she hath done what she could.' How many mistake the limit of their 'could!' Go on as you have begun, and you will develope the highest type of female character. That I have not said this much before, is because I am a man of few words; and you appeared to shun open praise."

Mr. Grant, seeing they were forgetting him, had, with native delicacy, stepped without the door, upon pretext of speaking to a passing laborer.

Ida was moved even to tears, by her guardian's unqualified encomium, so feelingly uttered. The esteem of such a man was, of itself a reward for her conflicts with self and outward temptations. She had so much to be thankful for! she said over and over, that day. She was at home! at Sunnybank! the air was purer—the water clearer—the birds merrier, there than anywhere else; and there was abiding tranquillity in the thought that she might live and die under the roof-tree that sheltered her cradle; an enlargement of heart and kindliness as she beheld her dependents rejoicing in her restoration to them; looking to her for support and happiness. And that mother's grave was there! She sat there a long hour at even-tide. The willow leaflets were just putting out, and the swaying of the flexile boughs was slight and noiseless. There was a hush in the air—not a dead calm—but a solemn pause, as if Nature had folded her busy hands to return devout thanks for mercies past, and gather strength for future labor. Ida was no sickly dreamer now. She knew life, as it is—a day! only a day—divide and sub-divide as we may,—the morning hallowed by some with early prayer—squandered by more in trifling; the noon, waxing to its height over reeking brows and panting chests, and straining arms; the evening, relaxing the strung muscles, and curdling the bounding blood, and bringing to each his meed,—righteous recompense for his deeds, fair or foul; and the night—black-browed angel, saying to the vexed brain, "Thy work is ended!" spreading his hands over the swelling heart-wave, and it is still! bidding the harassed body—"Sleep on now and take your rest." She knew life, and that to the God-fearing toiler in His vineyard, there is no rest until night. He is not denied the inhalation of the odorous breeze, and a pause in the shade to wipe his heated brow; but he must not swerve from his furrow to seek it. Flowers, whose kindred blossom in Paradise, smile up from the unsightly clods, and these he may wear in his bosom, leaving unculled the poppies and almond-laurel which flaunt near by; content in knowing but this, what is *his* work, and bending, training every power to the strenuous endeavor to do it.

Mr. Dana stayed but three days; his family prolonged their visit into as many weeks; nor would Ida have resigned them then, had not Emma been daily expected; for the school was a fixed fact. Accompanied and guarded by the faithful Will, Ida had explored the woods, gullies and old fields for recruits. Her determined spirit bore her out, or she would have thrown up the project by the end of the first day. She chose what Will called the "toughest cases" for her freshest energies.

"The Digganses" lived in a rickety hut, in the exact centre of a common of broom straw, mowed down to stubble, for ten feet around the door—said area populated at Ida's visit, by five white-headed children, three hounds, and two terrier puppies, a full-grown grunter and a brood of little ones, and half a dozen meagre fowls. The hounds bayed; the terriers squeaked their shrill treble; the pigs squealed, and made for the high straw; the human animals scampered squallingly, into the house; while Ida's horse—to complete the hubbub—set up a frightened neigh, and would have run, but for Will's grip. Without waiting for Mrs. Diggans' "Light! won't you?" she sprang from the saddle. The hostess came to the door with a greasy, steaming kettle in one hand, and the flesh-fork in the other. She deposited them upon the ground, wiped her hands upon her begrimmed apron, and offered her right. Ida blessed the ignorance of Fashion's laws in these regions, which did not compel her to remove her gloves. The cabin did not belie the promise of the exterior. It was dingy and dirty, scented with bacon and cabbage, and an indescribable smell, as of a musty cupboard, converted into a sleeping-room. Yet these people were not disreputable, in the ordinary acceptation of the word. They had never been convicted of theft or drunkenness. Indolence and improvidence kept them down, for they were never "up." They were as well off now as when they married; if the children came faster than the bread, they begged or borrowed of their "lucky" neighbors.

"I'm mighty pleased to see you!" said Mrs. Diggans, dusting a wooden cricket with the convenient apron. "How much you've growed like your mother. *Good* Fathers! I never see two folks more alike. You've done come home to live, I've heern."

"I hope so, ma'am."

"You didn't like town-folks, I 'spose?"

"Yes, ma'am; I have some good friends there, but I think my place is here."

"Um-*hum*! well—you ain't married?"

"Oh! no, ma'am."

"But you're goin' to be, I reckon?" slyly.

"Not that I know of. But how are you getting on, Mrs. Diggans?"

"Ah, Miss Idy! in the same old way;—can't never make both ends jine, but somehow we lives and fattens."

"How many children have you?"

"Six—my biggest girl is out, visitin' her father's kin."

"Is it possible! I must be growing old. I recollect when you were married. You wore your wedding-dress the next Sunday, and I thought it was so fine."

"I wonder if you do?" said the flattered Mrs. Diggans. "Who'd a thought it?—and you so young! One of my children's named after you—Ide-e-e!" with a car-whistle termination. "Come here this minute! I liked it, 'cause 'twas a pretty name—sort o' high-soundin' you know—Ide-e-e-e!"

Ida had occular evidence of this new beauty of her cognomen.

"And your mother was allers mighty kind to me—ah! she was a lady—every inch of her!—Ide-e-e-e! if you don't come 'long, I'll spank you well!"

And "Idee" sneaked in, fist in her mouth, and scraped her bare toes in a frightfully flesh-crawling, provoking manner, while her namesake informed her of their relation to each other.

"How old are you, Ida?"

"Going on seven;" answered the mother.

"Can you read?"

"Bless your life, Miss Idy! I don't have time to teach them, nor their father neither. Mercy knows how they are to git any learnin'. Poor folks don't need much, but its more *re*-spectable to know how to read and write."

"But you can read, Mrs. Diggans."

"I used to could."

"You do not object to their being taught if you are not troubled about it?"

"No-o. I reckon not—but who's a goin' to do it? thar's the rub!"

"I will have it done."

"*You*! Miss Ida! oh-oh! teachin' poor folk's chillen ain't for the likes of you. We've scuffled along without edication, and so must they."

"Say you will send them, Mrs. Diggans, and I pledge you my word they shall be as carefully attended to, as if they were the richest in the land."

She explained her plan. Mrs. Diggans demurred.

"She couldn't spar Maria Julia, and Anne Marthy was too little to walk so far;—then their clothes warn't fitten. She was mighty obliged, jest as much as if she had a-sent' em."

"I am *very* sorry," said Ida. "I came here first, knowing your attachment to our family. I am really desirous you should oblige me. I am *so* disappointed."

Mrs. Diggans relented. "If they had decent clothes, Miss Idy.—See them dirty rags!"

"Their clothing must be whole and clean, certainly. Promise they shall attend all the session, and I will give them a suit apiece."

"You're too good, Miss Idy—jest like your ma! We'll talk about it."

"I must have an answer now. My number is limited, as there will be but one teacher. How many shall I put down?" producing paper and pencil.

"Only two! but that is better than none. 'For the entire session,' Mrs. Diggans; I trust to your word."

"I keeps a promise when I makes it. Set 'em down."

"Hard customers, Mistis!" said Will, as they remounted.

"Rather, Uncle Will; yet I dread our next visit as much. Does Mr. Pinely drink now?"

"When he can get money or beg liquor. I feel mean, when he stops me in the road, to borrow a fourpence. 'Ah, Will!' he says, 'thriving and likely as when you drove your master's carriage after his bride—your late lamented mistis! You don't happen to have a fourpence in your pocket, my boy? Unfortunately, I'm out of change. Thank you, my fine fellow—I'll remember you my lad!' I can't deny him, Mistis. He knowed your father well, when they were both young men—a smart, handsome gentleman he was! and to think!"

"And to see!" thought Ida, as the house peeped through the trees, with unglazed windows, crumbling chimney, and sunken roof. It was presented to him by her father—a neat, comfortable cottage. His wife died of a broken heart; the children were saved from starvation and freezing, times without number, by her mother. How they subsisted now, was an impenetrable mystery; for the father never did a stroke of work, and loafed around the country, thrusting himself upon the hospitality of those with whom he had associated in former years, wearing his welcome—not threadbare, but into shreds, before he let go. In a beggar's garb, and soliciting alms from the slaves of his old companions, he retained the boastful swagger and ornate language which earned for him, in youth, the soubriquet of "Pompous Pinely."

The eldest daughter was sitting upon the door-step, dressed almost in tatters; her matted hair twisted up with a tinsel comb—a gift from her father, in a generously drunken fit; and the remnants of a pair of silk stockings hanging about a neatly turned foot and ankle. Her face was clean; and Ida could not but observe its beauty, as she blushed and smiled an embarrassed welcome.

"You have not forgotten me, Laura; but you have grown so, I scarcely knew you. Are you all well?"

"Except papa, who has a headache. Walk in."

"No, thank you. It is pleasant out here." She seated herself upon a block beside the door. "Where are the children?"

"Gone to look for strawberries."

"Isn't it too early for them?"

"I'm afraid so—but they wanted some so badly."

Ida suspected, from her stammering, that more substantial food would have been as acceptable.

"I came partly on business, Laura," she hastened to say, apprehending an irruption from the interior. "I am trying to get up a school in the neighborhood, to be taught at Sunnybank, by a friend of mine—"

"Miss Ross! do I in truth, have the felicity?" Ida groaned in spirit. "The softened image of my ever lamented friend!" continued the inebriate, whose headache was easily accounted for. Putting his hand to his heart, he heaved a profound sigh. "Ah! my dear young lady! may you have the inheritance of his transcendant virtues, as of his faultless physiognomy! Laura, my daughter—have you offered our guest refreshments?"

"Excuse me, sir! I have not time to partake of them. I was apologising to Laura for my first visit being a business call."

"She wants to open a school up at Sunnybank, papa. *Do* let us go!" cried the girl, eagerly. His face wore a mask of extreme concern.

"It cannot be! the righteous Fates can never be so oblivious to unparalleled excellence as to ordain that you—the solitary scion of an aristocratic race, shall be reduced by unpropitious vicissitudes, to the necessity of maintaining yourself by the arduous employment of imparting instruction to the juvenile mind!"

"A friend is to be the instructress, sir. I shall exercise a general supervision."

"What a mountain you remove! I trembled at the supposition that you were precipitated upon the frozen charities of a mercenary world. Ah, my young friend! the most shameful part of human hypocrisy is the heartless repudiation of unmerited exigency!"

"May we go, papa?" persisted the daughter. "I so want to learn!"

"My beloved! wariness is indispensable in the adjudication of a measure vitally affecting your intellectual progress. Is your friend versed in classical lore, Miss Ross?"

This absurdity was almost a match for Ida's forbearance. "Her recommendations cannot be impeached, Mr. Pinely," she said, spiritedly.

"I solicit no further assurance, Miss Ross, than your approbation of her qualifications. You have my paternal sanction, my daughter. Moderate your transports, my love!" She had clapped her hands. "Pray assign her extravaganzas to the intensity of her admiration of your lovesome self, Miss Ross. I blush at the trivialness of the reference—but my income is not what it was, when your father and myself were twin-souls. The remorseless falchion of Time cleaves down rank and fortune in his flight. The remuneration,—Miss Ross! If the scanty pecuniary assistance I can render your fair friend will ameliorate her hardships, my 'bosom's lord will sit lightly on its throne!'"

Ida curtly told him, "no tuition fees were demanded."

"That materially alters the aspect of your proposition. My munificent lady! this is a flagrant spoliation of yourself!"

"I do not consider it as such, sir."

"Your enthusiastic philanthropy misleads you. *I* cannot be an accomplice to this generous fraud. My children remain in their own habitation unless your friend accepts compensation for her toils."

Laura looked ashamed and sorrowful, and Ida restrained her indignant contempt. "We will not differ about a trifle, Mr. Pinely. The terms and time of payment are subject to your discretion and convenience. I may enter your little ones—Laura included? There are three, besides yourself, Laura?"

"They are docile to the flower-wreathed wand of moral suasion, Miss Ross, but may betray obduration if sterner means are employed. Of corporeal punishment we will not speak; the rod would fall barbless, from the lily digits of gentle woman."

"You will come to school, Monday week;" Ida was saying to Laura: "but do not wait until then to pay me a visit. I must have a long talk with you. Good bye."

Tears stood in Laura's eyes. Already she regarded her benefactress with feelings bordering upon devotion. Ida, in her sober ride, turning over the degradation and misery whose alleviation seemed impracticable, had no suspicion of the leaven she had hidden in the heavy lump.

CHAPTER XXIX

Anna Talbot's sketch of Emma's privations was not over-drawn. If her condition had been tolerable, an offer from Ida Ross, as she recollected her,—proud and unsociable,—would not have tempted her to change it. But Ida was honorable and liberal, despite her haughtiness; and in her uncle's family, she was an ill-paid under-servant. Ida sent her carriage and servants for her; and this regard for her comfort, while it called forth the contumely of her employers, raised her hopes of a friendly reception.

"There's my mistis in the porch," said Will, leaning down from his perch, to speak to his fair passenger. They were driving up an avenue, closed by a house, which, to Emma's modest eyes, was an imposing architectural pile. A haze dimmed her vision; in her agitation, she saw nothing of the awful figure Will pointed out, but the flutter of white drapery. The great yard-gates were open, and the carriage rolled over the gravelled circle which swept by the main entrance. She did not recognise the frank, sweet face that appeared at the carriage-door, but the voice was not to be forgotten. "I am *very* glad you are come!" it said, and the kiss and the embrace verified the welcome. "How changed!" was the thought of each. Emma was thin, and when the glow of the meeting faded—dejected. She looked, to Ida, like one who had been subjected to a constant weight, bending body and heart, almost to breaking,—as if the one feather more would end the torture. And her own spirit, gaining buoyancy day by day, under its discipline, gathered force from the necessity of restoring the lost elasticity to another's. She conducted her school-fellow to a chamber, once hers, and adjoining that she now occupied; divested her of her heavy hat and shawl, and commanded her imperatively to "lie down." Emma reposed her weary limbs upon a luxurious mattress; the breeze waving the spotless curtains, and whispering of green hills, and cool forests and violet banks; her hostess, after vainly attempting to persuade her that she required sleep—bathing her head with fragrant waters, and talking in inspiriting, affectionate tones, which were more than manna to her hungry heart. Mrs. Dana had gone the preceding day, and Emma was soon convinced that she had done a charitable—most meritorious deed, in arriving when she did; but she smiled, as she heard the lively voice dilate upon the "horrors" and "azure imps," that had infested the house while she was sole occupant—"always excepting my chaperon and *soi-disant* housekeeper, good Miss Betsey—*soi-disant* as I am, in point of fact, housekeeper myself. I have a great fancy to see to everything with my own eyes. We are retired here—I wrote this, you know—but there are some agreeable families within visiting distance. I am delighted at having a helper in the labor of receiving and returning visits; and my rides and walks will be doubly pleasant. Are you fond of out-door exercise?"

"Very—but I have neglected the duty for a year or two past."

"You shall not be so remiss here. I intend to be exacting. A gallop before breakfast, and a walk—not a promenade—before tea, will plant bright roses in these white cheeks. When you are rested, we will unlock our budget of news. Having been apart for so long, each will have a week's steady talk."

When she arose, revived in spirits and strength, she was taken over the premises "to see her home." Mr. Grant was introduced, and doffed his hat as to a queen; the negroes were respectfully cordial to the friend of their mistress; but more than all, Ida's bearing assured the trampled-down orphan, that she was here second to none—superior in command and importance to all, except the head of the establishment. It may have been the earnestness, which was the prevailing element of Ida's character, or her sympathetic nature, (Charley affirmed it was the latter,) which made it impossible for those who knew her, to be indifferent, or lukewarm in their sentiments towards her. Mr. Read, Josephine and Pemberton, having seen the wrong side of her disposition, hated her with a rancor, benefits nor patient efforts could appease. Her chosen intimates found no mate for their affection, but in their esteem and respect. Lynn's love for her was more like worship than that he entertained for Ellen—adored as she was; with Carry, she had no compeer of her sex; the exceeding tenderness of John Dana and his wife was a mystery to themselves; and in Charley's heart she had the highest place—taking rank even of the brother, to whom he had sacrificed his hopes of earthly bliss. Emma experienced, and yielded to the charm; she could not have resisted successfully, if she would; for Ida was determined to attach her to herself, and her indomitable resolution would have accomplished this, had her attractive qualities been less winningly displayed. From the moment of her arrival, Emma improved, and as the beautiful tracery of her character came out, to reward the warm rays love poured over it, Ida was confirmed in her satisfaction at her choice. She had not entire confidence in her ability to control the restive spirits, which had run wild, without rule or rein; but this fear vanished with a careful observation of her government and its results. If the "wand" was "flower-wreathed," it was no supple or brittle reed, to bend or snap in the storm. None, who had once rebelled against her mild authority, were ever inclined to repeat the offence. If, as had been asserted, Ida sought the Utopia of her fanciful dreams in her "return to Palestine," as she playfully styled it; if her ideas of country life were drawn from pastorals and romances, she would have sunk under the drawbacks and iron realities she encountered. Her influence over her servants was strong; but among so many, insubordination reared its head, now and then. The idle and sulky, deceived by her amenity and care for their welfare, appealed from Mr. Grant's decisions to her clemency; and with so much plausibility, that when this mode of undermining his laws was new, she was ready to sustain them. Consistent, however, to her principle of examining both sides of a question, she refused to reverse any decree, before hearing all the circumstances; and invariably, when this was done, ratified the original judgment. There were old and privileged supernumeraries who talked of her father's childhood, as a thing of yesterday; and volunteering the advantage of their experience for the benefit of the "poor chile,"—tossed their heads high at the idea of her controlling or enlightening them. Adding to self-righteousness, the whims and peevishness of age, they caused Ida more annoyance than the management of the whole estate besides; and hardly less than the never-ending vexations of the Digganses, and their neighbors of the same stamp, not to mention Pinely—most wearisome of all. He penned voluminous epistles, to complain of "a trivial oversight in her otherwise irreproachable system of philanthropy," or to convey a "father's acknowledgments for the soul-elevating teachings of which his beloved offspring were accipients;" and when they were unnoticed, his visits were frequent. She received him with distant politeness; and strove to repress his forwardness by chilling dignity—and he came again next day. At last he presented himself in the parlor, where were Emma and herself—so intoxicated, that he could not stand upright. His tongue was oily as ever, notwithstanding his limbs refused to do their office; and when Will entered, in answer to the vehement ring, he was holding the door with both hands, swinging it with him in his attempts to bow to the ladies, he was addressing as, "incomparable pair! whose supereminent enchantments are confessed by the most hebete of created intelligences."

Emma had shrunk into a corner, and Ida, her hand still upon the bell-rope—her brow frowning—spoke in a lofty tone, "Uncle Will! you will conduct this *gentleman* to the porch, and as much further as he shall see convenient to go. It is necessary to teach him to exercise some discrimination as to the times of his visits."

For Laura, the girls were strongly interested. Her progress in her studies was incredibly rapid; and their wretched home, if comfortless, was clean. She had no means of providing wardrobes or furniture; and Ida, hailing the dawning reformation, contributed as delicately as she could, such articles as they needed most. Laura's taste was good; and her aptitude enabled her to catch the ways and language of her friends, with fidelity and quickness. In six months after Ida's business call, she would not have been ashamed to introduce her in any company, however polished. But how was this to end? Would it not be wiser benevolence to content themselves with bestowing the rudiments of a common education, without exciting aspirations after pursuits, so incongruous with the occupations of her lowly station, as belles lettres, music and drawing? Ida put the objection down with an irreversible negative.

"The girl has a mind! and every intellect which God makes, should receive all the nutriment it can absorb. Let us give her her quantum, and in time she will reach her level. She is below it at present. If that odious father were out of her way!"

"He will be a drag to her as long as he lives;" said Emma.

"Yes, and alas! he is more fit to live than to die. You have read of the beggar idiot, who told Sir Walter Scott that he would be perfectly happy, but for the 'Bubly Jock,' (turkey gobbler,) that followed him everywhere. Pinely is my 'Bubly Jock,' I listen to hear him gobble whenever he comes near me."

"Laura has an uncommon talent for music;" said Emma.

"I have remarked it;" replied Ida, "and we have thought of the same thing, that her surest path to independence, and the position in society his vice has lost, is to qualify herself for a teacher. I waited to consult you before recommending it to her."

"And that delay was unnecessary. You can take my consent for granted in everything your judgment approves. Now, Laura has no motive but her love for knowledge and us. With a definite aim, she will surmount every difficulty, for her energy is as remarkable as her ability."

This was one of their twilight talks in the roomy porch.

"I believe," said Ida, laughing; "Miss Betsey fears the Ross pride is extinct in me. It costs her a twinge to see me teach my sable class, and she modestly hinted, this morning, that her chamber, or the dining-room would be a more proper place for their recitations, than mine. I represented to her that they were not there more than an hour in the day, and came in groups of three or four—one set retiring as another entered; and that they felt a pride in being neat and orderly, because they were in 'Mistis' room,'—but the dear old creature was not satisfied, although she held her peace."

"And you are the Ida Ross, whose pride kept the whole school at a distance!" exclaimed Emma. "How you were misunderstood!"

"Understood, my dear! if I appeared disagreeable and selfish. That was my dark age, Emma. How much has transpired since! how much of sorrow—how much of joy!"

"You are not unhappy now!" said Emma, in a tone of surprised inquiry.

"No, my love! happy and busy—and thankful for my Father's love and favors—not the least of which is His gift of a companion."

Carry had asked her a similar question during her first summer at Poplar grove—with what different emotions she had replied!

"But," she resumed, "the unbending will is not dead yet. Dr. Hall and lady called on me to-day, and I unfolded our prospectus of a Sabbath-school. The doctor pursed up his mouth in his quizzical way. 'The Church is four miles from you.'

"'But only three from *you*,' said I.

"'There is preaching there, on an average, two Sabbaths in a month. Will not that interfere with your instructions?'

"'Not at all, sir. We shall be through by the hour for public worship.'

"'But there will not be time to go to another church, where there is no service.'

"'Can't help it, sir. We must go home and read a sermon, seasoned by the consciousness of duty performed.'

"'You have a school-mania;' said he.

"'The grown trees are so stubbornly crooked, that I have no hope but in the twigs.'

"'A fair hit, doctor!' said Mrs. Hall. 'Submit with a good grace. He was wishing, the other day, for something to keep 'idle men' and children off of 'Satan's ground.' He is feigning objections, Ida.'

"'A bad game, doctor,' answered I. 'We *will* have the school, and what is more,—you for superintendent.'

"He remonstrated now in earnest, but we out-talked him. He and Mr. Latham are to circulate the information, and solicit aid and scholars."

"Who says unmarried women can do nothing in the work of the world's reformation?" said Emma. "How many in your situation, would be wrapped up in self, with a churlish delight that the claims of their fellow-creatures upon them were so feeble."

"A woman's heart, in its healthy state, must have something to love;" returned Ida. "The fountain is perennial, so long as its waters are drawn off. Stop their outgoings—stagnation—poisonous miasma—dryness ensue. The more we have to love, the better we feel—the better we *are*, Emma—for the closer is our approximation to the Being, who is all love!"

"This time, a year ago, I was disposed to think that in the economy of His Providence, crosses and trials were all His children's portion in this life. Sweetly has He rebuked my want of faith!" said Emma.

"*Not* a year ago," rejoined Ida, "His ways to me were past finding out. I wished to stay here in peaceful seclusion, and He sent me again into the world. The 'silver lining' of the cloud, impervious then, is already visible. Leaving out the experience I have acquired in that time, I should have commenced my residence here under a guardianship, which made interest and appearance the gauge of fidelity; should have missed Mr. Dana's invaluable assistance; have lost an opportunity to forget past grievances, and return good for evil—more than one, indeed. I had not heard then, that you were teaching, and should not, therefore, have thought of you as a co-laborer. Uncle Will would say we 'ought to be happy in the Lord's appointed way.'"

"There is no other path of peace," said Emma. "Yet I am foolishly ungrateful sometimes, in misinterpreting what He has done, and peering into the 'shadowy future.'"

"That was, formerly, my besetting sin. Now I have to guard against 'looking mournfully into the past.' What a world of meaning in those few words! And how like a trumpet-call to the 'world's field of battle,' sound the inspired exhortations of the same poet—

'Trust no Future, howe'er pleasant;
Let the dead Past bury in dead;
Act—act in the living Present!
Heart within, and God o'erhead!'

I can see the vigorous, upward fling of his arm, as shouting that last line, he shakes out his banner in the morning breeze! It thrills through every nerve, as I recite it."

"His is the true Bible philosophy," said Emma, "'living by the day,'—saying, as we fall asleep at night—

'To-morrow, Lord! is *Thine*,
Lodged in Thy sovereign hand;

And if its sun arise and shine.
It shines by Thy command!'

"Dear Lynn!" sighed Ida. "They sung that hymn at his funeral."

"'Looking mournfully!'" said Emma, in affectionate chiding.

"Yes! yet not repiningly. I was thinking, also, of the sure pleasure we have in the possession of our Father's love. We know that is pure, and cannot pass away; while our most sinless earthly attachments are enjoyed with trembling."

The Sunday-school, a novelty to all—the scoff of not a few, opened with fifty scholars and five teachers—Dr. and Mrs. Hall, Mr. Latham, a student of medicine and *protegé* of the former, Ida and Emma. Classing the children according to their capacity and attainments, the Doctor apportioned an equal number to each of his assistants, and planted himself before a form, containing ten of the most unpromising. "There must be an awkward squad," he said, afterwards, "and who is more fit to command it?" Reinforcements were on the ground by the following Sabbath. The number of pupils constantly increased; some who came to see remained to teach; and others were pressed into service by the energetic superintendent. Having induced him to put his hand to the plough, Ida gave over her exertions in that quarter; he drove as straight and deep a furrow as she could have desired. She was a teacher in an obscure corner, and nothing in her appearance or that of her class, distinguished them from the crowd, but when the thread-like rill widened into a flood, bearing broadly, steadily onward, the wonder and praise of its early opponents, she felt an honest pride in the reflection, that the witch-wand of Christian charity which had bent to the source of the stream was hers. Dr. Hall was mindful of this, and with the mistaken, but well-meant importunity of gratitude, begged her to occupy a more conspicuous post. She had contributed largely to the library, the selection of which was left wholly to her, and he entreated her to act as librarian. She declined, laughingly, and more positively, as he insisted; and at length, was driven to say, that "if it were for the actual good of the school, she would even do violence to her sense of propriety, and comply; as it was not, she hoped to be excused from occupying a stand, which was, for a lady, at best, but an honorable pillory." And the Doctor, finally comprehending what other men as wise and exemplary, are slow to admit—that to use one's talents does not imply the abandonment of the retiring modesty of womanhood—installed Mr. Latham in the vacant chair.

Ida was not too much absorbed in her numerous avocations to think of, and communicate with her absent friends. Her correspondence with Mrs. Dana, Carry and Charley was regular; John Dana wrote longer letters to her than to any one besides his wife; she heard, once in a while, from Alice Murray, and through her, learned that Mrs. Read was living in strict retirement at her father's, seeing none but her near relatives and friends; and that Richard was playing the lover to Lelia Arnold. "But," said the merry writer—"who angles for him, must bait one of these patent hooks, which hold, as well as catch." Ida sighed softly, as she read, and was unceasingly busy for the rest of the day; her infallible remedy for sombre thoughts. Mrs. Read had written once, while Ida was at Mr. Dana's—a mere note of remembrances and thanks. She might have supposed that Josephine had forgotten her existence, but for an uncomfortable suspicion that the cessation of Anna's friendly billets was owing to her influence. Ellen Morris wrote often, and spent a fortnight with her and Emma in August. Ida signalled Carry of the intended visit, and invited her to join in the re-union. She was eagerly expected each evening of Ellen's stay, and as often they looked in vain. The guest had been gone a week, before tidings came from Poplar grove. It was a double letter. Arthur wrote that the little Ida was recovering from an alarming illness. The crisis had passed now. They would have sent for her, but the child's danger was so imminent for many days, that there was no certainty that she would survive until a letter reached Sunnybank. "If she had died"—and the strong physician's hand had trembled as he wrote it—"I should have taken our Carry to you. It was a heart-breaking trial to her—I trust, not an unsanctified one."

Carry's was a blotted sheet, penned in agitation or haste, but its contents were cheering wine to Ida's soul. There was much said of her unworthiness, and thankless reception of the goodness which had followed her all the days of her life, and thanksgivings for her child's restoration, with slight allusions to her harrowing anxiety, while it was suspended 'twixt life and death. "Pray, dear Ida," said she, "that I may forever cling to the cross, to which I fled in my distressful hour!"

"Another!" said Ida, with tearful gladness. "Oh! blessed Redeemer! is there not room in Thy fold for *all*?"

"Surely," she replied to Carry, "None of us liveth to himself, and none of us dieth to himself. My darling name-child, (may she be one of the Saviour's lambs!) has, in her unconscious infancy, led her mother to Him. My own Carry! this is what I have prayed for from the first hour in which I prayed at all. If the angels in heaven rejoice over repenting sinners, shall not we, who have sinned, suffered with them, rejoice the more at their emancipation from bondage? By what various avenues of approach do we arrive at the Cross! our Hope! Some fly, scourged by fears of the wrath to come; some are drawn by the gentle cords of love—attracted by the majestic sweetness of the Saviour's smile; others, like you, for comfort in sharp and sudden sorrow; and others yet, with myself, having quaffed in quick succession, the beaded nectar that knowledge, worldly applause, earthly loves gave to our parched lips, come weary, distraught—our blood drying with the fierce heat of the poison, to lie down beside the still waters. Oh! my beloved! the delights of sin may entice, and cavillers ridicule, as false professors cast reproach upon our holy religion; but let us make it the one object of life—all duties and pleasures subservient to it; let us love it—work for it; never raising our hands, to sink again idly, but striking blows which shall tell our zeal for Christ's kingdom!

"I long to see you and your dear ones. If you cannot come before, you are pledged to me for a part—say the whole, of October. The entire family—my guardian and your sister, Charley and the 'wee ones' are to celebrate my majority then. My nominal majority— virtually, I am as free as I ever expect to be. Emma is a treasure to me, and she seems happy. Who could have presaged, in our school days, that we would live and labor together!"

CHAPTER XXX

Laura Pinely was practising her music lesson in the parlor one day, when the entrance of a visitor transferred the motion from her fingers to her feet. "I only glanced at him as he bowed to me on my way out," she said to Ida. "He is tall and handsome."

"Have you ever seen, Mr. Dana?"

"Yes ma'am, and it is not he. This is a younger man, and much fairer."

"Who can it be?" pondered Ida, crossing the hall. "I wish he had sent in his name; I do not like to be taken by surprise."

But she was, as Richard Copeland rose to meet her.

"I had no thought of seeing you!" she said, expressing her pleasure at his coming. "I did not know you were in this part of the country."

"Nor was I, yesterday."

"You have been riding all day; have you dined?"

He arrested her movement towards the bell. "What are you about to do?"

"Order refreshments for yourself, and have your horse put up."

"'Entertainment for man and beast?'" he responded, with a sickly smile. "I dined on the road—my steed ditto; and he can stand where he is for a half-hour."

"Half-an-hour, Mr. Copeland! You are not in the city!"

"But my visit must be short. How has the world treated you since our parting?"

"Excellently well!" said she, gaily, but secretly ill at ease at the alteration she observed in him. His manner to her was subduedly respectful; but a reckless, *blasé* air hung about him, token of carelessness or dissipation.

"Your friends at home are well, I hope," she said.

"Quite well. Helen—" the remembered cloud lowered gloomily—"sent her regards."

"And you may carry my love back to her. I will not repay formality by formality."

"Love?" questioned he, with a keen glance.

"Yes—why not?"

"What reason have you to love her?"

"Certainly no cause for dislike," she replied. "She treated me kindly."

"'A dizzy man sees the world go round;'" quoted Richard.

"Mr. Copeland!" said Ida, with a grave sincerity, that always unmasked dissimulation. "For the short time we are together, let us speak as friends, who understand each other. Or do you prefer that I shall meet you upon your own ground of satirical innuendo?"

"As *friends*, Miss Ida! you have proved that the name is not meaningless. But we do not understand each other."

"We *did*!" said she.

"Partially. You have risen—I fallen in the scale of being, since then. Your conduct to my unhappy sister, has imposed a debt of gratitude upon us—upon me, especially, which words cannot liquidate. This is the one subject of mutual interest to Helen and myself. She is, in effect, a cloistered nun; an unsmiling ascetic;—atoning for the sins of youth by penances and alms. This phase of piety is the larvae stage, I imagine, Miss Ross?" A grieved look answered the sneer. "Pardon me! if your charity can make allowance for one, who has become a doubter from extraneous influences, rather than nature. Helen and myself have never exchanged a word, except upon common-place topics, during her widowhood, until three days ago. I had avowed my implacable hatred of her lover in her hearing. Other members of the family, have caught stray rumors here and there,—sent out, doubtless, by Miss Read; but their unbelief in them being settled by my silence, and Helen's apparent affliction, they have not noticed them except by a passing denial. But Helen knew that I watched her, and her surveillance of me was as jealously vigilant. I have seen her face blanch in an agony of alarm at my quitting her for an hour; and the most tender sister never wept and prayed for a brother's return, as she did for mine. I should not have been here now, but for intelligence, received a week since, of Ashlin's death."

"Death!" ejaculated Ida, horrified. How had the "bold, bad man" gone to his account? Where was he *now*?

"He was killed in a duel in Bourdeaux," said Richard, coolly. "The villain escaped a less honorable fate by flight. Devoted as Helen was to him, the news was a relief,—removing as it did, her apprehensions of our meeting. So much for her. Thus ends the last chapter of that tragedy!" His countenance lost its bitter scorn.

"Miss Ida—before I met you, I never feared to speak what was in my thoughts. Policy or compassion may have deterred me—but cowardice never! I believed I had read every page in man's or woman's heart, and could flutter them with a breath. You were a study, taken up in curiosity, and baffling me by its very simplicity. You furnished me with a clue; but my skepticism cast it aside—to seek it again, and admit its efficacy in a solitary instance. Ingenuous in word and deed—you had yet, a hidden history. I felt it then, vaguely—not able to tell from whence the consciousness sprung. Can it be that virtue thrives only in the shade?"

He stopped again. Ida's face was crimsoning slowly with confusion and suspense.

"It *must* be said!" resumed he, desperately. "I may probe a wound, or touch a callous heart. Miss Ross! will you state to me candidly, the character of your acquaintance with Mr. Lacy?"

Ida's tongue was palsied. She would have given her estate for power to say—"He was my friend;" but it was denied.

"Then bear with me awhile. The evening of our introduction, I imparted to you the information of Lelia Arnold's engagement; and your deprecation of her trifling seemed only the detestation of a pure and upright soul. If I saw mournful pity in the eyes, which were often riveted by her beauty, I suspected no more. Before leaving Richmond, I heard that he had been—perhaps was then your lover:—the direction of your preference was not known. In my superior sagacity, I opined that my friend Germaine was his fortunate rival. Your rejection of his suit recalled the gossip I had not thought worth remembering. Lelia was Helen's confidante; knew of her betrothal to Ashlin, and surmised, if she was not informed of the rupture, when it occurred. After Mr. Read's death, my mother mentioned incidentally, that her influence had been exerted to the utmost, to persuade her friend to accept him. Until I heard that, I had laughed at her snares to entangle me—the only man, it was said, who was invulnerable to her arts. I despised her before, I hated her now; yet the county rung with acclamations over my capture; and the fair Lelia, in her exultation, was beguiled into an impolitic show of tenderness. I have her picture, her ring, her letters. I could dash them into the sea, without a pang, and would plunge after them, sooner than marry her. I designed a punishment for her falsehood in friendship and love; but all the while, was haunted with an indefinite thought that you were to be affected by the result. If your lover had been wiled away by her machinations, or more likely—if she had played upon his imagination and sense of honor, in an unguarded hour—I could free him. I intended to see you, and tell you this, but Helen hastened the execution of the plot. Breaking our accustomed reserve, she implored me to quiet her fears touching my marriage. A glimmering of Leila's treachery had penetrated her mind;—she mistrusted that she was playing me false, and that she had deceived others. I struck a key, which I knew would give a true sound—her love for you. She had heard your name coupled with his, she said; and once, a direct assertion of your attachment for him, but it was from lying lips. If I have

225

wearied and displeased you, intimate it. If not—here are the proofs to secure you revenge or happiness. Say the word, and the dupe is enlightened. She will not suffer more, that you connive at her disgrace. Her mortification will be public, and is inevitable. Where is Mr. Lacy?"

"I do not know, and would not tell you if I did!" cried Ida. "If I were dying of a broken heart, I would refuse the healing your cold-blooded scheme offered. She may be—I believe her unworthy of him; but when he sought her, he was shackled by no vows to me. He is not a vain boy, to be flattered into a courtship! if duped, she has cruelly deceived the noblest heart that ever beat. I honor him more for not discovering her snare, than you, for mastering her in duplicity. No! Mr. Copeland! I have no wrongs to avenge upon him or her—nor is it your prerogative, to retaliate for your, or your sister's injuries. We do not understand each other! You impute traits to me, which the weakest of my sex would blush to own; and I thought you generous—high-minded! 'Fallen,' indeed!" Her voice shook, and her head sank upon the table. The man of the world was confounded. The lofty tone of her principles lowered his plotted vengeance into unmanly spite.

He had been incited to it by the low standard of the sex, his sister's and her associate's conduct had set up in his mind; and a desire to betray the baseness of the currency the accomplished coquette was passing off upon society—backed by a justifiable displeasure at the evils of which she was the author.

"I am to understand that you disdain my offer to serve you?" he said, rising.

She looked up. "To serve me! how thankfully I would avail myself of such! I was hasty—unkind! Do not go yet!"

He sat down. "It is all so confused!" she said, apologetically. "You are engaged to Lelia Arnold, and do not love her:—yet you must have told her that you did!"

He colored, and did not reply.

"You are meditating a punishment for her—what has she done that you have not?"

"Falsehood—unprovoked falsehood is viler in a woman. I was driven to it."

"Viler in a woman—more despicable in a man! You should be above the petty vanity and ambition, that if cultivated, root up our better feelings. Selfishness, love of admiration, and in your case, pique, actuated her;—you have the bare plea of malice!"

"Miss Ross! malice!"

"Examine, and say if it is not so. Punishment, in this world, has cure for its object. Was this yours? or was it that she might endure the pain she had inflicted upon others?"

"Call it retribution."

"There is but one Retributive Being. He says 'Vengeance is mine!'"

"You are unsophisticated, Miss Ida. Your maxims are obsolete in the polity of the age."

"Because they are extracts from a changeless code. I am serious, Mr. Copeland. Your conscience assures you that you are in the wrong; that you have acted childishly—sinfully. That another debases God's gifts, is no reason why you should sully the fine gold of your heart. You have committed this outrage, or you could not talk of the sweetness of revenge."

"And *I* am serious, Miss Ida. Unjust, as you say I have been to myself, I have the manliness to recognise the superiority of a character—the antipodes of mine. I repeat, I regret my inability to serve you. Good evening."

"*Are* you going thus? What if we never meet again?"

"We part friends. Your reproaches, cutting as they were, have not diminished my esteem."

She could extort nothing more satisfactory. He would make no concessions—tender no pledges. Large tears gathered and dropped, as she beheld him mount and ride away; and other emotions than grief at her ill-success sent tributaries to the stream.

They prate senselessly who speak of forgotten loves or woes. As in neglected grave-yards, briars and weeds spring up, and delude the eye with the semblance of a smooth field, but when levelled to the roots, show the mounds they grow upon;—so above buried feelings, may wave memories and affections of later years—until some unforeseen event cuts, like a sickle-blade, through their ranks, and we see, with tears, as of fresh bereavement, the graves there still! Ida's was a brave spirit, but it trembled after the temptation was withdrawn. Richard had, unknowingly, been guilty of great cruelty in breaking the seal of her heart's closed chamber. Gingerly as he had handled its precious things, he had caused exquisite pain; and for hours and days, she felt that the door would not shut again. It was hard to smile—hard to concert plans for the future welfare of others, when before her, was blank darkness. But the whirling chaos was cleared and tranquillised in time; and even Emma was ignorant of the storm.

On the fifteenth of October, the heiress of Sunnybank would count her twenty-first birth day. The oldest negroes testified that it had been the custom in the Ross family, for an hundred years, to signalise such occasions with appropriate festivities; and Ida waived her wishes for a quiet visit from her friends; and tried to be as much interested in the proposed illumination and feast as if she were not the personage to be honoured. She worked more willingly when the Danas wrote that they were all coming, the Saturday before the fifteenth, which fell on Tuesday. Emma's scholars had a vacation of four weeks; and Laura Pinely was at the house most of her time. The two vied with each other in the number and elegance of the decorations of the premises.

"What upon earth!" exclaimed Ida, stumbling over a heap of green boughs in the back porch. Both girls screamed—"Oh! take care!" Ida sat down upon a bench, and untwisted a long streamer of running cedar from her ancle.

"What is this for!"

"To dress the pictures and looking-glasses," said Emma.

"And to festoon upon the walls," chimed in Laura.

"And loop up bed and window-curtains," finished Emma.

"My dear girls! if the President and suit were expected, your preparations would not be more formidable. Why trouble yourselves so much?"

"Trouble! *you* never incommode yourself for other people! oh no!" replied Emma, in severe irony.

"We love the bustle and excitement of fixing," said Laura.

"And what is there for me to do?" questioned Ida, stooping over the pile.

"Nothing! you are to play lady and hold your hands. It is difficult, because unusual work—but please try!" laughed Laura.

Miss Betsey came along, with a rueful face. "Miss Ida—there's a dozen loaves of cake, and ever so many snow-balls *wont* get in the big sideboard, no how!"

"Put them in the light closet, Miss Betsey. I hope we shall be able to eat it all!" she continued to the girls.

"Never fear!" said Emma. "Your Richmond party could consume it in a week. How many are there?"

"Let me see! Arthur, Carry and my pet—three—Mr. and Mrs. Dana, three children and Charley—nine. They will be here to-morrow night—Ellen Morris, Monday or Tuesday. I have invited Anna Talbot and Josephine—but do not expect them. Then for Tuesday evening—from the neighborhood—Dr. Hall and lady—and a friend, who shall be nameless—" pinching Emma's cheek—"the Strattons—Kingstons—Frenches—and oh! I gave Charley *carte-blanche* to ask any of my Richmond acquaintances—and all for what? To hear that Miss Ida Ross is—"

"'Free, white, and twenty-one!'" sang Emma, cheerily.

"Twenty-one! in four years, I shall be a spinster of a quarter of a century! Heigho!" She said it jestingly; but at nightfall, she was pacing the porch alone—Laura having gone home, and Emma asleep, wearied by her day's activity; and the thought returned to her. Twenty-one! the golden sands were slipping fast. The sky-meeting waves upon the horizon no longer blushed with sunset dyes, and nodded their bright crests, in luring welcome; her eyes were bent upon the regular swell of the Present, as she glided over it. The navigation of the unknown seas beyond, she trusted to the Pilot, who had engaged to see her safely to the desired haven. It was a holy, still hour.

Her swift step scarcely broke the silence—the firm, elastic tread of youth and health;—and an unruffled spirit was within;—a fulness of contentment and peace the world could not disturb or take away. She had conned that invaluable lesson—"It is better to trust than to hope."

"A letter, ma'am—no papers," said Will, sententiously.

"Thank you, uncle Will. Tell James to bring a lamp into the parlor, if you please. I almost dread to open this!" she said to herself. "My fears are always on the alert, to forebode evil to those I love. I *will* be courageous—*will* have faith!" and she walked resolutely into the lighted room. But the superscription sent a tremor to her heart—a minute elapsed before she opened it.

THE LETTER.

"I have come home alone, dear friend, leaving our Annie asleep in a foreign land. Her day of suffering closed in ease and peace; her 'good night' was as calm, as though she were sinking into a slumber of hours, instead of ages. A lonely, stricken man, I retraced the route we had travelled in company, to find that I had never indeed missed and mourned her, until I saw her empty chamber at home. Here—'I cannot make her dead!' Oh! the desolation of that word, when applied to one, in whose veins ran the same blood as in ours, who lived and loved with us—partaker of our individuality! As love is immortal, we would believe the frail clay to which it clings, imperishable too. But in our grief, there is a mingling of praise that her rest is safe—that a merciful Father is also wise, and will not, in answer to our selfish lamentations, restore her to an existence replete with pain.

"The date of the above—a month back—may surprise you. I wrote a fortnight after I touched my native shore; contemplating such a letter as one friend might send to another;—to inform you of my bereavement, and solicit the sympathy none ever ask in vain from you. I was interrupted to read a communication which has changed—not the tenor of this alone, but the current of all my anticipations. It was from Miss Arnold; an annulment of the contract between us; a step, she says, foreseen from an early period of our engagement, when she discovered that the heart, she thought she had surrendered to me, was wholly another's. I omit much that would be uninteresting to you; and which, in honour, I ought not to transcribe. Briefly then—the facts stand thus. She never loved me; and when the owner of her heart sued for her hand, she pledged it, and asked for a release from her previous vow. I have no inclination to animadvert upon her course—singular and inconsistent as it has been throughout—but am obliged to refer to certain particulars, to make clear the explanation which follows.

> "I have told you, Ida, that my attentions, from the beginning of our intercourse, until my conviction of your betrothal, were correct exponents of my feelings. I cannot deny that when compelled to acknowledge the uselessness of my efforts, I judged you harshly—was tempted to believe you an unprincipled trifler with my hopes, and the truth of your accepted lover. As my indignation and disappointment cooled before mature reflection, my faith in your sterling integrity revived.

"Not a word had escaped me which Friendship might not have dictated; and your manner to me was less confidingly affectionate than to Charley. You regarded me as a brother; and if in that capacity, any act or word of mine could conduce to your happiness it should not be withheld. Your committal of your lover's cause to me was a powerful appeal to every generous feeling. I solemnly resolved then, that you should never regret your implicit trust. At his death-bed, my thought was for you and him; at his grave, as I upheld your sinking form—my heart answering the heavings of yours, in our common sorrow—I renewed the promise never to desecrate the purity of your friendship, by a breath of a love, demanding reciprocation in that which had gone down with him into the tomb. In this illusion, I came home. You know whom I met here; and that her surpassing loveliness, her apparent artlessness and amiability captivated us all. Annie loved her fervently, and threw us together by many innocent manoeuvres—Dear girl! it was the blameless impulse of a loving heart—to unite two, who seemed to her hopeful perceptions to be destined for each other. I was amused at her fancy—then uneasy, lest it should be a restriction upon Miss Arnold's kindly feelings for the brother of her friend. I could not wound Annie by reproof or caution; so, after a while, descrying in Miss Arnold's demeanor, a touch of the dreaded embarrassment, I introduced the subject in a tone of light badinage. I may not describe the interview;—my sentiments and bearing had been utterly misconstrued. She did not express this in words, but her perturbation was unmistakeable. I reflected upon this unlooked-for disclosure with no enviable emotions. I was free; no hope ventured to point to you; and I might learn to love the beautiful, tender creature, whom I had unintentionally deceived. In honour—in conscience—in humanity—what could I do, but tell her that, although not offering the deep tenderness of a first love I would cherish her as faithfully, if not as fondly, as man ever did the woman he wooed and won? I cannot dwell upon the untold anguish of the moment when the fallacy of my impressions and reasonings was exposed. The tempter was at my ear. Violation of my plighted word—the downfall of her hopes were nothing! the barrier which parted *us* was down—the impossibility of our union was a chimera, dissolving in the beams of truth. You saved me! looking away from our divided lives, you reminded me that duty here writes our title-deeds to reward hereafter—and I submitted to the decree.

"*Now*—dear Ida!—but the rush of hope ebbs suddenly. The thought that flew towards you, the moment I was freed—now, that the slow weeks I allotted to rigid self-examination have rolled by—spreads its wings as eagerly still—but—you?

"What was I to you? what may I hope to be? I have ascertained that you are unmarried—are you heart-free? May I come to you? Dare I say—reply at once? I would not wring from you a hasty decision, but remember my suspense. May every blessing be yours!

MORTON LACY."

CHAPTER XXXI

Mr. Grant, wife and sister-in-law were "dear, nice old folks," who liked to see young people enjoy themselves, prim and staid 'though they were; and they had their fill of delight, that important Saturday; for three merrier mad-caps Sunnybank never held. Ida was the ringleader in the mirthful frolic.

"She's so pleased 'cause Mars' Charles is comin'," said Rachel, in a pretended "aside" to Emma and Laura; and Ida laughed, instead of reproving the gratuitous explanation. "I do want to see Charley—Bless him!" said she.

"Is he a *very* dear friend?" asked Laura.

"*Very* dear!" Ida emphasized as strongly;—"almost on a par with Carry. We will have fun while he is here;" and she launched into a recital of some of his freaks and stories; eliciting bursts of merriment from her listeners, which pealed even to the door of Miss Betsey's room, and hurried Mrs. Grant down stairs, "to hear what the joke was." The girls were upon the carpet in the middle of the large parlor, cutting pink and white paper roses. The graceful running cedar, they were to enliven, draped the walls, and hid the tarnished mouldings of the old portrait frames;—geraniums and mignionette breathed sweetly through the parted muslin curtains; but nothing was so fair in the dame's eyes as the centre group. Laura was a brunette—black eyes, nectarine bloom and pouting rosy lips—the handsomest of the trio; Emma's dove-like eyes, classic oval face and varying complexion placed her next. Ida sat between them, speaking with much animation of voice and action—the glee of a child, and the modulations of a clever elocutionist.

"Well!" said Mrs. Grant, when the narration was ended, "if you all ain't a happy set, I'll give up my judgment!"

"Don't do that, I beg!" said Ida. "We need it this minute, to tell us whether to mix these roses in the wreaths, or to dress this room with white ones, and the dining-room with pink." Mrs. Grant set her head to one side, and her hand upon her hip. It was a serious question.

"Well, I don't know exactly. Either way's very pretty. What do *you* say?"

"Oh! but we agreed to leave it to you. White ones look best by lamplight."

"*So* they do! Well 'spose you put them in here, as the party meets in the parlor."

"Thank you, ma'am. I am of the same opinion myself."

"And I"—"and I"—said the others; and Mrs. Grant, pleased at having, for once in her life, expressed a decided opinion, "reckoned Becky and Molly wouldn't beat them beds half enough if she didn't follow them up."

The impromptu "rose case," upon which Emma and Laura rallied Ida, was finished before dinner; and resolving themselves into a "committee of inspection," they visited every room in a body, with Miss Betsey and Mrs. Grant as rear guard. Even the wainscotted chambers were cheerful—snow-drifts of beds—and window-hangings lined with pink—stainless toilette covers; painted bouquets upon the fire-screens, and real ones upon the dressing tables.

"Sunnybank deserves its name to-day," said Emma, leading Ida to a window.

The October sun was everywhere; playing with the laughing cascade which fell over the rock, at the foot of the sloping lawn; carpeting the forest with tesselated gold; and the sheen of Ida's pine-grove was as of millions of burnished needles.

"It is brighter here!" said Ida, laying her friend's hand upon her breast.

"You need not say so;—your smile shows it. It is like sunshine itself."

"Shall I tell her?" thought Ida. "Not yet! he will be here in a few days—and *then*!"—and the heart-bound threw the blood, in a scarlet gush to her cheeks.

Love like hers is never selfish. When they were separating to dress, she called Laura into her room. Two dresses—a rose-coloured challé, and a white muslin were upon the bed. "No thanks, dear!" she said, as the delighted creature clasped her arms about her neck, in speechless gratitude. "You, who do so much for me and mine, deserve some token of regard. What! tears! Dry them instantly, and try your dresses. Ah! they fit! I thought we were nearly the same size,—so had them cut by my patterns. Emma! step in here! Are we not proud of our pupil?"

"She does not require fine robes to win praise from me," said Emma. "How handsome and becoming! just what one might expect from the donor."

"She is the best, dearest friend I have"—began Laura, smiling through her tears.

"Hush!" said Ida, threateningly. "Flatterers! both of you! be off and 'beautify' as Charley says. And Laura—do you hear? don't have eyes and dress to match! a contrast is better."

The main part of Sunnybank house was capped by a sort of belvidere, accessible by steps from the garret. Why it had been built was one of Ida's childish studies; and the acquisition of other knowledge was no help to the elucidation of this mystery. Emma said the founder of the mansion had an astronomical turn, and used it as an observatory;—Laura, that it was a belfry, from which the alarm-bell was sounded to collect the surrounding settlers, when an incursion was made by the savages; Ida's more matter-of-fact belief was that her ancestor had more fondness than taste for ornamental architecture, and so planned this tuft to the conical crown of his habitation. On the birth-night, this was to be illuminated; the brackets were prepared, and some of the candles in the sockets. Nearer and faster descended the darkness. Aunt Judy fidgeted from the kitchen to the house, and from the house to the kitchen, in mortal fear for the credit of her supper. Miss Betsey prognosticated upsettings and wheel-breakings, and "hoped the horses were sure-footed. That hill, the other side of Tim's Creek was *awful* of a dark night."

"I say, girls!" exclaimed Ida, "we will light the belvidere! They can see it six miles off. Anything but idle waiting!"

She was to stand in the yard, and direct the disposition of the lights—Laura, Emma and Will, who thought no whim of his "mistis" absurd, ascended to the roof. The breeze was at rest; and the rays shot forth, clear and straight, down the avenue, magnifying the proportions of the fantastic roof. The others came out to admire the effect with her.

"Hist!" said she. "Music!"

But there was not a sound.

"I heard it—I know!" said she, positively. "Come into the porch."

Another note was repeated by the hills. "I said so! they are coming—singing! Isn't that like Charley?" She distinguished voices as they approached;—Carry's soft alto; Mrs. Dana's soprano,—"Arthur—yes! that is his tenor—and Mr. Dana and Charley have the base!"

"The tune changes!" said Emma. "Auld Lang Syne—oh! how sweet!"

Ida's eyes were streaming,—her heart aching with joy. The carriages—two—and a buggy, drove up to the door; and with a scream of rapture she lifted Carry to the ground,—not knowing who came next—only that they were all there. All! no! where was Charley? She stopped upon the steps; Elle holding to her dress; one hand in Carry's, the other upon her guardian's arm.

"Charley! where are you?"

"Here!" with a muster-roll intonation. He raised her fingers to his lips—an unprecedented action with him—and holding them still, looked over his shoulder. "Here is a gentleman who is afraid you will shut your doors upon him, for coming without a special invitation."

"Mr. Germaine!" thought Ida, fearfully;—but his was not the figure that emerged from the shade,—nor the warm grasp, in which Charley, with a movement full of grace and feeling, placed her hand;—nor his the voice that said—"I do not doubt her hospitality, but my deserts."

"Do you forget your friends, that you expect a similar fate, Mr. Lacy?" said Ida.

His actual presence was the roseleaf upon the mantling cup of bliss. It did not overflow;—tumultuating passions were stilled into a calm, delicious ecstacy. She was more composed than she had been at any time since the reading of the letter,—saw everything, thought of everybody. Carry and Emma went up-stairs arm in arm, and Ida, her baby namesake, folded to her heart, was following Mrs. Dana, when she recollected Laura. She was standing, alone and overlooked, in the hall.

"Here, Laura! I confide my darling to your keeping. Gently! don't wake her. Is she not a lovely babe?"

"Beautiful!" said Laura, in proud gratification.

The sleepy children's suppers were brought up, and they were snug in bed before their elders were prepared for their meal. The gentlemen were in the yard, looking at the belvidere.

"Your beacon puzzled us considerably," said Charley to Ida. "It appeared to be upon the summit of a huge, shapeless height. We thought we had lost our road and wandered off to the Enchanted Mountains."

"Or that a remnant of Ghebers had an asylum among these hills," said Mr. Lacy. "You should have heard Charley's

'Fierce and high
The death-pile blued into the sky,
And far away, o'er rock and flood,
Its melancholy radiance sent!'"

"Was I the only rhapsodizer?" retorted Charley. "Who said, when a figure passed before the light—

"Hafed, like a vision, stood
Revealed before the burning pyre,
Tall, shadowy, like a Spirit of Fire,
Shrined in its own grand element?'"

"Why, that was uncle Will!" exclaimed Emma.

Amid the burst of laughter that replied, Charley pronounced poetry—"done."

"And having descended to real life, perhaps you do not object to more substantial food," said Ida. On the way to the house, some one took her hand.

"Has my impatience offended? I could not wait!" said a hasty whisper.

"No."

"Am I welcome?"

"In every sense of the word," was the ingenuous response. This was their plighting.

The sun was not up, when Ida raised the parlor windows next morning. Above the dun zone of forest, rested another, of silvery grey vapor, and higher, legions of fleecy cloudlets, from all parts of the heavens, hung motionless, as angels may hover, in rapt adoration, over the crystal walls of the New Jerusalem. He arose! the "bridegroom of earth and brother of time!" and her simile changed—as assuming roseate and golden robes, the expectant host wove themselves into a gorgeous causeway, by which he seemed to mount the heavens. So "Jesus left the dead!" the Sun of Righteousness burst His prison gates; and the shining ones sang the consummation of a world's redemption. She was reading her Bible, alternately with the resplendent leaf Nature unfurled this autumnal Sabbath, when a step dispelled her trance.

"Good morning!" said Mr. Lacy. "You are an early riser."

"There is my reward!" pointing to the scene without.

"May I participate, in virtue of my second-best claim?" asked he, with his own beaming smile, seating himself before she assented. Ida's trifling embarrassment was transient. His behavior, open and free, as of old, had not a tincture of reserve, or significance to indicate that he thought of their new relation. The beauty of our lower sanctuary; the upper, which it dimly shadows forth; Annie's sickness and death; the Christian's work and hopes—were the matter of their conversation; and as the rest assembled, they were spared the disagreeable sensation one feels at interrupting a tête-à-tête.

"Is it time to ring the prayer-bell, Ida?" asked Emma, as the last loiterer came in.

"I think so. We breakfast early on Sunday mornings, that we may be at school in season," she said to Mrs. Dana.

It was her practice to lead in family worship, night and morning. Arthur had performed this office the evening before, and the servants having collected in the hall, she motioned him to the stand, where lay the Bible.

"I am hoarse," he said. "Lacy!"

The person addressed reddened slightly, but conquering himself instantly, did as he was requested; and Ida, too, although not so easily, lost the identity of the man in the reader, and was prepared to join, with solemnity and fervor of spirit, in his prayer.

By Charley's contrivance, they rode to church in the light buggy. Ida condemned herself for the feeling of disappointment that fell suddenly upon her, as the school-house appeared; and more for the fancies which strayed—starry-winged butterflies into the machinery of her morning's duties; but her pupils were unconscious of the visitants.

"Is that your regular pastor?" inquired Mr. Lacy, as they were driving back.

"*Ir*-regular, rather—if you speak of the seasons of his ministrations. Presiding over three— I am not certain it is not four congregations, he preaches for us once a month."

"Who officiates the three other Sabbaths?"

"Sometimes the pastor of the Hill-side church. The second Sabbath is his day in course; but he lives twelve miles off. If he is among the missing, we catch up a circuit-rider, or go sermonless."

"'These things ought not so to be.'"

"I know it—but they *are*! Who is to remedy them? Palm-branch is a free church."

"And as often free of preachers, as of sectarianism, it seems," said he.

"More frequently. The war of polemic debate is waged as furiously there, as if the controversialists owned pulpit, pews and people. The number of communicants of our persuasion, in this neighborhood, is small; yet they are mostly persons in good circumstances, and able to have a church of their own, if they would think so."

"They should purchase this Palm-branch. There is more euphony than meaning in that name, when applied to a house."

"A free church, especially," answered Ida. "However, our Sabbath-school has vanquished its enemies, and may lead the church on to victory."

"Dr. Hall awards the merits of this enterprise to you. Has your residence here enlarged or contracted your sphere of usefulness?"

"Enlarged it. Not that this would be the case with most people. The city presents more facilities for benevolence generally; but my family had influence here; and my servants wanted a manager. There are more deprivations than I anticipated; the separation from my friends; want of general society; the dearth of books and intellectual recreations; and last and worst—abridgement of my church privileges. Still I do not repent my removal. My happiest days have been my Sunnybank life."

"Because you are in your right orbit. The evils you recount are not irremediable; we will discuss them at length, some day."

This was the only reference to the future, as theirs—into which he was betrayed all day; but it struck Ida dumb. She recovered her speech by evening; for she and Charley strolled in the garden, in close converse, until Mr. Dana sent Morton to warn them of the night dew. He perceived, as did the whole party, traces of emotion in her countenance; and Charley was very grave, although not melancholy. Music was proposed after tea; and Ida unlocked the parlor organ, a gift to Mrs. Ross from her husband, and still a fine instrument. Emma blushed so deeply at her nomination as organist, that Ida recalled the motion and occupied her accustomed place. Her fingers wandered; and Mr. Lacy, bending over to adjust the book, said softly, "Do not attempt to play, if you are indisposed." She smiled. "I am only weak and silly; I shall be better directly." And ere the first hymn was concluded her clear voice led the choristers, and the pealing chords rolled out in full strength and harmony.

The bell rang for prayers. Arthur glanced at Ida, and was arrested in the act of rising, by seeing her wheel a chair to the stand, and beckon to Charley. Yet more astounded were all that he took it. Unclasping the Bible, he read distinctly and reverently, a portion of its sacred contents; and they knelt with him at the mercy-seat. A stifled sob, and more than one sigh from surcharged bosoms, responded to his petitions; and Carry wept aloud at the "Amen." Arthur was equally moved. "God bless you, Charley!" was all he could say, as he wrung his hand.

"He *has* blessed him, and us," said Morton, joyfully. "I thought this would be the end of it, my good friend!"

"Not the end—the beginning!" said Ida, who stood by her adopted brother. "Only the beginning! is it not, Charley?"

"*You* were the beginning!" said he, smiling. "My mind has been made up for some time; but it was proper that she should be the first apprised of it. I was stubborn and rebellious; and the consistent practice of one private Christian did more to convict me than the preaching of the entire apostolic succession—Saints Paul and Peter to head them—could have done."

"O, Charley! you are Charley still!" laughed Carry.

"And always will be, I hope!" rejoined Morton. "Religion, my dear Mrs. Dana, does not *make* but *mend*, the disposition."

CHAPTER XXXII

Yes! "Charley was Charley still!" The brothers were walking the piazza, Monday morning; and John's smile and Arthur's laugh applauded the quaint humor which came from his lips, as freely as respiration of the air his lungs had inhaled. He was a consummate actor; and his self-command balked the sharpest scrutiny when he chose; but his spirits, this morning, were not feigned. Mrs. Dana, Emma and Laura made their appearance, and at length, Charley's flow of talk could no longer delay the inquiry "Where are Ida and Mr. Lacy?"

"'Brushing the dew upon the upland lawn.'" said Charley. "Gone to ride."

"When did they start?" asked John.

"Just as you shut your eyes for a second nap—luxurious citizen that you are. 'When will they return?'—query the second.—You will see them on the top of that hill in a minute."

They cantered down the avenue in gallant style. Ida was an expert rider; and her escort appeared to as much advantage on horseback as on foot.

"A handsome couple!" said Arthur.

Charley made no reply. "You do your teacher justice," he said, as Ida leaped to the ground, barely touching Mr. Lacy's hand.

"And more could not be said for master or pupil;" she answered, saucily.

"Morning rides are wonderful cosmetics!" he whispered, following her into the hall. She snapped her whip at him, but those mischievous eyes were too searching, and she ran off "to change her dress."

"I am for a walk to the river. Who accompanies me?" said John Dana. Ida held the taper at which he was kindling a cigar—his invariable after-breakfast luxury—and the flame was paled by her vivid glow, as Mr. Lacy said quietly, "I will, sir, with pleasure."

In an hour they returned, and the summons—"Mr. Dana's respects, and if you please ma'am, he wants the pleasure of your company in the drawing-room," robbed her of the last spark of self-possession. She stopped at the door, to muster courage; but her guardian had heard her step, and opened it from within. "I have no lecture for you," he said, passing his arm assuringly around her. "This is an event, we fathers have to bear, as best we may. I am fortunate that your choice has my unqualified sanction. You have acted wisely, nobly, my daughter."

"*Dear* Mr. Dana! I feared you would think me uncommunicative; but I did not know it myself until within a day or two."

"I am advised of the incidents of your drama. Never try to convince me again, that you are an unromantic young lady! What is your evidence, Mr. Lacy?"

She had not seen, until this speech, that he was present. She bestowed one look upon him, and the magnetic charm of his smile equallized her nerves and thoughts. Mr. Dana would have left the room, but Morton stayed him. In succinct and manly terms, he thanked him for the expression of an esteem, it should be the study of his life to merit. "I am aware, sir, that it is arrant boldness to ask more from your kindness; but you engaged to intercede for me in another suit." Ida looked up, hurriedly. The gentlemen smiled; and Mr. Lacy whispered a sentence in her ear.

"Oh no! no!" she ejaculated, "too soon!"

"Why 'too soon?'" It was John Dana, who drew her away from her lover, and pushed back the shadowing curls from her forehead. "Think of Mr. Lacy and myself as old friends, and speak out the language of your own warm heart. Why 'too soon,' Ida? Don't you know him well, enough?"

Another glance was the signal for another smile.

"Will you ever know him better?" asked Mr. Lacy.

"I think not," she replied.

"You don't like him well enough, then?" pursued Mr. Dana. The curls drooped over her face, and she was mute.

"Perhaps you do not like the idea of resigning your freedom the very day you gain it?"

"No, Mr. Dana! you *know* that is not it."

"What then?" Mr. Lacy secured her disengaged hand. "If this proposal distresses you, Ida, I revoke it without a murmur, and will abide your convenience, or inclination patiently; but if it is a question of expediency, you cannot suppose that Mr. Dana or myself would urge a measure, we were not assured was reasonable and proper. Your dearest friends are with you—what renders delay necessary or advisable?"

"But what will they say?"

"An odd inquiry from *you*! What potent 'they' do you mean?"

"Carry—Arthur—Mrs. Dana—Charley—all of them."

"Charley has been my abettor from the beginning. From him I learned your locality; and he warranted me a friendly reception, if nothing more. I should not have had the confidence to propose this immediate union, if he had not favored my ardent wish. You trust in his judgment in other matters—why not now? As for the rest of those you name—when did they oppose anything you advocated?"

"But your friends—your mother?"

"Is prepared to love you as a daughter."

"She wishes me to decide, I see;" said John, dictatorially. "Therefore, silencing all disputes—the fatted calf is slain—the neighbors are bidden—and I, as this perverse maiden's lawful guardian—setting my face, like a flint, against wasteful improvidence—decree an occasion for the feast, instead of a feast for the occasion; and as this must be, the sooner we are rid of the trouble the better. Not a syllable, Miss Ross! you are still a minor; and I will indict you for insubordination, if you are refractory. I am going to tell Jenny to air my white vest for to-morrow evening."

Emma, Laura and Carry were in Mrs. Dana's apartment; and when the clamour of amazement lulled, not a hand was raised in the negative.

"She deserves the best husband that can be given her;" said Carry, "and from my knowledge of Mr. Lacy's character, I expect he is almost good enough for her."

"He would have been my choice from among all the gentlemen of my acquaintance," answered Mrs. Dana, "as she and Charley will *not* make a match."

"Ah, Jenny! did I not say you would have to abandon that air castle?" said her husband. "It was the only essay at match-making I ever caught you at."

"What is it, Laura?" inquired Carry, as her face brightened suddenly.

"I was thinking how strange we should have decorated the drawing-room with white roses, when we were not expecting a wedding!"

The news spread like wild-fire over the plantation. "Young Mistis was gwine to be married!" and never did tidings of a splendid victory produce a grander jubilee. The Grants, Miss Betsey, and Will, as sub-steward, had the programme of the performances and actors; but with the crowd, the Lacy and Dana factions ran high, to the amusement of the wise. Aunt Judy's climax was reported at the dinner-table by Miss Betsey, who must have shared in the general delirium of pleasure, as this is the only authentic record of her ever having spoken in "company," unless "spoken to."

"'Well!' says Aunt Judy—says she—'Dany or Lacy—they's both mighty fine, pretty-spoken gentlemen. Either on 'em 'll do; but it's been a-runnin' in my head what a mussiful Providence 'tis, hur husband happened along, jes' when the cake riz nicer than any I'se made since ole Marster's weddin! And young Mis' too—poor, lone, sweet cretur! ah, chillen! things *is* ordered wonderful! wonderful!'"

"Don't blush, Ida! laughing suits the occasion better," said Carry, as every mouth spread at this apropos anecdote; and she did laugh merrily, as well as Mr. Lacy, who had tried to control his risibles until he heard her.

Ellen Morris arrived that night, attended by her brother, and at a feminine council, which sat until midnight, in the room of the bride-elect, a list of attendants was drawn up—Emma and Charley, Laura and Mr. Latham, Ellen and Mr. Thornton, who, she said, was certainly coming next day,—and Miss Kingston, one of the neighbors, with Robert Morris.

"Aunt Judy may well say, 'things is ordered wonderful!'" said Emma. "Who thought of this, a week ago? and here everything is arranged, as if expressly for a marriage. 'Not a screw loose or lacking!'"

"Ida will say it is a 'special Providence,'" said Mrs. Dana, "but Mr. Lacy and Charley had a hand in it."

"Who moved them?" asked Ida. "Depend upon it, my theory is irrefutable, because true. If a delusion, it is harmless and pleasant."

"You would make puppets of us;" said Ellen. "Chessmen—irresponsible for their motions."

"No, indeed! We are children, obeying a Father's orders, no matter how enigmatical; and having done our part, letting Him work out the answer to the puzzle. A so-called ignorant woman once furnished the best definition of Faith I ever heard;—'taking the Lord at his word.' It is safer to believe, than to argue, Ellen."

Aunt Judy's aphorism was bandied about on Tuesday until it was hacknied. Ida feared the appearance of her "Bubly Jock;" but her prime counsellor, Will, his stalwart arms bared to the shoulder, to turn an ice-cream churn, said confidently, that "she nor Miss Laura should be pestered with him that evening. I've got his written bond to stay at home, and eat the supper that will be sent to him. Mars' Charley and Mr. Lacy's been to see him too. They came while I was there, 'on a sociable visit,' they said, but before they went away, he was crying like a child—they talked so beautiful!"

The bridal paraphernalia was laid in array, and Emma and Laura tying up bouquets; Ida directing, but not permitted to assist.

"Ellen cannot find that arbor-vitæ surely!" said Emma. "I wish she had let me go!"

Ellen burst into the room, and flinging herself into a chair, laughed immoderately. "What has happened?" cried a trio of voices.

"The wheel of luck has turned! It is a 'wonderful ordering' that brings Josephine Read upon this, of all days in the year!"

"Josephine!" Ida seemed to behold a ghoul. She had invited her because propriety demanded she should not slight the daughter of her former guardian, after living in the house with her six years; then she was fond of Anna Talbot, and a separate invitation was not to be thought of. The possibility of her coming had not entered her mind. How could she present herself at the door of her, whom she had denounced as her mortal foe? Emma stood aghast, and Laura in bewilderment, at the dismay depicted in the faces of her friends.

"I am sorry for you, Ida," continued Ellen; "and if I were a magician, would whisk her off to Guinea in the time it would take me to say 'Presto!' but if you did not feel so badly, I would delight in her spiteful rage, when she knows that she has come to your wedding— and with Mr. Lacy! Oh! it is transporting!"

"Worse and worse!" said Ida, sorrowfully. "Unkind as she has been, I would not wound her; and she will never be persuaded that the insult was unpremeditated."

"'Insult!' forsooth! who is insulted, pray, but yourself, by the intrusion of a woman, who has reviled and backbitten you, until the town cried out against her evil tongue! Oh! the shamelessness of a wicked gossip!"

"Where is she?" questioned Ida.

"In the north chamber. Anna Talbot, Messrs. Thornton and Villet came with her."

"Charley said he asked them—and I am glad Anna is here—but oh! Josephine! and I am *en dishabille*! Emma, will you run up to them? you are at home."

"Willingly." The kind-hearted girl emptied her lap of the flowers.

"And explain everything," said Ida.

"Yes—make all right! Comfort yourself;" and away she flew.

Her face, upon her re-entrance, boded well for Ida's hopes.

"What did she say?" inquired the latter, anxiously.

"They were unpacking their trunks. Anna was very cordial—so was Josephine—for her. 'We concluded yesterday, to come up,' said Anna. 'Pa made a point of it, and Ida's letter was so kind and polite, that we finally determined to accept.'

"'And Mr. Thornton and M. Villet were so desirous to have some Richmond girls here;' said Josephine."

"Aha!" interrupted Ellen.

Emma continued. "Anna did not notice her remark. 'The maid tells me Ida is to be married;' she said, eagerly. 'What a trick she has played us!' 'The queerest part of the story is, that she is more surprised than any body else,' I answered—'They have not been engaged a week! You know the groom?'"

"'O yes! he is a noble fellow! I am rejoiced she is to marry him at last.'"

"And what did Josephine say to this?" asked the inquisitive Ellen. "You need not pretend you have told us all."

"Oh! nothing of consequence. She spoke very carelessly,—of his 'being nothing extra,' and 'she is welcome to him,' with no symptoms of unusual malice."

"Maybe she does not care now, having transferred her attentions to Mr. Thornton. That harp will hang upon the willow, too, or my name is not Ellen Morris!"

A note was handed Ida.

"'Ossa on Pelion piled!' from your countenance," said the volatile bridesmaid.

Ida read it aloud. "Villet is with Thornton. Will your plans undergo any alteration in consequence?

"M. L."

"Josephine is the loose screw, Emma spoke of. I would gladly add M. Villet and Anna to my train—"

"Do it, and let her fret!" exclaimed Ellen

"Oh, no!" said Emma, involuntarily.

"I cannot!" said Ida. She wrote upon the reverse of the billet—"Unless you object, the original order will be preserved."

There were no happier beings present that evening, than the acting host and hostess, and Carry and Arthur.

"I had resigned myself to Ida's perpetual spinsterdom," said Carry to her schoolmates. "She rejected several good offers from no apparent cause; and I imagined she had a prejudice against matrimony."

"She was very indifferent upon the subject;" said Anna. "She was a mystery to many. But those deathless friendships between ladies and gentlemen, are always suspicious, and I predicted how this one would end."

"Charley is delighted;" said Carry.

"Is that surprising?" asked Josephine, with a dash of irony.

"Hush! Here they are!" said Anna.

The clergyman stepped into the centre of the room. The fourth couple entered first.

"Only six attendants!" whispered Josephine, as Charley appeared in the doorway. A freezing night shut her in! through it she saw but two forms—a princely figure, his Antinous head erect in proud happiness—and the hated, injured rival, to whose house, curiosity and vanity had tempted her—the bridal veil falling in soft wreaths about her;—his bride! his wife! for emulous groups flocked around them.

"Oh! how could you deceive me so?" cried Anna, catching Emma, as Charley led her up. "Mr. Dana! we thought you were the bridegroom! The servant said—'Mars' Charley Dana!' Didn't she, Josephine?"

The frozen lips thawed into a stiff "Yes."

"Ah! how foolish in me to forget that Molly espoused the 'Dana cause!'" said Emma.

"And you believed the mistress would imitate the maid's example, Miss Anna?" returned Charley. "Are you inconsolable that I am single yet?"

"No! overjoyed! A change has come over my desperate spirit, since I discovered my mistake. Come Josephine! we must congratulate them."

Josephine was immovable. "I never pay congratulations."

"For decency's sake!" Charley heard Anna say, angrily. "Don't get into one of your surly humors to-night! Very well! stay where you are!" and she walked off with M. Villet.

"That sigh—what is its interpretation?" asked Mr. Lacy, of Ida, as they were watching and enjoying the lively company, which had none of the stiffness usual to weddings.

"Did I sigh? it was in thought—not in sadness, then."

"So I hoped. What was the weighty reflection?"

"I was running over the bridals and bridal-parties I have attended—each marking some important epoch in my history. At Mrs. Truman's—Ellen's sister—I met Lynn, and gained an insight into Charley's character."

"Those were pleasant data. Carry's was next—was it not?"

His chosen wife though she was, she hung her head. He had to bend to hear the faint accents. "I received a letter from you!"

"You may forget that. Go on."

"Mr. Read installed his new wife, and Lelia Arnold was her bridesmaid. Must I forget her also?"

"As I do—yes!" an unclouded eye answering hers.

"Mrs. Morris had a party in honour of her nephew's marriage; and a series of events succeeded, which occasioned me vexation and trouble; but I was not the principal actor."

"And the secret of another, you are not empowered to reveal. Right! The next?"

"Is this!"

"Out of three of the five you have mentioned, disaster and sorrow have arisen. The proportion of joy in this woeful life is variously estimated, from two-fifths to two-thirds. So we do no violence to natural laws, in assuming this to be a white mile-stone."

CHAPTER XXXIII

The stability of wedded happiness may be fairly tested in six years; and that number has elapsed since the wedding-eve at Sunnybank;—a month or two more—for hickory logs are heaped upon the carved andirons, and the arrowy blaze sheds a red glare upon a group of familiar faces:—Charley, unaltered, save that the benign lustre of his eye—formerly seen only by his best friends, has become habitual;—Morton Lacy, handsomer in the prime of manhood than as the slender student; and, her elbow resting on his knee, sits upon a low divan, his wife. If Time has dealt leniently with the others, he has acted repentantly towards her. She is younger, in face and manner, at twenty-seven, than she was at seventeen. Her husband's equal in many respects, and treated by him as such—she has never endured the servile subjugation of soul, which transforms intelligent women into inane, mindless machines. In yielding to his superior judgment, when in contrariety to hers, her will has parted with none of its strength in the bend which proved its pliancy. Submission is a pleasure, not a cross.

"I read to-day of a Mr. Latham, called to the —— street Church, Baltimore," says Charley. "Is it Emma's husband?"

"The identical personage!" replies Ida, with pride. "A high compliment to so young a preacher!"

"He is a man of superior talents," pronounces Mr. Lacy; "a divine of Ida's making."

"Of Mr. Lacy's, you mean—and maybe, after all, the Sabbath-school is entitled to the honour of teaching him that the healing of men's souls, not their bodies, was his vocation. Dr. Hall and I had a pitched battle whenever we met, over our interference with his pupil, until his trial-sermon, which was delivered in our church. The Doctor strode across the aisle, at the close of the services, wiping his eyes. 'I forgive you, madam, and that meddling husband of yours! My stars! what a parson I was near spoiling!'"

"Does Miss Laura meet your wishes, as Mrs. Latham's successor?'"

"Entirely. Mr. Lacy supports her authority, or the stigma attached to her father's memory would weaken her influence. She looks sad to-night. It is the third anniversary of his miserable end."

"He was burnt alive—was he not?"

"It is supposed so. He was found dead—his body partly consumed—upon the hearth of his room. Probably he fell down in a drunken fit. The blow was almost too great for Laura's reason. Natural affection covered the remembrance of all his faults. The children were taken by their mother's relations, to whom he would not allow them to go, in his life-time. Laura has continued with us."

"Still a passion for *protegés*! The last time I saw Miss Read, she inquired what your newest hobby was."

"What did you reply?" inquires Mr. Lacy.

"That ladies dismissed hobbies, when they were provided with 'hubbies—' an execrable play upon words, which she may have construed into an ill-natured fling at her single-blessedness."

"She ought not. *On dit* that Ellen Morris has supplanted me in your bachelor friendship; and she is not likely to marry."

"Any more than myself—but Ellen Morris is not Josephine Read. Old maids are a much-abused class of the community; I trust to her to redeem their character, but Josephine is a frightful counterpoise. If you had remained single!"

"But I didn't!" says Ida, smiling archly at her liege lord. "And you two have only yourselves to blame."

"And Lelia Arnold!" subjoins Mr. Lacy, teasingly. "There is another enchanting spinster, Charley."

Ida is grave.

"You observe my wife nurses her jealousy yet."

"I pity her, Morton! not for losing you,—but I shall always think that she loved Richard Copeland as sincerely as it was in her nature to do."

"Why dismiss him, then?" queries Charley.

"She had the credit of it. In my opinion, he made her discard Mr. Lacy by threats or blandishments; then punished her perfidy to him and others by violating his engagement."

"An unmanly act—but a just lesson! He is marvellously improved by his marriage. Was it a love-match?"

"I believe so. Alice is a lovely girl; just the equable temperament to balance his flightiness. What a contrast to his sister!"

"Has she taken the veil?"

"Alas! yes! She wrote to me, at her mother's death, that 'having lost both parents, and her brother's marriage making him independent of her cares, she should devote the remnant of her sorrowful days to prayer and expiation of her sins—if penitence and mortification could atone.'"

"*If*, indeed!" says Mr. Lacy. "Yet she is more sinned against, than sinning. Her remorse, much as it misguides her, is more creditable than her step-daughter's insensibility."

"Poor Josephine!" sighs Ida.

"Why 'poor?'" asks Charley. "You, of all people, have least cause to be sorry for her."

"I have most, because I know her best. She is not happy—never was—and never will be unless her heart is changed. I have not forgotten the misery of a part of my sojourn with her; yet I honestly preferred my to state hers."

"You are very unlike."

"Now, perhaps—and I thought we were then; but my mother's training was all that saved my disposition from adapting itself to Mr. Read's mould. She had no talisman. I wish she had a hundredth part of my happiness. A woman is so lonely without a home and friends! They are to us—I do not say to you—necessaries of life."

"She can gain them," replies Morton. "You did."

"To be taught the inadequacy of perishable things to satisfy a soul which must live forever!" muses Ida, gazing into the blaze. "I can apply literally that text—'Seek ye first the kingdom of God, and His righteousness; and all these things shall be added unto you.'"

"There are not many who can, in a temporal sense," says Charley.

"But who may not, spiritually? Why will men make a comfortless, doleful mystery of our cheerful, life-giving, home Faith? Why not think, write, talk of it?—"

"And *act* it?" interrupts Charley.

CPSIA information can be obtained
at www.ICGtesting.com
Printed in the USA
BVHW091959251218
536375BV00020B/1031/P

9 781523 395897